WINDBREAK

Stephen England

Also by Stephen England

Sword of Neamha
Lion of God: A Shadow Warriors Prequel Trilogy

<u>*Shadow Warriors Series*</u>
NIGHTSHADE
Pandora's Grave
Day of Reckoning
TALISMAN
LODESTONE
Embrace the Fire
QUICKSAND
ARKHANGEL
Presence of Mine Enemies
WINDBREAK

To the men and women of the Hostage Rescue Fusion Cell, for their tireless work in bringing Americans home, this book is respectfully dedicated.

"Arms are of little value in the field unless there is wise counsel at home."

~ Marcus Tullius Cicero

Chapter 1

11:03 A.M., Philippine Standard Time, December 3rd
Victory Baptist Church
Quezon, Bukidnon
Mindanao

". . .from whom all blessings flow, praise Him, all creatures here below. . ."

Shawn Braley leaned back into the cool metal of the folding chair, a contented smile on his face as he listened to Brother Emmanuel lead the congregation in song, a hundred voices raised in the praise of their Creator filling the small metal building that served as their church. *Praise Him*, indeed.

On any normal Sunday, the American missionary's own voice would have been raised with them, but he'd caught. . .something, on the flight back across the Pacific, four days before, and his usually robust baritone was a whisper of its former self. Best saved for the message itself.

He glanced over to where his wife Charity sat, in the front row of the assembled chairs, their infant daughter, Hope—only seven months old—nestled restlessly in the car seat propped up on the seat beside her. Her older sister, Faith, five years older and twice as restless—occupying the seat on the other side of his wife.

They'd gone back to the States for Hope's delivery in May, staying with his wife's family in Sacramento. Stayed longer than they'd originally had any intention to, ultimately deciding in August to remain and share Thanksgiving with family before returning to the Lord's work in Mindanao.

The first time they'd done it—for Faith's birth—he'd been concerned that it might cost them support, that their network of supporting churches might question their time away from the work.

But no one had cared—no one had even. . .*noticed*, it seemed, a revelation that had at once reassured and unsettled him. Then, or the next time, with the delivery of their son Timothy, now sitting with the Asuncion kids two rows in from the back. It seemed enough for American churches to throw money at the world's unsaved, and go back to sleep.

And perhaps his own heart had grown cold, in the process. It had been easier, this time, the pangs of conscience less sharp. He loved these people, he truly did—this was his *calling*. But he would have been lying to himself if he'd said it hadn't been easy to stay.

Lying to himself. Now there was one thing he was good at.

When he looked up, the song was finished, and Emmanuel Asuncion had turned to look at him, a curious look on the national associate pastor's face. "Brother Shawn?"

He forced a smile as he rose, clapping the shorter man on the shoulder as he moved to the small podium, laying his

Bible before him and leaning into the microphone as he gazed out over the faces of the assembled believers. His congregation. His *flock*.

And where had their shepherd been?

When he spoke, his voice was still hoarse, and faint. "Brothers and sisters. . ."

11:19 A.M.
Camp General Basilio Navarro, Western Mindanao
Command (WESTMINCOM)
Calarian District, Zamboanga City
Zamboanga del Sur, Mindanao

Jack Richards ran a rough, callused hand absently over the lower half of his face, feeling the stubble and grime of a five-day beard. It had been at least that long since he'd showered, and he hadn't slept in the past forty-eight hours. But it had been worth it.

The CIA paramilitary officer leaned back into the door of the interrogation room, his tall form cloaked in shadow behind the bright lights, eyes the color of obsidian staring daggers across the room to the slight, manacled form on the other side of those lights.

Ismin Ebrahim Mostapa.

Evil had so many faces, the Texan thought—and few of them, he had found through the years at war, looked anything like what you might imagine. Mostapa's own face was bland and unremarkable, lined with the approach of middle age, almost kindly—dark, deceptively gentle eyes, now bloodshot, weary with exhaustion.

Give him back his glasses—they had been left behind

when the raid snatched him from his bed in the dead of night—and it would be hard to see Mostapa as anything other than what he once had been, a decade and a half before. A pediatrician, with a thriving practice in Marawi City.

Little sign of the man he had become, since—the long chain of events that had led them to this place, in this small room. Beneath these lights.

No way at all to single him out as the man who had risen to become the Islamic State's "emir" in Mindanao in the months before Raqqa's fall. Presenting himself to the world as Abu Ismael al-Filipini, the head of the *Khilafah Islamiah Mindanao*, Mostapa had led his *mujahideen* back into the streets of his native Marawi eight months earlier, killing anyone who stood in their way.

They were gone now, for the most part, after a determined, five-month-long urban counter-assault from the Filipino military, but they had left devastation in their wake. Of late, Dr. Mostapa's main concern with children had been their murder.

He paused for another long moment, watching as the middle-aged man shook his head, answering yet another question in the negative—causing his interrogator to lean back in exasperation.

They would break him, with time—that was a given—but the information in his head was a perishable commodity, with a shelf life that was already running out. Something he knew every bit as well as they did.

Word of the raid would have already spread far and wide, and people in his organization would be scrambling for cover. For his team's mission here in Mindanao to be successful, they needed more than just Mostapa, cuffed and in holding after more than a decade of terrorist activity. They needed his *network*, dismantled.

They needed to be putting together target decks for further raids. *Now.*

A weary sigh escaped Richards' lips as he turned away, leaving the interrogation room past the pair of uniformed SAF Commando officers guarding the door, black ski masks covering the lower halves of their faces. Hard-eyed men with IMI Galil rifles chambered in 5.56x45mm NATO, the familiar winged scimitar badge of the Special Action Force visible on their uniform sleeves.

Police officers, legally speaking, but there was no mistaking the look in those eyes. They were *soldiers*, first and foremost. Good ones, as their performance in the Mostapa raid had proved.

Richards continued on down the corridor, reaching up to rub the fatigue away from his eyes. His presence here had reached the limits of its utility—he needed a shower, food, and sleep. Not necessarily in that order. The Filipinos could handle Mostapa from here—his team needed to regroup, get ready. For the next time.

11:23 A.M.
Victory Baptist Church
Quezon, Bukidnon
Mindanao

". . .we are called to rejoice, my brothers and sisters," Shawn Braley continued, the microphone carrying his raspy voice to every corner of the metal building—his hands gripping the edges of the podium tightly as he looked out across the faces of his congregation. "Even in the midst of our trials, as Paul and Silas rejoiced in the prison of Philippi. For our Lord has not given us the spirit of fear, but of power. . ."

And yet he was *afraid.* It had been fear, as much as anything else, which had kept them in the States so long this time, all through the five-month siege of Marawi City, a perilously short, four-hour drive to the west from their church here in Quezon.

He had met privately with Brother Frank, the pastor of their sending church—his wife's pastor, since her childhood—at the height of the violence, asking his counsel, whether they should return at all.

"You have a calling," the older man had told him, the faintest hint of reproach in his voice at the question. Moral certitude, so easy from half a world away. Seven thousand miles removed from the danger.

"And a family," he'd responded, sitting there in the pastor's study, surrounded by books, piled up at every hand. Unable to put his fears into words, the strange, unspeakable chill which gnawed at his heart every time he looked at the news. Every time he glanced into the faces of his children. His wife.

"As do the people to whom you were called," Frank Salazar had observed keenly, his words a two-edged sword, cutting to the quick. *"And they can't run."*

Brother Emmanuel—"Manny," as most people called him—had lost his brother Marcelo in the siege, Shawn reflected, feeling the eyes of the Filipino lay leader on him as he continued the sermon. A staff sergeant in the 1st Scout Ranger Regiment.

He'd started working with Marcelo before his departure for the States, one-on-one, leading him through the Scriptures. Endeavoring to bring him to the saving knowledge of Christ.

And then he had gone home, and Marcelo Asuncion had gone to war—his life, and with it, his chance of salvation, forever ended by a sniper's bullet as he led his men through the desolate streets of Marawi.

What if? A haunting question, and one which had cost him more than a few sleepless nights. *Guilt. Regret.*

". . .peace I leave with you, my peace I give unto you," he continued, his lips repeating the familiar words of the text, even as his mind drifted far away, lost in its own turmoil and remorse. "Not as the world giveth. . ."

And that was when Shawn Braley heard the first gunshot.

11:24 A.M.
Camp General Basilio Navarro, Western Mindanao
Command (WESTMINCOM)
Calarian District, Zamboanga City
Zamboanga del Sur, Mindanao

The SAF commandos were clustered around a laptop on the table in their ready room when Richards entered, conducting their own after-action review of the raid. Lieutenant Gregorio "Gringo" Mijares' voice characteristically low but animated as he gestured toward the screen, picking out details of the recorded footage from the ScanEagle UAV which had been in orbit over the target.

". . .here, at the western end of the compound. This corner, Tonyo," he was saying, his intense gaze fixed on the face of one of his squad leaders, "you allowed your team to take it too fast, without sufficient prep. If Mostapa's fighters had been waiting. . ."

It said much for the professionalism of the SAF that the rebuked sergeant accepted Mijares' words with a silent nod, with no attempt at justification. *"But they weren't. . .", "But our surveillance indicated. . .",* were things a lesser man might have offered in his own defense.

But a professional knew the first was luck, and the second. . .well, even with a UAV up, your surveillance missed things. Best not place your trust in anything you hadn't verified with your own two eyes.

"Jack!" Mijares exclaimed, looking up at the American's entrance. "They getting anywhere with him?"

Richards responded with a weary shake of the head, shrugging his ruck off his shoulder and dropping it on the bench in front of one of the security cages that housed the commandos' equipment. "Not when I left."

And he rather doubted they would, in enough time to make any difference. He had seen men like Mostapa before—men who were every bit as aware of that "shelf life" for the information in their heads as their interrogators.

Who knew you didn't have to hold out forever. *Just long enough.*

A low hum of voices in English and Tagalog continued from around the table as the Filipino officer left his men, coming over to where Richards stood, his fatigue pants still as torn and dirty as Richards' own. Infiltration had been. . .*fun.*

"It's not the end," Mijares said, looking up into the American's eyes. At 6'4", Richards towered over pretty much all of his counterparts in this part of the world, and

Mijares—a Cebuano from western Samar—was no exception, standing only a few inches over five feet. *Smaller target*.

It certainly hadn't changed the size of the fight in the man.

"Even if he doesn't break. . .in time," the Filipino went on, acknowledging the reality they had both faced, "we have other ways of obtaining the same end."

A nod. Their combined team had conducted an extensive and thorough site exploitation before the arrival of the Scout Rangers to occupy the compound, scooping up multiple computers and cellphones, including Mostapa's own. The intel value of all that alone, incalculable, *if* they could get at it.

Richards glanced down to see the Huawei smartphone in Mijares' hand, knew where this was going.

"I need you to reach out to your people, back at Langley. Your counterparts at Fort Meade. We don't have the personnel for this—not in the window we have."

A window already sliding closed, as both men knew. "What about the NICA's resources?"

A quiet nod. "Already en route. Policarpio's sending people down. But it's not going to be enough."

Fair enough. He knew that Mijares wouldn't have asked if he hadn't seen it as vital. He liked having to lean on American resources about as well as the average Filipino. *Less*. But the National Intelligence Coordinating Agency—NICA—had the responsibility of full-spectrum intelligence collection and analysis for the entirety of the Philippines, and as such, were stretched thin, dealing with a nearly five-decade-old Communist insurgency, the Islamist unrest in

Mindanao and points south, and an on-again, off-again adversarial relationship with Beijing.

"I'll contact Manila Station, Gringo," he replied as Mijares handed him the phone, glancing back over his shoulder to see Nate Carson enter the ready room, along with Gary Ardolino, one of the newest members of the reconstituted SAD strike team. "See what help they can offer."

He stared down skeptically at the phone, turning it over in his big hands, tracing a rough, callused thumb over the *Huawei* logo on the back of the housing. Chinese, like most of the rest of Mostapa's electronics kit—extremely common in this part of the world.

All of which increased the odds that, despite their best efforts, they could well hit the same stone wall with the tech that they had with the man.

11:25 A.M.
Victory Baptist Church
Quezon, Bukidnon
Mindanao

Pandemonium. Death. Shawn Braley's ears rang with the reverberation of gunfire off the metal walls of the small church, all but drowning out the screams. *Terror and pain.*

Blurred, kaleidoscopic images flashing across his vision— the muzzle of the pistol cold against his temple as the masked gunman dragged him roughly toward the door, fingers entwined roughly in the collar of his dress shirt.

Half-way there, he stumbled and almost went down— the gunman's hand all that kept him upright, looking down to realize that he had tripped on a body.

A Filipino woman, lying face-down in the dirt of the floor—blood soaking torn fabric, the back of her blouse ripped apart by the impact of multiple rounds.

He *knew* her—of that he was horribly certain, but he couldn't see her face, couldn't recognize her in the split-second before the pistol barrel jammed once more into the hard bone of his skull, the gunman cursing him in broken English as he dragged him toward the door.

Charity. His head came up in that moment, wrestling against the pressure of the gunman's hand, searching for his wife's face amid the tumult. He hadn't seen her—or their children—since those first moments of chaos, the back door of the church, suddenly kicked in. Bullets, filling the morning air. All of it, happening so *fast.* . .

And then he saw her, even as he was hustled out of the church and into the morning sunshine, being dragged toward the door by another masked gunman. Their little girl, Faith, pinioned carelessly beneath the man's other arm, her legs kicking, her young eyes wide with unaccustomed terror. No sign of their other children, a moan of fear and anguish escaping his lips. *Please God,* no. . .

He saw Brother Emmanuel stagger toward him, his face a bloody mask—shoved roughly through the door by one of the terrorists. Another gunshot piercing the morning, and for an instant, he expected to see his friend, his *brother* in Christ, fall to the ground.

But no, it was someone else paying that price—someone back in the church. Another friend, perhaps. Sorrow and a perverse sense of relief, warring with each other in his heart.

No time to indulge either emotion. He felt the hand in

his collar tighten, heard the back door of a utility van being wrenched open behind him—turned to catch a glimpse of the vehicle's faded grey paint in the seconds before the rough fabric of a hood scraped over his face, harsh words of Visayan echoing in his ears. *"Dali! Dali!"*

Quickly.

And everything went black.

3:45 P.M.
Camp General Basilio Navarro, Western Mindanao
Command (WESTMINCOM)
Calarian District, Zamboanga City
Zamboanga del Sur, Mindanao

". . .of course, Jack," Darren Lukasik responded, the backlit figure of the Manila chief of station visible on the secure video chat streaming over the screen of Richards' laptop, "I'll convey that request to Virginia presently."

Lukasik made a show of checking his wristwatch, and smiled. "Everyone who can make that kind of decision is asleep at this hour."

Richards nodded, leaning back in his chair. On the other side of the world, it was in the small hours of the morning.

"It also wouldn't hurt for our counterparts at the NICA to file the request formally," the station chief continued, glancing off-camera. "Just to facilitate the process. . .bureaucracy, you know how it is."

Knew it well, Richards thought. Whether the Company or the Corps, bureaucracy had been part of his daily existence for far longer than he cared to remember.

He also knew, as he was quite sure Lukasik did as well,

just how unlikely it was that such an official request would ever be submitted. Three and a half centuries of colonialism had left an indelible mark on this nation, and along with that legacy came a deeply-rooted reluctance to place itself once more in the debt of a great power. *Perhaps under the previous Filipino administration. . .*

But that too was history. And inescapable as all the rest. So backchannels it was. . .

Richards heard the door open, glanced away from the laptop to see Titus Granby enter the room, a towel wrapped around his waist—the African-American paramilitary officer's dark chest bare and heavily muscled, the wiry scruff of his black goatee still glistening with moisture.

The other new addition to the strike team, and a fellow Marine, Granby had grown up in the suburbs of Philly, developing a keen interest in martial arts in high school before joining the Corps at the height of the Iraq War, as the US military ramped up its recruitment efforts ahead of the "surge."

And then, ironically enough, he'd found himself deployed to Afghanistan for a tour in Helmand Province. The first of two such deployments before Granby had transitioned over to MARSOC—Marine Special Operations Command—making his way through Selection to become a Critical Skills Operator.

A "Raider," in the time-honored parlance which had come back into use with the disbandment of the old Force Recon companies—including his old unit, 1st FORECON, Richards thought quietly—and the integration of the Marine spec-ops units into the broader structure of Special Operations Command.

Richards had himself been a plank-owner of the newly-constituted Marine Special Operations Regiment, but by the time Granby had come along, the CIA had already come calling and Richards had left the Marines behind for good. As much as any man ever "left" the Corps.

For Granby's part, MARSOC had sent him back to Afghanistan after the completion of his training. Afghanistan, Iraq. . .and here, once before, as part of the now-defunct Joint Special Operations Task Force-Philippines—JSOTF-P—assisting the Filipino military in their counter-insurgency. His Tagalog was rough, his Visayan worse, but that still put him a step ahead of Richards, who spoke only a handful of words of either language.

And it was in the Philippines that he had first come to the attention of the Agency.

". . .but even so," Lukasik was saying, on-screen, the sound of his voice drawing Richards' attention back to the laptop, "the capture of Mostapa is a coup. He's been in our target deck for years."

Richards just nodded, his face impassive. Stay in this business long enough, you saw many such "coups." So many that it became hard to keep convincing yourself of their importance, as the war went on—heedless of your success.

"A success like this, first time out. . .you can be proud of your new team, Jack."

The ghost of a smile flickered across the Texan's face as he glanced back over his shoulder to where Thomas Parker slept, racked out in one of the bunks—catching a glimpse once more of Granby, pulling on a shirt.

That much, at least, was true.

6:07 P.M.
Somewhere in Mindanao

It seemed as though they might never come to a stop, every bump and jolt of the road communicating itself through the floor into Shawn Braley's tired, battered body—the back of his head still aching from where the gunman had struck him with the butt of his pistol before shoving him into the back of the van.

He and Emmanuel were back-to-back against each other on the floor of the van, their hands now zip-tied behind them—both men lying quiet, exhausted—in pain.

The jail of Philippi. The topic of his morning's sermon, now filtering back through Shawn's weary mind— reproachful. *Mocking.*

He couldn't bring himself to sing, not now—not *here*. Perhaps the words of his sermon had been for him, but he hadn't dreamed of needing them so soon, his eyes staring helplessly out into the blackness of the hood. The scenes of chaos back in the church playing over and again through his brain—defying his every effort to shut them out.

He had prayed for the first few hours, as his daughter sobbed, resisting her mother's best efforts to comfort her. But they had both fallen silent now, as if in mute resignation to their fate.

Where is all this going to end? Shawn asked himself for the thousandth time, fear prickling once more up and down his spine—wishing he could see his wife's face, even if only for a moment. He could hear her voice, soft and low as she spoke to Faith, but it wasn't the same as *seeing* her. Impossible not to ask if he ever would again.

Twenty years ago, it might have been different. Back then, while Americans in the Philippines were at times targeted for kidnapping, even by Abu Sayyaf, it was because of their perceived greater "market" value, ensuring that, at least, their captors had some vested interest in keeping them alive.

But that was all before 9/11, before the Filipino jihad had internationalized, like every other local jihad all over the world, with America the great enemy of all. *Before the Islamic State.*

Now, he knew, all bets were off. *All* bets.

The van shuddered to a sudden stop just then, and Shawn found himself holding his breath, at once hoping and fearing that perhaps they had run into a military patrol. Someone had to *know*, by now.

But then he heard the distinctive voices of their captors, masked only briefly by the creak of metal as the back doors of the van were jerked open.

"Come on, come on," a voice admonished him in broken English as he was pulled roughly to his feet, struggling to get his cramped legs back under him as the terrorist half-dragged, half-carried him from the van.

He heard his daughter cry out, turned halfway back toward the van before another cuff to the side of the head pushed him forward, the soft earth giving beneath his feet. And then he could feel Charity at his side, murmuring gently to their daughter. So close that he yearned to reach out and embrace them both, the plastic of the ties biting deep into the flesh of his wrists. *Please, Lord God, protect us. . .*

And another sound, strange and indistinct, the sound of. . .*waves?* He had no time to process that thought before the hood was ripped from him, the rough fabric burning his ears—leaving him blinking, staring west out across the water into the very dying embers of the setting sun.

They were standing on a desolate beach, his shoes half-sunk in the sand—his eyes meeting his wife's in that moment, seeing his own terror reflected in their depths.

And that was when he saw the fishing boat.

Chapter 2

7:46 P.M.
Camp General Basilio Navarro, Western Mindanao
Command (WESTMINCOM)
Calarian District, Zamboanga City
Zamboanga del Sur, Mindanao

". . .if you'll come right this way, sir," the Filipino staff sergeant directed, glancing back over his shoulder at Richards as the two of them proceeded down the stark, spartan corridors of the military base. "Everything is set up in the conference room, and your people have established the secure uplink with your headquarters in Virginia."

Of course. The AFP—Armed Forces, Philippines—might have been providing the room, but it would be their own Agency support element which would be responsible for handling all of their comms equipment. Allies or no allies, you didn't leave foreign nationals alone with sensitive kit.

They were nearly at the door when Richards heard his name being called from further down the corridor—turned to see Lieutenant Mijares hurrying toward them, a tablet in his hand.

"Jack! I need to speak with you a moment." He caught Richards' backward glance toward the door, and added, "*Before* you talk with your headquarters. It's important."

A nod. "Of course. . .what is it, Gringo?"

"This," Mijares responded, thrusting the tablet into his hands, an ABS-CBN news broadcaster already speaking on-screen as the commando officer nudged the volume up.

". . .was struck by gunmen during morning services at the church," the woman's voice intoned solemnly in perfect English, the camera panning over crumpled bodies scattered among rows of folding metal and plastic chairs, more than a few of the chairs riddled by bulletholes. "The attack left more than twenty dead, and nearly a half-dozen others are still missing and believed to have been kidnapped by the terrorists, including the pastor of Victory Baptist, American missionary Shawn Braley—"

"*And* his wife and at least one of their young children," Mijares interjected, an unusual intensity permeating his voice. Richards just stared at the images—the *devastation*—his lips compressing into a thin line.

"Do we have any idea where they are now?"

A shake of the head. "None."

6:53 A.M. Eastern Standard Time, December 2nd
CIA Headquarters
Langley, Virginia

"Make a note of that if you will," Director Bernard Kranemeyer said, glancing down the conference table to one of his staff operations officers. "We'll need Keifer to reach out to the Israelis, see what kind of *quid pro quo* can be arranged. I understand he's developed a solid working relationship with David Shafron, Avi ben Shoham's right-hand man—time to leverage that, if possible."

"Are we sure that's wise?" a woman's cool, dispassionate voice asked from his right, and Kranemeyer looked over into the face of Olivia Voss, his own recently-appointed deputy director. An old Agency hand who had cut her teeth in the Near East Division, Voss wouldn't have been his first choice for a deputy, but she knew this business inside and out. And had herself spent time in Israel.

"My money says that the Israelis likely have a better grasp on Russian activities in Syria than we do," Kranemeyer responded, nodding slowly. "If we're going to continue to run operations there against the remnants of the Islamic State, we need to know what they know. And Shafron is former ops—a good man."

A man I once served with, he thought but didn't add, remembering that night in the desolate wastes of Iraq's western desert, a lifetime ago. The winter of '01, long before the invasion. The young Israeli, and his team. *Young*. They'd both been far younger, then.

He'd been *whole*, he mused, subconsciously brushing a hand over the knee of his prosthesis, beneath the dress pants. Legacy of a later trip to Iraq. But that *was* another life.

"What about Richards?" he began, redirecting the focus of the discussion—glancing up toward the television screen on the far wall. "I understood we were supposed to have had his report. . .five minutes ago. What's the hold-up?"

"There seems to have been some kind of delay, director," the staff officer replied half-apologetically, seeming to consult the screen in front of him. "One moment, they're coming through now."

Kranemeyer cleared his throat, leaning back in his seat as the image of Jack Richards materialized on-screen, against the background of a conference room nine thousand miles away, in the heart of Camp Navarro.

"Congratulations, Jack," Kranemeyer announced with an easy smile. "Nice work out there. I've heard nothing but good from our counterparts in the AFP on the advisory role your team played in the Mostapa grab. Well done."

"Thank you, director," his team leader responded, but he could tell from Richards' expression that it was a mechanical reply. *Unfelt.* Something well beyond the Texan's usual stoicism.

"Sir," Richards began, another alarm bell joining the cascade in Kranemeyer's brain. Richards knew better than to call him *"sir."* "We have a situation."

9:06 A.M.
A coffeehouse
Ellicott City, Maryland

William Russell Cole stared out the window of the shop into the street, his coffee neglected and cooling on the table before him, eyeing the piles of grimy, three-day-old snow littering the edges of the sidewalks like wads of used-up tissue—a morose contrast with the gay pageantry of the town's Christmas decorations, the holiday music piping through the shop.

Matching the mood. He shook his head at everything and nothing in particular, lost in his own thoughts—soft gray eyes staring out from a face lined by the years, surmounted by an unruly shock of graying, nearly silver hair.

It had been months since the veteran FBI hostage negotiator had truly been troubled by the memories, but they were returning, inevitably, with the season. Memories of *failure*, of the chaos the previous Christmas had wrought. The horrors of the Vegas 12/24 attacks. . .and all that had preceded it.

He'd debated leaving the Bureau in the months that followed. Retiring, finally, after all the years. After all that he had seen in more than three decades of public service. Seen, and. . .*done*.

But then, despite it all, an offer had come to take a lead role in the FBI's Hostage Recovery Fusion Cell, a unit stood up in the last two years of the Hancock administration. An offer he couldn't have brought himself to refuse.

Even without a U.S. Special Presidential Envoy for Hostage Affairs, as provided for under PPD30, the policy directive which had created the HRFC—the incoming Norton administration hadn't bothered to fill the post for the entirety of their first year—the fusion cell represented the first real attempt by the federal government to unify hostage recovery into a whole-of-government effort, offering more substantial liaison with both foreign governments and the families of the taken.

An effort that had been needed for years, and one that he was proud to be a part of.

Russ glanced back across the table as his companion, a small, delicately-featured woman the better part of three decades his junior, returned her phone to an inner pocket of her purse, zipping it shut with a nervous gesture.

"Luke?" he asked, a raw, barely-concealed edge to his usually soft voice.

"Yeah." She looked away, hands clasped in front of her, refusing to meet his eyes. "I should be going."

"Tiff," he began hesitantly, unsure as ever of his ground, "you just got here."

"I know, I *know*," she responded quickly, almost angrily. "I just. . .I don't want to upset him."

Beneath the table, Russ' fingers balled into a fist, knuckles whitening in the effort to maintain control. *Where had his little girl gone?*

He couldn't see much of her in the woman that sat across from him, chewing at her lip. She had grown up on him as the years flew by, unnoticed. Become a wife and a mother. Her twin sons were the apple of his eye, the mirror of himself at their ages—a second chance he hadn't deserved. *But her husband. . .*

She still wouldn't look at him, fingers playing nervously with the cuff of her sleeve. She always wore long sleeves, these days.

No matter the weather.

"You need to get out, Tiff. *Leave* him," he said quietly, his eyes never leaving her face. "If not for yourself, at least for Andrew and Jon."

"It's not. . .he doesn't. . ."

"*Hasn't*," he corrected, his voice low. "They're young yet. Are you going to wait till he does?"

"*No!*" She seemed to surprise herself with the vehemence of the outburst, lowering her voice as she continued, "It's not that simple. It hasn't been like this, all along. Luke's not a bad guy, he just. . ."

Russ let out a heavy sigh, recognizing a refrain by now familiar. Having seen the bruises now discoloring her pale arms, he couldn't have brought himself to agree, but that was a fight he had yet to win.

"He needs help," he replied, looking across the table into his daughter's eyes. Reaching out to cover her hand with his own. "*Professional* help. And that's not something you can provide for him. And until he gets that help. . .you have to think of your own safety. And that of the boys."

"I can handle him," she responded, once again looking away. Her voice almost pleading. "Please believe me."

But he didn't. "Get the boys, Tiff, and get *out*. Come live with me, just until this all blows over—I have the room. The house has seemed empty since your mother. . .passed."

"I don't know."

"Think about it," he admonished, careful not to push too far. "Think about the Christmas we could have, together, the four of us. We—"

The phone on his belt rang in that moment and Russ bit back a curse of exasperation at the interruption, retrieving it to check the screen. *His boss.*

"I'm sorry," he said, glancing back at his daughter. "I have to take this."

A nod of resignation. "You always do."

There was no answer to that, and Russ offered none as he made his way through the tables toward the exit. Ice-cold air striking him in the face as he pushed open the door, stepping out onto the sidewalk.

"Yes?"

"Russ, we're calling everyone into the office. There's been an incident—at least two Americans taken hostage, possibly three."

"Where?"

"Mindanao."

10:36 P.M. Philippine Standard Time, December 3rd
The fishing boat
The Gulf of Moro

Darkness had fallen long ago, leaving only the weak luminescence of the waning moon—materializing occasionally from behind the layer of low-hanging cloud cover like a pale ghost, a faint glow sparkling in the turbulence of their wake.

Shawn Braley leaned back against the gunwale, listening to the waves lap against the side of the boat's hull, the soft throb of the engine, feeling once more the urge to piss—growing stronger with each passing hour, despite none of them having been given any water since the beach. Perhaps there wasn't any, which he found even more unsettling.

He could still feel the band of his watch encircling his wrist, just beneath the zip-ties. *"We are moral men,"* one of the gunmen had told him, drawing his attention to this, *"we will not steal from you. Neither will we touch your wife, or your daughter, or the other women. The Qur'an forbids all of this."*

And doesn't the Qur'an also forbid kidnapping? The murder of innocents? Shawn had wanted to ask, but he lacked the nerve to do so, the memories of the bloodbath in the church far too fresh.

"What are you planning to do with us?" he'd asked instead, struggling to look the man in the eye.

"That will be for the Emir to decide." He didn't know who that was, exactly, but he knew he had read of him in the news articles covering the battle for Marawi. *Were they being taken to him?*

He glanced over to where his wife sat, on the other side

of the deck, with Faith lying across her lap, sound asleep, having finally cried herself out. Someone, perhaps one of the other women, had given Charity a long piece of cloth to use as a *terong*—a head covering—but he could still see the shock, the fear in her eyes. She was holding herself together for Faith. *And for him.* And he had to do so for both of them. And the members of his flock.

If he could.

The murmur of voices in Visayan drifted back to them from the cluster of jihadists closer to the bow—talking and laughter, strangely discordant.

He turned his attention away from his wife, finding Emmanuel Asuncion staring at him from a few feet away, seeming to have collected himself better than any of the rest of them—either the Braleys or the other Filipino Christians, seven in all, who had been taken hostage along with them.

"Where do you think they're taking us?" he asked, keeping his voice low so as not to attract attention from the gunman in the stern, an assault rifle cradled loosely in the crook of the young man's arm, the brightly glowing cherry of his cigarette flickering in the night.

Emmanuel shook his head wearily, glancing up at the clouds. "One of the islands, likely. Basilan, Tongkil, Jolo. . .there are dozens of others in the archipelago, not all of them inhabited."

Endless places to lose themselves. Or any pursuit. Shawn just looked at him, unable to conceal his dismay. "They say they're taking us to the Emir, that *he* will decide what is to be done with us."

A nod. "The man calling himself Abu Ismael, most likely. Unless they belong to a rival group."

Shawn closed his eyes, steadying his voice. "And then? What happens?"

"Whatever our Lord allows," his friend responded calmly, resting his head back against the pile of crates and tarpaulin. "You and your family are valuable, for ransom or a political statement, either one. The rest of us. . .less so."

It took Shawn a moment to process Emmanuel's words, and then he shook his head. "No. Either we all get out, if it comes to that, or I stay as well. I'm not going to just *leave* you."

A quiet nod, his friend's eyes closing as he adjusted his position against the crate. "You will."

10:35 A.M. Eastern Standard Time, December 2nd
CIA Headquarters
Langley, Virginia

Bernard Kranemeyer stared a few moments longer at the photo before turning it over with a heavy sigh, replacing it in the briefing folder along with the other papers. Knowing the child's face was going to linger with him, far longer than the rest of the information in the packet.

Timothy Grant Braley. Four years old. An American citizen, born in Sacramento. Dead.

His little sister, Hope, seven months, found lying abandoned in the midst of the carnage, crying in her car seat, but somehow unscathed. *Physically, at least.*

No sign of either of their parents, or their older sister—other than the certainty that they were not among the dead at the church.

Little Hope was already en route to the US Embassy in

Manila, where she would be taken care of until family could arrive to bring her back to the States.

The case of her parents, already in the hands of the State Department, and presumably, the FBI's dedicated fusion cell.

"He was about the age of Adrian," Olivia Voss observed quietly, and Kranemeyer looked up to see her holding the photo. *That old already?* He could remember when her youngest son had been born. "Did you ever have children, Barney?"

He shook his head silently. There had never been the right time, or the right person. Or a world he wanted to bring them into.

She considered his response for a moment, seeming as if she was about to speak, then thinking better of it. "Richards' team is due to return Stateside in just under two weeks. If this situation still remains. . .unresolved, at that time, will you want them to remain in place? Just to keep our options open?"

Options. Kranemeyer shrugged. "We're not operating in the 'Stans here. What options we have. . .that's going to depend entirely on our hosts."

12:05 A.M., Philippine Standard Time, December 4th
Camp General Basilio Navarro, Western Mindanao Command (WESTMINCOM)
Calarian District, Zamboanga City
Zamboanga del Sur, Mindanao

". . .among those interviewed later saw the pair of gray utility vans driving southwest from Quezon, along the road— here."

"Toward the autonomous region," Titus Granby observed, earning a sharp look from the NICA officer delivering the briefing, a woman in her late forties. *Maricar de Rosales.*

He glanced over at Richards, shrugging almost imperceptibly, as if to say, *I've been here before.*

"That is indeed quite likely, Mr. . .?"

"White," Granby replied, a quiet smile creasing his dark face. The Autonomous Region in Muslim Mindanao—increasingly referred to locally as the *Bangsamoro*, or "Moro Nation"—was an independently governed region comprising five of the most predominantly Muslim provinces of Mindanao, a concession first extended by the Marcos regime in the '70s and finally made a reality by the administration of Corazon Aquino in 1989, all in a bid to finally bring the decades-long—*then*—Moro insurgency to an end.

Judging by the events of the intervening near three decades, reality had fallen somewhat short of those expectations.

"We consider it very likely that the militants would seek refuge in the ARMM, and have already begun liaising with the police regional office there to further our investigation."

Everything done by the book, Richards thought ironically, concerned that it might well stop there. All the *t*'s crossed, the *i*'s dotted, everyone's butt covered—and the hostages unreturned. *Likely dead.* The painful awareness that they were here as guests, nothing more, never far from the front of his mind.

Afghanistan, Iraq. . .a half-dozen other warzones, great and small, in the years since 9/11, it was easy to grow accustomed to dictating terms to one's allies. To more or less mandating what needed to be done, and doing it. Because you were more the law in their country than they were, and everyone knew it—the bad guys, most of all.

That wasn't the case here. Had been once, and for that very reason, could never be again. The legacy of the Philippines, a cautionary tale for Iraq and Afghanistan both. Or would have been, if anyone had bothered to look at it.

A legacy with consequences which still reverberated to this very day, more than a century later, Richards mused, listening to de Rosales' litany of bureaucratic assurances with only half an ear as he glanced across the table at Lieutenant Mijares. As he'd learned, only too well, shortly after his team's arrival in late October, laying the groundwork of his working relationship with the commando officer.

"My grandfather was here in '45," he'd observed late one night, going over intel with Mijares in the run-up to the Mostapa raid. Corporal Joshua Alvin Richards, 31st Infantry Division, XI Corps, fighting in Eichelberger's Eighth Army.

Two years out of high school in 1945, and a National Guardsman from Mobile, Alabama, Al Richards had led his squad into the dense, stifling fields of abaca outside of Davao City, just an hour's flight away, on the eastern side of Mindanao, rooting out Japanese positions as they worked to secure the island. Fighting and dying in that green, sweltering hell, lush, thick-stemmed abaca growing close as sugar cane, towering a dozen feet above the infantrymen's heads—reducing visibility to mere feet.

The first sign of contact, for many Americans, a rippling burst of machine-gun fire from among the plants, scant yards away. All that he knew from the history books—Al Richards had survived those fields to come home, living to the ripe old age of eighty-two, but he'd never once spoken of Mindanao. After the funeral, they'd found a Silver Star stuffed deep in the recesses of his desk, its ribbon faded with the passage of the years.

It had taken Mijares a long time to respond, and when he did, his soft voice was even quieter than normal. *Less soft.*

"My great-grandfather died at Balangiga—shot as a suspected insurrecto.*"*

It had taken the Texan a long moment to process the import of his colleague's words. To recognize that Mijares' memories went back further—the better part of another half-century—to a time when the people of his native Samar and the Americans had been anything but allies.

"I want no prisoners," the American commander, Jacob Smith, had told his Marines in that October of 1901, following a devastating insurgent attack on American forces in Balangiga itself. *"I wish you to kill and burn."*

And the Marines had done plenty of both in the days and weeks that had followed. That they hadn't gone as far as their commander's bombast would have allowed in turning Samar into a "howling wilderness" was to the credit of his Corps, but doubtless small comfort to the families of those they *had* killed—those Cebuanos who had found their homes burned down about their ears.

He'd nodded, then, in quiet acknowledgment of his partner's words. *"The Americans,"* he began, the words curiously disassociative, *"first came to the Philippines fresh from hunting my people."*

"Your people?"

"The Apache."

Chapter 3

It was their second full day on the water, the small fishing boat laboring through the open sea with not a trace of land in sight. Nothing at all in sight but the sky above and the ocean below—the afternoon sun burning down upon them with a pitiless heat.

The boat was overloaded with the ten hostages and their seven captors, riding perilously low in the water—a situation compounded by the amount of military equipment the terrorists had brought aboard with them, rifles, light machine guns, an RPG or two, and, heaviest and most incongruous of all, a mortar taken down for transport.

Far too heavy a load for such a small vessel, as Shawn knew all too well, having grown up in the Bay Area—most of his teen years spent aboard small craft. They'd be lucky not to ship water in a perfect calm. In a storm. . .

Storm. Was that to be his fate? Divine punishment, for having so neglected his calling, all through the years. For

32

having taken every pretext, every opportunity, to leave it behind. A modern-day Jonah, torn by fear and doubt, at war with God's commands. *Running the other way.*

Perhaps there was even justice to be found in that. . .and yet for so many to *share* this fate with him? *So many innocents?*

Faith had woken everyone the previous night, screaming out in terror in the midst of a dream. The pretty flowers of her little dress, still spattered with the rust-dark stains of dried blood from the massacre at the church. The blood of her friends, like as not—everyone at Victory Baptist had loved her like their own. And she had loved them, with the frank openness of a child who had never met a stranger.

All that was gone, now.

Shawn stooped down beside his wife and child, his wrists left unsecured during the daytime hours now, like those of the other men—gently smoothing Faith's dark, tousled hair back from her forehead. She might not have been asleep, even yet, but she was at least resting quietly.

He looked up to see his wife's lips moving slowly, as if in silent prayer. Perhaps for themselves—perhaps for their other children, Tim and little Hope, left behind.

Alive, he hoped, against hope. Everything had happened so *fast*, from that first shot—he'd been unable to find his family in the midst of the chaos, and not even Charity could tell him what had happened to their youngest children.

Or would.

4:13 P.M.
Quezon, Bukidnon
Mindanao

"Four minutes," Jack Richards announced, hands resting on his hips as the Texan visually measured the distance between the road and the front door of the bullet-riddled metal structure of Victory Baptist. That was how long the surviving witnesses estimated the kidnapping had taken, from the moment a neighbor not seventy meters down the road had watched the vans roll up, to the moment they had departed, their hostages shoved into the back of the vehicles. "They knew their business."

"Agreed." Thomas Parker removed his old, faded NYPD ball cap, slicking back his sweat-damp brown hair. A hard look in the former hedge fund manager's eyes as he surveyed the damage done to the building—envisioning the carnage that had unfolded within.

Parker's route to the Agency's Special Activities Division had been nothing if not unconventional, Richards thought, looking over at his old friend, but there was little trace left of the man he had been in the years before. 9/11 had changed them all, but Thomas Parker more so than most.

And they had both performed more than one such "grab" over the years—knew the mechanics of such an operation extremely well. "Do you think there's any chance that this was payback?"

"For the capture of Mostapa?" Richards shook his head, glancing over to see Granby, perhaps fifteen meters farther down the road, attempting to carry on a conversation with a local. "Unlikely."

They'd had the Filipino emir for less than eighteen hours when the church had been struck. It wasn't *impossible* for something like this to be laid on that fast—the church wasn't, after all, even remotely a hardened target, but it was improbable in the extreme.

They didn't even know with any certainty that these militants were part of the same group—the majority of the jihadist groups in Mindanao had been informally cobbled together under the label of "Islamic State-Philippines," of which Ismin Ebrahim Mostapa had been nominally the Emir, after their respective pledges of *bayah* to the Caliphate. But that was as an elusive a catch-all as "Abu Sayyaf," the more commonly-used metonym for Islamic insurgents in Mindanao and points south.

And that had all been before Raqqa's fall.

Since then. . .it was hard to say, and harder to determine just how much in control Mostapa had ever been. This was a part of the world which had always fought its own jihads, in its own way.

He'd wanted to interrogate Mostapa about the abductions, but that was a request which had yet to be granted. And there had been no claim of responsibility. No demands, as of yet.

So here they were, at the scene of the crime. . .

4:53 P.M.
The fishing boat
Gulf of Moro

"They're going to be okay, sweetheart," Shawn whispered, his arm wrapped around his wife's shoulders as they knelt in the stern of the fishing boat, their daughter now curled up asleep beside them, resting on a dirty, threadbare blanket one of the jihadists had produced from somewhere. "Tim and Hope. . .we have to trust that God will watch over them. He's far more capable of that than we ever could be, Charity. We have to *trust* in Him."

"I know." The reply seemed mechanical, somehow, her body shuddering with a silent sob as she reached down, smoothing out a wrinkle in Faith's dress. She was still in shock, Shawn told himself, unable even yet to completely shake the gnawing fear that she knew more than she was telling him, the strangest of walls having grown up between them over the last two days. The cold hand of despair, closing around his heart.

He looked around at the rest of the hostages, all gathered together in the stern, but no one was paying attention to the two of them in this moment. Emmanuel's eyes met his own for a brief moment, his expression unreadable, and then he too looked away. *Alone.*

It was a dark, oppressive feeling. He'd known something was different, returning to the Philippines this time, but he'd written it off as the clouded perceptions of jet lag and sickness, but his old friend wasn't what he had once been—the loss of his brother, perhaps his own sense of Shawn's desertion, altering their relationship irreparably. The chaos of their abduction, bringing it all to a head. *Crisis.*

"What are they going to do with us?" Charity asked, her voice thick with emotion. The question they had all been asking themselves, each other—*God*—ever since that first shot.

"Bang," a voice interjected, and Shawn looked up into

the eyes of the one they called "Aldam," one of the younger gunmen—a boy barely out of his teens, if that—standing there before them, his old, battered assault rifle held easily in one hand. Registering the laughing smile on his youthful face as he raised the index finger of his left hand to his temple, pantomiming the recoil of a shot, his head jerking back as if from the impact of the round.

Rough laughter breaking from his lips as he took in their reaction. His smile widening as he reached forward with his free hand, the muzzle of his rifle swinging free, dangerously close to Shawn's chest as he patted the missionary on the shoulder.

"Is joke," he said, grinning, his English broken, but only too clear. "Death won't be that simple."

10:32 A.M. Eastern Standard Time
J. Edgar Hoover Building (FBI Headquarters)
Washington, D.C.

"Good morning, people," FBI Director Kevin Chamian announced, gesturing for everyone to take their seats as he pulled out his own chair at the head of the conference table.

William Russell Cole traded a look with his own boss, Justin Valukas, the director of the fusion cell, as the two men sat down on opposite sides of the table. It had been nearly a year since FBI Director Eric Haskel had been found dead in his Georgetown residence, the victim of a massive stroke, and the following twelve months had been nothing if not tumultuous for the Bureau.

President Norton's first two choices for director had washed out in bitterly contentious Senate confirmation hearings, and it had taken until early June—after a senior

Democrat from Oklahoma had unexpectedly switched parties—for Chamian, a former US Attorney for Illinois' Southern District, to finally be confirmed as FBI director.

"So tell me, where are we at with the situation in Mindanao?" the director asked, arranging the papers before him as the HRFC's logo came up on the television screen behind him. An eagle astride the globe, against the backdrop of the American flag, a slogan just below the bird's outstretched talons. *One Mission. . .One Voice.*

Would that it could *ever* be so simple, Russ mused, only too aware that the bureaucratic hassles of coordinating multiple agencies remained ever with them, despite the fusion cell's best efforts.

"We know very little at this point," Valukas acknowledged, glancing up the table at Chamian. "Most of our information has come to us courtesy of the CIA, who apparently have a team on Mindanao, working in a support role to AFP units in the region."

That had hurt his boss to admit, Russ knew. It said something that even in this modern spirit of interagency cooperation, and despite their official role in the fusion cell, there wasn't a single Agency representative currently in this room.

"Our people in Manila are liaising with the Filipino government," Katherine Lipscomb, the fusion cell's lead representative from State, spoke up, her voice cutting across the conference room like a knife. Only a few years younger than Russ, she was a career foreign service officer and like him, had been contemplating her exit from civil service when the HRFC came calling. He was glad she hadn't. "At this time, they seem as much in the dark as we are. No demands, as of last report—no claim of responsibility."

"I understand there's some reason to believe that the Islamic State or IS affiliates in the area may be involved?" Director Chamian asked, glancing up from his notes.

"That is the Agency's working theory, yes," Valukas responded, nodding. "The attack on Victory Baptist bears all the hallmarks of an insurgent action, and most of the jihadist elements pledged their loyalty in one form or another to Abu Bakr in the months before Raqqa's fall. We've already dispatched agents from our West Coast offices to offer what support we can to the Braleys' family here in the States, and Russ' team will be leaving for Manila later this afternoon. By the time they're on the ground. . .we may have more answers."

Or at least more questions. That was the way of this business. If you got lucky, the one would lead you to the other. *If.*

"Good, good," the FBI director replied, his fingers clasped before him as he leaned forward, his expression growing even more serious. "You should all understand that, given the potential of IS involvement, the President has already brought JSOC into the loop. If we, or our Filipino counterparts—or the CIA—locate the Braleys, he wants to send in the SEALs."

11:23 A.M. Pacific Standard Time
California State University, Fullerton
Fullerton, California

"Mom's already seen it." The words brought a smile to Jason Guilbeau's face as his son turned the phone's screen toward him, showing him the Instagram post of the selfie the two of them had taken together not ten minutes before—his wife's handle now displayed below the image. *Of course she had.*

He and Dave were both smiling in the picture, which put to rest the old maxim that "the camera never lies."

It hadn't been the best of college visits, which was perhaps a function of his unexpected trip to the West Coast pushing up news that his son had intended to save for Christmas. That he was planning to walk away from his education, two years in, and had already applied—no, applied, and been *accepted*—to the LAPD.

That he would begin academy training in the fall, after finishing out his associate's.

It was natural, he supposed, taking another sip of his Pepsi as he glanced around them at the other college students clustered around picnic tables in the open-air courtyard of the campus' Carl's Jr., that you were never your child's hero. His father had been Cajun right down to the ground, a firefighter in Lake Charles, but Jason had dreamed of the sea from his earliest childhood. And when the opportunity had come to join the Navy, Guilbeau had left Calcasieu Parish behind for good, first for the fleet and then—after 9/11— the Teams.

Dave had grown up right here in California, during his dad's years with SEAL Team Three at Coronado, and had chosen to stay on the West Coast to continue working and pursue his education when Guilbeau was transferred to DEVGRU—the former Team Six—and the rest of the family moved east, to Virginia.

Now Guilbeau wondered if this had been part of it, all along—his son no more interested in the Navy than he had been in the fire department. It wasn't as though he had ever really wanted his son to follow in his own footsteps—a decade and a half of a war that wasn't going anywhere fast had cured him of that. But if you had to pursue a career in low-pay, high-risk public service, then for certain, *Navy* was the way to do it.

"Look. . .Dave," he began earnestly, what was left of his burger now forgotten on his tray. Wondering exactly when the boy sitting across from him had become a man. *During one of those deployments to Iraq, likely*, an unwelcome voice told him, but he shoved it away with an effort. "Finish out your four years, maybe get your bachelor's in criminal justice, if that's where you want to go with this. I'm willing to help you out, as I can. You'll be in a better position to—"

"No," his son replied, shaking his head—that Cajun stubbornness which had ever been a Guilbeau family trait, now manifesting itself in his son. "A criminal justice degree doesn't actually help you that much, not with where I want to go. I've talked with guys who have gone career, and you're better off just working your way up from the street, like you did in the Teams."

Yeah, like he'd done. It had taken him thirteen years to make E-8, and his salary now wasn't much more than double what it had been when he'd started out at the bottom. If he'd listened to his own father. . .he might have been able to put his kids through college without so much juggling. Dave's younger sister Briana was still a high school sophomore, but he already knew coming up with the money for her education was going to be a challenge. Unless he got out and went private, something he'd resisted doing for years. But he hadn't listened, and he could tell from the set of his son's jaw that history was repeating itself here. His father would have laughed.

"That's a hard path," he said finally, "and I still think that you'd be better off—"

The SEAL's phone vibrated hard against the table where he had laid it when they began eating, and he broke off in mid-sentence, glancing at the screen. *Dom.*

"Just give me a sec," he told his son reluctantly, recognizing the number—knowing ignoring it wasn't an option. "I have to answer this."

"Guilbeau here," he answered, shouldering his way past a pair of coeds as he walked out of the restaurant's courtyard and out onto the campus, staring west toward Gordon Hall.

"Command wants you back here, Jay," he heard his old friend and squadronmate Dominic Zamora announce, "most ricky-tick. Red has been activated."

6:43 A.M., Philippine Standard Time, December 7th
The fishing boat
Gulf of Moro

The speedboat had come alongside just after dawn, five more jihadists climbing aboard with the aid of a rope ladder as the gunwales of the fishing boat dipped ever more precariously toward the waterline. Something that didn't seem to concern any of their captors in the least.

It was strange, Shawn Braley thought, a curious sort of detachment filling his mind as he sat there in the stern, knees drawn up to his chest, reflecting upon it. These men should have spent as much time in and around the sea as he had, growing up in San Francisco. *More.* And yet, they seemed blithely indifferent to the very fundamentals of good seamanship.

Perhaps it was their trust in God.

He shuddered, gooseflesh dotting his exposed arms—his light dress shirt offering little protection against the morning chill. It would be hot before many more hours went by, but for the moment. . .

They had slept pressed up against each other the previous night, the three of them, huddled together for warmth, and finding it insufficient, even yet. Faith had wept, again.

A shadow fell over him, and he looked up into the eyes of one of the new arrivals. The *leader* of the new arrivals, if he'd judged the body language at all aright. A thin, sinewy Moro—he couldn't have stood more than 5'1" at most—the man wore a short-sleeved black t-shirt and camouflage pants, his dark hair flowing over his shoulders like a mane. Wiry dark hair clung to his chin in an untrimmed, patchy goatee, and a hard smile played around the man's lips.

"Manong Soleiman," he announced, as if by way of introduction, though he didn't extend his hand. "These"— he gestured expansively around the boat—"are my men."

9:51 P.M., Eastern Standard Time
Reagan International Airport
Arlington, Virginia

The Gulfstream G550 gleamed stark and white in the lights of the airport as it sat there alone to itself on the tarmac, the flight crew performing their final checks.

William Russell Cole stood by the stairs, bundled up against the biting winter wind in a heavy overcoat, finishing up the last of the half-smoke he had bought at the airport Ben's Chili. Most of his team was already aboard—a team comprising a half-dozen special agents, a pair of attorneys from the Department of Justice, a DoD lieutenant colonel tasked with being the team's liaison with the Filipino military, and of course Lipscomb's people from State. A dozen people in all, not counting himself.

Station Manila, headed up by a career CIA operations officer named Darren Lukasik, was supposed to provide intel support, and Ambassador Garner had instructions to give whatever assistance the embassy could provide. *Whole of government, indeed.*

He pushed the last bite of the chili-covered sausage into his mouth, glancing back over his shoulder to see an Air Canada Airbus A330 descending out of the wintry night sky on final approach. A silent ghost, the sound of its engines drowned out by the insistent, pulsating whine of the Rolls-Royce turbofans not ten feet behind his head.

Leaving the country now, like this, wasn't something he would have wished for. Not with everything on the line with Tiff and her. . .*husband.* The boys.

She'd told him she would "think about it," which was something she had told both him and her mother at least a dozen times before. All for nothing.

He'd thought, there in the coffee shop, that he might have made progress, but. . .well, one way or the other, he wasn't going to be around for Christmas. For a moment, he had even considered asking someone else to go, but those pictures, of Timothy Braley—it wasn't hard at all to see his own grandsons in the face of that little man, now gone on.

Someone had to bring his family back.

He wiped the grease off his hands with a napkin as another pair of agents carried equipment onto the plane, shoving the soiled paper into an outer pocket of his coat.

"Russ." He looked up to see Katherine Lipscomb standing in the open door of the Gulfstream, her blonde, graying hair tousled in the wind. "You coming with us?"

1:03 P.M. Philippine Standard Time
Camp General Basilio Navarro, Western Mindanao
Command (WESTMINCOM)
Calarian District, Zamboanga City
Zamboanga del Sur, Mindanao

Sixty-five, sixty-six. Sixty-seven. Richards' head came up as his tall, lanky frame rocked forward once again, hands clasped behind his head, elbows forward—catching a brief glimpse of Nate Carson holding his ankles down before he fell backward again.

Sixty-eight. Sixty-nine. Medical science had turned against sit-ups in recent years, and the US military was starting to adjust, but it had been one of the traditions of his Corps, and tradition died hard for any Marine.

Particularly when you could show up the Air Force.

Seventy. Seventy—"Time!" Titus Granby called out, holding up his phone, the *2:00* clearly visible on-screen.

Richards rolled over to one side and pushed himself up, taking the bottle of water Gary Ardolino extended to him and unscrewing the top.

"You're up, Airman," he announced with a smile, his breath still coming fast and heavy. Looking on as Carson laid down on the barracks floor, Ardolino taking up his post at his feet.

They were killing time here now, that was all. He knew

it and he knew his men did as well. But they were limited, by their orders—by the constraints of their relationship with their hosts.

He took a long drink of water, watching as the former Air Force PJ—pararescue jumper—began to knock out his sit-ups, finding a steady, methodical rhythm. No doubt about it, Carson was a good man—a veteran whose job it had once been to fly into some of the hottest fighting the War on Terror had had on offer, and bring the wounded back out. A man who had proved himself time and again over the last couple years with the Agency.

Didn't mean he was going to stop giving him crap about the Air Force.

Ardolino was the wild card here, much like Granby. Both of Bravo Team's new members had come to the Special Activities Division with impressive service records— Ardolino's service, like Mitt Nakamura's before him, with the 75th Ranger Regiment. But there was the military, and there was the Agency, and not everything transferred as seamlessly as an outsider might have imagined.

And Ardolino was more than a decade younger than Mitt—not even thirty yet, and his time in the Regiment had come well *after* their heaviest fighting in Afghanistan. He'd handled himself well on the Mostapa raid, but that had gone. . .smoothly, as raids went. They wouldn't all be like that.

"Thirty-five, thirty-six," he heard Parker count out, standing just on the other side of Carson, leaning up against one of the bunks. Their eyes met for a brief moment and he could tell Parker knew what he was thinking.

It wasn't like any of these men to just sit by when fellow

Americans were in danger, but here. . .they had little choice. The intel on the Braley kidnapping remained so very *limited*. Their scope for action even more so.

"Forty, forty-one. . ."

Lieutenant Mijares appeared in the open doorway in that moment, flanked by a couple of his men—Carson stopping in mid-sit-up as the Filipinos entered.

"I have been talking with my superiors, Jack," Mijares announced, taking in the scene before him. "Our interrogators have raised the issue of the Braleys' kidnapping with Mostapa and have gotten nowhere, but. . .Director Policarpio and General Gonzaga have both given their authorization: you can speak with him, as requested."

The commando lieutenant's face was hard to read in that moment, but Richards could tell he wasn't happy to be the bearer of this particular message. No doubt hating to admit defeat.

"Good," the Texan replied, choosing to ignore it. That particular battle was best fought another day. "I'll be right over."

"Tomorrow," Mijares corrected. "We will set up an interview for tomorrow."

And then he was gone once again, leaving the Americans looking at each other. *More delay.*

Richards turned back on Carson, still sitting there straight-legged on the floor. "Taking a break are we, Airman?"

2:32 P.M.
The fishing boat
Gulf of Moro

There wouldn't have been much of a way to relieve oneself on the fishing boat, even had it been less crowded. As it was. . .until "Uncle" Soleiman—the word *manong* meant "uncle" in Visayan—had arrived, the only real options were the hold of the boat itself, where most of the women had gone, and over the side, into the water.

He'd ordered the construction of a crude wooden platform out on the bamboo outrigger of the fishing boat, the innate Islamic respect for personal modesty allowing them to fabricate a screen out of tarpaulin.

Sweat beaded on Shawn Braley's face as he stood out there on the platform, the water just beneath him, the sun beating down from above—feeling the gentle motion of the boat beneath his bare feet. He'd discarded his dress shoes back on the beach, rightly judging them to be worse than useless from this point forward, but his feet were no longer as hardened and callused as they'd been as a teen.

He'd always been comfortable at sea, back then. Far more comfortable than he'd ever been in a pulpit. Or ministering to the people he'd been called to serve.

The thought made him uncomfortable, every time his mind returned to it, and that was far too often, these last few days. He zipped his fly, pushing aside the loosely hung tarp and making his way gingerly back across the boards— holding onto the rope the whole way. *One wrong step. . .*

Would they fish him out? That was an open question, and one he didn't care to find the answer to, given the level of seamanship he had witnessed so far. *If they could.*

Their fresh water, what there was of it, was stored in two fifty-gallon barrels near the wheelhouse, and Shawn made his way over to the nearest one, reaching in deep with a dipper. It was nearly two-thirds empty, and he felt almost guilty as he raised the dipper to his lips. Lukewarm water spilling over his stubbled cheeks as he drank thirstily.

When he looked up, Emmanuel was standing there at his shoulder. Shawn extended the dipper toward him wordlessly and the Filipino took it, but made no move to retrieve the water.

"Have you heard?" he asked, edging closer to Shawn—his voice low, his eyes flickering about as if in an attempt to locate the nearest guards. "They're worried. . .ever since Manong Soleiman arrived, I've heard them talking. They're saying the Emir has been taken prisoner."

Chapter 4

A chill night breeze stirred across the ocean, causing a shiver to pass through Shawn's body as he lay there in the stern of the fishing boat, stretched out beside his daughter and wife. He knew from the numb, tingling sensation in his right arm, wrapped around Faith's small shoulders, that it had gone to sleep even if he hadn't.

Wincing, he pulled his arm out slowly from beneath her body—cautious not to wake her, raising himself up into a sitting position there on the deck. Glancing about them in the darkness.

He could make out the forms of the other hostages lying around them. The members of his *flock*, as he had to keep reminding himself. The urge to withdraw into oneself, so very strong. Chris—Crisanto—one of his earliest converts, a businessman in his late thirties. His wife, Annalyn. Marivic and Connie, sisters, both married, who had attended services under Emmanuel for several years before the Braleys' arrival in Quezon. Jun, a heavy-set, middle-aged father of two, a *tanod*—or watchman—for a small *barangay* not far from Quezon itself. He'd only started attending in the last few months—Shawn had met him on his return, just a few days before. . .all this.

And finally, Chris and Annalyn's fifteen-year-old daughter, Dolores, a shy, withdrawn girl already as tall as her mother. He'd seen her and Faith playing together by the wheelhouse the previous afternoon, the first time he had seen his daughter smiling since the morning of their abduction—the years between them seeming to have been evaporated by the crisis.

He had to be strong for them, for *all* of them, not just his family. If he could. *God help me. . .*

His thoughts shifted back to his conversation with Emmanuel the previous afternoon as he stood, stretching out his aching limbs. What would it mean for them if the reports were true? If this. . ."emir" who had been supposed to decide their fate was now himself a prisoner? Would they be freed? Killed, out of hand? Or would Manong Soleiman—or some other local guerilla leader—now step up to broker his own deal?

That last seemed most likely, and he knew not what it would mean for them in the end. *Was it possible that things could even yet get worse?*

He saw it then, as he looked up, the looming shape of a jungle-covered coastline, dark even against the darkness of the night—perhaps five or six hundred meters off the port bow. *Land.*

5:02 P.M., Eastern Standard Time, December 7ᵗʰ
The Situation Room of the White House
Washington, D.C.

". . .and I assured Adam that we *would* recover the Braleys, no matter what," President Richard Norton finished, glancing around the Situation Room at his team. "That's a promise that I intend to keep."

Promises. If there was one thing he had learned during his stint as director of the HRFC, it was that promises were a delicate thing when it came to hostage situations, Justin Valukas thought skeptically, reaching for the glass of water on the table before him. Particularly promises which would be passed along directly to family members, as this one surely would be. Adam Cardwell was the dean of students at Liberty University, a former television evangelist and a prominent figure in the evangelical community. And a personal friend of the President, at least since very near the outset of Norton's campaign.

He'd already made an appearance on Fox the previous evening with Shawn Braley's parents, and there was little doubt that the President would soon feel the pressure, if he hadn't already.

A more skilled political operator might have avoided allowing himself to get painted into such a tight corner, but despite Norton's time in the Senate, his approach to politics remained, on the whole. . .unpredictable, leaving career political analysts even yet, as his first year came to a close, sharply divided—generally along partisan lines—on whether he was an unusually savvy chess-player, or simply a gambler who continually swung for the fences, swinging so hard and so often that one lost track of the individual balls.

The President's voice drew him from his thoughts, as Norton looked up once more from his notes. "It is Valukas, isn't it?"

"Yes, of course. My apologies, Mr. President," the HRFC head responded, flustered as he realized he had apparently missed the question. His hesitation earning him a dagger look from Director Chamian.

"What can you give us on your progress?"

"Not a great deal," Valukas confessed, shaking his head. "By morning, our time, my team will be on the ground in Manila. We're already liaising with CIA and NSA to see what intel they can provide on possible locations the Braleys could have been taken following their abduction, but so far. . .so far, Mr. President, I have very little. The process is in motion, but it will take time to bear fruit."

"General?"

All eyes in the room shifted toward General Nathan Gisriel, sitting near the head of the long table, three chairs down from the President. He had spent the last six months as the second of Norton's National Security Advisers, but he retained all of the command presence he had exuded during his career in the Corps, along with the clear-eyed realism which had made him such an effective commander of Marines in Afghanistan.

"I talked with JSOC not an hour ago and General Shulgach assured me that DEVGRU is mobilizing assets for deployment. Operation "WINDBREAK," Bragg is calling it. We don't have anything in the immediate AO, but Red Squadron has been on the West Coast working with Team One this past week. If you so determine, they can be forward-staged to Kadena."

"Time?"

"Based on Shulgach's assessments, I believe we could have a team on Okinawa within thirty-six hours of you giving the order, Mr. President."

"Consider it given. Director Chamian, if you—"

"Excuse me, Mr. President," the general interjected, his leathery face a mask as he cut the commander-in-chief off, "but there are. . .complications involved with utilizing military force in the Philippines. They are a treaty ally, and under their constitution—"

Norton just stared at him, shaking his head. "Americans are being held hostage, Nathan. And we're going to send Americans to get them back."

2:03 A.M., Afghanistan Standard Time, December 8th
Kandahar Airfield
Kandahar, Afghanistan

The American flag was lowered here now, William Russell Cole thought, looking back up through the open, bomb-blasted roof of the Kandahar TLS—Taliban's Last Stand—building into the darkness of the clear, cold Afghan night sky above.

A shudder ran through his body as he stood there for another moment, on the verge of leaving—the cold wind biting through his heavy coat as if it had been paper, a faint ringing of metal on metal striking his ears as the flag clips shifted back and forth against the pole, batted by the breeze. No doubt the flag would be raised again at dawn, but he wouldn't be here to see it.

Whether there had been any actual "last stand" in this

specific building was something already lost in the mists of history—as incredible as it seemed that such events now belonged to the realm of the historian—but Kandahar had been the last major stronghold of the Taliban in those final months of 2001, and US Special Forces and the Afghan fighters of Gul Agha Sherzai had overrun the airport in the first week of December, with the TLS building coming to take on a unique symbolism in the months and years that followed.

There was now a small 9/11 memorial in the courtyard to the rear of the bombed-out building, and he made a point to visit it whenever he passed through Kandahar, as he'd done more than a few times over the years—mostly during his time with the Joint Terrorism Task Force. Like he'd done tonight.

Kandahar Airfield had changed so much over the years, he reflected, walking back out of the TLS building and into the night. The once-raucous boardwalk, where hard-partying Coalition soldiers and airmen—men and women alike—had eaten at TGI Friday's, gotten drunk, and danced the night away in a surreal sanctuary from war, was now largely shuttered. Salsa Night was a thing of the past, and so was TGI Friday's, which had found itself replaced by a far humbler coffee shop and a Kebab House where you could still order pizza and Philly cheesesteaks.

Most of the people were gone too, the few thousand American support personnel who remained a mere fraction of the numbers the base had once boasted. Still tasked with the same mission as ever before, trying to bring some kind of resolution to a war which had begun before some of them were even in kindergarten.

The HRFC team would themselves be gone before first light, Kandahar serving as a convenient refueling station at the near-limit of the Gulfstream's range. *Next stop: Manila. . .*

3:42 P.M. Pacific Standard Time, December 7th
United States Naval Special Warfare Command
(NAVSPECWARCOM)
Naval Amphibious Base Coronado
Coronado, California

"You can't talk him out of it," his wife had told him the previous night, Senior Chief Petty Officer Jason Guilbeau thought, his eyes scanning the satellite imagery displayed on the screens at the head of the room as Red Squadron's commanding officer, Commander Eric Fichtner, continued his briefing. *"He's you."*

She was right, that was the worst of it. He wasn't going to change Dave's mind. *Trying* was only going to lead to the same result it had between him and his own dad. Bitterness, and years of estrangement.

Given his own absence over all those years at war. . .he wasn't going to risk pushing their relationship over that brink. He'd give him his blessing once he got back. Because the job was calling him away, once again.

". . .our intelligence at this time is exceedingly limited," Fichtner was saying, "but we believe the Braleys to have been taken by Islamist fighters linked to ISIS-P, serving under the command of this man, Ismin Ebrahim Mostapa, known in the American media chiefly by his *kunya*, Abu Ismael al-Filipini."

The SEAL commander took a step back as an image of Mostapa came up on-screen, revealing a diminutive figure with glasses, standing in a doctor's office. An old file photo, clearly. Fichtner turned back toward his men.

"The night before the hostage-taking, Mostapa was taken prisoner in a raid conducted by commandos from the Filipino SAF, though word around JSOC has it that our friends from Christians in Action were in on the raid as well."

That figured, Guilbeau thought, a sour smile creasing the SEAL's face. These days, when *wasn't* the CIA involved?

"That information, gentlemen, is classified TS/SCI, and does not, I say again, does not leave this room. As far as the world knows, al-Filipini remains at large, and it is in the interests of the United States for them to continue to believe that for as long as possible."

Of course. It was a familiar refrain, and one that never seemed to get them anywhere—the jihadist grapevine always got the word out, somehow—but Guilbeau found himself nodding as Fichtner continued.

"This tasking comes to us straight from the National Command Authority. Red Squadron is the closest mission-capable SMU, and I have assured JSOC that the Indians will get the job done."

Guilbeau glanced around the room, seeing the grim smiles—hearing the murmured *hooyahs*. This is what they did—this is what they had all been born to do. Killing bad guys. Bringing their own back alive.

He caught Dom Zamora's eye, saw his familiar, crooked grin and answered it with a smile of his own. They were going to get the Braleys out, one way or the other.

"Get your gear together," Fichtner went on, "anything you need to straighten out with your home life—make the calls. We're wheels-up at 2300."

9:12 A.M. Philippine Standard Time, December 8th
Camp General Basilio Navarro, Western Mindanao
Command (WESTMINCOM)
Calarian District, Zamboanga City
Zamboanga del Sur, Mindanao

Ismin Ebrahim Mostapa was already waiting in the small holding room when Richards and Mijares arrived, his hands manacled and resting on the table before him—a stone-faced SAF commando standing guard in the far corner of the room, a Glock 17 riding in a holster on his hip.

Mostapa looked up at their entrance, squinting back and forth between them, a weary smile passing across his face at the sight of the American. They were going to have to get him glasses, before his capture was announced and some human rights group complained.

"And the master arrives," the pediatrician exclaimed, raising his cuffed hands in a curiously mocking gesture.

Richards took a metal folding chair leaning up against the far wall and opened it with a single rough thrust of his arm, metal scraping harshly against the concrete floor as he dragged it into position, easing his lanky body into it.

"You take your orders from this man, don't you?" Mostapa asked, his English very nearly perfect, peering over Richards' shoulder at Mijares. "The government of Luzon has never *stopped* answering to the Americans for a hundred years, every time their masters tug at their leash."

To Mijares' credit, he didn't bite, simply leaned back against the window of the holding room, arms folded across his chest—his face impassive.

"A century ago," Mostapa continued, turning his gaze back toward Richards, "the Spanish sold you islands they did not possess, and once your soldiers had conquered them, you turned them over to the control of others who had never possessed them either. When will you learn. . .that *all of this* has been your doing?"

"The Braleys," Richards interjected quietly, his eyes dark as obsidian. Unreadable.

Mostapa ignored him. "My great-grandfather fought them until his last breath, in the jungles around Lake Lanao, killing two American sentries in one night with his *kampilan* and escaping unharmed. Two men, two blows."

"But he didn't escape in the end, did he?"

There was a flicker of pain, sadness in the pediatrician's weak eyes. The admission, slower to come. "No."

"And neither did you." The right or the wrong of it all was beyond his ken, the Texan reflected, his black eyes searching Mostapa's face. Seeing behind those pained, kindly eyes a man who had been responsible for so much death. So much loss. A doctor of children, who had turned from healing to murder. *Contradictions.* But only the results mattered now, not the grievances of a century gone by. He wasn't here as any man's judge, only to recover his own. His fellow Americans, thrust into harm's way. "We'll always win, in time. Now. . .the Braleys."

"But will you?" The smile was back, as he continued to ignore the question. "My great-grandfather fell fighting beside his *datu* at Bacolod. The sultan surrendered, but the

59

Moros did not—they held out for another decade, fighting your soldiers every step of the way. It was America's longest war, until you invaded the emirate of Afghanistan. . .and you haven't won there either, have you?"

"Shawn and Charity Braley," Richards repeated, refusing to take the bait as he leaned forward slightly, locking Mostapa's gaze with his own. "They were kidnapped Sunday morning by insurgents, along with their daughter and seven Christian Filipinos. I want them back."

"And you think I can help you?" Mostapa shook his head incredulously. "I was in your custody when you tell me they were taken."

"That doesn't mean you didn't know it was going to happen. A grab like that—your people had to have planned it out, well ahead of time."

A barely perceptible shrug. "Perhaps they did. . .you truly believe I'm important, don't you? That taking me has brought you some benefit, that it has *changed* anything. As if the cause of God could be brought down by stopping one man? You killed Emir Usama himself years ago, yet the jihad continues. You smashed our caliphate, and yet you accomplished nothing more than a man might accomplish by striking a pool of water with a hammer. The droplets of water fly. . .*everywhere. Alhamdullilah.* And now you have taken me, and you tell yourself that surely—this time will be different."

The definition of insanity, the Texan thought, unable to deny the validity of Mostapa's words. More than a decade and a half at war should have been enough for America to sort out that their decapitation strategy wasn't working. That you never simply killed your way out of any conflict.

But policy wasn't his concern, never had been. He was here to do a job, as ever before.

"Help me find the Braleys," he began, "use your knowledge and your influence to help bring about their safe return, and—"

"And what?" Mostapa asked, smiling. "You'll let me go? Do you really think me such a fool?"

"No," Richards replied stolidly. "You aren't going free— *couldn't*, even if my government desired it. We aren't in charge here, no matter what you may prefer to believe. What is in my power is to make your time of confinement better. . .or far, far worse. *Help* me, and you—"

An urgent pounding on the door of the holding room cut him off, with Mijares moving to answer it—the figure of a uniformed commando visible in the entrance, carrying on a hushed conversation with Mijares before the officer turned to Richards, motioning him out.

"What's going on, Gringo?" Richards asked when they were out in the corridor, the door closing once more behind them.

"Your embassy in Manila just received a call. From Shawn Braley."

10:27 P.M. Eastern Standard Time, December 7th
CIA Headquarters
Langley, Virginia

". . .demand the complete and immediate annulment of Proclamation No. 216 and the removal, by the end of the month, of all Filipino military forces from the *Bangsamoro*, including the islands of Mindanao, Basilan, Sulu, and Tawi-

Tawi. I call upon you, President Norton, to use your influence with the government on Luzon to bring about this outcome. If you fail. . ."—here Shawn Braley's voice faltered, choking out in what sounded like a sob—"My family and I will be executed."

"I'll give them this," Bernard Kranemeyer observed grimly as the audio finished playing, "they don't lack ambition."

He'd been at home when word came of the call, but he'd come back in—driving in through a cold December rainstorm that threatened to turn to ice before morning. Nothing was going to happen tonight, but he had to *be* here—to hear it all for himself.

"They're asking for the rollback of nearly a century of Filipino geopolitics," Laura Killinger mused aloud, twisting her pen back and forth between her fingers. "The annulment of martial law and the de facto independence of the Moro Nation—the *Bangsamoro*, as they refer to it in the text."

He had asked Carter to send over the best analyst he had on the Philippines account, and Killinger—a plain, soft-spoken woman in her mid-forties—was the answer to that request. She'd spent the better part of her twenty-one years in government focused on the Far East, specifically the Philippines, first with the State Department's Bureau of Intelligence and Research—the INR—and then with the CIA. There likely wasn't anyone in the building who knew them better.

From the other side of the table, Olivia Voss shook her head. Unlike Kranemeyer, she hadn't yet left when the call came in.

"Maskariño isn't going to go for that," she said,

referencing the Filipino president, Luis Maskariño. "He's from Mindanao himself, and fiercely proud of his heritage. He's going to hold on to the islands at all costs."

As indeed he had proven by his abrupt imposition of martial law—the mentioned Proclamation No. 216—upon taking office, Kranemeyer thought, recalling then that Voss had herself spent time at Manila Station a decade or so ago. No doubt she had stayed up with the region, as time allowed.

And she wasn't done. "If there was ever a chance to break away, it wouldn't be under this president. They have to understand that."

"They do," Kranemeyer announced quietly, looking up from his notes. The conclusion, only too clear. "They're laying down impossible conditions. . .and when they aren't met, they're going to execute the Braleys."

Chapter 5

"Good flight?" William Russell Cole heard the Embassy driver ask, popping the locks of the US government Suburban and opening the door. Russ motioned one of his agents in ahead of him, glancing back along the line of vehicles to see Katherine Lipscomb enter the SUV behind his.

"Long flight," he replied simply, shaking his head. Keeping this small convoy together on the ten-kilometer drive to the embassy would be a challenge, but right now that was the least of his worries. They'd been over the Indian Ocean when the news of the contact had come in, along with Washington's detailed analysis of the hostage-takers' demands.

None of them within the realm of possibility, as far as the Filipino government was concerned—he knew that much without being told.

That was a tough open. And even after the phone call, it

remained unclear just how open the jihadists were going to be to two-way communication, let alone any sort of genuine negotiation.

He buckled himself in, closing his eyes for a brief moment as the State Department convoy lurched into motion, pulling away from the parked FBI Gulfstream, the sleek white fuselage of the business jet gleaming as though painted with fire in the final dying rays of the sun.

Now the work began. They'd know more after reaching the embassy, after they'd had time to conference with the ambassador and—perhaps more importantly—Manila Station.

The Suburbans pulled out into heavy traffic on Ninoy Aquino Avenue, surrounded by other cars, motorcyclists, an occasional jeepney—a bright red bus bearing the logo of *JTB Tours* looming up along the right side of their lead vehicle.

They'd be working closely with the Agency on this one, given their existing relationships with the Filipino mil/intel communities, despite hostage recovery overseas remaining firmly in the domain of State.

A bureaucratic mess of intertwined equities, even with the creation of the fusion cell. *Before that. . .*

It wasn't the first time he had done business with the CIA—he'd worked with them plenty during his time with the JTTF, most memorably one time in Peshawar—but it had never been by choice. *And last December. . .*

Well, last December—West Virginia, everything surrounding the road which had led to Vegas—was best left in the past, Russ acknowledged wearily, leaning back in his seat, glancing out through the heavily-tinted windows of the SUV as they flowed north with the traffic. It hadn't been anyone's finest hour, let alone his.

It was the negotiations that broke down which you remembered, long into the night—years later. The times you had *failed*.

And he could only hope, as the State Department convoy sped north up Roxas Boulevard, the median lined with towering palm trees, that this wasn't going to be one of those times.

6:03 P.M.
Camp General Basilio Navarro, Western Mindanao
Command (WESTMINCOM)
Calarian District, Zamboanga City
Zamboanga del Sur, Mindanao

"All those demands," Gringo Mijares mused, a thoughtful look in the commando officer's eyes as he scooped some of the pork adobo into his mouth with his hand, "and not one mention of Mostapa."

Richards nodded quietly, the mild spice of the pork and rice filling his mouth as the two men sat alone in one corner of the base cafeteria. "I noticed."

"That means the hostage-takers either aren't part of Mostapa's group, or. . ."

"He's as unimportant to them as he suggests," Richards finished, reaching for his cup.

"He's been their commander, these last few years, we know that from our intelligence—Marawi was his doing, all those casualties we took during the siege."

"Doesn't mean they want him back. You know how this goes, Gringo—you take out one, and everyone else below him sees it as their day in the sun." *Until we drop a Hellfire on their head,* the Texan thought but didn't add. For that itself sometimes created more problems than it solved. Like it had in the Sinai, not six months before.

"We will find your people, Jack," Mijares said earnestly, brushing grains of rice away from the corner of his mouth with the back of his hand. "And when we do, we're going to go get them back."

"I know you will." Richards reached for another handful of the pork and rice, glancing briefly at his watch as he did so. Knowing DEVGRU was already en route. . .

4:03 A.M. Hawaii-Aleutian Standard Time
A USAF C-17 Globemaster

Jason Guilbeau felt the massive airframe of the Air Force transport shudder as the KC-135 Stratotanker's refueling drogue decoupled from the port on the top of the Globemaster's fuselage.

He had made the mistake of watching a video of inflight refueling on-line one time, years back, and watching that obscene mating dance had robbed him of any peace of mind he might have once enjoyed during these flights. Aircraft the size of these had no business within *miles* of each other in the air—let alone. . .touching.

The SEAL rubbed a hand nervously over the knee of his AOR2 pattern camo uniform trousers, glancing around the fuselage at his fellow operators. Deploying Red Squadron to Kadena was no small feat of logistics, involving the transportation of not only the Squadron's fifty SEALs, but another forty mission support personnel, who would supplement those already in place on Okinawa.

A glance at his dive watch told him that they were still an hour out from Joint Base Pearl Harbor-Hickam, where they were going to pick up a task unit from SDVT-1, the Seal Delivery Vehicle Team stationed at Pearl. Another couple dozen SEALs, along with their own support team and headquarters element.

Which was to say nothing of the SDVs themselves, small manned submersibles used to deliver SEALs from either a submarine or a surface ship to their target. "Small" being a very relative word, Guilbeau thought, glancing sourly around the fuselage of the Globemaster—each of the SDVs measured twenty-two feet in length. They'd all be sitting on the floor by the time this was over, which probably wasn't that much worse than the narrow bench seat he currently occupied. Four hours in, and it was already digging painfully into his butt. *Four hours.*

They'd have another nine after leaving Pearl before they touched down on Kadena, refueling at least one more time in mid-air. He'd spent far too many hours in these planes over the years, flying out to war. Never came to like it.

He leaned back against the fuselage, glancing over to see Dominic Zamora's eyes glued to the tablet in his lap, going over the last intel they had received just prior to departure. First contact from the hostages since their abduction, not that it gave them much. Not even a general location, at least not yet—the call had been made from a satphone, and getting location data from those could be interesting.

All of the squadron's firearms were stowed, in the heavy equipment lockers lashed down to the center of the Globemaster's deck, but the chief petty officer wore his tomahawk on his belt. They all had them—Red Squadron's insignia was an Indian warrior, after all—but few of the SEALs carried them into the field.

He'd never had any use for them, himself—fine craftsmanship, to be sure, but a throwback to a peculiarly vicious kind of fighting he had no desire to ever engage in himself. He had given his to David, on his twenty-first birthday.

But Dom. . .Dom was a wild man.

Always had been, he reflected with a smile, remembering the first time their paths had crossed, in the Helmand, back when they'd both been on Team Three.

He'd known then that he'd met more than a friend—a *brother*. And when Dom had found his way to DEVGRU, not long after Guilbeau's #2 on the assault team had been sidelined in a training accident, he knew he'd found his replacement.

They made a good team.

Dom looked up then, shaking his head as he glanced over at Guilbeau. He said something, but it was lost in the incessant roar of the Globemaster's engines, and Guilbeau cupped his hand up against his ear.

"WINDBREAK," Dom repeated with a grin, louder this time—shoving the screen of his tablet toward his senior chief, the JSOC codename for this hostage recovery op displayed at the top of the classified document. *Operation WINDBREAK.* "Sounds like someone up top ate too many beans—I mean, come on, who picks these names, Senior?"

Guilbeau laughed at that. "A computer, *esé*. Just a computer."

10:37 A.M. Eastern Standard Time
The Situation Room of the White House
Washington, D.C.

". . .we've already submitted a formal request to the Emiratis to obtain the location data for the call," Justin Valukas said, looking up from his notes to meet the President's gaze. "We don't yet know if they'll be cooperative."

It just had to be a Thuraya. He'd had his fingers crossed that it would prove to have been an Inmarsat phone when word of the call came in—they were commonly used in East Asia, and getting a British company to cooperate with the FBI under circumstances like this wouldn't have presented any real challenges. Something the terrorists likely had sorted out for themselves.

The UAE—where Thuraya Telecommunications was based—offered the Bureau an entirely different problem-set, particularly given the administration's at-times abrasive approach to the Gulf States over the last year, something which seemed best left unsaid.

"Can't you track them anyway?" Richard Norton demanded incredulously, shaking his head as he glanced down the table. "Can't the NSA monitor that sort of thing?"

"If they call back, Mr. President, now that we have an idea of the number and service going in. . .there are certain protocols we can pursue which might give us at least an approximate location," Valukas explained, choosing his words with care. No one at this table labored under any illusions as to what Norton preferred to believe when it came to the surveillance capabilities of the intelligence community. "But we don't know that there will be another call."

"Unbelievable. You're telling me that you can monitor the phone calls of every American citizen, you can *store* their information in perpetuity—but you can't find a handful of jihadist tribesmen out there in some jungle using a satphone?"

"It's not that simple, Mr. President, we—"

"I've heard enough, thank you, Mr. Valukas," Norton shot back, cutting him off as he turned toward his National Security Adviser. "General?"

"DEVGRU's Red Squadron left Pearl thirty minutes ago, Mr. President," Nathan Gisriel replied gravely, "after being reinforced by a task unit from SDVT-1."

"Good, good," Norton smiled, every trace of his temper fading away at the general's words. "I know they'll get the job done. The SEALs are phenomenal warriors. You've seen 'Act of Valor,' Dennis?" he asked suddenly, glancing over at his chief of staff.

"I have, Mr. President."

"Great movie—one every American should see. Men who didn't have to *act* like heroes. As soon as the intelligence community gets their act together," Norton's gaze returned briefly to Valukas, "I want them to get in there and get the Braleys out."

11:37 P.M. Philippine Standard Time
Basilan Island
Autonomous Region in Muslim Mindanao (ARMM)

"We're going to help you, Mr. Braley—just stay with me here, and let me—"

Shawn Braley turned over on his back, suppressing a

hacking cough as he stared up through the darkness at the roof of the small shelter. The words of the female State Department employee running back through his mind. *Hope.* Manong Soleiman had ripped the satphone from his hands at that moment, and turned it off—silencing her voice. *His* message had been sent, and that was enough.

Somewhere off in the darkness, he heard a muffled curse—the sharp slap of a hand against flesh. With their arrival on the island, the mosquitoes—the absence of which had been one of the few blessings of the sea—had returned in force. He had already been bitten a couple times on his exposed arms, and, worse, once on the sole of his bare foot.

They had hiked in-land from the coast for most of the day, deeper into the densely forested jungle, after several of Manong Soleiman's men had taken the fishing boat back out to sea. Shawn had no real idea where they were, to be honest. Basilan, yes—a small island separated from the southwesternmost coast of Mindanao by a strait not more than nineteen kilometers across at its widest point—the eastern coast, given the position of the sun all day, as it slowly sank behind the mountains in the west. *Beyond that. . .*

He had been here once before, with Emmanuel, looking to plant a church among the Chavacanos of Lamitan, a small city on Basilan's northern coast. They hadn't stayed long— the church plant had turned out a failure, amid strong opposition from the local priests—but he'd seen enough to know: Basilan was a bigger place than it looked on a map. More than big enough to get lost in.

"We're going to help you," he heard the woman say over again in his head, and this time it was joined by a prayer. *God, let it be true. . .*

Chapter 6

The R.C. Worley Prayer Chapel
Liberty University
Lynchburg, Virginia

". . .and in conclusion, Father God, we trust in you, that you will watch over our brother and sister, Shawn and Charity, and bring them safely home to us, Lord, along with those of your children who were taken prisoner with them, that you would restore them to their families once again. Father, we are gathered here in this chapel where Shawn and Charity were joined together before you, claiming your promises of protection over your servants, that you will lift them up from out of this pit of despair and establish their steps upon the rock. In the precious name of Your Son, our Lord Jesus Christ. Amen."

Adam Cardwell rose from his knees, his joints protesting bitterly against the exertion—turning toward Tim Braley even as Shawn's father, his face wet with tears, reached out to embrace him. "Thank you, Adam. *Thank you.*"

"There's no need," Cardwell replied, holding the older

man close as he choked out his thanks. He had never met Shawn, but he felt as though he knew him now. "We're going to be here, every morning, interceding before the Lord. . .until they are returned to us. No matter how long that takes."

This time, they had prayed all through the night, the dean of students thought, dismissing those gathered with a brief word of thanks as he reached for the cup of coffee, his eyes bloodshot from lack of sleep.

He had been grateful for just how many students had turned out, though not all had stayed the night—joined together in prayer for two Liberty alumni who had gone to do the Lord's work, half-a-world away.

"We'll be flying back to Sacramento late tonight," Tim Braley went on, his hand on Cardwell's shoulder. "We need to be there. . .Timothy's body will be arriving tomorrow."

He nearly broke down once again at those words, the thought of his grandson—his namesake—coming back to America in a box, so very soon after having seen him leave. *For the last time.*

Cardwell grimaced at the thought, unable to keep from thinking of his own children, now in their late teens. "Of course. We'll do everything in our power, Tim—I have another meeting with the President this coming Wednesday morning. We won't let Shawn and Charity be forgotten by their government, that I can promise you. Everything else, well. . .that's in God's hands."

6:14 P.M. Philippine Standard Time
Basilan Island
Autonomous Region in Muslim Mindanao (ARMM)

They had walked all day, *again*—a strain that was telling on all of them. The captives, at least, Shawn had to admit—scooping up the last of his rice with his fingers and tucking it between his lips. His own feet were raw and blistered, despite one of the older guards, a greying Moro named Khadafi, loaning him a well-worn pair of *tsinelas*—flip-flops.

It was an act of generosity that had taken Shawn by surprise, all the more so when Khadafi had looked at Faith, riding on her father's shoulders, and handed her a piece of mangosteen candy, produced from somewhere deep within the recesses of his faded camouflage military jacket.

The jihadists, by contrast, seemed to be having no trouble keeping up the pace—not even the teenager, Aldam, who was laboring under the weight of the mortar strapped to his back, the better part of another fifty pounds in addition to his normal load.

The afternoon before, they had heard the sound of gunshots, a scattering of small-arms fire, faint and indistinct—off to the north. They'd been in an open field when the first firing began, and Manong Soleiman had hurried everyone across and into the trees, forcing the captives to stay down as his fighters fanned out, rifles at the ready.

They had even set up the mortar, which delighted Aldam as much as it seemed absurd to Shawn. Surely they—whoever *they* were—were well out of range.

They'd all stayed there for the better part of three hours

under the shelter of the trees—a merciful rest—slapping at mosquitoes and listening to the occasional desultory burst of gunfire drifting down to them on the breeze.

It was, Manong Soleiman had eventually concluded, a skirmish between other *mujahideen* and an AFP patrol. No threat to them, at least not immediately, and he'd pushed everyone back on their feet. *Back on the march.*

It was tantalizing to think of help that close, so close you could hear the sound of their guns. But he knew he would never have been able to make it, not and leave Charity and Faith behind him. And taking them with him on any kind of escape attempt would have been an impossibility, Faith in particular.

He leaned back against the trunk of the tree behind him, finding himself still hungry after what had passed for their supper. They had spent the latter part of the afternoon laboring up this hill from the fields below, finding a deserted farmhouse at its crest, surrounded by trees.

Manong Soleiman had taken up residence within, along with a handful of his fighters, leaving the rest of them to sleep on the ground outside—though a few of the jihadists had found hammocks somewhere and strung them between the trees. Somewhere, he heard the sound of women's voices singing, soft and low—Emmanuel had led the group in hymns several times over the last few days. Something *he* should have done, if he'd possessed the voice. *And the faith.*

"She's still hungry, Shawn," he heard his wife say, looking back to see her sitting there in the gathering twilight, just a few feet away. He had given a part of his rice to his daughter—would have willingly given it all, had he not known that he would be carrying her tomorrow. He had to keep up some of his own strength, if any of them were to survive.

His cough seemed to be getting worse, the sickness he had picked up on the plane trip back across the Pacific now only exacerbated by the stress of their kidnapping—the chill and exposure of the nights.

"Everyone is," he replied helplessly, the despair in her voice cutting him to the quick. He knew the words sounded cold, but he didn't know what else to say—or how to say it.

He wanted to reach out, to comfort her, but before he could speak another word, something caught his eye and his breath caught in his throat, looking out across the valley to see tracers flickering in the growing darkness. Too far off to hear the shots, this time—but you could *see* them, lethal fireflies flashing through the night. He stood, taking a few steps toward the brow of the hill to get a better look, the motion attracting Khadafi's attention. The older guard moved toward him, as if to check his movement, a warning look in his eyes.

"Unsa ang nahitabo?" he asked in Visayan, stopping short. *What's going on?*

"Manong Soleiman's men," Khadafi replied shortly, a smile creasing his bearded face as he hefted the Type 56 in his hands. "They're engaging the government soldiers, Shawn—drawing them away from us. You don't need to worry."

No need to worry. He just stared at the man for a long moment, as if unable to believe his ears. Then, collecting himself, he stepped closer, a faltering, hobbling step—his legs still protesting against the exertions of the day. "My daughter. . ." he began, "she's still hungry—the food. . ."

"I will try to find something for her," the older man replied, glancing past him toward where Faith was snuggled up against Dolores. "I have an *apo nga babaye* of my own, not much older than your girl." *Granddaughter.*

He smiled, his gentle demeanor belied by the weapon in his hands. "Children. They are a gift from God. Go back and sit down, Shawn. . .I will find something."

Jun sidled over to him as he returned to his seat on the hard, rapidly cooling ground—a furtive look in the eyes of the heavyset watchman as he glanced around them, seeming to mark out the positions of the nearest fighters.

"They're close, the soldiers have to be close—they weren't far at all from the trail this afternoon." He paused, as if mustering up the courage to continue. "I've been watching them, Pastor Shawn, the last few nights—the guards. I think I can get away. . ."

7:03 P.M.
Camp General Basilio Navarro, Western Mindanao
Command (WESTMINCOM)
Calarian District, Zamboanga City
Zamboanga del Sur, Mindanao

The call had come in thirty minutes before. Richards didn't know just how long the Filipinos might have been sitting on the intelligence before that—how long it might have taken them to weigh out what they intended to share with their American counterparts—but they *had*, and that was what mattered.

". . .according to our intelligence, the targets are currently located in this house here," Maricar de Rosales was saying, gesturing to a small, squat concrete-block structure outlined on the satellite map thrown up on the massive screen behind her, "in the Marabico *barangay* of Sultan Mastura. Abu Jainal is a known lieutenant of Mostapa, and had fallen off our radar since Marawi—we believed, in fact, that he might have died in the siege. Based on this sighting. . .it would appear not."

"And here," the NICA intelligence officer paused, clicking her remote to advance to the next screen, bringing up a surveillance photo—clearly taken from street-level, perhaps a passing car, "parked outside, to one side of the building, we have a grey utility van very similar in appearance to the vans reported outside the church in Quezon on the morning of the kidnapping."

That got Richards' attention. He shot a sharp look at Thomas Parker, their eyes meeting across the table. *Could it be?*

"Are the Braleys there?" If they were, and the Filipinos were already ready to launch. . .this was going to complicate things with Washington.

"We don't consider it likely," de Rosales replied, turning toward him. "It's a small residence, as you can see—it would be hard to accommodate the number of hostages, and we see few signs of guards being posted as one might expect if they were holding people inside."

All of which meant very little, Richards realized, unable to overcome his growing dislike of the intelligence officer. They might very well have split up the hostages—it would have made tactical sense to do so. Guards could be hidden. And Sultan Mastura was nearly four hours southwest of Quezon, near the Moro Gulf. Inside the autonomous region, which meant that even under martial law, the NICA's surveillance capacity would be limited.

"At this point, we're looking at a snatch-and-grab," she continued, "similar to our raid on Mostapa, though less elaborate. Collect or kill Abu Jainal, sweep the site for intel. Anything we can learn about the hostages, or the broader *Khalifa Islamiah* structure. Lieutenant Mijares has of course been instructed to account for the presence of hostages in his tactical plan, should our intel change."

Richards looked over at Mijares, taking in the commando officer's expression at a glance. He wasn't comfortable with the way this was unfolding, any more than Richards was.

"The assault teams will depart this base at 2130 hours, and stage for the assault at the coast near Parang. . ."

"Help me out here, Gringo," Richards said quietly, as the two of them exited the ready room together at the end of the briefing. "You know good and well what this could turn into."

A nod, as Mijares turned to face him. "This isn't my call, Jack. My men have been ordered in—the decision was made above my head."

"The NICA?"

"Above theirs, too, though it's their intel that is making it possible. Manila wants this wrapped up, Jack— Maskariño wanted to announce the capture of Mostapa in the next week as a success of his government's counter-insurgency strategy, and the coverage of the Braley kidnapping is taking all the attention in the foreign press."

Everything in war was political once you got down to it,

Richards thought, staring at his counterpart. There was no use in trying to convince yourself otherwise—no extricating the means from their ends.

"I'll call Washington," he said finally, casting a glance at Thomas Parker as he emerged into the corridor behind Mijares, "and get my team ready to roll out."

To his surprise, the commando officer shook his head. "No, not your team. You, and one other officer."

"Why?" This wasn't making any sense. "We all went out together to get Mostapa, my team and yours. We've operated together."

Mijares looked back and forth between the two Americans, his face betraying his exasperation. "This isn't about your people, Jack. It's about the fact that the media spotlight is on this time, in a way it wasn't when we grabbed Mostapa. This has to be *our* op."

Politics, again. As inescapable as all the rest. "I'll take Granby."

9:13 P.M.
The Embassy of the United States
Ermita, Manila
Philippines

"I am told that the President is awake and has been apprised of the latest developments," Ambassador Reuben Garner announced, sinking heavily into his chair as he glanced around the room, taking in the assembled group of FBI agents, other HRFC personnel, and CIA officers. "He's proposed placing a personal call to Luis Maskariño in an effort to put the brakes on tonight's raid, but I just got off the phone with Secretary Guidote, and . . .Maskariño isn't going to be accepting any calls this evening."

William Russell Cole swore softly, glancing over at Darren Lukasik in time to see the CIA chief of station frown and shake his head.

Maskariño's term in office had been characterized by an off-again, on-again pugnacious attitude toward engagement with the United States, but this. . .this took it to another level.

Indeed, he and his team hadn't experienced a great deal of substantive cooperation from their Filipino counterparts in the Department of Foreign Affairs since arriving in Manila two nights previous. Russ had hoped, by now, to be on the ground in Mindanao itself, working to set up negotiations with the militants, but with the island under martial law, that was proving to be a mess of red tape that Lipscomb and Garner's combined efforts had as of yet proved insufficient to unsnarl.

"I spoke with several of Policarpio's people earlier," Lukasik observed after a moment, referencing Ugalde Policarpio, the NICA's Director-General, "and they seem convinced that none of the hostages are actually in Marabico. That this will be a straightforward raid."

Russ looked up, shaking his head. "We'd all better pray they're right."

11:04 P.M.
The Gulf of Moro

Jack Richards leaned back against the hard seat of the UH-1H Iroquois, staring out through the window into the darkness of the night, only faint traces of the moon filtering through the heavy cloud layer to glint off the waters of the gulf, the rhythmic pounding of the Huey's main rotor filling the cabin.

Another helicopter was just visible there, maybe fifty meters off their port side—running blacked-out like their own, a hundred meters off the deck. There were three of them in all, loaded with commandos and support personnel.

It had been a while since he'd flown in one of these—over a year—and the sight of the familiar silhouette had brought back memories of that ill-fated cross-border op into Iran which had set them all on the road to Jerusalem the previous September. *The road to betrayal.*

It was nearly impossible to say, looking back, whether the warning signs had been there all along—or whether that was something you only perceived in hindsight, once the cracks had opened into fissures, swallowing you up. Had anyone told him, going in, that that helicopter ride into the Islamic Republic would result in the loss of three of the Special Operations Group's finest—one dead, one forced out, one turned traitor—before the dust had finally settled, he would have thought they were mad.

But it had been the world itself gone mad, instead. Zakiri and Sarami had come home in body bags, the traitor and the honored dead. And Harry Nichols. . .

Nichols' was the story without an ending—*yet*. No one knew where he was, ever since that bloody finish on the docks of Aberdeen, when he'd left the perpetrator of the Vegas attacks in a smoldering pile of human meat, torn apart by a suicide vest.

But Nichols hadn't been wearing the vest. And he'd disappeared after that, using all the skills the Agency had ever taught him to simply. . .vanish, into the night. A trail gone cold.

A part of him hoped it would stay that way. Nichols had been a brother, but after all that he had done in the UK—after all the *bodies* he had left behind him in his quest for vengeance—no good could come from his return. Only the bitterest of reckonings. That wasn't an end any man wished to see for his brother.

He glanced over at Titus Granby, sitting there beside him, and got a tight-lipped smile in return. All that was nothing but history to Granby, who had still been in training at the Farm when the world had fallen apart—and hardly even history. The Agency never made a point of publicizing its failures.

It had everyone else for that.

Men lived, men died, men disappeared. . .and the war went on. Like it did tonight, he mused, briefly checking the luminous dial of his watch. *Ten minutes to feet dry. . .*

11:43 P.M.
Basilan Island
Autonomous Region in Muslim Mindanao (ARMM)

"Father, watch over my brother Jun—may you guide him through the camps of our enemies, and bring him to safety. May you use him, Lord, as an instrument of your deliverance. . ."

Shawn's body convulsed with a wracking cough as he lay there on the cold ground beneath the trees, feeling the chill seep into his bones through the threadbare blanket. He had prayed over Jun before the two men had parted—Shawn back to his wife and child, the watchman back to his blanket. *Temporarily.*

He didn't know how long Jun intended to wait before making his attempt, but he found his entire body tensed as if in anticipation for the moment. A moment, that, if Jun were successful, he probably wouldn't even be aware of until the morning.

*If he wasn't. . .*he felt his body shudder, and this time it wasn't from the cold. Should he have advised him to stay put? To wait for rescue? They hadn't been mistreated, yet. Not really. The food was limited, for sure, but Manong Soleiman's fighters weren't eating that much better. And the Filipinos were likely in less danger than he and his family if they stayed. . .they didn't have the same value as a political statement and Manong Soleiman had already broached the subject of ransoms, for them.

But he'd said nothing of the sort, just knelt down and prayed quietly with the watchman, a man he hardly knew. Hoping against hope that he would succeed—that he could be the means of salvation for them all.

11:03 A.M. Eastern Standard Time
Naval Support Facility Thurmont—Camp David
Frederick County, Maryland

It was good to get away from the city, even if only for the day, Richard Norton thought, hands shoved into the pockets of his dark slacks as he stood in the sun room of the Aspen Lodge, staring pensively out through the fine-falling snow toward the pool, an addition made to the presidential retreat during the early '70s. *The Nixon years.*

The press was comparing him to Nixon, but that was something they had done ever since the early days of his campaign, playing the similarity between their names into an odious smear. Despite his commitment to greater government transparency, a contrast with his infamous predecessor which couldn't have been more blindingly obvious. They would have done the same thing to any Republican president, of that much he was sure—certainly the Hancock administration had never faced the kind of scrutiny that his government was subjected to on a daily basis.

And his task was complicated by the reality that not everyone in this town—or even in his own government, he reflected darkly, the face of Vice President Kenneth Havern materializing before him—wanted transparency of the kind he had promised the voters. He had known that, going in, but even so. . .implementing his legislative agenda had proven far more difficult than he ever could have imagined, the bureaucratic inertia nearly impossible to overcome.

He had told those closest to him that putting a former CIA deputy director on the ticket was a disastrous choice—but Havern's comforting centrism had been the only way to squash a brooding rebellion of the party establishment which could have split the election three ways and returned Roger Hancock to the White House.

It had been a devil's bargain he had regretted bitterly ever since the night it was made, and the relationship between President and Vice President had only grown more chilly over the course of their first year. It wasn't uncommon in Washington for friendships to be forged—or simply to survive—despite deep policy differences, but Norton had always despised the kind of politician who put on a show for the cameras and then went golfing with his political "enemies" the next weekend. All of it, kabuki theater of a kind this nation had sickened of long ago.

That wasn't for him. For Norton. . .enemies were enemies, when the cameras were off, as when they were on. And the Vice President was looking more like one with every passing day.

"What's the latest from the Philippines?" he asked, glancing back past the figure on the couch to where his chief of staff, Dennis Froelich, stood by the door.

"Nothing as of yet, Mr. President. We're still ninety minutes out from the takedown of the target, according to the timetable passed along by Ambassador Garner."

"Let me know the moment we hear anything from Manila," Norton advised, pacing away from the window. Maskariño's refusal to take his call had rattled him—he was the President of the *United States*, for the love of God, and yet this. . .this former *mayor* from an island half the world had never heard of had the audacity to slap away his outstretched hand.

"Of course, Mr. President."

The Braley family had reached out through the HRFC's family liaison, requesting that they be given the chance for input on any proposed rescue attempts, along with an implied veto of any actions they felt might further endanger their loved ones. Which was ridiculous—even *he* didn't have a veto over the actions of the government in Manila. The most powerful man in the world, and he couldn't alter what was about to happen on the other side of the globe. . .not one bit.

"The NSA can tell you what an American messaged their wife while eating breakfast," he spat angrily, returning to perch on the edge of his recliner, "but they couldn't find a handful of jihadists in a jungle fast enough for me to send in the SEALs ahead of this Filipino upstart. This is about *survival* now."

"Excuse me, Rick?" Senate Majority Leader Scott Ellis asked from the couch, looking surprised at Norton's last line. "What do you mean?"

"I mean that I want SB286 back on the table, first thing come the new year. This isn't just about the principle of the thing, not anymore, the promises I made to my voters. This is about survival—*my* survival. They are trying to take me down, Scott."

"The intelligence community?" Ellis' voice betrayed his incredulity, a grimace passing across his face. "Rick, I don't really think—"

They had been friends, once, during Norton's own time in the Senate—members of the same coalition. They had campaigned for each other, been in each others' homes—their families had grown close, Norton reflected with a pang, glancing back out through the doors of the sun room to glimpse Scott's teenage children building a snowman on the veranda, one of the girls leaning in to take a selfie with the crudely-shaped figure. When his own son had died of a drug overdose in junior high, he and Leslie had taken Scott's much younger children as their own.

All of which made this betrayal the more painful.

"That's right," he fired back, his face flushing with anger. "You don't think. And so long as I am President, Scott, you will address me with the respect due the *office!*"

"Look, Ric—Mr. President," Ellis stopped short, his eyes reflecting surprise. Taking a deep breath as if to collect himself. "I'm simply saying that it's not helping anyone's legislative agenda when you come across paranoid like this, what with your public comments about a 'deep state,' and the suggestions that people in your own government are out to get you. You would help your party a lot more if—"

"What would you suggest they were doing in the Sinai, Scott?" Norton asked quietly, his voice now deceptively even—his hands pressed flat against the arms of the recliner to keep them from trembling. "Allowing me to embarrass myself like that. What are they doing now? We know what the intelligence community is capable of doing. . .when they have the *desire*. But they don't."

"Mr. President, what you're suggesting—"

"The intelligence bureaucracy of this country is a cornered animal," Norton continued, cutting the Senate Majority Leader off. "They know what I promised to do, and unlike those who preceded me. . .they know I meant it. That *scares* them, Scott. The most powerful security apparatus in the world, and they're *scared*. What do you think that means? We're locked together now, in a struggle to the bitter end. Either I take them down—or they take me down."

"I hear what you're saying, Mr. President," Ellis replied at long last, a tactic Norton recognized as familiar from their Senate days. *Hear*, not *agree with*. "But right now. . .I simply don't have the votes."

"Then *find* them."

Chapter 7

1:24 A.M. Philippine Standard Time, December 11th
Marabico, Sultan Mastura
Maguindanao, Philippines

Six minutes. Richards adjusted his NODs, staring down the gentle, sloping hillside a hundred and forty meters toward the small *barangay*, and their target building on the far side of the road which ran through the center of the village. Picking out the figures of the SAF commandos, flitting like ghosts between the buildings—moving into position, enveloping the target.

"We should be down there, man," Granby observed, leaning back into the side of the rusting, abandoned jeepney on the crest of the hill, his voice nothing more than a whisper. "You know it, and I know it."

Richards just nodded, Granby's words drawing a sharp glance from their minder, one of Mijares' junior NCOs, crouched a few feet away. He did. But they were bound to abide by the wishes of their host nation. . .until they weren't. And Washington hadn't taken those particular gloves off. *Yet.*

He heard the *clucking* of chicken just then and glanced down through the NODs to see the disturbed fowl scampering out of the way of Mijares' men, setting up a racket as they scattered into the street.

Come on. His breath caught in his throat, eyes straining to pick out any signs of further disturbance in the village as he saw the commandos freeze in place, ghostly statues— weapons trained outward. All it would take was one person, investigating the noise.

And then he saw a door begin to swing outward. . .

1:26 A.M.
Basilan Island
The Autonomous Region in Muslim Mindanao (ARMM)

How long he had lain there, awake, looking up at the dark clouds drifting by above the tops of the trees, Shawn had no idea. He had nearly fallen asleep a couple times, overcome by the sheer exhaustion, but each time he had come back awake with a start—reproaching himself bitterly for the lapse. *Could you not watch with me one hour?*

Was Jun already gone? Had he slipped out, hours before, leaving Shawn to continue his vigil, pointlessly, alone? The missionary turned over on his side, suppressing a heavy cough as he did so—staring out through the trees in a futile attempt to locate Jun's form. He could discern the shapes of the hammocks their captors had strung up in the trees, but it was too dark to make out anything else.

"Shawn. . .are you okay?" he heard Charity ask softly, her voice hushed so as not to disturb their daughter. He hadn't realized that she was awake, and wondered briefly who else might have heard his cough.

"I'm fine," he replied, a self-evident lie. He was sick, and getting worse the longer they spent exposed to the elements. If only Jun could get help, could get them *out* of here. "It's just—"

And that's when he heard it, from off toward the other side of the farmhouse—a rough shout, breaking through the stillness of the night. Followed by a burst of gunfire.

1:27 A.M.
Marabico, Sultan Mastura
Maguindanao, Philippines

Disarming and securing the local *barangay tanod*—village watchman—had been the work of seconds, Richards thought, his NODs picking out where the man lay zip-tied, face-down in the dirt of the street. One of Mijares' men standing over him, gun in hand. *Precious* seconds, but it was done and had been done quietly—that was the important thing.

He might be an innocent, he might be one of Abu Jainal's fighters. They'd sort that all out later, at their leisure. For now. . .Richards' eyes picked out the SAF assaulters stacking up on the entrance—heard the murmured Tagalog of the sniper team positioned on the brow of the hill maybe ten meters off to their right, maintaining overwatch.

Another squad of the commandos was holding a perimeter back of the target building, in place to trap any squirters—anyone who might even think of getting away.

It was a solid tactical plan—there wasn't anything about it that he would have changed had he been tasked with leading the assault himself, other than that *he* would have been down there, with Mijares.

He felt Granby shift restlessly at his side, knew the strain of waiting was telling on them both.

Then a crackle of static came through his borrowed earpiece, Mijares' voice hoarse and low, "*Go! Go! Go!*"

As if in acknowledgment, the sound of an explosion rippled up the hillside toward their position, the metal door of the target structure flying inward, torn off its hinges by the force of the blast. Part of the concrete-block wall appearing to collapse inward along with it, forcing Richards to question the size of the charge used. Demolitions had always been his forte.

But Mijares' men were up and in right after the blast, the muzzles of their weapons leading the way—relying on the surprise and disorientation of the explosion to incapacitate their targets.

Taken off-guard, asleep, the urge for *flight* was going to be far stronger for most than the desire to fight back—Richards knew that much from hard-earned experience. It was just basic human nature, and the best tactical plans always did their best to both account for and exploit the weaknesses of man.

Yet even so, as he stared down on the squat concrete-block outline of the target structure, he heard a shot. Followed by another. A long, ragged burst of gunfire, ripping apart the night.

And then silence—an agonizingly painful silence which couldn't have lasted more than forty seconds, but felt like an eternity. Broken only by Mijares' voice, coming over the comms 'net.

All clear.

2:03 A.M.
The Embassy of the United States
Ermita, Manila
Philippines

"So that's that," William Russell Cole conceded grimly, bringing the cup to his lips and draining the last of his now-cold coffee. "It was a dry hole."

Ambassador Garner let out a heavy sigh, shaking his head as he leaned against the conference table, his elbows pressed heavily into the wood, the sleeves of his dress shirt rolled up above the elbow. It had been a long night at the chancellery, a long night and a fruitless one. "No sign of the Braleys."

"Or Abu Jainal." Russ looked over at the sound of the station chief's voice, nodding slowly. Lukasik looked about as haggard as the FBI agent felt, and small wonder after the night they'd all had.

The NICA's intelligence had been accurate, as far as it went. The missionaries hadn't been at the target location—nor was there any clear indication, as of yet, that they ever had been. It had been, as promised, a straightforward raid.

A raid whose actual target, Mostapa's lieutenant—Abu Jainal—hadn't been there either. The SAF operation had netted them a grand total of four militants of dubious rank in the ISIS-P hierarchy taken prisoner, and a fifth shot dead resisting capture.

"The SAF commandos are still on site along with my officers," the CIA station chief continued, "conducting site exploitation."

They may yet find something—the clear subtext of Lukasik's words, even if he left it unsaid. And perhaps they might—coming up through the Bureau, Russ had worked far too many investigations to discount the value of physical intelligence collection. . .but that was going to be a question for another day.

He glanced over at the ambassador and saw him nod. *Time to call it a night.*

3:01 P.M. Eastern Standard Time, December 10th
Aspen Lodge
Naval Support Facility Thurmont—Camp David
Frederick County, Maryland

"So you're telling me they failed?" President Richard Norton demanded, arms folded against his chest as he stared toward the television screen mounted on the other side of the Camp David conference room.

"Site exploitation is ongoing, Mr. President," NCS Director Bernard Kranemeyer replied, his face impassive on-screen. Disturbingly calm, Norton thought, unable to conceal the dislike he'd felt for the man ever since his testimony during the Sinai hearings.

If the deep state had a face, it was that of Bernard Kranemeyer, of that much the President was sure—but he was also a consummate professional who commanded the respect of his community, and had given Norton no reason to remove him.

It wasn't that he *needed* a reason, exactly—Kranemeyer, like any other IC executive, served at the pleasure of the President—but he was laboring under enough media scrutiny as it was, and firing a war hero wouldn't play well with the party base. Particularly one who, like Kranemeyer, had lost a limb in his country's wars.

"Our Filipino counterparts," the DCS was saying, "remain confident that valuable intelligence will be gleaned from the raid, but yes, neither the main target nor the Braleys were located at the target location."

Norton swore softly, shaking his head. He felt alone in this room, just him, his chief of staff, and the disembodied voice coming from the speakers, the face on the television screen. He had come to Camp David to spend a quiet Sunday in the mountains, but now he felt himself missing the comforting murmur of his advisers. The knowledge that there was someone he could turn to—lash out *against*. Even Ellis was gone, hiking the trails with his wife—apparently needing his own "space" after their contentious meeting earlier.

"You need to find them," he said suddenly, looking up again to glare across at Kranemeyer's image on-screen. "Quickly. Before the Filipinos do. I won't tolerate this kind of incompetence leading to their deaths."

5:34 A.M. Philippine Standard Time, December 11th
Basilan Island
The Autonomous Region in Muslim Mindanao (ARMM)

Pain. Shawn Braley doubled up from the impact of the kick, a hacking cough tearing at his empty lungs as he gasped for breath, struggling to shield himself against another blow.

Instead, he felt a hand entwine itself in his hair, jerking his head up from the hard ground—his eyes opening to find Manong Soleiman's face only inches away from his own, silhouetted dark against the first rays of the dawn. "You sent him away," the guerrilla leader spat, drops of moisture flecking Shawn's face. "You told him to try to escape us. . .my men, they saw you talking."

"No," the missionary managed, honestly enough, fighting against the pain, hearing Faith sobbing in the background—his wife's soft voice as she struggled to comfort her.

He hadn't *told* him—he just hadn't *stopped* him. Wasn't sure he could have, even if he'd wanted to. And they hadn't found the watchman yet, despite the chaos that had reigned in the small farmhouse camp for the last four hours, since Jun's escape attempt had been detected.

Shawn still wasn't sure how he'd managed to get away, plunging down the hillside in the darkness—a sporadic flurry of gunfire pursuing him out into the night. But it had taken the dazed, sleep-deprived jihadists valuable minutes to collect themselves after their initial reaction—eight men fanning out across the cassava fields in an ultimately fruitless pursuit.

Thank you, Father. He was watching over them—*all* of them. Four hours Jun had been gone, now—the soldiers they'd been forced to evade the previous day hadn't been *that* far off. It might take most of the day, but he could reach them. *Bring them back.*

Manong Soleiman shook his head in disgust, thrusting the missionary's head back against the cold, hard ground with a rough gesture, pain exploding through Shawn's skull.

He lay there, moaning, struggling to get his breath back as he listened to Soleiman bark orders to his men, ordering them to pack up and prepare to move out. Knowing that another hard day was ahead of them—that his body was beginning to break down under the strain.

But help was on the way.

7:34 A.M. Japan Standard Time
Kadena Air Base
Okinawa Prefecture, Japan

". . .the raid resulted in the capture of four low-level militants, and the death of a fifth. The SAF took no casualties."

"And it was a dead end," Jason Guilbeau observed, leaning back into the chair as he looked across the desk into the eyes of his commanding officer.

"It was," Fichtner nodded, glancing briefly around the confines of the small office. It wasn't his—belonged to some Air Force lieutenant colonel home on leave, just another one of the dozen or so small pieces of real estate around Kadena which DEVGRU had commandeered upon arrival two days before. *Hurry up and wait.*

It was a familiar routine, by now, if one that never failed to chafe. There were times Guilbeau wished he was back on Team Three, forward deployed once more—not held in reserve to put out fires, forever awaiting the signal.

A faint smile passed across his face at that thought. Maybe he *had* followed in his father's footsteps, after all.

"The AFP have some good people in their spec-ops units," Fichtner went on, conversationally, "particularly their SEALS. I did cross-training with their Special Warfare Group some years back when I was with Team Five, and they've gotten better since. But when the spooks get the intel wrong. . ."

Then everyone has a bad day. Guilbeau nodded, remembering some of his own experiences with the Agency in Afghanistan. He'd worked with the CIA on several occasions over the years, and it had always been an uneasy relationship. They had their own way of doing things in the field, and it didn't always mesh with Naval Special Warfare.

"But that's not why I called you in here today, Senior," the CO said, his tone of voice shifting as he straightened in his chair, looking Guilbeau in the eye. "I've been advised by JSOC that the command authority no longer believes that the cooperation of our AFP partners is guaranteed, and we've been ordered to prepare contingency plans allowing for both a smaller footprint, and a covert infiltration of the target, once one is identified."

And that changed the ballgame, the senior chief thought, grimacing at the words. They'd counted on the support of the Filipinos—they *were* an ally, after all. *If they couldn't. . .*but Fichtner wasn't done.

"General Shulgach has already covered the bases with CINCPACFLT, and the USS *Michigan* has been detached from CARSTRKGRU 5 to support our operations."

We get to lock out of a sub. It wouldn't be the first time, for any of them, but it wasn't Guilbeau's favorite way of infiltrating a target. The *Michigan* was an old *Ohio*-class boomer which had been laid down at the height of the Cold War, and like more than a few of the *Ohios*, had been converted to an SSGN in the early 2000s, replacing each of its original Trident nuclear missiles with seven much smaller Tomahawk cruise missiles, better suited for supporting America's conventional operations during the War on Terror.

All but two of the launch tubes, that is. The remaining two had been converted into lockout chambers for special operations personnel. *Them.* The SDV boys were going to be earning their pay. . .

"The *Michigan* is currently based out of Fleet Activities Yokosuka, and if the balloon goes up, that's where we'll be headed." Yokosuka, Japan—the home of Carrier Strike Group Five—the US Navy's only permanently forward-deployed carrier strike group, headed up by the *Ronald Reagan.* "And Senior. . ."

"Yes sir?"

"Keeping this low footprint is going to cut down the number of men we can deploy operationally. Basically just a pair of assault teams and the SDVs. If it comes to this, Senior. . .I want you to take tactical command of the op."

Chapter 8

The soft sand gave under Jack Richards' booted feet as he ran down the beach, legs pumping—his tall frame bent forward into the crisp sea breeze.

A Marine Corps cadence streaming over his earbuds as he glanced off toward the south, out past the wharf toward the open sea, spotting a *Jose Andrada*-class coastal patrol boat making its way back in toward Naval Station Romulo Espaldon, the headquarters of Naval Forces Western Mindanao, just adjacent to the WESTMINCOM base itself.

He had fallen asleep on the flight back, despite the cacophony of the Huey's engines throbbing just behind his head. His Corps training coming into its own once again—years out in the field giving him the ability to go to sleep all but on command. You slept when you could, wherever you could.

Because you never knew how long it might be before you could do so again.

Now. . .he had no doubt that the cables were flying fast and thick between Manila and Washington, but there was little he could do about any of that. He and his team were due to leave Mindanao in five days, and he had yet to receive any clarity on whether their stay would be extended past the original deadline.

A part of him wasn't sure it should be. They weren't accomplishing anything here—not so long as the AFP kept them on such a tight leash. Might as well leave the Filipinos to it, as hard as that decision would be. Not that it would be his to make. He would go where he was sent, as in the Corps, so now. When he was sent.

He stopped in the shadow of the wharf, the crashing surf washing over his boots—hard black eyes staring out across the water toward the faintly visible outline of Basilan, dark against the blue horizon, a scant eight kilometers across the straits.

The Braleys were here, *somewhere*. That much he knew. Mindanao itself, Basilan. . .Jolo—any one of scores of other small islands in the Sulu Archipelago, stretching away to the southwest for three hundred kilometers.

So much territory. *Too much*, to strike out blindly, even if he'd had authorization.

And wherever they were, time was running short.

10:42 A.M.
Basilan Island
The Autonomous Region in Muslim Mindanao (ARMM)

The sun was already high in the sky above as Shawn Braley stumbled through the cassava fields, his hands now tied behind him, the rope biting deeply into the soft flesh of his wrists. His wife's hand on his shoulder, doing her best to steady him. Faith was somewhere behind them, with Dolores, no doubt—she and the young Filipina had been inseparable, these last few days.

You never realized just how much of your balance was in your arms until you could no longer use them, he thought, staggering forward—his throat raw and his head light, as if it were floating somewhere in the clouds high above him. *Dreaming.*

But their captors were taking no chances on another escape. He, Emmanuel, and Chris were all tied up now—they were less concerned about the women, or so it seemed.

His side throbbed with pain with every halting movement—his ribs were bruised, of that much he was sure. Would probably have been broken if Manong Soleiman had worn boots, rather than the open-toed *tsinelas*.

"You're burning up," he heard Charity murmur, pressing an ice-cold hand against the damp, matted hair covering his temple. Concern written across her face as he turned to look at her. The last few hours, the chaos surrounding Jun's escape—his beating at the hands of Soleiman's men—seeming to have broken through the spell that had fallen on her in the hours and days immediately following their kidnapping.

"Of course," he responded, shaking his head, every word an effort. His throat was dry, but their water was limited, and he had just had a drink not that long before. The sun was beating down on them all, burning away the chill of the night. *What did she expect?*

He stumbled just then and she caught him, her face only inches away from his when he looked up. The anguish and sorrow in her eyes, cutting him to the bone.

"We're going to be okay," he whispered hoarsely, so low that only she could hear. He wasn't capable of much more, and yet. . .he had to say something, to strengthen himself, as much as her. "God is watching over us, sweetheart—even now. He's going to bring us all back together with Tim and Hope once again. *Jun got away.*"

She turned her face away from him then, her body seeming to convulse in a soundless sob. Her fingers digging into the flesh of his shoulder with a strength born of desperation, as if she feared to ever let him go.

And a cold, gnawing chill gripped his heart at the sight— a fear he had managed to repress ever since those moments following the shooting at the church. "What is it?" he asked, lurching forward in the soft ground of the field—struggling to face her. Yearning to reach out and touch her, to find in her embrace the comfort for his fears. "Tell me."

Charity looked back and he could see her face was wet with tears. A shake of the head answering his question—or refusing to. He heard Aldam's voice crack out like a whip, urging him on, but it rang distant and hollow in his ears and he paid the teenager no heed, all of his attention focused on his wife. His voice raw, and pleading, once again, *"Tell me."*

Another sob, her shoulders shaking in her anguish. "He's

gone, Shawn," she moaned, the secret she had held in her heart, for so many days, breaking forth like water through a shattered dam. "Our son. . .is gone."

No. He had known it somehow, even yet—but he had convinced himself it was a lie. Stress and exhaustion, playing tricks on his fevered brain, tormenting him with the illusion of loss. Perhaps it still was. He backed away from her, shaking his head—his words finally finding voice. *"No, no. God, no."*

Another step back, and his foot caught on something— a rock, a clod of earth, a *root*. And he was falling, a curiously weightless sensation overcoming him in the split-second before he slammed into the earth, driving the breath from his body.

He lay there, disoriented, unable to move—to know *why* he should move—staring up at the sun past his wife's face as Charity shook him, struggling with what remained of her strength to help him back to his feet.

A single word, running over and over again through the murky shadows of his brain as he lay there, unheeding. *Tim.*

1:34 P.M.
DILG-NAPOLCOM Center
Quezon City, Metro Manila
Philippines

"No, that's simply unreasonable. You can't ask my government to cede sovereignty over its territory in exchange for the lives of two of your citizens."

"Three," Katherine Lipscomb responded, her eyes hard and unyielding as she stared across at Ismael Robredo, the

Secretary of the Department of the Interior & Local Government (DILG). "And we're not asking you to cede sovereignty—simply that you would, in conjunction with our team, open negotiations with Abu Sayyaf for the safe return of the Braleys."

"And Abu Sayyaf has made the startpoint of those negotiations very clear." Robredo shook his head, his lips compressing into a thin line. "Your country doesn't negotiate with terrorists. Why would you insist that we should?"

William Russell Cole looked away, out the window of the government skyscraper, the north face of the still-unfinished Skysuites Tower just visible in the corner of his field of view. *Your country doesn't negotiate with terrorists.*

There was a story to be written there—how a throwaway line in a Ronald Reagan speech had unwittingly become *de facto* US hostage policy. Fitting, perhaps, for a culture built around the TV soundbite—now, the tweet—good for a president who had needed to maintain his reputation as a hardliner, but in practice, it had done little but complicate the jobs of men like him. And hadn't really been true, even then.

"Mr. Secretary," he opened, trading a brief look with Lipscomb as he turned his attention back to Robredo, "many times, we find that these groups—or elements within them—*are* open to other forms of concession or compensation, given the right approach. All we ask of your government is that you initiate contact."

4:06 P.M.
Basilan Island
The Autonomous Region in Muslim Mindanao(ARMM)

At some point, Shawn didn't know when, the tears had simply. . .stopped. Replaced by a deep, throbbing ache, somewhere deep within his heart—a pain that surpassed any physical pain he had known in the days since they were taken. The fever clouding his brain until it was only the anguish which remained, the only sensation sharp enough to penetrate the fog.

Tim. He hadn't spent as much time with him as he'd wanted to—even during their time in the States, away from the day-to-day pressures of the ministry, there had always been meetings to attend, places to speak. A thousand little things, all of them so very important. And he'd told himself that it would be different when he was older, when they could do more together. That he would *make* the time.

And now. . .that was all at an end. Tim was never going to be any older. They were separated, even if only for time and not eternity.

He moved as if in a trance, his hands still bound behind him—his steps halting. One foot in front of the other, again and again.

Through the delirium, he could hear Charity's voice, somewhere off to his left—arguing with first Khadafi, then Soleiman himself—snatches of their conversation, filtering past the haze.

". . .if. . .don't get help. . .he's sick. . .he's going to die out here. . ."

Perhaps so. He hardly knew whether he cared, anymore—

it *would* be the quickest way to see Tim, once again. And that seemed to matter more than anything else, just now.

His brain hardly even registered the first shot—the whiplash *crack* of a rifle bullet ripping through the humid afternoon air.

It was only when one shot became two, then bursts of fire tearing through the air around them—when he heard the shouts of Soleiman's men—that he realized what was going on. *They were being rescued.* Jun had gotten through. They were safe.

He looked up to see a bullet strike the forehead of the militant just ahead of him, ripping through the young man's skull and out the back in a fine spray of blood and brains, dropping him into the cassava plants practically at Shawn's feet. His eyes wide as they stared emptily up at the missionary.

Another bullet whipped past his head as he stood there, seemingly rooted in place—struggling to clear the fog from his brain, to *find* his wife and daughter.

Aldam's shouts of anger and fury reached his ears, and Shawn glanced over to see fire blossom from the muzzle of the teenager's Type 56, his long, jet-black hair flowing over his shoulders as he squeezed off burst after burst. He was standing exposed in the open field as he fired, the mortar tube still strapped to his back, until one of the older men grabbed him by the shoulder, forcing him down.

Shawn looked off to the north, saw the line of soldiers— spread out among the trees bordering the edge of the field, a few figures advancing into the open. *Freedom.* So very close.

A cry broke through the haze and he looked back to see Khadafi scoop little Faith up in his arms—the older man holding her protectively against his chest, her arms wrapped around his neck as he returned fire with a pistol, firing off-hand as he moved westward, toward the shelter of the trees.

Then a hand was on Shawn's own shoulder, an urgent voice in his ear, forcing him onward, out of the line of fire.

A window of opportunity, open. *And closed.*

6:37 P.M.
Camp General Basilio Navarro, Western Mindanao
Command (WESTMINCOM)
Calarian District, Zamboanga City
Zamboanga del Sur, Mindanao

"Basilan?" Jack Richards asked, following his Filipino counterpart down the stark, brightly-lit corridors toward the detention facilities.

"So he says," Mijares replied, casting a glance back over his shoulder at Richards and Parker. One of the prisoners snatched the previous night had broken under interrogation and was singing like the proverbial canary. "He claims that they were taken by men loyal to Uncle Soleiman—*Manong* Soleiman, as he is known."

He exchanged a glance with Thomas. That name didn't ring any bells. "He's a fairly low-ranking KIM lieutenant—or was, prior to our capture of Mostapa," Mijares went on, referencing the *Khalifa Islamia Mindanao,* clearly reading the lack of recognition in his counterparts' eyes. "It's hard to say where he'll land in the hierarchy as it reshuffles, particularly with such valuable hostages under his control."

"Does the prisoner have any idea where Soleiman is holed up on Basilan?" Richards asked, reflecting back on his morning run on the beach—staring across the straits at the very island in question. "Basilan" narrowed it down, but it still left them with a lot of territory to search. *Too much.*

A shake of the head served as reply. "He's just a shooter, nothing more—he knows Uncle Soleiman by reputation only."

"But he was willing to talk." The skepticism must have been audible in Richards' voice, because Mijares paused, his hand on the door leading into the detention center itself.

"Not everyone who joins Abu Sayyaf is a true believer, Jack. You know that, you've worked counter-insurgency before. You both have. Some people do it for the money—others are forced to join up at the point of a gun, aimed at them, or their families."

Richards nodded. It was a familiar refrain, its truth complicated by the fact that the number of people claiming they had been "forced" once they were themselves taken prisoner was almost certainly larger than the number who actually had. *Like Nazis in post-war Germany. . .*

But none of that mattered, just now. If this man truly had the information they needed to secure the Braleys. . .Richards didn't care about the rest. It would be left for the Filipinos to account for his sins.

"I will ask you both to remain on this side of the glass as we go in," the commando officer continued, glancing between the two Americans. "One of my men will act as interpreter as we—"

A voice from down the corridor cut Mijares short, an enlisted man wearing the muted single chevron of a private first class on the sleeve of his uniform hurrying toward them.

"Sir," he began, handing what appeared to be a hastily-scrawled report over to Mijares, "we've just received communications from Major Ocampo."

Richards felt himself tense at the mention of the name, and looking over at Parker, he saw his own concern mirrored in his partner's eyes. Nehemias Ocampo was in operational command of the Philippine Army's 10th Infantry Battalion. *On Basilan.*

If anyone had come across the hostages, alive or *dead*. . .it would have first gone through his headquarters.

It seemed to take an eternity for Mijares to finish scanning the report, looking up at the Americans as he finished. "Earlier this afternoon, elements of the 10th Infantry stumbled across an Abu Sayyaf contingent about ten kilometers to the southwest of Tuburan."

He extended the sheet toward Richards, inviting him to read it. "They're saying they've recovered hostages."

7:02 P.M.
The Blackbird, Nielson Tower
Makati, Metro Manila
Philippines

". . .thank you both so much for meeting with me here tonight," Debra Patterson said, a wan smile crossing her face as she toyed absently with her silverware. "I know you're both terribly busy."

"Helping you," William Russell Cole replied, reaching across the table to briefly cover her hand with his own, "is our job, Debra. We're here for you, and all the rest of your family, as you need us."

"Thank you," Charity Braley's older sister responded,

and he could see tears welling in her eyes, held bravely in check. Debra was eight years older than her younger sister, and looked the part of the Midwestern Sunday School teacher, wife, and mother of three that she was. "Shawn brought Charity here for their anniversary last year. . .the photos were so beautiful. We don't have anything like this in Linton."

That wasn't hard to believe, Russ thought, the lighting low and soft around them as he glanced out the rounded windows of the converted airport tower—through the trees toward the bustling streets beyond. In 1941, Nielson Field had been the headquarters of the Far East Air Force, an ill-fated organization stood up scant weeks before Pearl Harbor. The FEAF had been cut to pieces in the months that followed, most of its personnel eventually swept up in the final resistance on Bataan.

And in the years that followed the war, Metro Manila had grown up around the old military airfield, swallowing it whole. Runways becoming roads, and the tower—a restaurant.

"I want to assure you, Debra," Katherine Lipscomb said, laying down her fork, "we are doing *everything* in our power to get your family back. We will not rest, so long as they are in captivity."

Russ nodded his assent, noting Lipscomb's judicious choice of words. *No promises.* They were dangerous things to make, in this business. Particularly with the lack of cooperation they had experienced with Secretary Robredo, earlier in the afternoon.

"God bless you, both of you." Debra's voice choked off, and she reached for her water, taking a long sip as she struggled to compose herself. "I'm staying here, in the Philippines, until they. . .until it's over. It's the least I can do."

Her mother—Charity's mother—had come with her, but she had left days earlier, flying back to the States with little Hope. There wasn't much her presence here could effect. . .but perhaps it would serve to put additional pressure on the Filipinos. He wasn't going to be the one to tell her "no," at the very least.

"I received a call, earlier this afternoon," she went on, picking at her food. "They wanted a ransom."

Russ stiffened, his posture suddenly rigid as he lowered the fork of lamb rendang back to his plate, untouched. But it was Lipscomb who spoke first. "You heard from their kidnappers?"

"That's what they said," the woman replied, shaking her head helplessly. "I have no idea how they got my number, but they sent me a picture of Shawn and Charity."

"Do you have it with you?" Russ asked, cursing inwardly that she hadn't notified the embassy at once. *Or at least her HRFC family liaison.*

You never knew what you were getting into, working with families—the combination of raw emotion and ignorance of proper procedure making for a potent cocktail. He remembered a case he had worked back in the early '90s—the family of the victim, a sophomore at Duke, hadn't bothered to tell the Bureau of the ransom demand for *weeks*, imagining somehow that they could handle it on their own. That it would be better that way.

She nodded, digging her phone from her purse and unlocking it, briefly running her thumb across the screen for a moment before handing it over to the two of them.

Both Shawn and Charity were visible in the picture—but *not* their daughter, Russ noticed, unable to suppress a growing sense of disquiet—sitting by themselves in the shade of a tall marang. The camo-clad legs of someone, presumably a guard, visible in the upper right-hand corner of the frame.

There was no indication that they knew they were being photographed, which struck him as curious by itself—but there was no difficulty in making out their faces. And Shawn was clearly in bad shape, his own face bearing the marks of a beating—visibly being supported by his wife, even sitting there on the ground, his hands apparently tied behind him.

"Seeing them like that. . ." Debra's voice choked out in a sob and she shook her head, wiping away hot tears of anger with the back of her hand. "They asked for twelve million dollars."

He could tell that the sum had staggered her, but it was far from abnormal. The Islamic State had demanded $132 million for James Foley alone—a case which had ended in the worst possible of outcomes. He hadn't been involved, but he knew the agents who had. Knew that the HRFC itself was a nearly direct response to what the US government perceived as its failures in the Foley debacle.

That didn't change what he had to say. "I must caution you, Debra," he began, exchanging a brief glance with Lipscomb, "that the HRFC cannot be involved in any payment of ransom to a Specially Designated Terrorist Group. We will, of course, continue to do everything in our power to negotiate their release by other means, but in this. . .you'll be on your own. You will have to hire someone private to run things on that end—there are companies that handle this sort of thing."

Something of a growth industry, he had to admit, in the age of the Islamic State. And its far-flung affiliates.

"I understand," she nodded, blowing her nose into a tissue. "I'm sorry to break down like this—I spoke to our lawyer before coming here."

So her first call had been to their lawyer, Russ thought, his face impassive as he listened. *Better and better.*

"He said that there would be legal concerns—that such a ransom could be construed as material support for terrorism. That we, or those who helped us, could find ourselves in jeopardy. . .that can't be *right*, can it?"

Material support for terrorism about summed it up. Kidnapping had always been a for-profit enterprise, but the Islamic State had industrialized it, as they had so much else, bringing in a significant chunk of their operating expenses through ransom payments.

"He is right," Katherine Lipscomb interjected, "but it is not the policy of this administration—or any prior US administration—to prosecute family members for doing what it took to recover their loved ones."

Which still left the other thousand or so people contributing to the GoFundMe out there twisting in the wind. . .but that was likewise uncharted territory, legally speaking. Their world, changing more rapidly than the law could keep up.

Russ opened his mouth to add to Lipscomb's remarks, but at that moment, his phone began to vibrate within the inner pocket of his suit.

"Excuse me," he told the women, rising to wend his way

through the clustered tables of other diners as he made his way toward the door. "Yes?"

"Russ, are you with Mrs. Patterson?" *Darren Lukasik's voice.*

"Just excused myself," Russ replied, pushing open the door of the men's restroom. "You can talk freely—what's going on?"

"Word came in from WESTMINCOM in the last hour—their forces got into a firefight on Basilan earlier this afternoon with Abu Sayyaf fighters, believed to be part of Soleiman's group. They recovered two hostages, and the body of a third."

The body. Russ swore softly, struck afresh by the sense of failure. Debra Patterson's face, rising before him. The grief, and yet the *resolve* in her eyes. "The Braleys?"

"We don't yet know."

Chapter 9

Another shock jolted through the frame of the jeepney as the vehicle went over a bump, and Shawn Braley groaned despite himself—leaning heavily against his wife's body. Feeling her breath on his cheek.

He was warm, far warmer than he ever should have been, temperatures without plummeting as the night deepened—sweat beading on his forehead, but he knew the chills would hit soon enough. And once they started. . .they would never stop. Across from them in the darkness, he could make out the figure of Manong Soleiman, lounging against one of the bench seats on the other side of the bus, with Khadafi beside him, a rifle in the older jihadist's hand, his eyes ever watchful. *Guarding them.*

Curses in Visayan filled his ears as the vehicle went over another bump and in his mind, drifting absently through the delirium of fever, he found himself hoping one of the jihadists riding on the jeepney's roof had been shaken off.

Everything after the running gun battle in the cassava fields was a haze, but he remembered reaching the shelter of the marang trees. Bullets still cutting through the air past their heads, seemingly fired indiscriminately.

They'd realized only then that the sisters—Marivic and Connie—had been left behind, somehow separated in the confusion. Perhaps they had made a run for it. He hoped so—hoped someone, somehow, had managed to find deliverance from this nightmare.

Then a bullet from one of the soldiers' rifles had come whining through the trees, striking Chris in the throat—dropping him like a rock, leaving him drowning in his own blood as he struggled to speak.

They'd torn a wailing Dolores away from her father's body even as more rounds came in, killing another of Manong Soleiman's fighters. Aldam had scavenged mags from his corpse, shouting curses back through the trees as he reloaded.

And they had run, all of them—hurried along by Soleiman's men, until the gunfire faded into the distance and they could slow down once more, by which time Shawn had felt nearly dead.

Where they were now, how far they had come, where they were going. . .he had no idea. The garishly-painted jeepney had arrived a couple hours after dusk, with a stone-faced young Moro at the wheel, after Soleiman had placed a series of increasingly-agitated calls on his satellite phone, to someone—other Abu Sayyaf commanders, presumably, soliciting aid.

He only wished that, along with the vehicle, they could have sent someone who actually knew how to drive.

A few minutes later, his head rocking back and forth listlessly against Charity's breast with the motion of the vehicle, Shawn felt the jeepney slow—a shout of alarm coming from one of the fighters on the roof. He glimpsed Manong Soleiman's hand steal to his pistol, heard voices without. Loud and authoritative.

Soldiers. A military checkpoint—it had to be.

He struggled to push himself up, to rise—knowing that even now could be their moment of salvation. Surely there would be no way for Soleiman's fighters to hide, stacked up as they were on the roof, their weapons barely concealed, if at all, beneath blankets.

The big Colt 1911 out in his hand, and his knapsack slung over his shoulder, Soleiman pushed open the back door of the jeepney and disappeared into the night as Khadafi took up a crouching position in the door—rifle aimed outward.

More voices, Soleiman's among them—rising and falling as if in the midst of an argument, the words indistinct, lost in a stream of rapid-fire Visayan. And then someone laughed.

"All right, all right," he heard an unfamiliar voice say. "Go on, then."

When Soleiman reappeared in the jeepney, taking his seat across from Shawn as the vehicle lurched once more into motion, the knapsack was gone.

And Shawn knew, as sure as if he had witnessed it with his own eyes, his heart sinking deep into the pit of his stomach. *The soldiers had accepted a bribe. . .*

11:43 A.M. Eastern Standard Time
The Oval Office of the White House
Washington, D.C.

"This is unacceptable." The President stopped pacing for a brief moment, hands on his hips as he paused by the *Resolute* desk, glaring back at the small group of men and women occupying the two sofas. "Completely unacceptable. That could have been Shawn Braley. Or his wife."

It was the calmest thing Norton had said in the twenty minutes since the meeting had gotten underway. Not that he was wrong. Justin Valukas pursed his lips, his eyes drifting back toward the photo of the dead man in the file folder lying open on the coffee table in front of Bernard Kranemeyer. Crisanto "Chris" Parada, age thirty-seven, a married father whose wife and daughter were presumably still hostages of Abu Sayyaf.

Dead, somehow, a casualty of the firefight between the terrorists and the Filipino Army. The official line out of Manila, currently, was that he had been executed by his captors when they were cornered by the terrorists, but that seemed inconsistent with what other information they had about the gun battle.

"We cannot allow this to happen again," Norton stormed, glancing from face to face as Valukas busied himself with his notes. "If the Braleys are still alive, we cannot give the Filipinos another chance to. . .foul this up."

Easy enough to say. *Stopping them*. . .hard to say how that could be accomplished. It *was* their country, after all.

"I will be meeting here, in the Oval Office, on Wednesday with Adam Cardwell," the President went on after a moment's pause. "I need to be able to tell him that we are making progress—real progress."

"I need you, both of you"—his glare flickered between Kranemeyer and Chamian—"to find the intelligence I need to send in the SEALs."

"Obtaining authorization for direct action from Manila may prove problematic, Mr. President," Aaron Sorenson interjected, every eye in the room shifting toward the Secretary of State.

"We don't *need* authorization, Aaron," Norton fired back, his hands resting on his hips. "We are the *United States of America*."

There was a pause between each word, the way he said it, every successive word receiving a more intense emphasis. "We will do what it takes to bring our people home, and if Maskariño knows what's good for him, he'll go along with it."

"Mr. President, with respect." This time, everyone turned to look toward the slight, middle-aged woman sitting at Kranemeyer's side. "While it's true that Luis Maskariño's personal style is more confrontational than we've become accustomed to dealing with from Manila, on this issue make no mistake, he *does* speak for his nation. The legacy of colonialism is still incredibly real in the islands, as are the memories of the American involvement of the last century, and all it brought, the bad along with the good."

Valukas smiled, despite himself. He had worked with Laura Killinger before, during her time with the INR—State's intel arm—and knew her to be as outspoken as she was competent.

He was almost surprised that Kranemeyer had brought her

into a principals meeting, but it was Kranemeyer, after all. The man was nothing if not an enigma—as close to a black hole as it was possible for anyone in the Beltway to be. Those dark eyes of his, a vacuum from which no light escaped.

The President stopped pacing once again, shooting a dagger-sharp stare in Killinger's direction. "'Colonialism'? Seriously? If I wanted a lecture on the past misdeeds, real or *imagined*, of this country, Ms.. . .Killinger, I would turn on CNN."

"Respectfully, Mr. President," the analyst pressed on, undeterred by the display of anger, "when your predecessor signed the Enhanced Defense Cooperation Agreement with Manila, it was met by heavy protest. The cultural memory of our prior involvement in the islands is still something which carries weight with the Filipino body politic, and will influence how Maskariño reacts to actions taken by this administration."

"*My* administration, Ms. Killinger," Norton corrected, his voice hard and unyielding. "The Marxist Left is going to protest, there as here—it's what they do."

From the opposite end of the far sofa, Nathan Gisriel cleared his throat, drawing Norton's attention as the general leaned forward, elbows resting on his knees as he clasped his hands together before him. "The concerns Ms. Killinger raises are not without validity, Mr. President. A direct military action in sovereign Filipino territory—no matter how covert, because we certainly would not be concealing the recovery of the Braleys after the fact, would undoubtedly have diplomatic repercussions. Maskariño has already made overtures toward Beijing since coming to office—this could drive him directly into their arms."

With everything that flowed from that. . .the loss of a major ally in the Far East, a strategic partner in the effort to stem the swelling tide of Chinese influence in the western Pacific. Valukas had never specialized in the region, but you didn't have to be a specialist to grasp the long-term ramifications of such a step.

"Then perhaps," Norton went on after a moment's pause, "it's past time for Manila to get off the fence. And choose their friends."

1:25 A.M. Philippine Standard Time, December 12th
Camp General Basilio Navarro, Western Mindanao
Command (WESTMINCOM)
Calarian District, Zamboanga City
Zamboanga del Sur, Mindanao

". . .for over an hour, until losing contact with the terrorists approximately—here." Lieutenant Mijares used a pencil to draw a short line across the large terrain map of Basilan spread out on the table before them, illustrating the general route.

Three kilometers, Jack Richards thought, glancing at the map scale. It was tempting to criticize the Filipino detachment for not being able to pin their enemy down in that time and space, but it was hard to judge without being there to view the battlefield for himself. And it was just as well that they hadn't.

Ocampo's men were grunts, not commandos. They didn't have the kind of training necessary for hostage recovery, and if they had succeeded in running Manong Soleiman to ground. . .

"The deputy chief minister of the autonomous region, Mujiv Dimaporo, has already filed a complaint with Manila over the afternoon's violence," Mijares continued, shaking his head. "Insisting that the major rein in his men."

"Dimaporo?" Titus Granby asked, looking up from the terrain map. "He was MILF, right?"

Richards heard a muted chuckle from Ardolino, but Mijares simply nodded.

Granby swore softly at the admission, shaking his big head. "Last time I was here, we were fighting those guys. Now he's in government."

And round and round it went. The Moro Islamic Liberation Front had spent more than two decades fighting for the liberation of the *Bangsamoro* after their predecessor organization—the Moro National Liberation Front, or MNLF—had laid down their arms in 1987, making their peace with the administration of Corazon Aquino.

A fight which had come to an end a few years prior, when the MILF officially laid down their own weapons at the culmination of years-long peace talks with Manila, driving their remaining hardcore fighters into the ranks of Abu Sayyaf—itself a former MNLF splinter group—or the *Khalifa Islamiah Mindanao*, Mostapa's organization.

"The rescued women will be brought here in the morning, to be fully debriefed before being reunited with their families."

"Good," Richards nodded. They needed to get the information out of their heads fast, before the trauma erased anything valuable. *If it hadn't already.* "I'd like the opportunity to speak with them, if I may."

"Certainly."

"Lieutenant." It was Granby again, a curiously intent look on the Marine's dark face as he studied the terrain map, rubbing a hand through his wiry black beard. "The Tenth had elements in blocking positions here. . .here. . . and here, right?"

Mijares took a brief look at the map. "Yes. We continue to maintain military checkpoints throughout the *Bangsamoro* as part of our agreement with the ARMM."

"If Ocampo's soldiers have already swept this area toward Tipo-Tipo, and he had other elements set up to control the roads. . .how did Manong Soleiman get through?"

3:05 A.M.
Basilan Island
Autonomous Region in Muslim Mindanao (ARMM)

Fire. Heat. It felt as if his feet might go out from under him at any moment, the fiery glow of a burning flare casting strange, flickering shadows across Shawn Braley's face as he swayed there, his bare, blistered feet sinking into the sand of the beach, Charity's grip on his shoulder the only thing keeping him upright.

The fishing boat that bobbed out there in the rolling surf was larger than the one that had brought them to Basilan, but not by much. Then again, there were fewer of them, now. Marivic and Connie, gone, presumably rescued. Jun, escaped—to bring help that had fallen just short of their salvation. Chris, dead.

Along with Tim. The knowledge of his son's death, a congealed ball of ice in the pit of his stomach. He might well join them soon.

It seemed strange to him—all of the lights, as though the terrorists had no concern of being spotted. Perhaps they had bribed the navy, like they had those soldiers at the checkpoint.

A man came splashing in to shore, wading through thigh-deep water to reach them, his camouflage pants soaked and clinging to his legs. "Manong!"

"*Salaam alaikum*," Soleiman greeted, reaching out a hand to pull him onto firm land. *Blessings and peace be upon you.*

"*Wa alaikum as-salaam.*" And upon you be peace.

No one was coming for them, Shawn realized, catching Emmanuel's eye as he was prodded forward. Jun's attempt to bring help, futile in the end. The barrel of the Type 56 in Aldam's hands jabbed hard into the Filipino's back, nearly sending him sprawling into the surf. The teenager's laugh loud even over the sputtering crackle of the flare.

"Come on, come on." Khadafi's voice in his ear, a hand on his shoulder—the water swirling around his ankles, then his knees as Shawn stepped deeper into the surf. Uncertain, faltering steps.

Farther toward the boat, waiting for them out there, beyond the crashing waves. *Deeper into the night.*

10:12 A.M. Japan Standard Time
Kadena Air Base
Okinawa Prefecture, Japan

". . .Basilan Island, forty square kilometers of terrain, mostly mountainous in the center of the island. Somewhere in here, gentlemen," Commander Fichtner announced to his SEALs, gesturing toward the map, "are the Braleys."

"So when do we go get them?" Guilbeau heard Dom Zamora ask, glancing over to see his second-in-command standing poised there, not five feet away, hands on his hips. The waiting had been grating on them all, but Dom's impatient streak was never far from the surface.

It would disappear once they got into the field, as Jason knew from long experience. Once he was doing something, Dom could take his time if that's what was needed, but to do *nothing*. . .that cut against the grain.

They couldn't even train here at Kadena the way they would have done back in Virginia.

"We don't yet have authorization from Manila," the SEAL commander replied, turning to focus on Zamora. "And if our own command authority clears us to proceed without it. . .we're going to need better intel."

Guilbeau felt himself nod. It was a small island, but far too large to go running around blindly, particularly with Philippine Army units in the AO. They needed something precise, and ideally near the coastline—unless command was willing to switch over to air assets for the infil.

"At the time of their brush with the AFP, Manong Soleiman's fighters were located here, southwest of Tuburan toward Tipo-Tipo. The AFP after-action report estimates his strength at fifteen-sixteen MAMs, maybe less."

Military-aged males. A relatively small group, all things considered, but enough fighters to prove a hassle in a firefight, if it came to that.

"Senior Chief," he heard Fichtner say, realizing suddenly that the commander was addressing him. "I want you and your people to go over Basilan with everything we have—

terrain maps, satellite, everything. Familiarize yourself with the AO. If you find something you need and don't have, have the Agency make themselves useful and get it. Get to *know* that island."

11:34 A.M. Philippine Standard Time
Camp General Basilio Navarro, Western Mindanao
Command (WESTMINCOM)
Calarian District, Zamboanga City
Zamboanga del Sur, Mindanao

". . .and when the firing started—when the soldiers came through the trees, I didn't know what to do. I froze," Marivic Torralba admitted, choking up as she reached up to wipe away a tear from the corner of her eye, the trauma of the memories still far too fresh. The reality of her rescue, as yet not quite *real.*

Richards sat quietly on the other side of the table, giving her space to recover. She had to want all of this to be over, and in this moment, he was just another part of her ordeal.

"Connie took me by the hand and pulled me along—Soleiman's men, they were too distracted to stop us as we ran. I heard someone shout out a few minutes later, but we were too far away—to get to us. . .the soldiers would have shot them."

He nodded. He knew all this already, from the notes the Filipinos had taken on their prior debriefing session with the sisters, but it was her story and there was nothing to do but let her tell it. *Her way.*

"What about Shawn and Charity Braley?" he asked when she paused, reaching out to take a drink from the bottle of water on the table between them. "How have they fared, through all of this?"

A shadow seemed to pass across Marivic's face at the mention of the Braleys, but it was hard to know how to account for it. "It has been difficult, for both of them—as it was for all of us. They lost a son, you know, in the shooting, but Shawn didn't know that, until the last day. I had tried to tell Charity that she should tell him, but she could barely believe it herself, and he was so sick. . ."

"Shawn?"

A nod. "He was sick when he came back, some kind of flu or. . .something. It was Pastor Manny who kept us together, the months they were gone—and since the attack."

Emmanuel Asuncion. A married father of two who had, according to to Marivic's sister, started the work in Quezon before the arrival of the American missionaries, and kept it going during their absence. Richards nodded his recognition of the name, encouraging the woman to continue. It was strange that he hadn't found more references to the man in the bulletins posted on the Braleys' mission website—no references at all to him as the founding pastor of Victory Baptist.

"Those nights—the cold, I could hear him coughing. He looked as though he were going to die." She swallowed hard at that, her face still pale. "I thought we were all going to die. If Jun hadn't escaped. . .if he hadn't *found* the army. . ."

The clock was ticking, Richards thought. *Faster now.* If Shawn Braley's condition was as bad as she described, their time was short.

Abu Sayyaf might try their best to keep their hostages alive, but their best might not be good enough. And they might not even try, if all this was intended to end in an execution anyway. "Did Manong Soleiman make any attempt to procure medicines for. . ."

He stopped then, only then registering what she had just said. "What do you mean, 'escape'?"

She looked at him strangely, shaking her head. "Jun— the watchman—he escaped, and brought the army to us. That's how they found us, how they rescued Connie and I."

"I see," he replied simply, scrawling a brief note on the pad before returning to his questions. A reminder to mention her words to Mijares, but he knew, even without asking—a dull ache settling in the pit of his stomach.

He had read the after-action report from Ocampo's soldiers. And there had been no mention of any escaped hostage. . .

Chapter 10

9:27 A.M. Philippine Standard Time, December 18th
Edwin Andrews Air Base
Zamboanga City
Zamboanga del Sur, Mindanao

"It's him," Gringo Mijares acknowledged reluctantly, running a hand over the lower half of his face as he turned away from the half-unzipped body bag, the stench of decomposition seeming to spread out to fill the airplane hangar. Richards heard one of the SAF commandos retch and shook his head, a grim sadness in his dark eyes.

It had been six days since Marivic Torralba's report had sent them out looking for Jun Santos. Seven since the rescue. Seven. . .or eight, the reports conflicted, since the middle-aged watchman had made his escape from Manong Soleiman's men. A brave man. *Or so he once had been.*

It was hard to say how long he'd lasted, but at some point, judging from the slash wounds on the bloated corpse—the savage blow to the side of the neck which had all but decapitated him—he had run into more Abu Sayyaf.

Maybe Manong Soleiman's men, maybe not. Hadn't

made much difference, either way. He'd died, alone, in the jungle—only to be found the better part of a week later, his body already in an advanced stage of decomposition, as Nehemias Ocampo's soldiers swept the island in an increasingly futile search for the remaining hostages.

And Washington was getting impatient, Richards thought, turning away from the body as a priest in Philippine Army uniform zipped the bag back up, beginning to say prayers for the dead—Parker and Granby falling in behind him as the three of them walked out past the ungainly shape of the twin-tailed OV-10 Bronco light attack aircraft parked at the other end of the hangar.

An American design dating back to the late '60s, it once had provided forward air control to his own Marine Corps, but had been retired well before his own enlistment. So here it was, still fighting, fifty years on, on the far side of the world. There was always going to be a war.

His team had already been extended a week past their original departure date, despite the lack of the updates. There had been no communication from Abu Sayyaf, no further ransom demands made of the family. No propaganda videos featuring the Braleys as props to advance their captors' message. Just. . .*nothing*. Utter silence.

He knew that the powers-that-be back at Langley suspected the Braleys might already be dead, that this. . .silence might be nothing more than an attempt to drag it all out.

It was hard to say they might not be right, given what the sisters had been able to tell them of Shawn Braley's condition, a week before. If Manong Soleiman hadn't found some way to get that fever under control. . .

He heard a soft curse escape Granby's lips, looked over to see the Marine shake his head. "Man, I haven't seen a body that bad in years. . .Afghanistan, probably. Maybe not even there—if there was one thing the hajjis were good at, it was retrieving their dead."

Granby paused a moment before adding, "That dude risked a lot to give those people a fighting chance—he deserved better."

There was a murmured assent from Parker, his face pale—the smell of death lingering around the three men as they emerged into the open air—but Richards said not a word, his jaw set as they made their way back to the vehicles.

A man's just deserts had to wait for the next life, he reflected, his mind still with that priest—beginning to pray over the resealed body bag. This life—this life didn't care at all what any man *deserved.*

And it wasn't going to care about the Braleys one lick more than it had about Jun Santos.

9:32 A.M.
DILG-NAPOLCOM Center
Quezon City, Metro Manila
Philippines

". . .you don't understand the situation in Basilan, Ms. Lipscomb," Ismael Robredo countered, rising from behind his desk to pace over to the window. "The MILF laid down their arms, and *became* the government of the ARMM. We made peace, but the relationships didn't go away. It's still a tribal society, in much of the autonomous region, and those connections run deep."

"Then you need to increase the pressure." William Russell Cole could hear the weariness in Katherine's voice as he looked up, sliding his phone back into the inner pocket of his sports coat. Neither of them had gotten much sleep. Still nothing from his daughter, not since the previous night—he had yet to convince Tiff to make the move to his place, and now she was saying that there was no point, if he wasn't going to be there for Christmas anyway.

And there was no way he could tell her he would be, not a week out, with so much yet hanging in the balance here. The situation, essentially unchanged.

If anything, it was getting worse, with the recovery of Jun Santos' body—a day before. *Another one down.* That made two hostages dead now, the odds that the Braleys were still alive, shrinking with each passing day.

"A Moro isn't going to betray his family because Luzon tells him to," Robredo replied, turning from the window of the skyscraper to face them, his hands spread out before him. "Mujiv Dimaporo? He's been an integral part of the peace process, these last few years, but his second cousin's son fought with Mostapa during the siege of Marawi City. Would he have given him up?"

It was a rhetorical question, clearly. No doubt the Filipino government had *tried*.

"The present administration," Ismael Robredo continued, referencing the Maskariño government, "has succeeded beyond anyone's expectations in its handling of the crisis in Mindanao."

Those expectations must have been low indeed, Russ thought skeptically, given that less than three months before, a major city on the island had been held by militants loyal to the Islamic State. But the Interior Secretary wasn't done.

"But that success. . .is fragile, and easily reversed. And make no mistake, while Dimaporo and the rest may no longer endorse violence in pursuit of their political ends— they want to see martial law lifted, just as much as the leadership of Abu Sayyaf. They won't regret *any* pressure placed on Manila, so long as they're not called to answer for it. And they won't be."

"So you're telling us that your government won't act," Katherine observed, leaning back against the couch.

"I'm telling you," Robredo said, coming around the front of his desk, "that we *have* acted. And that you should not expect miracles."

"We don't expect miracles, we expect the cooperation of an *ally* in recovering our citizens." They'd been in the country for ten days, and even Lipscomb's patience was wearing thin in the face of Manila's stonewalling.

But if her patience was thin, Robredo's was gone—the look on the Interior Secretary's face as though she had slapped him. "An ally?" he demanded, taking a step closer to both of them, gesturing angrily with his right hand. "Is that how you view us? Is that why your President Norton has sent out three tweets in the last five days, promising to send in the US military to recover the hostages? The SEALs? On our soil?"

Russ kept his face neutral with a mighty effort, and could see from Katherine's expression that she was struggling to repress a curse.

The President's tweets had come up at every single meeting they'd had with their Filipino counterparts since the first one had gone out, and Lipscomb was no more fond of

Norton's approach to foreign policy than the average careerist at State, to begin with.

"He's trying to bring public pressure to bear on your government," she replied finally, her hands folded together in her lap. *"He's bluffing,"* she had maintained back at the embassy, several days prior, discussing the tweets in a conference meeting with the ambassador. *"He's not actually going to send them in—not without Manila green-lighting such an operation."*

It wasn't a confidence Russ could bring himself to share, Lipscomb's ingrained institutional commitment to international norms, to the rules-based order to which she had dedicated her life, blinding her to the reality that she was now serving a President whose commitments were far more. . .transactional. *All* of them.

"That's not going to work the way he thinks," Robredo replied, an unusual intensity creeping into the Interior Secretary's voice as he stood there before them. "He's backing Maskariño into a corner, forcing him to dig in further or appear nothing more than a puppet of Washington. Tell your president, this will *backfire.*"

It would be nothing more than many others had told him before, Russ mused, and Norton had yet to listen to any of them. *Perhaps this time. . .*

"And perhaps the answer to our problem is to be found elsewhere," the Interior Secretary said, returning to his desk. "I understand the family has received a ransom demand from the group responsible."

Russ' head came up at that, taken off-guard. They had insisted with Debra Patterson that the family allow the HRFC to handle all communications with the Filipino government, and she had agreed. *Or so they'd thought.*

"If a way could be found to come up with those funds. . ." Robredo's voice trailed off, the implication of his words, only too clear. It would solve many problems, for all of them. *If the Braleys were even still alive.*

"The US government can't be involved in such an effort," Russ began, but Robredo cut him off with a gesture.

"Of course, of course. . .I understand that's why the family has hired a private security corporation to handle their negotiations."

The FBI special agent's lips pressed together into a thin line as he looked over at Lipscomb. Still more they hadn't been told—it was what he had recommended at their dinner meeting, but he had expected her to keep them in the loop. The family was pursuing their own agenda, it would seem, and complicating the fusion cell's work of recovery in the process. Robredo glanced at his watch.

"I am told their representative should be arriving in Manila on a flight later this evening."

4:18 P.M. Japan Standard Time
Risner Gym, Kadena Air Base
Okinawa Prefecture, Japan

Rap music pounded in Guilbeau's ears as he leaned back into the incline bench, a heavy dumbbell in each hand as he pressed out toward the ceiling, rotating his wrists until they reached full extension.

"You saw the photos, didn't you, Jay?"

The senior chief lowered the weights to his chest and pushed them back out before answering Dom's question, holding them out before him, his arms burning with the strain.

"I did," he replied finally, lowering the dumbbells to his sides and setting them on the floor. He reached for his bottled water before glancing over to where Zamora stood, not three feet away in the noisy, crowded gym, spotting for Melhorn, another of the SEALs.

"He was a brave man," Dom continued, his dark eyes burning with anger. "Brave as any one of us."

Coming from someone as proud as Dom, that was quite an admission, but Guilbeau nodded. For a civilian with no training to have mustered up the courage to do what Jun Santos had done, in his effort to get help for the other hostages. . .that took guts. *A coward might still be alive.*

He shook his head, wiping the sweat from his forehead with a crumpled t-shirt as he took a drink of the water. Every friend he'd ever lost had been brave—that's what had taken them to their deaths, that bravery, what had placed them in harm's way in the first place.

Would be him, one of these days, like as not. You never knew when your time was up, had no way of seeing it coming.

"Yeah," he agreed, choosing not to say everything else that filled his mind. "He was one of the good ones."

Guilbeau felt someone's eyes on him, looked over his shoulder to see a young airman—not much older than his own son—glaring at him, clearly waiting to use the incline bench he was sitting on.

He didn't say a word, just held the stare until the younger man quailed, a soft chuckle escaping his lips as the airman retreated to the machines, beginning to stack rusty weights on a lat pull-down machine as he attempted to chat up a petite brunette. *Air Force.*

"A brave man," Dom repeated, a dark intensity filling his voice, "and they butchered him like an animal. If I get close to Soleiman, I'm burying my tomahawk in the skull of that son of a—"

"Dom," Guilbeau warned, his head coming up suddenly. This wasn't Afghanistan, and even there. . .damage control had been difficult. "Zip it, bud."

Zamora's eyes flashed fire and he stepped away from Melhorn, motioning for him to rack the weights. "Look, Jay," he said, stepping in front of Guilbeau, "I know how you felt about how things went down in the Mohmand, but I'm asking you—look at that photo, and tell me that isn't what *they* deserve."

Guilbeau set down his water, rising to his feet to look the chief petty officer in the eye. "I'm telling you how it's going to be, Dom. My team, remember?"

"*El Degüello,* Jay," Zamora spat, arms folded across his chest, seeming not to hear him. *Or care.* "I'm from Texas, and while my people might have been on the wrong side at the Alamo. . .they had that much right. *No quarter.*"

8:13 A.M. Eastern Standard Time
CIA Headquarters
Langley, Virginia

"We can't keep them in place indefinitely, Barney. You know that." Olivia Voss leaned back in her seat, staring across the conference table at Kranemeyer. "Things are heating up in sub-Saharan Africa, you've seen the reports—

same as I have, not to mention the continuing chaos in Syria. The media stopped paying attention after Raqqa fell, but the Islamic State didn't go away, they went *underground*."

Kranemeyer nodded. The simple truth of it was that the "shattered" Islamic State still had significantly more fighters on the ground in Iraq and Syria than the old AQI had possessed following its "defeat" the better part of a decade prior. And far more money.

"We don't have enough personnel to go around as it is. Certainly not enough to leave one of our SAD teams parked on Mindanao for a month, waiting on. . .what, an execution video to make its way onto the darknet?"

A grimace passed across Kranemeyer's face at the question. Olivia had always had a way of getting to the point. He couldn't fault her logic, though—it was the very argument he had himself used with Richards, in urging him to get his new team trained and mission-ready, back during the summer. *We can only sustain our current op-tempo so long with a team down, Jack. And the missions aren't going away.*

So they hadn't. And now that they had gone a week without fresh intel on the Braleys—four days past the original end date of Richards' liaison mission with the AFP—it was getting hard to justify the team's presence. Either to himself, or to the Filipinos, Kranemeyer mused. Because they were getting antsy about the Agency's continued involvement, all the more so in the wake of the President's aggressive tweets about sending in the SEALs.

"All right," he said finally. "Manila willing, we'll keep them in play another four days. We don't pick anything up by then. . .bring them all home for Christmas."

Everyone except the Braleys, he thought grimly, hearing

Olivia's brief assent as she rose, pushing in her chair. *If they were still alive to be brought home.*

10:04 P.M., Philippine Standard Time
Emirates Flight EK404
Final approach to Ninoy Aquino International Airport
Manila, Philippines

He'd been in Dubai when the call came in, the man thought, looking out the window of the Boeing 777 as it descended out of the night sky—all of Metro Manila spread out below them, ten thousand glittering lights ending only in the sea, back out there over his left shoulder to the west.

Brent Kruta leaned back into his seat, tugging restlessly at the cuffs of his dress shirt. He'd spent eight years out in the field as a CIA paramilitary operations officer, and these last nine months, transitioning into the private sector, had been challenging in more ways than one.

The expectation that he would wear a suit while conducting company business was perhaps the least of those concerns, but it was the most omnipresent one. That would no doubt change, if he could ever get back out in the field, but for the moment. . .well, he would be representing the company to the Braley family and their representatives, and it was important to make a good impression.

Make a good impression, and avoid making any promises he couldn't keep. He'd do what he could, try to reach out to the hostage-takers, and negotiate their release with what ransom the family was able to come up with. If they were still alive to be released, he reminded himself grimly. That was another, all-too-possible, outcome to all of this, and one he couldn't hide from them.

He dug into his shirt pocket, extracting a business card and glancing at it in the dimmed lights of the cabin. Business cards—that was another innovation that he hadn't been accustomed to dealing with in his years with the Agency.

The logo in the center of the card was just visible in the dim light, rays of a sun spreading out from behind a large, Norman-style kite shield. The words *"To keep the world from burning"* were inscribed in neat, flowing script just below the shield, and above it, one could read the name of his new employer.

The Svalinn Security Group, LLC. . .

11:37 P.M.
Jolo Island, Sulu Province
The Autonomous Region in Muslim Mindanao (ARMM)

Heat. A damp, feverish fire, seeming to race through his veins, filling him up—sweat pouring from his face as he ran, his eyes wide and staring—searching for something, anything. Tim.

He heard the sound of gunshots, the whispering whistle of death about his ears, saw a man's head explode before him— felt his own face spattered with blood and brains. And he was running again, running through the field of cassava, a field suddenly littered with folding chairs and broken bodies—a roof over his head and a cross mounted on the far wall. Screams echoing over and again in his ears, moans of agony and pain.

He saw him then, not far away—standing bewildered among the crowd, the small frame of a boy disappearing from sight in between the legs of bystanders. Saw him disappear, ran after him, the fire still burning through his body like a furnace—but something seemed to catch at his foot and he fell, sprawling, into the water of a field that had become the sea, the taste of brine filling his mouth. A soundless cry escaping his lips as he struggled to rise, desperately weak. "Tim!"

And the boy turned back toward him, as if at the sound of the cry, his face visible for the first time—a face that was nothing more than a bloody death's-head mask, distorted by the impact of a rifle round.

Grinning and laughing at his horror in the brief second before the figure turned away to become the child once again, running away from him through the crowd of dead and dying.

He stretched out a hand in desperation, as if he could reach his son, as if he could somehow bring him back—and he was falling once again, hurtling through space, sea and field and church all melting away to be replaced by nothing but the abyss, a darkness filled only by his own screams. "Tim!!!!"

Shawn Braley awoke sobbing, his body soaked with sweat and reeking with urine—still moaning out his son's name helplessly.

He felt a cool hand on his arm, heard a woman's voice in his ear, but he couldn't recognize it, couldn't shake off the hand, even as he lashed out desperately with what remained of his strength. And then the darkness descended once more. . .

1:07 P.M. Eastern Standard Time
Naval Support Facility Thurmont—Camp David
Frederick County, Maryland

". . .and Lord, we would pray that you would watch over your servants, Shawn and Charity—their daughter, Faith, for we know that children are precious in your eyes, Father.

That you would lift them up and grant them strength, and peace even among their trials. . ."

President Richard Norton shifted uncomfortably on his knees, the strain of the position already wearing on him, his elbows resting on the pew before him as Adam Cardwell continued to intercede with God beside him.

It was to be hoped that he wasn't expected to follow him, Norton thought, his gaze flickering restlessly around the chapel as the prayer continued. He hadn't prayed—seriously *prayed*—in a very many years, and he'd never felt quite sure anyone was listening when he had.

He made eye contact briefly with Curt Hawkins, the lead agent of his Secret Service protective detail—standing there gravely silent in the center aisle of the chapel, between the pews, flanked by another pair of agents.

". . .we would pray, Father, for the family of Jun Santos, a martyr in your service, Lord," the Liberty dean of students prayed, his hands clasped together against his forehead as Norton watched, feeling awkward and out of place, even here. "Greater love hath no man than this. . ."

The Evergreen Chapel was one of the more recent buildings at Camp David, dedicated by the former President George H.W. Bush in 1991. A place of worship, of spiritual sanctuary, for the President of the United States.

This was the first time he'd set foot within its walls since taking office, and Norton found himself glancing curiously about him even as the prayer went on—lifting his eyes to take in the massive stained glass windows that rose up on both sides of the chapel, the art taking the form of a pair of trees, flanking the sanctuary, their boughs spreading out toward the peak of the chapel's roof.

The Tree of Life, over on the far side of the chapel, and here, on the side where the president would sit during services, bearing a stained glass representation of the presidential seal in the midst of its branches. . .*The Tree of Knowledge.*

A bitter smile played at Norton's lips, wondering if the artist could have possibly appreciated the irony of the choice. He had never before felt so helpless as he'd felt upon becoming the most powerful man in the world, never felt so utterly. . .destitute of knowledge.

When you were powerful, people derived their own power from keeping you in the dark, from *managing* what you knew, controlling it. It was how an unelected bureaucracy of "professionals" had managed to wrest control of the American government from the hands of the people it had been elected to serve.

A bureaucracy he had campaigned against—dedicated his political career to opposing. And yet here, at the apex of his power. . .he found himself helpless *without* them.

". . .in your name, Father God, we pray. Amen." The President composed himself just in time as Cardwell opened his eyes, reaching out to place a hand on Norton's shoulder, squeezing it firmly. His cheeks damp with the evidence of his tears.

"We are going to receive an answer to our prayer," the dean of students said as both men rose to their feet—Norton's joints stiff and protesting after kneeling on the hard floor, "and I believe that God is going to use you as the instrument of His will to bring this to pass."

He told you that? The President wanted to ask, but bit his tongue, starting to answer in another way before Cardwell cut him short. "We supported you all that way, Rick—all through the primary, and the election that followed, because of our belief that God had brought you to the forefront of American politics for just this time in our history. Now, I think, we know why."

We supported you, Norton heard, reading the determination shining there in Cardwell's eyes, along with the tears, *and that support can be as easily withdrawn as it was extended.*

Message received.

"Hancock wouldn't have cared, wouldn't have been willing to do what was necessary to get them back," Cardwell continued, referencing Norton's predecessor, "but I know that you do. And will."

The President nodded, clasping Cardwell's hand in his own. "Lord willing."

11:04 A.M. Philippine Standard Time, December 19th
Jolo Island, Sulu Province
The Autonomous Region in Muslim Mindanao (ARMM)

". . .God, from whom all blessings flow." The sun was already high in the morning sky, streaming through the jalousie windows as Shawn Braley came awake, the sound of voices singing in Visayan echoing hollowly through his brain as though in some dream. *"Praise Him. . ."*

Praise Him.

He opened his eyes, unsure for a moment of where he was or how he might have gotten there, and struggled to turn over on his side, feeling the coarse fabric of the military blanket scrape against the bare skin of his back with the movement.

A soft, cool hand descended on his arm and he looked up into his wife's eyes, kneeling there at his side, the sound of the singing continuing on in the background even as she announced, "You're finally awake."

". . .praise Father, Son, and Holy Ghost. . ."

"Your fever broke, Shawn," she continued, and he could see the weariness, the relief in her eyes, "in the middle of the night, and we've been waiting for you to wake up, ever since."

It came back to him, then, in a flood—all that had happened over the course of the last six days, or at least all that he could remember of it.

He'd drifted in and out of a feverish delirium for most of the two days and two nights they'd spent on the water, traveling south-southwest, the commandeered fishing vessel—larger and more powerful than the one that had originally spirited them away from the coast of Mindanao—covering the hundred-plus kilometers of ocean between Basilan and Jolo with comparative ease.

It had been a long voyage, for all that, marked as the first by thirst and insufficient food, in those rare moments when he'd been able to eat anything. Once, he remembered vaguely, they'd had to double back—a Philippine Coast Guard patrol vessel visible on the horizon. . .the hostages' hopes rising along with their captors' fears. But it hadn't come after them, and night had fallen soon after, bringing with it a stiff, ice-cold breeze.

Last night wasn't the first time his fever had broken, but he'd slipped back into it every time, the exposure and cold of the nights at sea taking their toll on his weakened body—the highs and lows blurring together into one persistent haze.

He could remember someone giving him medication of some sort, the day before—or was it two?—their arrival on Jolo bringing them back to some kind of civilization, and a network which could offer Manong Soleiman sanctuary. Perhaps that was what had broken the fever, in the end.

"We're still with them, aren't we?" he asked, glancing around the narrow confines of the small concrete-block room as he struggled to collect himself. *To discern the truth from the delirium.* Still remembering Tim's little face, like Death itself, disappearing into the carnage.

She just nodded, reaching out to touch his hand, looking pale and haggard. Her hair a tangled, matted mess where it was visible under the ragged *terong*—none of them had truly been able to *bathe* since their abduction, their every movement under the eye of Soleiman's guards. And the women had had the worst of it, with the jihadists' rigid insistence on their modesty.

"And. . .Tim?" Shawn asked, a raw, pleading edge creeping into his voice as he looked at her. Ice-cold fingers seeming to wrap themselves about his heart. *God, let that have been part of the fever.*

But she shook her head, the fingers closing themselves into a fist—as if to squeeze the life from him. *God, Tim. . .*

"And the girls?"

"I don't know, Shawn," Charity responded, a raw despair in her voice as if she was on the verge of breaking, "you've asked so many times."

Had he? "Faith is with us, you know that, she's out there. . .singing right now with Manny and the others. He's looking out for her and Dolores both now."

Dolores' father was dead now too, Shawn realized, the

memories trickling back. Seeing Chris collapse into the undergrowth of the jungle's edge back there on Basilan, a soldier's bullet through his throat.

But his wife wasn't done, the distress visible in her eyes as she continued. "Hope. . .I don't know, God help me, I don't *know*. I lost her, Shawn—I panicked, with all of the shooting, and people running everywhere, I panicked and I *lost* her."

He reached out his hand to grasp her own, seeking to comfort her, yet overwhelmed by his own sorrow. And he could feel her shrink away from his touch, almost visibly withdrawing within herself. He opened his mouth to speak, but he was still so tired—the fever leaving him exhausted, weak as a child, in its wake.

"Sweetheart, I—"

Someone pushed the door open before he could say another word, a young Moro entering the room with a grimy Chinese-made Type 56 assault rifle slung carelessly over his shoulder. He took a look at the two of them, at Shawn lying there on the bed—and put a hand to the door, murmuring a few words in Visayan to someone without. He wasn't one of Soleiman's men, Shawn realized vaguely, at least not one of those that had been with them on Basilan.

Another moment, and another unfamiliar guard entered the room, followed immediately by a third man, taller than either of the other two—clearly the leader, and just as clearly, *not* a local.

"You're awake," he observed, running a hand over the thick growth of his dark beard, his English rough and heavily accented, "finally. I am Abu Nazih al-Tunisi. And you. . .are now my guests."

Chapter 11

1:24 P.M. Philippine Standard Time, December 20th
Camp General Basilio Navarro, Western Mindanao
Command (WESTMINCOM)
Calarian District, Zamboanga City
Zamboanga del Sur, Mindanao

Jack Richards closed the last of the folders he had received from the National Intelligence Coordinating Agency with a heavy sigh, running a hand across the rough stubble of his beard as he leaned back in the chair, looking down at the files spread across the floor of the barracks. He was missing something—they all were. They *had* to be.

"What do you hope to accomplish?" Maricar de Rosales had asked him when he'd first put in the request for the files, the skepticism clearly visible in the NICA intelligence officer's eyes. *"You're a door-kicker, not an analyst."*

He was more or less *both*, in truth—officers of the Agency's Special Activities Division were usually prior-military types like himself, cross-trained as intelligence officers. There were exceptions, like Nichols, but they were few and far between.

Nichols. His brow furrowed at the memory of his former team leader. *What would he think, if he were here? What would he be doing?*

He'd probably be over there, on Basilan, running afoul of the Filipinos in an effort to get the Braleys back, no matter the odds. He'd always had a knack for bending the rules, for getting *results*, no matter what it took. *Until one day. . .they had bent until they had broken.*

And Nichols, right along with them.

That wasn't the way he could lead this team—the Agency couldn't take any more body blows, not with the scrutiny they now found themselves under from the top. They were under a microscope.

He bent forward, elbows resting on his knees as his dark eyes scanned the files—heavily redacted, all of them. It had taken him the better part of a week to obtain them, and it seemed as though his Filipino counterparts had spent most of that time removing everything they didn't want him to see.

It was routine enough, if no less maddening for all that—even the closest of intelligence partners were cagey when it came to the details of their sources and methods, and the US-Filipino partnership had known better days.

Still. . .there had to be something here, the big Texan thought, some connection they were overlooking. Basilan simply wasn't *that* big of an island—even with a sympathetic populace, hiding that many hostages wasn't going to be easy. Not with the intensive sweep of the island Ocampo's troops, backed by the SAF, had conducted over the course of the last week.

Unless they were no longer on Basilan. That was the

question, of course—one he had posed, some days earlier, to a Philippine Navy captain at the nearby Naval Station Romulo Espaldon, receiving in return the confident assurance that any such attempts on the part of Manong Soleiman would have been intercepted by Navy or Coast Guard patrols.

It rang hollow. Even as a littoral force, the Philippine Navy was something less than impressive—they simply didn't have the ships. It didn't seem at all impractical that Soleiman could have slipped through.

But he would have to have had somewhere to run. . .

A *pinging* sound from his laptop caught Richards' attention and he rose, moving over to where it sat open on the card table in the center of the room. It was the secure video chat program, announcing an incoming "call" from Manila, and Richards reached for his headset, slipping it on before clicking *Accept.* Darren Lukasik's visage materialized on-screen a moment later, the station chief's face weary, his necktie loosened at the throat.

"Jack," he began, leaning in toward his camera, "are we secure?"

A nod. The Filipinos had left him alone for most of the day, and as for his team. . .Parker and Carson were off at the base gym, and Granby and Ardolino had flown out to the other side of Mindanao the previous night with a team of SAF commandos on a low-side intelligence-gathering op in Saguiaran, a small municipality in Lanao del Sur—an attempt to justify their continued presence in-country in the eyes of Manila. This was as secure as it got.

"What's going on?"

"We've had a development," was Lukasik's cryptic reply.

"An American businessman flew into Ninoy Aquino two nights ago from Dubai. An old friend of yours. . ."

1:47 P.M.
Jolo Island, Sulu Province
The Autonomous Region in Muslim Mindanao (ARMM)

It all still seemed a bad dream, Shawn Braley thought, a product of the fever. As though he had found himself falling off a cliff, a fall that never seemed to end as he hurtled farther and farther down.

"The Arab isn't one of us," Khadafi had said earlier that day, stooping down to look Shawn in the eye as he rested there in a plastic chair in the courtyard. *"But he's in command, now."*

There had been a touch of regret in the older Moro's voice, whether from simple nationalistic pride, or concerns for the future—their future—Shawn couldn't say. It didn't change the reality that in his retreat south, Manong Soleiman had left his own territory behind. A move which had forced him to accept the sanctuary of a rival leader like Abu Nazih, a Tunisian-born jihadist who had apparently fought in Syria before being dispatched east by the Islamic State.

How a man like that had managed to supplant the local Abu Sayyaf leadership was something Shawn didn't pretend to fully understand. His years in the Philippines had been spent trying to reach the hearts of its people, not sorting out the geopolitical intricacies. And very little of his outreach had extended into the Muslim areas of the island, for his own safety, as well as that of his family.

How well that had worked out. He found himself unable to repress a surge of anger and grief at the thought, lost in despair, as he stared across the courtyard to where Abu Nazih's men stood guard. He had devoted his *life* to serving God, and this was how it was all going to end. In the loss of his son, and perhaps his daughter. The deaths of he and his wife.

But did you? A voice asked from somewhere deep within, haunting, reproachful. God? The remnants of the fever? *Truly? Then why did you leave My people, so often? For so very long?*

3:18 P.M.
Cotabato City, Manguindanao
The Autonomous Region in Muslim Mindanao(ARMM)

The middle-aged Moro brushed away an imaginary fleck of dust from his white polo shirt, a skeptical look in his eyes as he put his hands together before his chest, fingers tented. "I don't know if I can help you."

"But you know who can," Brent Kruta said, leaning back in his seat, bringing the glass of thick mujiv tea to his lips. It wasn't a question.

The taste of the tea reminded him strangely of marmalade, strong notes of lemon and orange pervading his mouth as he sat there, regarding the man closely. *Talk to Jim,* his contacts in Manila had told him, *he should be able to put you on the right track.*

If he would. Hadjiman "Jim" Palalisan had been active in Mindanao politics for thirty of his fifty-five years, rising as high as ARMM vice-governor a decade before. He had accomplished little of that by being over-generous.

"Perhaps," came the reply, eventually—almost reluctantly. Palalisan's face like stone as he looked across the cafe table at the American. "You've raised the money?"

"Not all of it," Kruta replied, shaking his head. "Not yet."

Likely not ever, he thought skeptically, but didn't add. The family's fundraiser was well on its way to its first million, but that was still far, far from what had been demanded by their captors. Whether the evangelical network which had first rallied to the support of the Braley family would be able—or willing—to come up with that kind of cash. . .or whether they would choose, instead, to leave their fate in the hands of the Lord, remained to be seen.

"Then what are you doing here?" the Moro politician asked, reaching for his coffee. "Besides wasting my time and your own."

Kruta bit back the angry retort that came first to his lips, reminding himself once more of what he *was* doing here. Of its importance. "I'm here to negotiate with their captors—if I can make contact with them. You can help me with that."

Palalisan smiled. "Can I?"

"Look," the former intelligence officer began, setting his cup of tea on the table between them as he leaned in—the awning above shading both men from the afternoon sun, "you're not fooling anyone, least of all me. . .everyone in Mindanao knows how Jim Palalisan got where he is today. You played an active role in the MILF back in the oughts, and your business ties to various figures in the Abu Sayyaf command structure are also no secret. You might not have taken a hand when Mostapa's *muj* overran Marawi, but you smiled. You're no terrorist—not anymore—but you're next-door to one."

The smile was gone, a wary look entering Palalisan's eyes. *The kind of man I would have killed, once upon a time.* Kruta shook his head, knowing those days were now behind him. That this was the reality of going private, that he would now spend his days negotiating with men he once might have shot.

"I may know someone who can help you," was the Moro's cautious reply, "but you're going to need to make it worth my time and trouble."

"I believe that can be arranged."

5:01 P.M.
Jolo Island, Sulu Province
The Autonomous Region in Muslim Mindanao (ARMM)

"What do you think this is going to mean?" Shawn asked quietly, dipping his fingers into the bowl of rice and bringing a handful to his mouth. The food had gotten better since their arrival on Jolo, but it still wasn't even remotely enough to replace the weight he had lost across those days in the clutches of the fever.

Charity was across the courtyard, with Chris' widow Annalyn—out of earshot. He hadn't dared bring this up where she could hear.

Emmanuel Asuncion shook his head, favoring the missionary with a critical glance as he licked the last few grains of rice from his fingers. "What do you mean?"

"It's been almost two weeks," he responded, an edge of desperation creeping into his voice. Two weeks since Manong

Soleiman had forced him to place the phone call to the embassy in Manila, listing the group's demands for their safe return.

Two weeks, and less than ten days until the deadline came up, as Aldam had reminded him a few hours before. The teenager, alone among Soleiman's men in seeming to have found himself right at home here—hanging around Abu Nazih's handful of foreign fighters like a starstruck groupie in the presence of his rock stars.

"Two weeks," he repeated, as if somehow unable to believe it himself, "and nothing has happened. No one has done *anything*. And now. . .we have Abu Nazih. Is anyone coming for us?"

The lay pastor's face darkened. "Manila will never agree to those demands, Shawn—you had to know that, going in. Unless someone *finds* us. . ."

His voice trailed off, a cold shudder running down Shawn's spine. *They were going to die. They were all—*

He looked up to see Emmanuel staring at him, reproach in the Filipino's eyes. "These people need you, Shawn— those who are left, they need you to be strong, to face this with the faith you told us of, so many times. This time, you can't run away. . ."

6:37 P.M.
Camp General Basilio Navarro, Western Mindanao
Command (WESTMINCOM)
Calarian District, Zamboanga City
Zamboanga del Sur, Mindanao

"Kruta?" Thomas Parker asked, the look on the New Yorker's face clearly incredulous as he turned to face Richards. "What's he doing here?"

"The family's exploring all their options, it would seem." Richards shrugged. "Word is that they had reached out to a private security company to handle negotiations for them. Apparently, that company was Svalinn."

He heard Ardolino curse softly, and nodded. *Yeah.* Kruta wasn't the only paramilitary operations officer the SOG had lost to the private sector in recent years, lured away by the kind of salaries and corporate perks the Agency couldn't dream of offering.

And given their own prior. . .connections to the CIA, the Svalinn Security Group was one of the principal offenders. For some men, it seemed, a flag simply wasn't enough.

"And Lukasik wants you to make contact?"

"That's the general idea," was Richards' laconic reply. "See what he's found. What he's willing to share."

If anything.

9:37 A.M., Eastern Standard Time
NSA Headquarters, Operations Building 2A
Fort Meade, Maryland

"Barney," a familiar voice greeted Kranemeyer as his NSA minder led him through yet another set of security doors into the maze of the cubicle farm deep within the blue-black, copper-clad tower known as Operations Building 2A, one of the four main structures which comprised the National Security Agency Headquarters complex on Fort Meade.

"Josiah," the DCS responded, turning as the NSA's deputy director of SID materialized from among the cubicles, extending his hand. "Josiah Galvin. It's been a long time."

"Too long," Galvin agreed, a smile in his dark eyes. The African-American bureaucrat was a few years Kranemeyer's senior, his mustache and what little remained of the hair on the top of his head long since turned silver. He'd joined the National Security Agency right out of college in the late '80s, and stayed with the agency ever since, rising steadily through its civilian ranks to join the leadership of the Signals Intelligence Directorate. "How was the drive?"

"It was on the way," Kranemeyer replied simply, still able to feel the cramp in his remaining leg from the trip. "I fly out of BWI for Hartford at noon, hitching a ride on a government flight. So show me what you've got."

"The funeral?" was Galvin's tight-lipped question, and Kranemeyer nodded.

"He was a good man."

Better than you even know, Kranemeyer thought, but he contented himself with a brief nod of assent. "A dying breed, around this town."

A snort, as the NSA official turned, leading the way deeper into the building. "You're telling me."

A few contractors looked up at their passage, but only for a brief glance before returning to their work—the detritus of office life visible around their workstations here, as at Langley. Family photos, half-eaten fast food, the occasional bobblehead.

Kranemeyer spotted one of the current President and suppressed a smile, even as Galvin led him through yet another layer of security, turning aside into a conference room filled with NSA personnel gathered around a long table—most of them with laptops or secure tablets in front of them, several scribbling down notes.

"Ladies and gentlemen," Galvin began easily, gesturing for Kranemeyer to take a seat near the head of the table. "Barney Kranemeyer, Director of the Clandestine Service. Company man, but don't hold that against him. He's here to be brought up to speed on our most recent intel on Manong Soleiman."

He took his own seat at the conference table's head, nodding toward the SID's chief of S2A, the South Asian division. "Garrett, will you lead us off?"

10:41 P.M. Philippine Standard Time
Jolo Island, Sulu Province
The Autonomous Region in Muslim Mindanao (ARMM)

"He wants what?" Shawn Braley heard his wife's sharp intake of breath, still unsure he had heard Annalyn correctly.

The Filipina hostage had slipped back into their sleeping quarters only ten or fifteen minutes before, taking her place on the other side of the Braleys, beside Charity. Her quiet sobs as she lay there, soon rousing both of them.

"I'm to be *sabaya*'ed," she repeated quietly. "He—Manong Soleiman—wants me to become his wife."

"But that's impossible," Shawn heard himself say, still feeling weak and sluggish in the wake of the fever. "You're already. . ."

Not anymore, he realized, too slowly—watching Annalyn shake her head sadly. Remembering the sight of Chris' body, slumping into the jungle undergrowth, shot through the throat. Shot by their *rescuers*.

Annalyn, widowed in that moment—and placed, in the same horrific instant, beyond the protections of the morality of a man like Manong Soleiman. Even so, her next words took him even further off-guard.

"He wanted Dolores," she said, her words drawing a strangled cry from Charity, the sound stabbing Shawn to the heart. He knew she had come to view Chris and Annalyn's fifteen-year-old daughter almost as her own over the last few weeks, the violence forcing them all together. . .bringing their girls closer than ever before. The implication of Annalyn's statement, only too clear.

She had offered herself in place of her daughter. *God. . .*

He reached out, laying a gentle hand on her forearm—feeling her shrink away from his touch.

"We won't let you be separated from us," he said, his voice soft, almost pleading. With her, with himself. *With God.* "We have to stay together, get through this—*God* will bring us through, all of us. He will find a way. You believe that, don't you?"

A nod, more felt than seen in the semi-darkness, a long, shuddering sigh escaping her lips—her hands reaching out to clasp his and his wife's, holding on with a strength born of fear. Of desperation. She believed, hope against hope—she believed.

Did he?

10:58 P.M.
Al Nor Hotel & Convention Center
Cotabato City, Manguindanao
The Autonomous Region in Muslim Mindanao (ARMM)

"And you believe his intel to be legitimate?" Brent Kruta leaned back on the half-made bed of the small hotel room, the phone pressed against his ear.

He nodded, knowing the woman sitting more than five thousand miles to the west in another hotel suite in Istanbul couldn't see the reflexive gesture. "I think it's the best we've got, ma'am."

And had only cost them a few thousand dollars to obtain. He'd met greedier corrupt officials than Jim Palalisan in his day. "I'm to be driven to the meet in the morning."

"I had understood that your government already had negotiators in Manila," Palalisan had observed a few moments before their parting, a shrewd look in the Moro's eyes. *"And yet here you are, as well."*

"My government doesn't negotiate with terrorists," he'd replied calmly. The inference, only too clear. *We do.*

"Be careful out there, Brent." Another nod. Heidi had said the same thing, when he'd talked with her, a few hours earlier, though his wife knew less of the details than his boss. *As ever before.* Some things hadn't changed *that* much. "We don't need Abu Sayyaf ending up with a fourth American hostage on their hands."

Svalinn didn't need those kinds of headlines, the clear, unwritten subtext in those words. *Message received.* He was sure that he would find such a captivity even more uncomfortable than his employers. "My contact has offered to act as guarantor for my safety, to and from the meet."

"Can you trust him?" The woman's voice was cold, analytical. Echoes of the case officer she had once been, years before becoming a CEO. Some instincts never died.

"As far as I need to," he responded after a moment's consideration. "He's comfortable."

Comfortable men didn't make good martyrs, he had

learned, and Jim Palalisan was far too comfortable in his current lifestyle to risk the amount of heat that would descend on his head if an American businessman vanished from under his protection.

Businessman. It still didn't seem right to think of himself that way. Not with the stakes remaining this high. Her next words only serving to confirm those thoughts.

"Our former employers have taken an interest in your presence."

11:21 A.M. Eastern Standard Time
Naval Support Facility Thurmont—Camp David
Frederick County, Maryland

". . .based on which, Mr. President, we have credible reason to believe that the Braleys are no longer on Basilan."

"But not a location?" President Norton asked, stopping short, hands resting on his hips as he stared across the long table of the Laurel Lodge conference room toward the wide television screen, the sleeves of his dress shirt rolled above the elbow.

"No, sir." On-screen he saw the NSA director, Admiral Samuel Palochak, shake his head. "Not more specific than Sulu Province, generally—well to the south of Basilan."

"I know where it is, Admiral," Norton snapped, unsure even as he spoke why he had done so, given that he wasn't at all certain that he could have located the islands on a map, but Palochak's tone. . .

The man was his own appointee, but he wondered at times if that had been a mistake. If there even was anyone better he could have chosen, or if they were all corrupted.

"Please, continue. You were saying?"

"They're being discreet, as far as that goes," Palochak went on, clearing his throat, "but the increase and changing nature of the chatter among these groups over the last week is significant. We haven't found them, but we have a much better idea where to look."

"Is it enough to send in the SEALs?"

The Admiral frowned, visibly shaking his head. "Respectfully, Mr. President, it's not my place to advise on. . ."

"It isn't." Norton's head came up, glancing down the conference table toward where his national security adviser, Nathan Gisriel, sat, dressed almost as casually as the President—the knot of his necktie visible just above the general's sweater. "My advice, Mr. President, as previously expressed, would be to turn all this over to the Filipinos, everything the NSA has garnered from these intercepts. Our intelligence collection capabilities greatly exceed those of Manila, but it still *is* their country. Allow them to act on our intelligence."

"If they will," the President retorted, shaking his head darkly. They weren't facing the same stakes.

"Even if they won't, Mr. President," the national security adviser countered, "this intelligence isn't specific enough to enable us to mount a recovery operation. Not yet."

"If we were to get such intelligence, Nathan, just how quickly could we move the SEALs into position?"

Gisriel's brow furrowed in thought. "Five hours, minimum, for DEVGRU's Red Squadron to stage to Fleet Activities Yokosuka. . .from there, Mr. President, I'd say at least the better part of three days to reach the Sulu

Archipelago, and that's with the *Michigan* running at flank speed, a practice we normally wouldn't endorse in the PLA(N)'s backyard, even with operations not directed at the Chinese. Four would be more reasonable."

Days? Norton just stared at the general, certain that his surprise was visible on his face. It was far longer than he could have imagined. . .hours, he had thought, at the most. *Had this been a part of the plan, all along?* To narrow his choices, place him in a position where his only choice was to do what *they* wanted?

He took a deep breath, reaching out for the glass of water that sat by his chair. "Get the wheels in motion, general. If we obtain actionable intelligence, I want the SEALs in position."

Chapter 12

9:48 A.M. Philippine Standard Time, December 21st
Cotabato City, Maguindanao
The Autonomous Region in Muslim Mindanao (ARMM)

Getting leave from the Filipinos had been a challenge, Jack Richards thought, unscrewing the cap off the Powerade as he pushed open the door of the 24/7 convenience store and stepped out, his ball cap shading his eyes against the sun as he took a drink—scanning the street bordering the commercial center. Though not, perhaps, as difficult as actually finding the man they had come here to meet.

Sinsuat Avenue was filled with the usual mix of traffic he had come to expect from the Filipino urban scene—trucks, a sprinkling of SUVs, a man on a scooter buzzing by, a jeepney bearing the logo of the nearby Awang Airport. A large dump truck filled to the brim with sacks of animal feed rumbled past, several teenage Moros perched precariously atop the load. No sign of Kruta, anywhere.

He glimpsed Granby across the street through a hole in the traffic, standing near the arched entryway for the Cotabato Regional and Medical Center, right beside a faded sign proclaiming March to be "Rabies Awareness Month." The muscular black man was hardly an inconspicuous choice for a surveillance op, but it wasn't like he had a lot of choice. None of his people exactly blended in here—himself most of all.

And this hadn't been supposed to be a surveillance op—his words to Gringo Mijares still echoing in his ears as he took another sip of the Powerade. *"I just want to talk to him, Gringo. One old friend to another. Nothing more." "Then why do you need Granby?"*

He'd shrugged. *"Buddy system. I don't intend to end up another statistic in the autonomous region."*

It hadn't been a joke—Cotabato wasn't the safest of locales, even now, with martial law in place and the military crackdown which had followed the Braley abduction. Richards glanced to his left, toward the entrance through the strip mall-like commercial center which led to the parking lot for the Al Nor Suites beyond. He and Granby had counted no less than half-a-dozen private security guards in their visit to the hotel lobby on arrival a couple hours earlier, all of them armed. And that was in addition to the handful of PNP police officers they had seen on the streets, carrying M16 rifles, a level of caution not unwarranted with Marawi less than a four-hour drive north.

Caution Kruta seemed to have himself thrown to the wind in leaving the hotel a few hours prior to their arrival—alone, according to the staff. Picked up by a car.

What were you thinking, Brent? Richards asked himself, raising the energy drink once more to his lips. He hadn't known Kruta *that* well, despite running a small handful of ops with him over the years, but he'd always respected the man. Recommended him to Kranemeyer, actually, for the command slot he now himself held at Bravo, after Mitt was sidelined by his injuries.

But Kruta had already left the Agency by then, having departed for Svalinn while Richards and the rest of the team were in Egypt. Going private after nearly a decade with Langley. He wasn't sure what he had been thinking then, either. Nothing for it but to ask the man himself, when he came back. *If* he came back.

In the meantime. . .they were drawing attention to themselves, the longer they waited in the open. He pulled his phone from the back pocket of his jeans, shooting a quick text to Granby. *Let's get off the street.*

9:59 A.M.
Jolo Island, Sulu Province
The Autonomous Region in Muslim Mindanao (ARMM)

"We have to find some way to help her, Shawn. We *have* to." There was desperation in Charity's voice, a palpable fear that gnawed at Shawn's heart, unable to keep from envisioning what might befall her if anything happened to him.

Khadafi had brought them their breakfast, a few hours before—a vinegary paste of cassava, steamed in banana leaves. But the older militant had only shook his head when Shawn had brought up Annalyn, his eyes grim and hard. *"It's part of the deal, between Soleiman and Abu Nazih."*

"Deal?" Shawn had found himself asking, unsure he even wanted to hear the answer. *"What kind of deal?"*

Khadafi had taken him by the shoulder, his voice hushed,

barely above a whisper as he'd responded, *"Manong Soleiman made a mistake in coming here—in taking refuge with this foreigner. He cannot control this situation, any longer."*

Then it was under control before? When you took us? When Chris—when my son—were murdered? The words had been so close to spilling out, but he'd kept them locked away, fearing to presume too much on what kindness the older man displayed.

"Abu Nazih wants American hostages—the freedom to make his own demands, his own deal," Khadafi had gone on after a moment's pause. *"Soleiman wants. . .a way out, without admitting that he was taken for a fool. A new wife will do."*

"I don't know how we can," Shawn acknowledged now, shaking his head at the memory. *If Khadafi had been telling the truth. . .*

"Why did you tell her that God would find a way?" Emmanuel asked from a few away—his back pressed against the concrete block of the wall, his knees drawn up toward his chest. He had grown thinner over the weeks, his face worn and haggard, but his voice was still strong—he had led the hostages once again in singing in the courtyard the night before, until one of Abu Nazih's Libyans had come out and put a stop to it, his men far more rigorous in their enforcement of Islamic strictures than Manong Soleiman's Moros had been.

"I-I don't know," Shawn stammered, taken off-guard by the sudden question. It was only the three of them in the small concrete house now—the girls outside somewhere, playing in the walled courtyard. Annalyn keeping cautious watch. "It just, I don't know. . .it just seemed like what I should say. To comfort, to reassure her."

"She doesn't need your reassurance, Shawn," the lay pastor replied, opening his eyes to look across at the Braleys. "She doesn't need the platitudes you brought with you from America."

Shawn flinched, the rebuke hitting him like a physical slap. Wanting to protest, to lash out against the unfairness, the *injustice* of it all. But he had known the emptiness of the words, even as he'd spoken them. *Felt* their insufficiency, no more genuine comfort to her than to himself.

Emmanuel took a deep, shuddering breath, kneading his swarthy brow with his fingers. "The faith of the American church, of those who sent you to us. . .it's not enough out here, and she needs to be prepared, to face whatever may come. Whatever God may *allow* to come."

10:07 A.M.
DILG-NAPOLCOM Center
Quezon City, Metro Manila
Philippines

There was silence in the office of the Secretary of the Interior as Ismael Robredo pored over the open folder, his face a study in contrasts as he read. Surprise alternating with indignation and anger.

William Russell Cole exchanged a glance with Katherine Lipscomb, sitting across from him on one end of the sofa— both of them awaiting the first breaking of the storm.

It hit a moment later, Robredo's eyes flashing as he glanced up from the folder, jabbing a forefinger down into the paper. "How were you able to obtain this? You were spying on us—on the Philippines? An *ally?*"

"If they want to be treated like an ally," Darren Lukasik had observed sharply back at the embassy, in response to Lipscomb saying virtually the same thing, *"they should act like one."*

The career foreign service officer had responded with equal heat, pushing back hard against Lukasik's assertion, but there was none of that visible in her demeanor now. *Close ranks*, Russ thought, *move forward*. A united front.

"That's not necessarily true, Mr. Secretary," she replied, gesturing to the folder of intel garnered from NSA intercepts lying in Robredo's lap. "While it is true that the individuals listed as being surveilled were themselves Filipino citizens and believed to be on Filipino soil at the time of the surveillance, the *networks* they used to communicate are global, and as such, legitimate targets of our National Security Agency."

"That still does not give you the right to—"

"We have found the terrorists you've been looking for, Mr. Secretary," Lipscomb replied, her voice still as calm as could be, "and better yet, we haven't told anyone it was us. Do with that what you will, but we anticipate the safe and soon return of the Braleys."

Robredo shook his head in exasperation, glancing back and forth between the Americans. "This doesn't tell us where they're being held, Ms. Lipscomb—your people haven't *found* anyone. This is—"

"Enough to go on." Katherine Lipscomb reached down, brushing an imaginary piece of lint from the leg of her crisply-pressed blue pantsuit. "Ismael, let me be perfectly straightforward with you. . .you understand the situation we're dealing with in Washington, the pressures being brought to bear. If your government doesn't act, ours will—and that's not an outcome you or I want out of this."

Russ caught Lipscomb's eye as she spoke those final words, knowing the truth neither of them had the authority to divulge to their Filipino counterpart. Washington was *already* acting.

11:31 A.M. Japan Standard Time
Fleet Activities Yokosuka
Kanagawa Prefecture, Japan

Towering orange-and-white cranes dotted the skyline of the military base as Jason Guilbeau stepped from the Navy bus which had brought his assault teams from the nearby Yokota Air Force Base, after the three-hour flight from Kadena.

A bus they'd had to wait nearly an hour for, their arrival apparently lost in the bureaucratic shuffle. That was the military for you. *Maximum efficiency.* The story of his life. With luck, their equipment had arrived in better shape—the SDV guys had caught an earlier flight and should already be loading their minisubs into the pair of Dry Deck Shelters on the *Michigan*'s deck, just aft of the sail.

Out beyond the cranes, looming against the horizon like Godzilla come to lay waste to Yokosuka itself, Guilbeau could see the USS *Ronald Reagan*, the flagship of CARSTRKGRU5.

A floating city in its own right, the *Nimitz*-class aircraft carrier towered nearly twenty stories above the waterline, dominating the landscape and dwarfing both the surrounding buildings and every other ship in the base.

The power of the United States Navy, never more on display than in that single image. It was a stirring sight, even for a sailor who had left the blue-water Navy behind the better part of two decades prior.

"That's just a big target, *jefe*," Dom Zamora observed, hefting his ruck over his shoulder as he came up behind him, predictably unimpressed. Unlike Guilbeau, he had gone straight into BUD/S on enlistment, without having spent time in the fleet beforehand. It showed.

Even so, Guilbeau thought, casting a glance behind him as the rest of his men filed off the bus, he couldn't argue that he was glad the transport to their objective would be more. . .covert.

Their objective. They didn't actually have one yet, a reality that left Guilbeau more than slightly uneasy as they prepared to embark.

"It's about moving assets into place," Fichtner had told him, in a private meeting between the two of them, following the full squadron brief. That didn't change the fact that the new intelligence was painfully thin. . .the NSA intercepts, at least those he'd been briefed on, revealing little but a sharp spike in chatter about the Braleys—and their presumed captor, Manong Soleiman—emanating from Islamist commanders in the Sulu Archipelago, particularly Jolo, the main island.

If that was *all* the spooks were going on. . .well, he and his men had their orders. Time to find their ride.

12:04 P.M. Philippine Standard Time
Al Nor Hotel & Convention Center
Cotabato City, Maguindanao
The Autonomous Region in Muslim Mindanao (ARMM)

". . .and thanks once again for all your help, Mr. Palalisan. My company, and the family, is deeply grateful." That none of that was true seemed less than relevant, Brent Kruta thought, ignoring the Moro politician's parting words as he stepped from the SUV onto the pavement, Palalisan's bodyguard holding the door open for him.

He was used to saying what needed to be said, that one remaining constant whether you were cajoling an asset for the government or brokering a deal for a private corporation. Your job, to tell people what you needed them to hear.

Graft, corruption, and uncertain loyalties aside. . .he wouldn't have gotten nearly this far without Palalisan—needed to keep him on-side for as long as possible. As long as it was *necessary*.

And it was necessary a while longer—this morning's meeting, only the opening round of negotiations. But he *was* dealing with the right people, as the less than day-old photo of the Braleys had proven.

He brushed dust from his suit jacket as the SUV drove off, circling the parking lot to return to the exit—noting only then the presence of a large black man leaning up against the side of a blue Toyota not far from the entrance, a ball cap and shades obscuring his face, seemingly absorbed in his phone.

Another American? The odds of that being natural seemed vanishingly small, all of the old instincts from years in the field coming back to the fore in a rush—his eyes scanning the parking lot as he made his way toward the Al Nor Suites.

He's on his way in, the text from Granby read—Richards' eyes coming up to scan the modern, elegantly-appointed lobby, taking in the small knot of Muslim women gathered near the concierge desk, their heads covered with brightly-colored hijabs.

There. He was on his feet in a moment, covering the floor with long strides—his hand already out almost before Kruta even saw him, clasping his old colleague's hand firmly as he wrapped the other arm around the man's shoulders, clapping him on the back. "Brent!"

"Jack." Kruta disengaged himself from the hug with an effort, a smile seeming to force its way onto his face as he looked up at the Texan. "Had no idea you were within a thousand miles of here. . .good to see you, brother."

The first was the truth, the second was a lie, as they both knew well. But Kruta was recovering fast, his training never far from the surface. "That quarterback in the lot—one of yours?"

"He's a Marine, but yeah," Richards replied, unsurprised that the former paramilitary had noticed, "he is. Good man."

"A Marine?" Kruta nodded appreciatively, the smile becoming marginally more genuine. He had done his own time in the Corps, the Texan recalled, with the 15th MEU in November of '01 when they had launched an amphibious assault off the decks of the USS *Peleliu*, flying nearly four hundred miles deep into Afghanistan to seize the airstrip which would become known as Camp Rhino. "I'll have to buy him a drink."

"He'd like that, I'm sure," Richards smiled, "but later." He glanced around, recognizing that their exchange had drawn every eye in the lobby. "You have somewhere more private we could talk?"

12:21 P.M.
The Embassy of the United States
Ermita, Manila
Philippines

"That could have gone better," Katherine Lipscomb announced with a heavy sigh, dropping her handbag onto a chair in the chancellery conference room.

It had been a rough morning, that much was beyond dispute, but even so. . .Russ shook his head. "Not really. There was no way Robredo was going to take that news well."

No one liked being spied on, and even the closest of America's allies never enjoyed the reminder that it was far from a marriage of equals.

"The important thing was how we handled his reaction," Russ continued, placing both hands on the conference table as he leaned forward, looking at Lipscomb, "and you did so masterfully. He's going to move on this new intel—he doesn't have any other choice."

"That's what concerns me," his State Department colleague replied, the strain visible on her face. "What if we didn't leave him any other choice?"

He recognized what she was saying in that moment, realized that he should have seen it earlier himself. His negotiating latitude was so limited here, working with a foreign government—most of the mission thus far, in the bailiwick of State—that he'd allowed it to blind him to one of the constants of his trade. *Never back them into a corner.*

"Manila isn't going to give Manong Soleiman what he wants," Lipscomb went on after a long moment, staring reflectively toward the window. "It's totally impracticable and Maskariño would never agree to it, even if it was. We haven't succeeded in developing alternate lines of negotiation, given the stance of Robredo and his department, and we have no reason to believe they've done so without informing us. That means if they feel they're being backed into a corner. . .the military option is the only one they have left."

Lipscomb's phone began to ring in that moment, the sound jarring them both from their thoughts as she retrieved it from the inner pocket of her suit jacket, glancing at the screen for a brief moment before answering it.

"Yes?"

12:24 P.M.
Al Nor Hotel & Convention Center
Cotabato City, Maguindanao
The Autonomous Region in Muslim Mindanao (ARMM)

"So you were in the Helmand too?" Brent Kruta asked conversationally, glancing back at Granby as he drew the blinds screening the hotel room's balcony. "What timeframe?"

"Back in '08," the CIA officer replied, "first deployment after I joined the Corps." He shook his head, an ironic smile spreading across his dark countenance. "I joined on a surge bonus. . .didn't make it to Iraq for years."

Kruta laughed. "That's the military for you. You joined for the surge?" He swore, chuckling as he glanced at Richards. "By that time, I was already out. . .where you finding these kids, Jack? What's happening to our Corps?"

Granby joined in the laugh, but Richards just smiled, watching his old colleague closely as he shrugged off his jacket, throwing it on the hotel room bed.

"It's their Corps now," he said quietly. "Going to be their Company soon enough."

"God's truth," Kruta acknowledged, his fingers loosening the knot of his necktie and undoing his collar at the throat. "Makes me glad I got out when I did. . .you get to my age, you can only handle so much change, Jack. You'll see."

"Maybe." Richards shifted position restlessly as Kruta stripped the tie from around his neck, folding it carefully before dropping it onto his discarded suit. "Why don't we get down to business?"

"Business?" Kruta feigned surprise, the smile still there but all of the humor gone from his eyes as he glanced between the CIA paramilitaries. "You mean this wasn't a social call, Jack? You're breakin' my heart."

"Cut the crap, Brent. You know why we're here."

"The Braleys?"

"Ding, ding," Granby quipped, drawing a look of annoyance from Richards as he nodded in response to Kruta.

"Langley tells me that Svalinn was contracted by the family to conduct ransom negotiations with the hostage-takers. And Svalinn sent you."

"All accurate, so far as it goes. The Company must be

178

getting efficient in its old age. Or maybe," Kruta inclined his head toward Granby, "there's something in this new blood thing. Still doesn't explain what you're doing here, in my hotel room."

"The Agency is looking for intel on the Braleys' current location, whether they're even still alive. Anything that could enable us to effect their rescue."

Kruta just held his gaze for a long moment, hands shoved into the pockets of his dress pants—conflicted emotions playing across the former intelligence officer's face. Then, finally, "They're still alive."

"You've verified that?" A nod. "How?"

"The usual way, Jack, how do you think?" Kruta shook his head, taking his hands from his pockets and spreading them wide. "They'd printed out yesterday's home page from WaPo—had her holding it, in the picture."

"How'd they look?"

"Bad." The sarcasm was gone from Kruta's voice, his tone telling Richards volumes about just how bad the picture must have been. Brent was a father, after all. "All of them, but him most of all. Looks like death warmed over. Couldn't get them to open up on what he's been going through—if they knew—but I've seen that look before. He's only going to last so long without dedicated medical attention."

"Then we need to get him out."

His old colleague started to nod in agreement, but drew himself up short. "No. . .hold on there, Jack. There's no 'we' about this. You have your job, I have mine."

Richards traded a glance with Granby. "Sounds to me like it's the same job. Might as well work together on it, share what intel we have."

A harsh, humorless laugh broke from Kruta's lips. "Langley's sharing now? That's a first." He put out a hand before Richards could respond. "Doesn't matter, I was in your shoes long enough to know that's a one-way street. But it's not the same job, Jack. The family doesn't want a raid, they don't want pipe-hitters kicking down doors. They just want their loved ones back. Svalinn's contract here is to negotiate a ransom payment—a simple exchange, money for freedom. That's it."

Richards just looked at him, his obsidian-black eyes flashing like coals of fire. "And you were in my shoes long enough to know exactly where that money is going to go, and what it's going to do. How many more people it's going to kill. You're trading three lives for. . .God knows how many. They might not be American, next time, but they'll be just as dead."

The shot struck home, he could tell by the look on Kruta's face. But the former paramilitary shook his head nonetheless. "Come on, Jack. You're not going to stand there, look me in the eye, and tell me you've never, in all your years with the Company, handed over a bag full of cash to a bad man and walked away, not knowing what he intended to do with it. Only hoping that what you got for it was worth the price someone else was going to end up paying. You have, I have—this kid," he indicated Granby with a gesture, "has or will if he stays in long enough. It's the *business*."

"It is," the Texan nodded. "But this time, you *do* know. You can't tell me that's the same."

"Maybe. What's your alternative?"

Richards traded a glance with his partner. "Glad you asked. . ."

180

1:43 A.M. Eastern Standard Time
CIA Headquarters
Langley, Virginia

"Tell me what we're looking at," Olivia Voss announced, striding into the conference room just off the Clandestine Service op-center and closing the door behind her. She was dressed far more casually than anyone at Agency Headquarters could ever remember seeing her, if about what one would expect from someone woken up in the middle of the night—jeans and a thick grey sweatshirt, her dark hair pulled back in a ponytail.

"We heard from Lukasik's people at Manila Station forty-five minutes ago," Danny Lasker replied, gesturing up to one of the battery of digital clocks mounted up on the far end of the conference room—its read-out giving the local time in the Philippines. As duty officer, it had fallen to him to make the call, bring her in. "They'd received a new call from the Braleys' kidnappers at approximately 1315 hours local."

"Manong Soleiman?" Voss asked, taking her seat at the head of the table and gesturing for the rest of the gathered officers to sit down.

"Abu Nazih."

Voss shook her head wearily. "That's not ringing any bells, Danny."

"Didn't for me either, when Manila Station first made contact," Lasker replied, glancing over at Nicholas Patsakos, a middle-aged father of two who was their ranking analyst on the Asia desk and had, like Voss, been at home in bed when the call came in. He wasn't making any friends tonight. "How about you lead us off, Nick, give us the rundown?"

"Abu Nazih al-Tunisi is a relatively new player on the Southeast Asia scene," the analyst began, running an absent hand through his tousled hair as he consulted his notes, "a veteran of Syria believed to have left Raqqa just a few months before its fall. It's not known whether he was dispatched to support or supplant Mostapa's leadership of IS elements in Mindanao, but he popped back up on our radar in East Kalimantan in late July, when he narrowly escaped a Kopassus—Indonesian SF—raid on the compound where he was staying. Fast-forward a month, and we received our first concrete evidence of his presence in the Sulu Archipelago, where he and his small cohort of foreign fighters seem to have successfully supplanted one of the local commanders, a man known to us only as Abu Yasser. We—"

"Do we have a good understanding of what territory this Abu Yasser controlled?" Olivia Voss asked, leaning forward, her elbows resting on the table as her gaze shifted back and forth between Lasker and Patsakos.

"Roughly," was the reply. "We believe most of his influence was centered in the municipality of Indanan, on the main island of Jolo—on the outskirts of the capital itself."

"So, beyond corroborating the NSA's intercept intelligence and giving us a better idea where the Braleys might likely be found. . .how exactly does this impact our situation?"

Lasker cleared his throat, tapping a finger nervously against the wood of the conference room table. "The demands have changed."

2:49 P.M. Philippine Standard Time
Awang Airport
Cotabato City, Maguindanao
The Autonomous Region in Muslim Mindanao (ARMM)

"That went well." *Yeah*, Richards thought, hearing Granby's sardonic comment as they stood together just outside the terminal, watching the Cebgo Airlines twin-engine turboprop taxi in for a landing. *Their flight.* Or would be, once it had refueled.

It hadn't. Kruta's response to their suggestion that he wear a GPS micro-tracker sewn into his clothing when he went to Jolo to negotiate with the jihadists in person, an angry refusal which left little room for discussion.

Not that he hadn't known it was a long shot, going in. Their request, an additional risk even he would have hesitated to assume, if someone had asked it of him. Brent. . .well, Kruta had put in his time, served his country for a lot of years. No dishonor in that.

"If you had distracted him," Titus Granby went on after a moment, his muscular arms folded across his chest as he turned to face Richards, "I'm sure I could have planted the tracker on him."

The thought had crossed his mind—that much he couldn't deny. It might have even worked, and he was somehow certain that Nichols would have greenlit the idea without much hesitation.

But he wasn't Nichols.

"And when they found the tracker?" he asked quietly, his black eyes hidden behind the dark lenses of his shades. "What then?"

A grimace. They both knew *what then*—a one-way ticket to an orange jumpsuit and a video going up on the darknet.

"A man puts his life on the line," Richards continued, "he deserves to know why. And to make that decision for himself."

Particularly when that man was a fellow Marine. *One of their own.* The brotherhood.

Granby started to respond, but whatever he was about to say was lost as Richards' phone began to vibrate insistently, a WESTMINCOM ID code coming up as he glanced at the screen. "Yes?"

"Jack." It was Mijares, an unusual excitement in the lieutenant's voice. "You need to come back here as soon as possible—we've just received new intel."

Richards glanced out at the turboprop, still disembarking passengers. "Just waiting on our flight."

Chapter 13

"I had hoped to see them home by Christmas," President Richard Norton announced out loud, to the room, to himself, and no one in particular, taking a long slow sip of his coffee as he stared out the window of the Aspen Lodge, into the thick Maryland woods beyond. The snow was mostly melted now, in the wake of the previous two days' warm-up—leaving behind only a few scattered patches in the shadow of the evergreens, the white standing out in the half-light of the dawn. It wasn't going to be anyone's postcard Christmas, least of all his.

"You've done all you could, Rick," a woman's voice replied from behind him, and he turned to see his wife of twenty-eight years, Leslie Kreider Norton, standing there in the shadow of the doorway, still in her housecoat—her chestnut-brown hair disheveled from sleep. He had been up for more than an hour, throwing on a light brown polo shirt and jeans before receiving the first of several calls from

Langley. "All anyone could have done."

"And they're still in the hands of terrorists," he spat, shaking his head, regretting the anger with which he spoke the words even as they left his mouth, but unable to suppress it. "Nothing I've done has made a difference, Leslie. *None of it.*"

The more power you held, the more keenly you felt your impotence when all that power simply. . .ceased to matter. Like it had now.

The throbbing sound of helicopter rotors had faded away off to the west almost ten minutes before, no doubt the Agency Sikorsky, coming in for a landing on the Camp David helipad.

The folder lying open on the low coffee table in front of the sofa contained the basic outline of the new developments which had begun to unfold with the overnight call to the US embassy in Manila from the Braleys' new captor—but the CIA had insisted that the DCIA himself should fly up to Camp David to brief the President in person. *David Lay.*

A careerist who now held the unusual distinction of having served three presidents as DCIA, Lay was one of the few people in Washington whom Norton trusted even less than Bernard Kranemeyer, the two of them together representing so much of what he had campaigned against all throughout his time in the Senate.

It was in his power to remove Lay, as Kranemeyer, but his advisers had cautioned against such a course—in both cases. Lay might not have been a war hero like his counterpart at the Clandestine Service, but he commanded a respect in both the intelligence community and DC political circles few others possessed. And he had lost a daughter in the Vegas attacks only a month before Norton took office, which made attacking him openly. . .politically unwise.

The President stifled a curse, glancing behind him to find that his wife had vanished, no doubt gone to get changed. He should do the same, he thought, suddenly regretting the informality of his chosen attire. Before the CIA arrived at the lodge.

8:22 P.M. Philippine Standard Time
Camp General Basilio Navarro, Western Mindanao
Command (WESTMINCOM)
Calarian District, Zamboanga City
Zamboanga del Sur, Mindanao

Abu Nazih. The piece they'd all been missing, now fitting into its place—the jigsaw puzzle coming together before them, even if the resulting picture was no prettier for all that.

Richards recalled the name from the NICA files he'd gone over, two days before—though he could recall nothing in them which would have linked Manong Soleiman directly to the Tunisian. Perhaps that had been in the redacted portions.

". . .according to our best intelligence," Maricar de Rosales was saying, gesturing to the large, highly-detailed military map spread out on the table before them, "Abu Nazih's influence is concentrated here, in the area surrounding Maimbung—about eleven kilometers south of Jolo proper, particularly this compound, circled here, although there are others believed to be under his control to the west, toward Talipao and along the road toward Panamao."

"How many?"

De Rosales looked up, seeming taken off-guard by the question. It had been clear from the moment he'd walked in that none of the Filipinos were thrilled by their continued presence, and would just as soon have proceeded *without* briefing their CIA counterparts. In their place, he'd likely have felt the same. "I beg your pardon?"

"How many compounds are we looking at, exactly?" Richards repeated calmly, holding the NICA intelligence officer's gaze.

"At least three. Possibly four to five." *That was a lot of targets,* he thought, trading a glance with Thomas Parker. A list they were going to have to narrow down.

"The lines on Jolo have become blurred since Abu Nazih's arrival," de Rosales went on, seeming compelled to explain the uncertainty, "with some of the local commanders rejecting his attempts to assert authority outright—his appeal is mostly with the youth, the next generation of fighters, those raised on more global-oriented jihadist propaganda."

Made sense. He noticed she didn't reference the Islamic State, despite Abu Nazih's own past ties—hewing to the official party line out of Manila, that the Islamic State did not have a presence in the Philippines, a party line they had maintained throughout the siege of Marawi and all the carnage Mostapa had wrought in the ISIL name. *See no evil.*

"How do you expect to pinpoint his actual location?"

"Tomorrow morning," she responded, clearly prepared for that question, "our military partners will perform an aerial reconnaissance by UAV of the target sites. We're confident that will give us the results we need, either by direct visual identification, or by analyzing patterns of life against what we would expect if Abu Nazih or his foreign fighters were to be found in the area."

"And then?" Richards glanced between de Rosales and Mijares. "What's the plan?"

It was Mijares who took the question, stepping forward to the table, his hands clasped behind his back. "Then we're going to go in and get them out—tomorrow night, if all conditions have been met. My men, in three helicopters, with additional support personnel flying into Jolo to stage at the airport. We'll set down outside Maimbung and infiltrate the target on foot, hitting it in the early morning."

Not a bad plan, depending on exactly how it was executed—and the SAF were professional enough to carry it off. *But.*

Richards cleared his throat, knowing his duty in this. "My government has been quite clear that it wishes direct military action by the AFP to be used only in last resort."

"Then," Mijares replied, his eyes grim as he stared across the table at the Americans, "your government needs to decide whether they are prepared to meet Abu Nazih's demands."

7:31 A.M. Eastern Standard Time
Naval Support Facility Thurmont—Camp David
Frederick County, Maryland

". . .instead of the territorial concessions aimed at Manila previously demanded by Manong Soleiman, Abu Nazih al-Tunisi's demands are directed at the United States," Olivia Voss continued, turning her laptop toward the President, "and concern the release of several members of the Islamic State hierarchy currently in US custody, namely, Mirsad Imamović, Abu Muhammad al-Andalusí, and Khaled Talib Husayn al-Zubaydi."

David Lay watched, leaning back into the cushions of the sofa as Norton shook his head slowly. "I've never heard of any of these men."

That hardly came as a surprise, the DCIA thought, concealing his inner grimace behind an impassive mask. Richard Norton hadn't been elected President for his foreign policy chops, and to be fair. . .it would have been unreasonable to expect this level of granularity from most any American President, certainly any of the three he had served.

"Mirsad Imamović," Voss responded, "was born in Bosnia-Herzegovina—then Yugoslavia—and, as a teenager, was swept up in the fighting in that country in the early '90s. We believe that is where he first came into contact with the jihad, through the groups of foreign *mujahideen* who came to support Bosniaks like Imamović in the fighting against the Croats. When he fled BiH in 2004, it was to avoid standing trial on charges of war crimes. We first came across him in Iraq, two years later, fighting under the banner of Abu Ayyub al-Masri in AQI's rearguard action against the US surge and the *Sahwa* militias."

A "rearguard action" which had turned out to be more effective, in the long run, than all their efforts to crush it. Lay winced, the memories of those days still fresh. The *hope* they had known. Hope shared by their allies in Anbar, those *Sahwa* militia leaders—most of whom were now dead, wiped out years before as the Islamic State came washing back into the province like the return of the tide.

He was getting old, and tired of all this—though he knew part of it was the dread of facing this first Christmas since Carol's death. His daughter, shot dead by a sniper's bullet in the Christmas Eve attacks on Las Vegas, an anniversary now only three days away.

Still, his days were numbered and he knew it. There was only so long he could keep this up.

". . .we had reports of his death in 2007 and again in 2009," Olivia Voss was saying, an intent look on her face as she held the President's focus, "but he resurfaced in Syria four years later as part of the Islamic State's Shura Council, and was appointed by Abu Omar al-Shishani, presumably on the strength of his military experience, to head up one of their largest training camps in northern Syria. After the fall of Raqqa, he attempted to flee Syria, but was captured in early August."

"So we *do* have him, then? And the others?" President Norton asked, his brow furrowing as he glanced between Voss and Lay. Kranemeyer's deputy glanced in Lay's direction, as if expecting him to answer the President's questions, but he simply nodded imperceptibly for her to continue. The future of the Agency was in the hands of others now—her generation, stepping up to the roles of senior leadership they'd spent twenty years preparing for. He was only here to facilitate, to back her up. *If necessary.*

"Not officially, sir," Voss replied carefully, the look on her face clearly indicating that she knew just how thin this ice could be, with this president. "Imamović was captured by local militias coordinating with US Special Forces, and transferred into Agency custody. He's currently being held for us by King Abdullah's *Mukhabarat* at a prison in Jordan's Ma'an Governate. We have never publicly acknowledged our role in his capture and ongoing detainment, nor that of the other two."

"So he's what. . .hoping to use the Braleys as a pawn to force our hand—acknowledge that we were, in fact, involved?" Norton shook his head in exasperation. "I made my commitment to smashing the Syrian caliphate clear in the campaign, and it was a promise kept. We *won*. How is this a problem?"

Another look between the two officials, and this time Lay took the signal, leaning forward in his seat. "The problem we face, Mr. President, is that our Jordanian counterparts do not necessarily adhere to international conventions on interrogation methods. And Abu Muhammad al-Andalusí is a Spanish citizen. . ."

9:03 P.M. Philippine Standard Time
Jolo Island, Sulu Province
The Autonomous Region in Muslim Mindanao (ARMM)

"What does this mean now, Shawn?" he heard his wife ask quietly, her back pressed up against the concrete wall, her face shadowed in the glare of the Coleman lantern set on the low table on the other side of the small room that served as their cell.

It was a long moment before he replied, trying to find some words of hope, of encouragement, to share with her. Trying and failing before opting for the truth instead. "I don't know."

He could hear the despair in his own voice, wanted to

reach out and comfort her, but he had no comfort to give. Abu Nazih had explained little. . .simply handed him the script and had him go over it a few times before they'd stepped out into the courtyard of the compound with the satellite phone to place the call to the embassy.

Even so, he'd managed to stumble over the words more than once on the call—his voice still weak from the sickness and exposure which had so nearly cost him his life, the hesitation earning him a rifle butt in the ribs from one of the foreign jihadists, who clearly thought he was stalling for time.

Shawn reached down, touching his side gingerly—wincing with the pain, even now. An angry blue-black bruise spreading out over his flesh the last time he had lifted his shirt to check.

"He wants to trade us for. . .terrorists from Syria, I guess." None of the names had been Filipino, that much he was certain of, at the very least.

Abu Nazih and Manong Soleiman had been arguing when the guards led him in, but the Moro had broken off at his entrance—firing a few angry curses in the direction of Abu Nazih before retreating before the advance of his foreign fighters. Perhaps another disagreement over the fate of Annalyn; Soleiman had still been talking with her when they'd emerged into the courtyard to make the call.

Shawn had tried to make eye contact with her in the moments as Abu Nazih set up the call, but her attention had been focused on the Moro leader, a look of resignation on her face.

"Will they. . .will they do that?" It was a question he had already asked himself, so many times since he'd first read the script. The first demands had been of Manila, and they had demanded so *much*. These demands had been made of their government, and surely the release of a few prisoners. . .

"I have no idea."

9:31 P.M.
Camp General Basilio Navarro, Western Mindanao
Command (WESTMINCOM)
Calarian District, Zamboanga City
Zamboanga del Sur, Mindanao

"So that's where we stand now," Jack Richards announced, hands resting on his hips as he stood there in the barracks room, looking around at his men. "Our AFP counterparts are still playing hardball, so I've only been given authorization to take along two officers on tomorrow night's op. Parker, I want you to stay here and head up our continuing liaison operations with the SAF. Do what you need to do to justify our continued presence, within our mission parameters."

"Right on." Thomas Parker nodded, touching two fingers to his forehead in a mimic salute. "You got it."

"Granby, I want you with me," Richards continued, looking the Marine in the eye. "See this through. And Carson, your PJ training could come in handy. . .we don't know what shape the hostages are going to be in, but from what Brent said, it doesn't sound promising."

"What *did* he say, exactly?" Parker asked, a skeptical glance on the New Yorker's face. There'd been no time—an SAF vehicle picking them up at Zamboanga International, bringing them directly back to be briefed on the latest developments since the Braley call.

"Not enough," Richards replied simply. There wasn't much time now, either. And for all he might understand Kruta's reasoning, that didn't mean he had to agree with it— or respect his refusal to work together. A man with *access* could have made all the difference.

On the other hand, it was hard to know with whom, precisely, Kruta had been negotiating. If it had been the possibly late and unlamented Manong Soleiman, he might be as far out in the cold now as anyone else.

"Ardolino," he went on after a moment, "you'll stay here and back up Parker. The rest of you, get your gear together, pack for tomorrow night. Mijares' proposed wheels-up is 0100."

Catching the red-eye, he thought as his men dispersed to carry out their orders, hoping against hope that Washington was staying on top of this. Because someone had certainly lit a fire under the Filipinos. . .

10:27 P.M.
Masjid Sultan Hassanal Bolkiah
Cotabato City, Manguindanao
The Autonomous Region in Muslim Mindanao (ARMM)

The trip from his hotel in Cotabato had been a twenty-minute *habal-habal*—motorcycle taxi—ride west along the banks of the Tamontaka River as it flowed out into the waters of the gulf. Waters now lurking out there in the darkness to the west of the mosque's sweeping grounds as Brent Kruta swung his leg off the saddle of the battered Suzuki at the gate of the compound—squeezing his driver's shoulder and handing over half of a thick roll of 100-peso notes.

"Wait for me," he instructed the young man over the throbbing roar of the *habal-habal's* engine, flashing the remaining half of the notes in his face. Hard to say whether he would.

Coming here was an undeniable risk—he'd spent another long Signal session conferring with his superiors at Svalinn after receiving Jim Palalisan's seemingly urgent call, and they'd shared his skepticism, ultimately leaving the decision up to him. But if things had changed. . .he needed to know.

It was that simple, sometimes. *For you shall know the truth, and the truth shall set you free.* The motto of his old Agency, even if they had known, well as anyone, that sometimes it was lies that kept you alive—truth that got you killed.

Perhaps the catch was that *you* would know the truth.

The *masjid* was huge—rising out of the flatlands and marsh lining the coast of the Moro Gulf as though it had sprung, like Venus, fully-formed from the sea. Small white lights at the top of each of its four towering minarets blinking steadily in the night, as a landmark to pilots. The architecture—more than a dozen golden domes rising out of the massive white structure itself, seeming to glow in the moonlight—reminded him of a visit to Brunei, years back. *Company business.*

The portico looming ahead of him through the fronds of the palms lining the approach was lit by floodlights, the glare of the floods revealing a trio of blacked-out Toyota Fortuners parked beneath, at the top of the curved, sloping drive, a small group of men clustered around the hood of the foremost SUV. At least one, maybe more of them carrying long guns—Kruta making out the familiar shape of an M4 carbine as he made his way forward, up the incline.

Palalisan's security detail, like as not—based on his experience of the morning, the man tended to roll heavy. Take no chances.

A wise old fox.

"Mr. Kruta," the foremost man challenged as he entered the circle of light, taking a hand off the M4's grip and raising it, stopping him short. He recognized the voice—the man's face backlit by the floods, thrown in shadow—Palalisan's head of security, a former AFP officer introduced to him only as "Mohd."

No sign of Palalisan, but that wasn't surprising—particularly as Mohd motioned one of his men forward. He wouldn't emerge from the vehicles until his men were assured it was safe.

Kruta raised his arms away from his sides in a crucifix pose, holding them as the Moro patted him down, searching him for weapons. He didn't have any—had thought of buying a gun earlier, after the call, but hadn't, for exactly this reason. He wouldn't have retained it long enough for it to do him any good.

The rough frisking lasted maybe thirty seconds before the man stepped back, waving the all-clear. He saw Mohd speak into his phone—Palalisan emerging a moment later from the rear Toyota, spreading his hands as he advanced. "Thank you for coming to meet with me, Mr. Kruta. When we spoke this morning, I did not anticipate that it would be necessary to meet again so soon. But our circumstances have. . .changed."

The mosque was far less impressive from close up, Kruta noted absently, moving into the shadow of the portico. The white paint already faded and peeling in places, grime building in the eaves.

Standard practice for the Philippines, near as he could tell—build big and flashy, run it into the ground, build new. Rinse and repeat. Granted, the climate didn't help.

"How so?" he asked, every fiber of his body poised and alert—mentally noting the positions of the politician's bodyguards.

"The deal—our deal—is no longer on the table. The hostages," Palalisan said, a strange look of embarrassment seeming to spread across the Moro's swarthy face, "are. . .well, let me just say that—"

"Are they still alive?" Kruta demanded, more sharply than he'd intended. Behind Jim Palalisan, another bodyguard stepped out from behind the cover of the rear SUV, an M4 in his hands. And this guy was rocking an M203 grenade launcher on the forend of his weapon, the former CIA officer noticed incredulously, marking the glint of the 40mm grenades themselves in the bandolier slung across the man's chest. Hopefully he had enough sense not to use them to "protect" his boss, not here. . .he'd splatter them all across the portico if one of those went off.

"They are, they are," the politician replied quickly, raising his hands to gesture for calm. "But they are no longer under our control."

Our control, Kruta thought, noting Palalisan's use of the possessive. So much for the purported separation between the former MILF leader and the current crop of terrorists.

"The Tunisian has asserted his own authority over them,

backed by his fellow Arabs," Palalisan continued, "and issued his own demands to Manila. Trading the hostages for money. . .is not something he's open to discussing."

Kruta shook his head in disbelief, glancing from Palalisan back to where Mohd stood by the hood of the lead Toyota. "Are you kidding me? You seriously brought me all the way out here in the night to tell me that it's over, that there's nothing more you can do for me?"

"No," the politician replied, "not exactly."

Chapter 14

"They're doing this to me deliberately," Richard Norton announced, staring across the table of the small Hickory Lodge restaurant at the RNC chairman as he put down his club sandwich for the fifth time since he'd begun eating. He'd taken maybe three bites. "This is about embarrassing me, Jeff—has been, ever since that disaster in Egypt over the summer. Ever since my bill died in the Senate. They want me to be a one-term President."

He'd had the same conversation with his wife, earlier. The CIA executives had left three hours before, but he hadn't found himself able to focus on much else since they'd left, to the point of rescheduling his call with the President of Ecuador. He would have canceled this early lunch with the RNC chair if the man hadn't already been en route.

"The intelligence community, Mr. President?" Jefferson Van Dorn asked, his eyes narrowing as he reached up to daub his lips with a napkin. Leslie hadn't had to ask. A small, soft-spoken man from Sweetwater County, Wyoming who had spent the better part of the last thirty years of his life in Republican politics, Van Dorn favored a military-style high-and-tight haircut which left his ears protruding incongruously from the now-graying stubble.

"Of course," Norton replied, leaving off the curse he wanted to attach to the end of that sentence. Van Dorn might have looked faintly ridiculous, but he was a shrewd political operator, and an ally Norton really couldn't afford to do without. Not now—not with so many enemies already circling.

"The security bureaucracy is entrenched, to be sure," Van Dorn replied, putting down his napkin by his plate, "and they have their own way of doing things. But to ascribe these actions to malevolence, to some sort of evil master plan. . ." He smiled. "When you've worked in and around this town for as long as I have, it truly becomes hard to give them credit for that much competence."

"Maybe that's the problem," Norton said, the smug smile on Van Dorn's face like sandpaper scraping across an open cut.

"I beg your pardon?"

"You've been here too long." The President pushed back his chair, rising his feet. "Too long to see what they're really doing. This is all an attempt to use this hostage situation to paint me into a corner, to make it look as though I *approved* this—this abuse of detainees."

He paused, taking in the look of surprise on Van Dorn's face. The smile was gone. "If I acknowledge that we've been holding these terrorists in Jordan, and agree to the trade, I look like a fraud. If I don't. . ." his voice trailed off for a moment, becoming almost plaintive when it re-emerged. "I can't allow them to be executed, Jeff. I *need* this win."

The RNC chairman shook his head, seeming on the verge of replying when Dennis Froelich appeared in the doorway. "Mr. President, you have a call. On the secure line."

1:22 A.M., Philippine Standard Time, December 22nd
Al Nor Suites
Cotabato City, Manguindanao
The Autonomous Region in Muslim Mindanao (ARMM)

"Any word from the boss?" Brent Kruta asked when his call finally connected. "She asked to be kept updated, and I've been trying to reach her for an hour, no dice."

"She had dinner with a business contact tonight at the Râna in Istanbul, Brent," a man's deep baritone replied from more than six thousand miles away in Brussels. *Arne Kornbech.* Svalinn's operations officer was a Dane, a former Jaeger who had gone private after fifteen years in the *Jægerkorpset.* "I imagine she's still there. What's going on?"

Kruta reached up, rubbing a hand through the bristles of his close-cropped hair. "I don't know, Arne, and that's what bothers me."

"You had the meet with Palalisan?" Kornbech had been on the conference call earlier. "Everything go smoothly?"

"I'm still alive." That was something, but Palalisan's manner. . . "He says the hostages are out of his control, that al-Tunisi's using them as leverage for some sort of crazy prisoner swap he wants to pull off."

"Syrian jihadists," Kornbech acknowledged. "We know."

The former Agency officer shook his head in mute disbelief, moving over to the window of his hotel room, the phone tucked against his ear. "And you didn't think I might need to know that?"

"Easy," was the Dane's reply. "Intel only came through an hour ago. Our networks are good, but it takes time for things to leak. Bottom line, yeah—the game has changed. So our boy's out in the cold?"

"I'm not sure. He implied that there were still options on the table, but I wasn't able to get him to move beyond generalizations and a promise to stay in touch."

"You think he was implying that al-Tunisi can be bought, same as Soleiman?"

"Maybe." Kruta reached up, brushing the blinds gently to one side as he gazed down into the parking lot, half-expecting to see Richards or one of his other old friends from the Agency still down there, watching. He wouldn't know all of them. "Or maybe something more kinetic."

3:54 P.M. Eastern Standard Time, December 21ˢᵗ
St. James Episcopal Church
New London, Connecticut

"You've made it clear to the command authority that his opposite number won't even be awake at this hour?" Bernard Kranemeyer asked, feeling the December cold seep through his gloves as he rested a hand on the heavy ironwork of the railing just outside the door of the historic red-brick church, pressing the phone to his ear with the other.

"I understand that has been communicated by the President's advisers, yes," Olivia Voss replied, a weary edge to her voice. "He's insistent that he speak personally with the Filipino president at the earliest possible opportunity, which is still a few hours away. If Manila will go for it."

A fairly massive *if*, the director mused, given Maskariño's earlier obstinance, and the signals this move by the Filipinos toward direct military action sent. Above his head, the Episcopal flag snapped angrily in the bitter December breeze, a red cross against a snow-white field, its Madonna blue canton nearly concealed in the flag's rippling folds.

The wind, obscuring Voss' next words in a burst of static. ". . .the Bureau's sending down their people from the HRFC to Mindanao, should arrive in the morning. Finally got clearance from the Interior Secretary."

Hard to say what good they'd be allowed to do, but. . .he supposed it wouldn't hurt to have a hostage negotiator on-scene. Or as close to the scene as the Filipinos would let them get.

"What about Shulgach?" he asked, choosing his words carefully as another pair of late-arriving mourners mounted the steps behind him, disappearing into the church.

"JSOC is being kept in the loop," his deputy replied. "Lasker reached out to Fort Bragg as soon as word came in."

"ETA?"

"Not soon enough, not the way this is moving. The *Michigan* won't be in position until the night of the 24th, local, at the earliest."

Kranemeyer's lips compressed into a thin, bloodless line. The geography, their undoing in the end, as it had been for so many before them. There was simply no way around it.

He glanced up at the ornate Gothic Revival architecture of St. James' bell tower, its cross-topped spire piercing the winter sky high above his head—hearing the solemn, funereal sound of an organ drifting out on the breeze as the door behind him opened and closed once again.

"I have to go, Olivia. The service is beginning."

5:23 A.M. Japan Standard Time, December 22nd
The USS Michigan
East China Sea, a hundred miles northwest of Okinawa

"I say let them handle it, then." Petty Officer Vic Kuznicki shook his head, glancing around the small wardroom at his fellow SEALs—meeting Guilbeau's eyes for a brief moment. "If that's how it's gonna be. They know the terrain, the language. It's their AO."

Dom Zamora swore loudly, an angry glitter in the chief's eyes as he glared over at Kuznicki. Cramming this many men—twenty SEALs, including the SDV operators—into the narrow confines of a boomer along with the hundred and fifty-plus sailors and officers already aboard was bound to create tensions, no matter how many times they'd all done it before.

And the intel picture was only getting worse every time they came to comms depth.

"They're Americans, Vic," Zamora spat, as though that sufficed for an answer. Perhaps it did. Made bringing them home their responsibility, no matter how messy it was shaping up to be.

"Never said they weren't, Chief. That doesn't change the reality—we're going in blind."

He wasn't wrong, and Jason could tell by the look in Dom's eyes that he knew it—an op like this, SOP was to train for weeks, preferably on a full-size model of the target. *This time?*

The intel boys had yet to even tell them where the target was, and they weren't going to be building any models in this steel tube three hundred feet below the waves. *Or training.*

Might be that Vic was right—the hostages might be better off if the Filipinos went on in and got them out. But it didn't matter.

"We have our orders, gentlemen," he interjected, cutting off Dom's angry reply. Looking around at his men as he continued, "And we're going to execute them, to the very best of our ability. The situation is the far side of ideal, not going to lie, but we'll overcome that, like so many times before. We're going to bring the Braleys home. If the Filipinos get there before we can stage, well. . .that's how it'll go. Not much we can do about that—time to focus on what we *can* change. Get back to going over every scrap of intel we have, make the most of it."

"Hooyah, Senior."

7:14 P.M. Eastern Standard Time, December 21ˢᵗ
Naval Support Facility Thurmont—Camp David
Frederick County, Maryland

". . .'and ours is a cause far larger than the United States of America, a *human* cause, wherever men seek to live free—a freedom guided by ideals and guaranteed by strength'. No," President Norton announced, an exasperated sigh escaping his lips as he closed the folder, dropping it on the coffee table. "That's not going to work, Lydia, we're going to need to go with something else—you've made me sound like Bush."

He cursed softly beneath his breath, leaving his speechwriter Lydia McKinnon sitting on the couch as he rose, pacing across the floor of the Aspen Lodge's sunroom. "I need a speech, and I need one *now.*"

The President turned, looking back at her—hands poised assertively on his hips as he stood there in front of the door. "I'm leaving for Vegas in less than twenty-four hours, and I'll be speaking at both the Bellagio and the crash site of Delta Flight 94 on Christmas Eve, not to mention the other speeches. I need to know what I'm going to say."

"Well, Mr. President, if you'll just look over what—"

"I have to get the tone of this right, Lydia. I took risks, this last year, in my response to the attacks on taking office. I didn't expand the surveillance state, didn't go to war—we dealt with those directly behind the attacks, and we moved on. That's what we did—what America elected me to do. America doesn't want another crusade." He paused. "But the wounds are still fresh, and now, with Americans being taken hostage overseas. . ."

There was anger written across his face as his head came up, shooting a glare toward the living room. "Dennis!"

"Mr. President?" Dennis Froelich asked, appearing a moment later from around the corner. The White House chief of staff was, like the president, in his shirtsleeves—a marked departure from his usual Washington uniform.

"Have you people had any success reaching Luis Maskariño yet?"

"Not yet, Mr. President." Froelich glanced at his wristwatch. "It is still very early morning over there, sir. I'm sure Ambassador Garner is doing his best to—"

"I don't care about anyone's *best*, Dennis, unless it gets results. I want to talk to the Filipino president."

8:31 A.M. Philippine Standard Time, December 22nd
Edwin Andrews Air Base
Zamboanga City
Zamboanga del Sur, Mindanao

There was a light cross-breeze blowing across the runway, bearing with it the slow-ebbing chill of the night and raising the gooseflesh on Richards' forearms as he leaned back into the canvas seat of the AFP military jeep. The deep whine of twin turbojets filling the air as a narrow-bodied Airbus A319 in the yellow-and-white livery of Cebu Pacific taxiied for takeoff from Zamboanga International, which shared the runway with the military airbase.

Overhead, the sun climbed higher into the cloud-obscured sky above the city, but there was little warmth in it.

And somewhere out there, amidst the clouds, was the Bureau's inbound flight.

"You were right," he heard Granby announce from the back of the jeep.

"About what?"

"Yesterday. Kruta." There was an unusually earnest look on the younger officer's face as Richards half-turned in his seat to face him. "I thought it was stupid not to exploit our opportunity with him—plant a tracker and let him lead us to the Braleys. But I see now you were right. He was one of us, once."

One of us. The brotherhood, and all that went with it. *Honor.* Even among spies. Richards shrugged. "It worked out."

They hadn't needed Kruta, after all. Not with the call, and the Filipinos' intel.

He hesitated for a long moment before continuing, his native reticence very nearly holding him back. "But there's gonna be times, you'll find, when doing the right thing doesn't 'work out.' And you're still going to have to do it— find a way to live with the consequences. *Somehow.* That's when this business gets hard."

8:42 A.M.
The Gulfstream G550
On approach to Zamboanga International Airport

The last twenty-four hours had been a frenetic bustle of activity, ever since Abu Nazih's call had arrived at the US embassy, William Russell Cole reflected, glancing out the window of the Bureau jet into the gray haze of the low-hanging clouds as the Gulfstream descended toward Zamboanga International.

Lots of shuttle diplomacy between State and their opposite numbers in the Maskariño government. More meetings with Ismael Robredo, culminating in one particularly bitter exchange, but he'd eventually signed off on Russ' departure for Mindanao. *Finally.* Two weeks after their arrival in Manila.

He'd gotten a message from his daughter in the middle of it all, asking if he would be coming home for Christmas—had to tell her that wasn't going to happen, not now, three days out, with the situation still in flux. Even if the Filipinos' rescue operation came off tonight. . .it just wasn't happening.

Russ let out a heavy sigh, even as he felt the familiar *bump* of the Gulfstream's landing gear meeting the runway. He had hoped to be there for her, for the kids, but he was *here*, instead. His last message to her, urging her to move out anyway—to take up the offer of his place for Christmas—going unanswered, as before. She wasn't going to leave Luke now, during the holidays. Or after them.

He had to accept that, somehow. Accept it and move on with his mission. He was here, after all—had a job to do.

The Gulfstream decelerated as it rolled down the runway, taxiing toward one of the military hangars, and Russ could see several AFP vehicles parked nearby, as if awaiting the arrival of him and his fellow special agents. A tall figure—far too tall to be a local—reclining in the front seat of the foremost jeep.

He was waiting for Russ when he came down the steps of the business jet, dwarfing the Filipino officer at his side.

"Lieutenant Gregorio Mijares, Special Action Force," the police commando said unsmilingly, stepping forward to shake Russ' hand. "Welcome to Mindanao."

So that's how it was going to be. *No different than Manila.*

"Jack Wilson, CIA," the tall man added, offering a firm handshake—a grim, tight-lipped smile. There was something familiar about the man, Russ realized, looking up into those obsidian-black eyes. . .as though he had seen him somewhere before. Perhaps he had—he'd worked with the Agency a handful of times during his tasking with the JTTF.

"You'll come back with us to Camp Navarro, Agent

Cole," the Filipino lieutenant announced, gesturing to the waiting vehicles. "We have accommodations set up for you and your fellow agents."

"I understood we were to accompany you tonight," Russ replied, looking the man in the eye. "To Jolo."

"That remains to be determined by my superiors and yours, Agent Cole—if you do, it will be along with the other support personnel on the transport. Come, let's go."

It was as he was turning away that it struck him—the sudden realization taking him by surprise.

"I *know* you," he said, the surprise still written on his face as he turned back toward the tall man. "You were in Vegas, last Christmas—during the attacks."

If he had taken him off-guard, there was no sign of it in the man's impassive countenance. Just a slow shake of the head. "No, sir, I wasn't. I'm afraid you've taken me for someone else."

9:34 A.M.
Malacañang Palace
San Miguel, Manila
Philippines

In the days of the Spanish, when the Malacañang had served as a temporary summer residence for the Governors-General, the Rizal Room had been a bedroom, but it had been transformed into a study in 1935, when the complex had become the official residence of the President of the Philippines upon the establishment of the Commonwealth.

The desk was still the same one which had been installed by President Manuel Luis Quezon y Molina, the second president of the Philippines, on his arrival in the office, President Luis Maskariño thought, tracing a hand idly over the ornately carved wood of the desk's surface as he pressed the phone against his ear, a deeply skeptical look spreading over his saturnine countenance as he listened.

A short, stocky man in his late sixties, Maskariño had first risen to political prominence in Davao during the People Power Revolution of 1986, which had driven the Marcos regime from power and brought democracy back to the Philippines.

He'd weathered the storms of those years—weathered them and won, becoming the mayor of one of the Philippine's most violent cities, a city he had transformed with an iron fist into one of the safest in the world. Or so he had convinced the media, at least. Perception, he had found, was everything in life—particularly in politics.

It was said that he had killed criminals with his own hand during his days in Davao, a rumor he deliberately chose—in a fashion that would have done credit to his counterparts across the Pacific—to neither confirm nor deny.

Through it all, he had *survived*, while the much younger man on the other end of the secure line had done. . .what? Cast a few votes in the American Senate?

"This is not your country, President Norton," Maskariño observed acidly, his face twisting into a grimace as he turned away from the window—the light of the Commonwealth-era chandelier playing strangely across his visage. "And my people are no longer your little brown brothers. You would do well to remember that."

The other end of the line fell suddenly silent, and the Filipino president smiled to himself. He still remembered the stories from his own youth—the stories of his Moro grandmother, who had been alive when the Americans had come to the island for the first time, bearing with them fire and sword, destroying the power of the local *datus* in their lust for conquest.

All because of some scrap of paper which had been signed some six thousand miles away—in a place his people had never heard of. The Americans were so used to seeing themselves as liberators, that the sound of someone daring to speak the truth shocked them into silence.

"Tonight's raid," Maskariño went on before the American president could recover, "will proceed as planned by my military commanders. If you wish to avert it, President Norton. . .I suggest you empty your secret prisons and come to terms with this terrorist. Before I kill him."

Chapter 15

"Can we even secure their release in the time we have remaining, if I were to make that decision?" President Norton asked, looking up from his notes to glance around at his advisers.

"Mr. President," Nathan Gisriel began, from his position a few seats down the Laurel Lodge conference table from the president, "Imamović and al-Andalusí both have *American* blood on their hands—that we know of—and al-Zubaydi is likely in the same boat. I would not advise this course of ac—"

"I was not asking for your advice, general," Norton spat, cutting him off with an angry look, "I was asking if it was *possible*. I don't want to release these animals any more than you do. But I do want the Braleys brought back home—safely."

It was clear from the look in his eyes that Gisriel wasn't happy with that response, but he would simply have to get over it, Norton told himself, taking a deep breath as he

214

struggled to restrain the anger he still felt after his call with the Filipino president.

A contentious conversation which had accomplished precisely nothing—as his advisors had warned, he remembered unwillingly.

"I have been made to understand, Mr. President," the acting Director of National Intelligence, Bob LeClair, began, glancing up over the rims of his reading glasses, "that the CIA has already reached out to the Jordanians, to begin laying the groundwork for those negotiations. Naturally they will only proceed on your order."

Naturally. Like they had in throwing them in there in the first place. Norton shook his head. He'd wanted to believe that LeClair would have made a good choice to take over the ODNI permanently—the man was a former Green Beret and had come to the post from his position heading up the National Counterterrorism Center. But his last few months in the post had confirmed that whatever good qualities LeClair might have possessed in his military service, he'd gone native in the intelligence community.

"Speaking of the Agency," Norton continued, glancing at a hand-scrawled note he had made on his pad while talking with Maskariño, "President Maskariño mentioned something about the CIA while I was on the phone with him. . .some Agency operation in Davao back in 2002? He provided no details, but it was clear that it was something which angered him greatly."

"Michael Meiring," the voice of the Secretary of State replied from the speakers, Sorenson's image visible on the television screen mounted at the far end of the table. "A treasure hunter who was injured in an explosion in Davao in that year—he had apparently made some claim of Agency ties, and the resulting incident, which took place while Maskariño was mayor, has fueled a great deal of his animosity against the US."

Clearly. "But this Meiring. . .he wasn't actually CIA?"

"No, sir."

Or so you would have me believe, Norton thought, holding Sorenson's gaze for a long moment.

"This would all, I believe," LeClair interjected, as if to break the awkward silence, "have been in your background brief on Maskariño, Mr. President."

There was an implicit rebuke there, in the acting DNI's comment, but the President chose to ignore it, bristling even as he refocused on his notes. Maskariño's words—as pompous and insufferable as the Filipino president had been on the phone—had held the ring of truth. *The CIA never went anywhere without causing trouble. . .*

1:03 P.M. Philippine Standard Time, December 22nd
Camp General Basilio Navarro, Western Mindanao
Command (WESTMINCOM)
Calarian District, Zamboanga City
Zamboanga del Sur, Mindanao

"Pan the camera left fifteen degrees," Richards heard Mijares instruct the fatigues-clad AFP drone operator, the soldier's hand moving up to manipulate the joystick controlling the UAV's camera. "And zoom in further, if you can."

There were armed guards visible at this compound at least, long-haired young Moros dressed in an eclectic mix of sports jerseys, jeans, and camouflage. The previous one—the primary location, according to the NICA's intel—had been a total dry hole, with no sign of life visible at all.

Even so. . .the presence of armed men signified exactly nothing, as their Filipino counterparts knew full well. They needed more. A *lot* more.

And overhead reconnaissance had its limitations—a grim reality they always had to face. He'd been there for the launch, a few hours prior, as an AFP chaplain sprinkled holy water over the pair of small ScanEagle UAVs in the moments before they rocketed from their catapults.

He had added a prayer or two of his own as the diminutive drones disappeared into the clouds above. That they might find their targets. That the Braleys would be brought home in safety.

"What are we seeing from the other drone?" Richards asked, glancing over at the opposite bank of screens. Both UAVs were orbiting their targets from nearly nine thousand feet in the air, far too high up to be heard from the ground— the skies over Jolo, blessedly, far more clear than those over Zamboanga City.

"Much the same," the SAF lieutenant responded. "Jolo is full of Abu Sayyaf—they have strongholds all over the island. But al-Tunisi. . .he has not been accepted by all of the local commanders, who view him as an outsider. His influence is limited to the area immediately around Maimbung."

He has to be here. The unspoken subtext of Mijares' words. *Somewhere.*

It was never quite that simple, Richards knew. The reality on the ground, never as straightforward as even the best intel made it seem. He moved across to the other monitors anyway, scanning their screens as if he could make something out that everyone else was missing.

The compound revealed there beneath the circling ScanEagle was smaller than its fellow, situated in the jungle with dense undergrowth and groves of massive palms scattered all around, surrounded by a head-high wall of concrete block with a single main gate on the eastern side toward the road, large enough to accommodate vehicles.

One primary building nestled in the northwestern quadrant, a squat, rectangular concrete-block structure rising two stories above the compound and surmounted by a faded red corrugated metal roof. Two guards were posted at its door, dressed in a mix of civilian clothes and military fatigues like the others, and the resolution of the streaming imagery was high enough to make out their weapons—a Kalashnikov of some kind, probably a Chinese knock-off, in the hands of the man on the right, and carried loosely in the crook of the other man's arm, an M1 Garand. A weapon which had probably come to the Philippines around the same time as his grandfather, the Texan reflected. And still as lethal as ever.

There was another pair of guards patrolling in the open space between the main building and a much smaller, perhaps even single-room, concrete-block building across from the main structure toward the south. A small, seemingly rickety equipment shed situated in the shadow of the wall beneath a towering palm in the southwestern quadrant rounded out the compound's structures—an old Nissan Navara parked between it and the gate, the pickup truck's frame visibly spattered with mud from the rutted dirt road which led into the compound.

"That guy's not a local," Granby observed suddenly, his voice at Richards' shoulder alerting him to his presence. He was pointing toward a guard leaning up against the side of the smaller building—a rifle slung casually over his shoulders as he smoked a cigarette. *Sure enough.*

The man was visibly taller than his counterparts, and his kit looked newer—more expensive. *One of Abu Nazih's foreign fighters?* Richards opened his mouth to speak, to call Mijares over, but it was in that moment that the door of the main building opened and a trio of figures emerged together into the sunlight.

Another pair of tall, well-equipped guards who, like their friend, were obviously not Moros. And stumbling along, shoved along between them—an equally tall man whose features were unmistakably Western. . .

1:07 P.M.
Maimbung
Jolo Island, Sulu Province
The Autonomous Region in Muslim Mindanao (ARMM)

Once he might have thought of escaping, as Jun had—even with the danger involved, the risks that all three of them might not get out. The fear of death, so very strong.

But the fever had broken him, Shawn Braley realized, stumbling as one of Abu Nazih's Libyans shoved him in the back, the man's rifle butt connecting just above the kidneys.

A harsh laugh escaping the Arab's throat as he cried out in pain, nearly going down.

He was no longer dreaming of getting away, of *surviving*—no matter what he might have tried to tell

Charity, or Faith, when she curled up in his lap at night, seeking shelter and comfort in his very presence. He dreamed only of an end to it all. . .all of the pain, submerged in oblivion.

"Your friends back in America—they have raised more than three million dollars for you and your family, Mr. Braley," Abu Nazih had said, a curiously satisfied expression on the jihadist's face as he sat there, resting his elbows on the surface of the small card table which served him for a desk. A satisfied expression which had twisted into a sneer as he regarded Shawn there on his knees before him. *"Manong Soleiman had demanded twelve for your release."*

That was the first he had heard of any of it. He'd had no idea that there were other negotiations underway, that a ransom had been placed on their heads. *And people were responding. They* cared.

Abu Nazih's next words had dashed any hopes he might have begun to nourish. *"But you Americans must learn a lesson. . .not everything can be had for a price."*

He staggered forward, still gasping in pain from the blow to his kidneys, toward the door of the small concrete-block building which had served as their prison—only for one of the Libyans to stick forward a foot.

The ground came rushing up to meet him, the impact of his body hitting the dirt greeted by guffaws of laughter—the pair of foreign fighters sauntering away casually toward the gate. *Just leaving him there.*

Shawn rolled over on his back, groaning with pain—lacking the will to rise as he stared up into the clear blue sky above, as if somehow expecting to find deliverance there.

But there was nothing there, out beyond the fronds of

the palms, only a few white wisps of cirrus, blown rapidly across the lower stratosphere. Paradise.

Hell.

He heard a small, tear-filled voice calling out for *"Daddy,"* and felt Faith's small hands against his chest, pulling helplessly at his shirt. Her voice plaintive and fearful.

"I'm okay, sweetheart," he lied, unable to prevent a groan escaping his lips as he rolled onto his side—struggling to pull himself up. And then Khadafi was there, at his side, the older Moro's arm under Shawn's armpit, helping him to rise.

He had known that Khadafi had stayed behind when Manong Soleiman and most of his other fighters had departed at daybreak, taking Annalyn with them, but. . .*even so.*

"Thank you," he managed, putting a hand out against the concrete block for support, hardly able to find the words as the grey-haired militant stooped down beside his crying daughter, speaking to her in a soothing voice as he produced a piece of hard candy from somewhere within the recesses of his ruck—shucking it of its dirty wrapper as he extended it toward the little girl.

Khadafi looked up then, as she took it, his eyes meeting Shawn's. "Of course."

4:12 A.M. Eastern Standard Time
CIA Headquarters
Langley, Virginia

"So we have positive ID on at least two of the three American hostages?" Olivia Voss asked, rubbing her eyes wearily as she rested an elbow against the conference table. She had slept in her office—such sleep as it was, no more than a couple hours.

"That is correct, ma'am," Richards said from the other side of the world, his voice coming through the speakers of the conference phone in the center of the table. "We were able to clearly ID both Shawn and Faith Braley as present at the target compound.

"But not the wife?" Voss asked, glancing around the table at her subordinates. Two out of three wasn't bad, as the saying went, but if the raid failed to get *everyone*. . .

This wasn't one of those things you could hope to do twice.

"Not yet." She saw Lasker grimace, and glanced up at the clocks on the far wall, one of which was set to Philippine Standard Time. The sun would be going down soon, severely limiting the UAVs' potential for target identification. And the Filipinos were moving.

"What's your assessment, Jack? What's your gut telling you?"

There was a long pause before Richards answered, seeming to weigh his words carefully. "I think it's likely that they're keeping all three together, particularly with the presence of the Braleys' daughter at the site."

Likely. That was about as good as it got in this business. "And the other Filipinos?"

"I don't know." Richards' tone of voice told her he hadn't spent a lot of time considering it. As cold as it sounded, the Filipino hostages were Manila's concern, not theirs. "Local civilians have shown up on the ScanEagle's feed of the compound, but as far as I know, none of them have been positively ID'ed as the hostages."

"Understood."

4:42 P.M. Philippine Standard Time
A Cessna 182 Skylane
Over the Moro Gulf

The sun was already setting over the waters as the small private plane slipped between the clouds, the pilot holding a steady course south-southwest, two hundred and six degrees.

Brent Kruta glimpsed the island of Basilan far off to the north, a dark mass of land barely visible among the red-and-purple-tinged clouds as night fell.

He leaned back in his seat, glancing over at Mohd as the security chief sat there, playing some game on his phone. The man was his escort for. . .whatever this was, but when the boss had finally gotten back to him, it had been with orders to see it through.

Which was how he found himself on this small charter, with a flight plan filed for Jolo Airport.

"Just how do you propose to reach an agreement with Abu Nazih?" he'd asked Palalisan at their last meeting before departure. *"Even Manong Soleiman wanted more than three mil."*

The Braley family's GoFundMe was nowhere even close to its goal, but Palalisan had been insistent. *"There is a way—leave it all to me. The time has come for all of this to end."*

"How do I know I can trust you?"

"You can't, of course," the older man had replied, a shadow passing across his broad face, *"but I have no desire to end this life I enjoy. And I know very well that it* would *end if I were to betray our agreement."*

He wasn't wrong there, Kruta mused, turning his attention back to the window. If anything went wrong,

Palalisan's life was coming apart. It was the same argument he had made to the boss, some days earlier.

Now, as he found himself flying toward Jolo, he hoped it had been a good one.

11:03 A.M. Arabia Standard Time
Al-Jafr Prison
Ma'an Governate, Kingdom of Jordan

From somewhere down the corridor, a man's scream reverberated along the polished tile lining the walls—a strange, torturous sound, barely even identifiable as human.

Mirsad Imamović shuffled forward, ignoring the pathetic sobs which followed the scream, arm-in-arm with his balaclava-masked guards in Jordanian Armed Forces uniforms, each of his steps small, furtive, hobbled by the heavy manacles securing his ankles.

His hair, long and matted after months in captivity, fell forward into his eyes as he walked and he shook his head contemptuously, struggling to clear his vision.

Al-Jafr had been closed more than a decade before, or so the world had been told. The world still believed the infamous prison permanently closed, part of the Hashemite kingdom's long-running program of penal reforms.

But everything had changed after the Arab Spring, as those few Middle Eastern rulers lucky enough not to be dragged through their streets clung desperately to power, and began looking for dark holes into which to throw their problems.

Al-Jafr had been one of those holes. And the world, trembling before the rage of a region committed as never before to the struggle of Allah, had asked few questions.

Imamović's lips curled into a sneer. The hole had been dark, the beatings—like that inflicted on that poor nameless devil down the corridor—severe, but Al-Jafr had not broken his will to resist, any more than the savage murder of his older brother by Croat militias had unmanned him, all those years ago in the former Yugoslavia.

He had found his faith in those dark years, and it remained his strength and his support now, here, in this hole.

They turned off the main corridor and down another to the side, equally dark and poorly-lit, one of his guards releasing his arm and proceeding ahead to open the door before them.

The other soldier shoved him brusquely forward into the side room, nearly forcing him off-balance.

When he recovered himself, he looked up to see a black man in a business suit—an American by the look of him— standing on the other side of a small table, casually smoking a cigarette.

Imamović recoiled at the smell of the smoke, feeling the gnawings tug at him. He'd smoked for years, all through the war with the Croats, and no matter how many times he shook the addiction, how long he went without, he was never truly. . .*free*.

He could feel the rage surge within him, as much at himself as the American's casual insolence.

"Hello there, dead man," he snarled, the words coming out in rough, unpracticed English. None of his other guards dared uncover their faces around him—recognizing the threat he remained, even *here*.

"Well that's not very nice, Mirsad," the man replied, taking a long draw on his cigarette and exhaling smoke across the table into Imamović's face as the guards forced him into a folding metal chair across from the American. "And here I was, come to take you home. The name's Stone, Central Intelligence Agency. Home. Or somewhere." A smile, white teeth glistening in an expression which struck Imamović as nearly feral. "I forgot. . .you don't have a home anymore, do you? Care for a smoke?"

6:27 P.M. Philippine Standard Time
Camp General Basilio Navarro, Western Mindanao
Command (WESTMINCOM)
Calarian District, Zamboanga City
Zamboanga del Sur, Mindanao

". . .the first two helicopters will land here, and the third. . .*here*," Gringo Mijares announced, indicating the circles on the map which marked a pair of small clearings in the dense jungle growth that carpeted the hillsides west of Maimbung—perhaps half-a-kilometer apart, and three klicks from the target compound. "From there, we'll push in to envelop the compound on all sides, securing a perimeter here."

It was a reasonably solid plan, so far as it went. Richards looked across at Granby and saw him nod, taking it all in. There was always the risk that someone was going to hear the helicopters coming in and place a cellphone call to Abu Nazih, but there wasn't much of a way to get around that. This wasn't Afghanistan—they didn't have a lot of room to work with.

"The hostages—at least those we have identified," the SAF lieutenant continued, "are being held in this structure here, on the southern side of the compound. The guards seem to be loosely posted around the compound, and we've seen no evidence of any of Abu Nazih's people actually in the building with the hostages."

"What's their strength?" one of Mijares' NCOs piped up, glancing up from the map.

"Fifteen to twenty men, at our best count. Possibly more." That was at least half-a-dozen more than had been present when they'd first ID'd the Braleys, Richards reflected grimly—about an hour before sunset, a Toyota pick-up had driven up to and through the gates of the compound, armed men spilling out of the bed, locals every one. Reinforcements, apparently.

The last thing they needed.

"Colonel Segovia has been apprised of our operation," Mijares continued, clasping his hands behind his back as he looked around at his men, "and instructed not to take his people near the compound without prior authorization."

"Are you sure that's wise?" Richards asked, taking a step closer to the map table. Lieutenant Colonel Flaviano Segovia was the commander of the 32nd Infantry Battalion, the primary AFP unit charged with carrying out counter-insurgency operations on Jolo.

Clearing an op by the principal commander in the AO was nothing if not SOP, but given the Philippine Army's legendary reputation for corruption. . .they ran risks by expanding the circle of knowledge too far. But it was best not to take that tack with Mijares, not *here*, in front of his men.

"If Abu Nazih's network is monitoring the AFP—and you can be certain they are," Richards added, "they're like to notice what *isn't* there as well as what is."

"And if one of Segovia's patrols stumbles across the compound in the next five hours, they'll do more than notice," the SAF lieutenant pushed back. "It's the only way, Jack."

"It seems necessary," William Russell Cole spoke up from across the table, "to point out that we do not yet have confirmation on Charity Braley's presence at the compound. Nor positive ID on any of the remaining Filipino hostages. If we hit the compound, only to find out that they are being held at a secondary site. . ."

Mijares was stone-faced. "Agent Cole, you will allow us to worry about our citizens. As for Mrs. Braley. . .it seems likely that if her young daughter is there, then so is she."

The assessment he had given Voss, hours earlier. He hoped he'd been right.

"And if you're wrong?" the FBI hostage negotiator pressed, concern written in his eyes. "If there's a raid, if we recover some of the hostages but not all, they *will* panic and execute the rest."

"The decision has been made on the best intelligence available to us, Agent Cole," Mijares replied, a tinge of irritation slipping through the mask. "And it has been made."

He turned toward Richards. "We're wheels-up at 0100. Be at the airbase."

7:03 P.M.
Maimbung
Jolo Island, Sulu Province
The Autonomous Region in Muslim Mindanao (ARMM)

Dusk had fallen across the jungle, the chill of the oncoming night slowly settling in over the compound.

The chill of death. Shawn Braley shivered, leaning forward in the small plastic chair—a grimace of pain distorting his face at the movement. He'd sat too long, his muscles cramping. The bruises across his lower back and kidneys already purpling from the beating.

Across the compound from where he sat, toward the main building, the fire blazed up as someone threw wood on it—their form silhouetted against the flames. There was a handful of men clustered around the fire for warmth, most of them with weapons slung across their shoulders—fighters, all of them. Another truckload had showed up an hour before, Khadafi walking out to meet them as they drove in through the gate. Men he knew, perhaps, though the geography made that seem unlikely.

"Will you go?" Emmanuel Asuncion asked quietly from the other chair a few feet away, the glow of the distant fire reflected in his dark eyes.

"What?" Shawn asked, startled by the sudden question. Charity had spent most of the day trying to console Dolores over her mother's departure, and the men had found themselves trying to spend as much time outside as they could without drawing abuse from their captors.

"If they get what they want—if your government releases the prisoners they're holding—will you go?"

"I don't. . ." Shawn's voice trailed off, struggling to sort through the emotions roiling within him. Scarce daring to hope, yet knowing the cruel reality of that hope. What—*who*—it would mean leaving behind. "They won't."

He glanced up into the fronds of the overhanging palm, black against the gathering twilight. Avoiding Emmanuel's gaze, aware that he hadn't answered the question. Not *truly.*

"But if they do? If they come through, and you can go free. . .what then?"

Shawn opened his mouth to reply—opened it and closed it again, unable to speak the words that were on his lips, to repeat the assurance he had given so readily back there on the boat. Knowing now it had been a lie. *I'm not going to just leave you.*

Another moment, and he was spared the necessity of responding as Khadafi emerged from the semi-darkness off toward the main building, bearing little Faith in his arms.

"Keep her close," the older Moro warned, handing her off to Shawn as he rose—every muscle of his body protesting against the sudden movement.

He nodded, patting her back as she wrapped her arms sleepily around his neck. *How she had wandered off to begin with. . .*

"Keep her close," Khadafi repeated, a curious edge to the man's voice as he adjusted the sling of his rifle around his shoulders—looking Shawn straight in the eye. "And whatever happens tonight, whatever you might hear. . .stay inside."

And then he was gone.

Chapter 16

12:36 A.M., December 23rd
Edwin Andrews Air Base
Zamboanga City
Zamboanga del Sur, Mindanao

The Philippine Air Force Airbus C-295's twin Pratt & Whitney turboprops were already spooling up, their throaty roar filling the air as Jack Richards dismounted from the AFP jeep, waving off their military driver.

The area around the military transport was filled with activity—pallets of equipment being unloaded and carried up the ramp into the belly of the aircraft. Zamboanga International itself was now closed down to all non-military traffic, the trio of UH-1H Iroquois helicopters which would ferry them to the target warming up not far from the Airbus on the runway which Edwin Andrews shared with the airport—the distinct sound of the Hueys' two-bladed rotors chopping the air adding to the cacophony of sound enveloping them.

Richards slung his ruck across his back, gesturing for Granby and Carson to follow as he led the way toward the

Airbus, spying Mijares standing near the foot of the ramp.

"Nearly thought you weren't going to make it," the SAF lieutenant announced, reaching out to shake Richards' hand. A smile on his face as he looked up into the Texan's face, but it never made it all the way to his eyes, and there was something in his voice that told Richards he wouldn't have been upset if they hadn't.

"Traffic," Richards replied ironically, glancing past Mijares into the plane. Truth of it was that he'd spent the better part of an hour on the horn back to Langley and Manila, alternately, as the powers that be attempted to sort out what their will *was*—never mind how he was supposed to implement it.

It was clear that, no matter the competence of the SAF, Washington wasn't comfortable with the Filipinos taking point on the tactical end of this operation. It was also clear that, with the bit between their teeth and a hard location for at least some of the hostages, there wasn't going to be much way to stop them.

He glimpsed William Russell Cole standing there not far from the Airbus and started to move toward him, his fellow officers falling in easy step behind, but Mijares raised a hand to stop them. "I'm going to have to ask you, as I asked your FBI, to leave behind or turn over your comms equipment for the duration of this op. We have to ensure operational security—make sure this is a unified effort."

Richards heard Granby curse behind him—stopped short, looking down into his counterpart's eyes. "That's not happening. Not without authorization from the top."

"You have twenty minutes."

12:43 A.M.
Jolo
Jolo Island, Sulu Province
The Autonomous Region in Muslim Mindanao (ARMM)

In the dimly-lit street below, a man on a bicycle veered around a lumbering truck, prompting a sonorous bellow from the truck's horn as the offender pedaled hard away, barely dodging a jeepney puttering along in the opposite direction.

There was gunfire then, a long, extended burst, but it came from the television in the room behind him. Brent Kruta shook his head, letting the curtain fall back in place as he turned away from the window—traffic here was like traffic in Pakistan, where he'd spent an inordinate amount of his time with the Agency. There was no left or right, there was only *road*—to be taken up and dominated as aggressively as possible.

He shoved both hands into the pockets of his slacks, glancing back toward where Mohd lay stretched out on the hotel room's lone bed watching the television—the Moro's full-size Glock visible protruding from the inside-the-waistband holster within his jeans.

They'd been at the hotel for the last five hours, but neither man had slept and he suspected sleep was not in their cards, given how frequently the bodyguard looked away from the Steven Seagal film he was watching to check his phone.

He had expected a hassle at the airport over Mohd's weapon, or simply his own presence as a Westerner, but the AFP soldiers had simply waved them through. Presumably Jim Palalisan's doing, like all the rest.

Palalisan. It was hard to know exactly what game the former vice-governor was playing, far more certain that there *was* a game.

One way or the other, Kruta suspected that a fair bit of the three million-dollar ransom was destined for Palalisan's pockets. *Somehow.*

On-screen, a crazed Jamaican reversed a pistol-gripped Mossberg and charged Seagal, waving it like a club—a stupid tactic that met its deserved end a moment later as the actor sent his opponent careening over a store counter.

The former CIA operations officer allowed himself a small smile. He'd grown up on action movies himself, loved them as a teenager, but he'd found reality. . .very different. Reality, he had learned, involved a great deal of this—long nights without sleep, just waiting. And he was tired of waiting.

"So what's the plan?" he asked, stepping deliberately in front of the television. Annoyance flickered in Mohd's eyes, but he muted the film, swinging his legs off the bed.

"The plan, Mr. Kruta," he replied, tucking his shirt over the gun as he prowled over to his backpack, stooping down to rummage through its interior, "is to wait for a call. Those are my orders, along with keeping you safe."

He found what he was looking for a moment later, a small stainless steel hip flask visible in his hand as he stood back up. Hardly surprising—Palalisan hadn't struck him as the fundamentalist type, and neither were the men he surrounded himself with.

"Pretty sure I can do both," Mohd added, smiling at Kruta as he unscrewed the cap, "while watching a movie. And enjoying a drink."

He took a long pull, making a face at the strength of the liquor. "Join me?"

Kruta shook his head in the negative. "After this is over, I'll buy you one. Who are you expecting to call?"

"Manong Soleiman."

12:56 A.M.
Edwin Andrews Air Base
Zamboanga City
Zamboanga del Sur, Mindanao

"I need an answer, ma'am," Richards pressed, an index finger pressed into his right ear in a vain attempt to shut out the roar of the Airbus' turboprops as he glanced out from the shadow of the hangar, noting the last pallets of equipment being loaded aboard, SAF commandos already waving off the extraneous Air Force personnel. *Go time.* "Because someone has to make this call, and if it's mine to make, this mission is getting scrubbed."

He paused to take a breath, shaking his head in exasperation. Their Agency support team had already arrived from Camp Navarro to secure their comms equipment if they *didn't* take it with them—they certainly weren't turning it over to the Filipinos—but this was insanity. They didn't operate without secure comms, not in this world.

Not with the tightrope they were walking with their Filipino counterparts—and the President's desire to send in the SEALs. And the last thing they needed was another international incident which could be laid at the Agency's doorstep.

"I'm sorry but that's not an option," Olivia Voss replied

after a long moment's silence. "We need eyes on this operation, whatever goes down—the command authority has made that abundantly clear. And I need you to be those eyes."

The President. Richards shook his head. "Respectfully, ma'am, eyes aren't much good without a mouth."

"Improvise, Jack," Voss shot back, and he could hear from her voice that the deputy director's exasperation was rising to match his own. "Beg, borrow, steal. Send smoke signals, if you have to. Just find a way."

12:32 P.M. Eastern Standard Time, December 22nd
Joint Base Andrews-Naval Air Facility Washington
Prince George's County, Maryland

The December sky above was bleak and gray, bearing the promise of snow, as the Sikorsky VH-3D Sea King currently designated by the call sign "Marine One" set down, its tires meeting the tarmac with a clearly perceptible *bump*.

President Norton barely noticed, staring out the window as the helicopter taxiied forward to within a hundred meters of the looming blue-and-white fuselage of the Boeing VC-25 bearing the presidential seal on its nose, the other two helicopters settling down around them—another Sea King and a smaller VH-60N White Hawk.

The concept was that any actor with mal intent along the flight path wouldn't be able to determine which helicopter actually carried the President of the United States—confusion which would doubtless prove small comfort to the crew of whatever helicopter *did* end up being the target.

"Have we heard anything from Mindanao?" he asked

distractedly, glancing back over his shoulder at his chief of staff, sitting in the seat across from him. They were leaving for Vegas within the hour, ahead of the memorial events on the 24th.

Dennis Froelich shook his head. "Not since we left Camp David, Mr. President. The Filipinos should be en route to the target, but they haven't granted us real-time access to their feeds, so we're flying blind until we hear from them."

Afterward, the President thought bitterly. After it was all over, his fate sealed. Along with that of the Braleys. . .

1:36 A.M. Philippine Standard Time, December 23rd
Maimbung
Jolo Island, Sulu Province
The Autonomous Region in Muslim Mindanao (ARMM)

The compound was still—the soft murmur of voices from the guards posted up at the gate barely audible, blending in with the song of crickets from the surrounding jungle. Somewhere off among the trees, a hornbill cried out, its familiar insistent *ta-rik-tik* repeating itself over and again.

Shawn Braley shifted restlessly on his blanket, listening to Emmanuel's steady, regular breathing on the blanket to his right—unable to get to sleep. It was the pain, he had told himself, the fresh bruises making it even harder for his battered body to relax.

Pain. But more than that, it was unease. . .at his inability to answer Emmanuel, his unwillingness to face the possibility that he might be asked to leave them behind. Ignoring it, in the hopes that it would just go away. That he wouldn't be subjected to that trial. *Knowing he would fail.*

And then there had been Khadafi, and his cryptic warning. *Whatever happens tonight. . .*

The missionary rolled over onto his left side, biting his tongue to keep from crying out. He'd never been able to sleep flat on his back, even if any other position hurt.

He could just make out the curve of his wife's body in the darkness of the concrete-block structure, her back turned to him as she lay there, her arm wrapped around their sleeping daughter. Dolores, lying another foot or so away on her left, all of them in a row.

The guards' voices were no longer audible, Shawn realized vaguely, some distant part of his brain recognizing that the compound had grown quieter still. The hornbill itself, falling silent.

And that was when he heard the first shot.

1:43 A.M.
A UH-1H "Huey"
The Sulu Sea

Below their landing skids, the waves licked black in the moonless night, seeming to reach out toward the low-flying helicopters, as if to draw them into their dark embrace. A void, waiting to swallow them up.

Jack Richards bent forward, resting his elbows on his knees as he glanced around at the paint-blackened features of the SAF commandos surrounding him, his own face now as black as his eyes. The faces were hard and intent beneath the paint, the eyes of men who had seen battle before. These weren't raw conscripts, but professional soldiers.

Whatever doubts he might have harbored about the

wisdom of conducting the raid based on their limited intel, he didn't share Washington's concerns about the men carrying it out.

Richards straightened, easing his Elitool-manufactured CAR-15 back against his chest on its two-point sling, nodding across to where Granby and Carson sat facing him on the opposite bench. Only Granby acknowledged the nod, and only just—both men undoubtedly absorbed in their own thoughts. *Fears.*

He still felt it, after all these years, that dark frisson of excitement bordering on the edge of terror, a man's constant companion as he rode into battle.

There should have been Wagner playing somewhere, he thought, glancing out the open door to glimpse one of the other Hueys flying in formation not thirty meters off their port side. That memory, of Robert Duvall's helicopters descending on a Vietnamese fishing village, still one of his strongest associations with the Huey, ever since he had first watched *Apocalypse Now* at the age of eleven. That, and Iran.

He felt a hand on his forearm, looked up to see Gringo Mijares reaching across—the Filipino lieutenant's voice lost in the pounding roar of the rotors filling the cabin, pulling back his hand to raise them both, closing and opening the fingers of both hands once. Ten minutes to feet-dry.

After that, they'd be at their designated LZs in no time.

Richards settled back against the seat, his knuckles white against the pistol grip of the CAR. *Time to dance.*

1:45 A.M.
Maimbung
Jolo Island, Sulu Province
The Autonomous Region in Muslim Mindanao (ARMM)

Rescue. That had been his first thought, when he'd heard the shots—a scattering of small-arms fire breaking out around the compound, to the accompaniment of shouts of alarm. The anguished screams of their captors, dying around them.

Shawn Braley stumbled forward, his face lit by the flames leaping from the main building, Khadafi's hand on his arm as the older Moro hurried him along—Faith clutched tight against the man's broad chest, his Type 56 slung over his shoulder.

He felt something soft give beneath his bare feet—his sandals abandoned in the concrete house in the rush when Khadafi and the others had come for them—looked down to realize he had stepped onto the stomach of one of the Libyans, lying dead there in the short grass and mud of the compound. The man's face was blank and staring, his throat a bloody mess—slashed through with a knife. He had never seen it coming.

Whatever happens tonight. . .

There was another burst of fire off in the night, and Shawn ducked his head reflexively, but it was simply one of the Moros, standing near the equipment shed, emptying his rifle into a corpse as if to assure himself of its death, a savage cheer escaping his lips.

And then he saw him, standing there backlit by the flames—the dark, mane-like hair streaming wild over his shoulders. A long kampilan in his outstretched hand, its naked blade smoking with blood. *Manong Soleiman.*

Nightmare. His brain struggled to process any of it, and there was no time, in any case. The Toyota pickup which had arrived at the compound the previous afternoon was pulled up just within the gate, and Khadafi pushed him roughly toward it, handing off Faith as he turned back to hurry the others forward.

She whimpered and buried her face in her father's chest, attempting to shut out the horror. The memories, no doubt, of that morning in Quezon—where all this had begun.

Khadafi was back in a moment, gesturing for Shawn to climb into the open bed of the Toyota—bellowing toward one of the Kalashnikov-carrying militants sitting over the wheelwell to help him up when he hesitated. *"Tabang! Dali, dali!"*

Give him a hand. Quickly!

1:54 A.M.
The UH-1H "Huey"
Patikul
Jolo Island, Sulu Province
The Autonomous Region in Muslim Mindanao (ARMM)

Palms swayed and danced beneath the helicopters, buffeted by rotor wash as the transports swept in over the jungle, maintaining their formation just over the treetops.

Just over the treetops, Richards observed, noting with a distinct sense of unease that it felt as though he could reach out and brush the fronds with his hand. It was hardly his first time flying nap-of-the-earth, but all those had been with American pilots, and there was something to be said for your own people, no matter how much respect you might have for foreign counterparts.

He hoped the chopper pilots were up to the training standards of the SAF. *Hoped.*

Wouldn't be long now, he mused, glancing off to the north to make out the dormant volcanic crest of Bud Dajo, looming black against the darkness of the night. Another two or three minutes to the LZ, then another twenty to thirty minutes to regroup and cover the last few kilometers to the target on foot.

With luck, they should hit the compound just before 0230 hours—well-nigh the deadest time of the night. If Abu Nazih had sentries posted, and it was best to assume that he would, they'd be fighting sleep.

They would—something, some movement, caught Richards' attention in that moment and he looked over to see Mijares bent over, pressing a hand to his ear as he apparently struggled to listen over his headset, the roar of the Huey's Lycoming turboshaft filling the cabin. Drowning out all else.

He saw the lieutenant shake his head, disbelief and fury written in the lines of Mijares' blackened face in the moments before he removed his headset, throwing it angrily to the floor of the cabin.

Then he felt the helicopter lift, coming up hard off the treetops as it banked away toward the north—toward the dormant volcano. And Jolo beyond.

"What's going on?" Richards demanded, knowing it was futile—the words barely even reaching his own ears, swept away in the tide of noise.

But he met Mijares' eyes, saw him mouth a silent reply—

the night seeming to grow palpably colder at the lieutenant's words.

Return to base.

Chapter 17

"What in *God's* name happened out there?" President Norton demanded, pacing back and forth restlessly in front of the penthouse suite's windows, casting an angry glance back toward the secure conference phone in the center of a glass table positioned a few feet back of the plush sofa in front of the fireplace.

"We're as yet not certain, Mr. President," was Bernard Kranemeyer's entirely unsatisfactory reply from the other side of the continent. "We are still liaising with our Filipino partners in the NICA, trying to assemble a coherent picture of the reality on the ground. I spoke with Director Policarpio myself, only a half hour ago."

The President bit back a curse of frustration and anger, glancing about the suite—unable to escape noticing how his team looked away, avoiding his eyes.

This week had been *meant* to be about remembrance—about commemorating those lost in the Christmas Eve

244

attacks a year before, and vowing resolve for the path ahead.

Having a test of that very resolve filling up the headlines instead was. . .both ironic and terribly inconvenient, particularly given that he had no idea what to do. Even more so *now*.

"Tell me what you *do* have," Norton ordered, pulling out a chair from the table and collapsing into it, his back to his advisors. The jet lag was telling on him, he knew that, and this promised to be a sleepless night.

A sleepless night as he prepared for one of the biggest and most important speeches he'd ever had to deliver, now less than a day and a half away.

"About eight hours ago," the Director of the Clandestine Service replied, "around 0200 local time, the SAF raid on the target compound was aborted when overhead reconnaissance revealed that some kind of. . .attack was already underway, with the muzzle flashes of automatic weapons clearly visible, and the main building—not the one, Mr. President, where the Braleys were believed to be held—set on fire."

"And they *aborted*?" the President demanded incredulously, staring at the conference phone. "With the hostages clearly in danger?"

"It was chaos, sir," Kranemeyer replied, that imperturbable calm never leaving his voice. "Injecting another thirty armed men into an ongoing firefight with no clear intel was only going to get people killed. Possibly including the Braleys. In the SAF's shoes, I would have made the same call."

Typical, Norton thought, unable to suppress a weary grimace. The CIA's bureaucratic culture was nothing if not risk-averse.

"And where are we at *now*, director?"

"Backed by a detachment from the Philippine Army, the SAF swept the compound at daybreak, and recovered nearly a dozen bodies, most of them badly mutilated, including the beheaded corpse of Abu Nazih, whose head was recovered more than a kilometer down the road, in even worse shape than the body."

That got the President's attention, bringing him bolt upright in the chair. "Al-Tunisi? He was among the dead?"

"He was."

"Then that. . ." Norton paused, struggling to process his new reality, to *accept* it. "That means that any thought of the prisoner swap, the deal he had tried to negotiate with us, is. . .off the table."

"Likely yes, Mr. President," came the grave response from the other end of the line. "Tellingly, all the bodies recovered from the compound were Middle Eastern, according to the intel we're receiving from the Filipinos. Not a single local among them."

The director paused, as though that were self-explanatory, but Norton found it as opaque as everything that had gone before. "I don't. . .I'm afraid I don't understand. What are you saying?"

"I'm saying that from the available intel it would look as though Abu Nazih and his foreign fighters were wiped out, to a man. By their own allies. A night of the long knives. . ."

11:36 A.M. Japan Standard Time, December 23rd
USS Michigan
Luzon Strait, thirty miles south of the Batanes

"So they're in the wind." It was a statement, not a question, a look of weary resignation settling over Dom's face as he stood there in the officers' wardroom of the *Michigan*, glancing between his team lead and the *Michigan's* CO, Commander Derrick Piasecki—a thin, lantern-jawed figure in service khakis, standing there with hands poised on his hips.

"Seems like," Jason Guilbeau nodded. The transmission had been brief, and vague—stripped of nearly all detail. But it was enough to know that the Filipinos had failed. That the Braleys' location was once again. . .unknown.

A bad situation, somehow become even worse.

"It means we're still in the game, though," he observed grimly. "Still have a mission. What do you have for us, captain?"

Piasecki ran a hand across his chin, seeming to consider the question for a long moment. "We'll be off Luzon in a few hours—make our way down the west coast through the Mindoro Strait. . .if we keep running hot, we could arrive on-station by tomorrow evening. But I don't like it. We're running a risk going this loud, this hard. We aren't alone out here."

"Noted, sir." Piasecki's sonar officers had been tracking multiple contacts over the last twelve hours, including at least one suspected PLA(N) vessel. The CO's concerns about being shadowed by the Chinese couldn't have been more alien to the war Guilbeau had spent the last decade and a half fighting, but he supposed the man had a point. Not that it mattered. "We all have our orders. Just get us there."

10:54 A.M. Philippine Standard Time
Jolo Airport
Jolo Island, Sulu Province
The Autonomous Region in Muslim Mindanao (ARMM)

The airport was shut down completely to all incoming or outgoing air traffic, Colonel Segovia's grunts from the nearby Camp Bautista holding a tight perimeter around the terminal north toward the Gandasuli Road.

It was hardly the most subtle of approaches, Richards thought, casting a critical glance toward the big Airbus parked on the runway before turning his attention back to the screen of the laptop set up in the bed of the deuce-and-a-half military truck which was serving as the centerpiece of Mijares' temporary command post.

Then again. . .subtlety had gone right out the window around 0200 hours, along with their plan for rescuing the Braleys.

". . .were able to track the vehicles west from Maimbung for several kilometers," Maricar de Rosales was saying, her voice coming faint through the tinny laptop speakers, forcing Richards to lean in closer. "Then they split up, and we lost them."

"You lost them?" There was an edge in Mijares' voice, an edge of irritation exacerbated by exhaustion. "Even with them splitting up, you had to at least have been able to track *one* with the UAV."

"We were," de Rosales replied, the hesitation visible in

her face, even in the jerky video feed over the secure satellite uplink. "We lost it in the jungle northwest of Talipao."

Out toward Bud Dajo, Richards realized, conjuring up a mental map of the island from their planning sessions as he glanced out toward the jungle-covered crest just visible eight kilometers away to the southeast of Jolo proper, a lush green cinder cone rising two thousand feet above sea level.

The site of one of the most notorious battles of the counter-insurgency more than a century before, with nearly a thousand Moros, men, women, and children, massacred by American soldiers who had fought their way up the crest to rain down fire into the crater below. There had been only a handful of survivors—none, according to some accounts.

Could it be. . .?

He heard Mijares asking, "The trucks we saw at the compound were open. . .you weren't able to identify which one the Braleys were forced into?", heard the NICA officer's fainter *"no,"* but his attention was no longer on the ongoing briefing, but on the mountain, off in the distance.

They needed to recon that crater. Preferably without involving the Filipinos, he reflected, hoping the same thought hadn't occurred to Mijares or de Rosales.

He just had to find a way to make contact with Langley, and he was fairly certain that Voss' "smoke signals" weren't going to cut it.

Out of the corner of his eye, he saw Granby walk over from the perimeter, an unusually intent look on the paramilitary's face.

"I've been talking to Segovia's people," he announced, his voice low as he approached Richards. "Found a couple who were pulling security here at the airport yesterday. They say an American flew in last night on a private charter, along with a local heavy, presumably as bodyguard. The American matches Brent Kruta's description."

12:03 P.M.
Jolo
Jolo Island, Sulu Province
The Autonomous Region in Muslim Mindanao (ARMM)

"They *are* still alive, aren't they?" Brent Kruta demanded, pacing over to the window of the hotel room as he pressed the phone tight against his ear, struggling to clear the anger from his voice. Emotion wasn't going to help, not now, he told himself. He should have seen this coming—should have *realized*, somehow.

From the other end of the line, back in Mindanao, Jim Palalisan sounded incredulous. *Hurt*, almost. "But of course they are, Mr. Kruta. That was our deal."

"Our deal. . ." Kruta shook his head as he glanced back at Mohd, leaving the sentence unfinished. "So this was your plan, all along? *This?*"

"Our late friend was not a reasonable man." Nor had Abu Nazih been a Moro, which was more to the point, the former CIA officer grasped. He was an outsider, who had attempted to put the aims and goals of a faraway jihad over the more immediate concerns of these islands. And they'd killed him for it. But Palalisan wasn't done. "He could not be negotiated with. Our uncle can."

"Then where is he?" That was the sticking point now—the expected call from Manong Soleiman had never come, at least not to them, though it appeared that Palalisan had received some communication from the militant leader.

"Other interested parties flew into Jolo last night," the Moro politician acknowledged by way of reply. "And things are very hot right now."

No kidding. The increase in military activity on the small island was palpable, with the airport shut down and the Airbus C-295 with PAF markings parked in the middle of the runway, a trio of Hueys clustered around it like sleeping dragonflies.

Palalisan wasn't telling him anything he didn't already know.

"I can make that go away for him," he said after a moment's pause, choosing his words with care. Knowing the dangers here, all too well. Dangers the man on the other end of this phone could only mitigate, not eliminate entirely. "I have the money, ready to be drawn upon. . .we can make the trade. And once it is made, he will no longer be nearly so important to those parties."

That was only true in part, and he suspected Palalisan knew it as well as he did. Knew it, and likely didn't care, so long as he got his cut of the ransom.

"His representatives will meet you this afternoon, on the shores of Lake Seit. Can you make it there?"

A moment's reflection, and he nodded. *In for a penny. . .* "We can."

"Good."

It was in that moment that he heard vehicle doors slam down below, heard an authoritative voice barking out commands.

He traded glances with Mohd, seeing surprise and concern wash over the bodyguard's dark face.

"Got to go."

12:07 P.M.

Infantrymen were much the same the world over, Jack Richards thought, striding down the dimly-lit corridor of the hotel with a quartet of Colonel Segovia's soldiers at his back and Granby unobtrusively—to their escorts, at least— pulling rear security.

That bluntest of instruments, excellent for one's purpose. As long as that purpose didn't demand much in the way of subtlety. He should know—he had been one, and for all that the Marines were the world's finest light infantry, they had shared many of the foibles of all the rest.

Their chance of handling this quietly had gone out the window from the moment of arrival, when the Filipino grunts, their corporal at their head, had bailed out of their vehicles and immediately begun ordering bystanders about in tones that could have been heard half over town—leaving Richards to reluctantly uncurl his long legs from the back of the jeep and follow them in.

He raised his hand now, standing back and to the side of the hotel room door as he rapped hard on the thin partition.

Silence. No response from within, just the sound of someone—or *someones*—moving around.

"Take it down," he instructed casually, inclining his head toward the door. "And remember your orders."

No shooting.

Chapter 18

". . .as I told you back in Cotabato, Jack, I can't help you." Kruta shook his head, gesturing to where the Moro bodyguard sat on the floor, the long barrel of one of the soldiers' M-16s in his face, his cheek bleeding profusely from a wicked gash over the cheekbone. "And after the way you've handled things, coming in hard like this. . .no idea why I would."

"And yet here you are," Richards observed grimly, not a trace of a smile on his saturnine countenance. "A very long way from Cotabato."

"I'm just doing my job. Like you are."

"Like I am." He considered that for a long moment, glancing back toward the bodyguard—a man Kruta had identified only as "Mohd." Reading the defiance flashing in the Moro's dark eyes. The Philippines would have to be one of the last places on earth not to have implemented a national identification system. No way to verify or disprove. . .*anything.* "No, Brent, that was the case once, but it isn't now. You're not fighting for a flag anymore, and you're not here because they're your fellow citizens. You're here because you're getting paid."

There was anger written in the former intelligence officer's face, but Richards found he didn't care. Private mil/intel companies like Svalinn hovered around the intelligence community like vultures, poaching good men from a pool that was already desperately shallow. Leaving the rest to carry on. . .come what may. "This isn't a game anymore. People are getting butchered out there. Not people I really care about just now. . .but that could change at any moment."

"Then get out of my way, Jack, and let me do what I came here to do. Like I said back in Cotabato, the family's not in the mood for thrilling heroics. They just want their loved ones back, and, yes, that is what I'm getting *paid* for."

"So that's why when Abu Nazih cut you out of the process, you paid Manong Soleiman to wipe him out?" Richards asked shrewdly, watching his former colleague's eyes. "Is that it? That what happened out there, last night?"

"I had nothing to do with any of th—" Kruta began to respond, his mouth closing suddenly, like the steel trap he had just walked into. *Come on, Brent, you're losing your edge.*

Richards looked over to where Granby stood near the door, caught the paramilitary's barely perceptible nod.

"You have twelve hours, Brent. Think it over—come and see me at Camp Bautista. After that. . ." He inclined his head toward the soldiers. "The island's still under martial law, and the authorities won't need that strong of a reason to approve your detention."

A jeepney scuttled past, its horn blowing angrily to clear pedestrians out of the way as the CIA officers exited the hotel with their military escort, moving back out toward the AFP jeeps and the pair of soldiers left guarding them.

Half-way there, Richards put a hand on Granby's shoulder, his voice low and urgent. "You got the phone?"

A nod.

"Good man."

6:23 A.M. Arabia Standard Time
Muwaffaq Salti Air Base
Azraq, Zarqa Governorate
Jordan

"I trust you had no difficulties at the prison, Mr. Stone," the young *Mukhabarat* officer said smoothly, the thin dark mustache gracing his upper lip giving his swarthy face a sinister aspect in the early morning twilight. Clark Gable he was not.

Steven Walker shook his head, withdrawing a pack of Newports from an inner pocket of his suit jacket and placing a cigarette between his own lips before offering one to his Jordanian counterpart. The two of them, standing together beneath the wing of the aging Mitsubishi utility transport, watching the sun begin to stagger reluctantly over the horizon like a man waking up with a hangover.

The prison hadn't been a problem, it had been the more than two-hour drive to the air base which had been nerve-wracking, despite—or perhaps because of—his Jordanian Armed Forces escort, their small convoy racing northeast along dark, near-deserted highways with all the maschismo-fueled finesse he had come to associate with drivers in the Middle East.

And now here they waited. The black man lit up and handed his faded Bic over to the Jordanian—feeling the taste of the menthol pervade his mouth as he took a slow drag.

They were vulnerable here, he thought, glancing down the runway toward the perimeter of the airbase. *Exposed.* Less so than they had been on the open road, but even so. . .he wasn't going to be happy until they were in the air. The three prisoners now cooling their heels under guard in the aircraft—Mirsad Imamović and his buddies—had lots of friends in this part of the world.

By all rights, they should have cleared Jordanian airspace by sun-up, but here they sat. . .successive directives from Langley countermanding each other overnight until finally he had been ordered to hold up completely. By all rights, he never should have been here at all, the forty-five-year-old Atlanta native snorted, taking another drag.

Freeing terrorists. He'd spent eight years with the Central Intelligence Agency, on the tail-end of another twelve with the US Army, most of it in Special Forces. He'd hunted terrorists, killed his share. . .but freed them? Never. *Until now.*

Some things, a man shouldn't live long enough to see.

He'd much rather have pitched them through the open door of the Mitsubishi in-flight, answered once and for all whether terrorists could fly.

His sat phone began to pulsate just then and he took a

step away from the plane to answer it, listening intently—a smile spreading across his dark face even as he did so.

"Back they go, Abdallah," he grinned, turning back to his Jordanian counterpart as he ended the call. "Deal's off. Let's go share the good news with our friends."

1:05 P.M. Philippine Standard Time
Station Manila
The Embassy of the United States
Ermita, Manila
Philippines

"Washington is going to wake up in about five hours," Darren Lukasik observed ruefully, sneaking a glance at the rightmost clock on the far end of the conference room, set to Eastern Standard Time. "And when they do, they're going to want answers. Tell me we have something to give them."

"Not near enough," his deputy replied, reaching up to scratch his scalp through his thinning, prematurely gray hair. Still in his late thirties, Matt Campisi looked at least a decade older, and had the world-weary air to sell it. "Getting intel out of the NICA is like pulling teeth—the last they've given up is hours old. No workable leads, and no comms from our people or the Bureau."

"If their intel is reliable," Carla Souders interjected from the far side of the table. A soft-spoken mother of three who was on the far side of forty-five, Souders ran Station Manila's liaison with the NICA. Her skepticism was well-founded. "We'll be able to form a better judgment on that in another three or four hours, after the next sat overpass."

That was something. *Precious little.* Lukasik grimaced,

running a hand across his chin as he looked around at his team. Forcing their field personnel to go dark had cut them off at the knees, as the Filipinos knew well—and as much as he would have liked to be able to sit back and enjoy the FBI's discomfiture, he had more at stake here. *More to lose.*

"Jolo is a small island," he said after a moment's consideration. "And the AFP has a large presence. There can't be that many places for them to hide the Braleys."

"Basilan was also a small island," Campisi countered, a strained, weary expression on his usually dour face.

And they had gotten away there. The unspoken subtext of his deputy's words. The chief of station swore softly.

If they could pull off that stunt again. . .well, another hundred miles of open, trackless ocean west, and you ran into Indonesia. If the Braleys disappeared there, their captors taking shelter among Indonesia's numerous jihadist militant groups—the diplomatic situation would become exponentially more complicated.

As if it wasn't already.

"Reach out to Policarpio, if you will, Carla," Lukasik instructed, scrawling a note on the pad before him. "On my behalf. See if he's willing to meet, yet today."

Perhaps the NICA head would prove more cooperative in person.

"That may be difficult, Darren. . .the DG is a busy man on the best of days, and after last night, he may not want—"

Whatever Souders had been about to say was lost as the conference phone on the table in front of him buzzed with an incoming call.

"Sir," he heard his personal assistant say over speakerphone as he punched the button, "we just received a call from Jack Richards. Unsecure line."

"What did he say?"

"Two words—he wasn't on the call for more than fifteen seconds. *'Overflight: Pompeii.'*"

2:34 P.M.
Camp Bautista, Jolo
Jolo Island, Sulu Province
The Autonomous Region in Muslim Mindanao (ARMM)

"We will find them, Mr. Wilson," Lieutenant Colonel Flaviano Segovia promised, leaning back in his office chair—the collar of his BDUs damp with sweat from the tropical heat. A short, white-haired, almost neighborly, figure in his late fifties, Segovia's dark eyes radiated an intense seriousness from behind the thick lenses of his glasses. "Tomorrow morning, my men will sweep the island, west to east. We will turn over every rock. *Every* rock."

"Colonel—" Richards began, but Mijares cut him off, rising to his feet.

"Colonel, such action is more likely to endanger the hostages than effect their rescue. I must insist that you continue to keep your men on a short leash, and that you do not—I repeat, do *not*—interfere with SAF operations."

Segovia turned his attention toward the commando officer, staring at him for a long moment before replying. "The security of this part of Sulu is my responsibility, *lieutenant*. Not yours. I—"

"And this operation falls under the domain of the SAF," Mijares retorted, his hands on his hips as he glared across the desk at the lieutenant colonel. He extended a hand, gesturing toward the phone on Segovia's desk. "Call WESTMINCOM—ask to speak to Police Brigadier General Gonzaga. Tell him that you intend to jeopardize the safety of the remaining hostages by carrying out a military operation with your regular troops."

Turf wars, Richards thought, keeping his face studiously neutral as he sat there, looking on as the argument continued. He'd never known a bureaucracy—military or civilian—without them.

He hoped that Langley had understood his brief, cryptic message. That they would follow through on it, without getting tangled up in their own bureaucratic red tape. There hadn't been time for anything more, and he could only hope that the NICA's surveillance of cellular traffic in Sulu was. . .less than comprehensive.

"Mr. Wilson," he heard Segovia begin, refocusing his attention on the AFP lieutenant colonel at the sound of "his" name, "I understand my men escorted you on your visit to the hotel of the American—Mr. Kruta—earlier today. Was your mission successful?"

Richards shrugged. "Such as it was. He knew very little."

3:07 A.M. Eastern Standard Time
CIA Headquarters
Langley, Virginia

Kranemeyer would be arriving inside the hour, Olivia Voss thought, casting a brief glance toward the bottom right-hand corner of her computer screen before reaching for her nearly-empty coffee cup.

He'd gone home not five hours before, long enough to

get a shower—some sleep. On his return, she'd head out to get a few hours' of sleep herself, but for this moment, she had the watch.

This wasn't how she had anticipated spending her sons' Christmas vacation, but after all these years. . .perhaps the unexpected should have been second nature. Shane—her ex-husband—had picked Alex and Adrian up from her mother's two days prior, he and his parents stepping in to fulfill *her* promise of taking the boys to Disney World for the holidays. His job, far more flexible than hers, these days.

She drained the last of her coffee, making a face. It was a promise she should have known better than to make, but wait another year or two and Alex would be too old to truly enjoy it.

And Shane. ..well, Shane had his moments. Their marriage had fallen apart the better part of five years before, Adrian's birth the result of one of their last serious attempts to put things back together.

But her husband had already been on his way out of the Agency by that time—one of the last remaining things they'd had in common, a shared reality which had sustained them for the better part of a decade across the thousands of miles of separation which had taken them from Afghanistan to Latin America, to Germany and Iraq. Both of them driven—by ambition, by a fiercely idealistic sense of duty which had ultimately proved stronger to the mission than to each other.

The belief that their actions could change the world—leave it a better place, somehow. A belief that had ultimately led Shane out of the intelligence community and into the private sector, taking up a job with Acheron International, a prominent mil/intel company with headquarters out in Herndon. His stubborn insistence that she follow him, both of them working as a team once again, the final straw that had precipitated their divorce.

Perhaps it was just as well, she reflected, closing a window and opening the latest message from JSOC, giving the Agency the updated position of the *Michigan*. West of Luzon now, staying just outside the twelve-mile marker as it made its way down the coast at a speed which had to be giving CINCPACFLT an ulcer, never mind the *Michigan*'s CO.

She never would have been picked for deputy director with a spouse in the private intel sector—not even considering Acheron's cozy relationship with State. The conflict of interest there, far too obvious.

So here she was, enjoying the perks of life at the top. *Even more sleepless nights.*

Her intercom buzzed, the abrupt sound bringing her attention back to the present, her assistant's equally weary voice announcing, "Daniel Lasker to see you, ma'am."

"Send him in."

"We just heard from Lukasik," Danny Lasker announced a moment later, appearing in the door of her office. "They've initiated a request to NROC to focus on the volcanic cone of Bud Dajo on the next satellite overpass over Jolo. Apparently they received a call from Richards."

Smoke signals, Voss thought, unable to suppress the weary smile that crossed her face at Lasker's words. *Good work, Jack.*

4:11 P.M. Philippine Standard Time
Lake Seit
Jolo Island, Sulu Province
The Autonomous Region in Muslim Mindanao (ARMM)

Sweat trickled down Brent Kruta's face as he stood in the open door of the old second-generation Datsun Patrol, an arm propped against the doorframe—watching the children play near a cluster of corrugated metal buildings not thirty meters back along the road toward the sea, chasing a chicken around the yard with shouts of laughter and excitement. Off to the northeast, out over the Sulu Sea, clouds were gathering, foreshadowing rain. It might have seemed welcome, but he knew the tropics. Rain wasn't going to cut the heat. Not for a second.

Viewed from above, Lake Seit's dark waters stood out midnight blue against the lush green of the surrounding jungle—a vaguely heart-shaped crater lake less than half-a-kilometer inland from the sea, back over his right shoulder to the north.

"They're late," he announced sourly, glancing over to where Mohd leaned against the Datsun's hood.

The bodyguard acknowledged the observation with a nod, reaching up to adjust the sling of the M-16 cradled in the crook of his right arm, a spare 20-round mag sticking out of the back pocket of his jeans. He'd come back to the hotel earlier with both rifle and vehicle, answering no questions about where he'd obtained either.

And his phone was gone. That last, a large part of what was fueling Kruta's indigestion. The phone had disappeared in the wake of Richards' "visit," which meant it had either been purloined by an opportunistic AFP grunt—a possibility not at all remote—or else. . .*Richards.*

Which meant the CIA would know as much about his contacts with Palalisan as he did—likely more, given that it was *Mohd's* phone.

Movement caught his eye and he glanced up to see a pair of vehicles moving in from the north along the road, a mud-spattered Nissan pickup leading the way, several men visible in its bed. *Armed.*

"We've got company."

Mohd put the phone away, shifting the buttstock of the rifle against his shoulder as the truck and the dark blue Ford Everest following it rolled to a stop not twenty meters away, near the buildings. The children, vanishing like ghosts—the chicken now abandoned to run unmolested.

Kruta shoved the creaking door of the Datsun shut, taking a few steps away from the vehicle—keeping his hands conspicuously in the open as young men spilled out of the Nissan, forming a rough approximation of a perimeter. The former Marine E-5 was unimpressed.

Then the door of the SUV opened, and a long-haired man in his late thirties emerged from the rear seat, a Chinese Type 56 Kalashnikov clone slung around his shoulders. *Manong Soleiman*, Kruta guessed, watching how the other militants reacted to the presence of their leader. Svalinn hadn't been able to provide any photos.

It was a surprise to him that the man had chosen to come in person, but he didn't have long to dwell on it as Soleiman approached Mohd, unleashing a rapid-fire stream of Visayan on his fellow Moro, only the stray loanword of English making its way through the language barrier to Kruta—the anger, all too apparent. *Something was going wrong*, he realized, feeling every muscle of his body tense—watching the body language of the other militants. *On edge.*

"What's the problem here?" he demanded, taking a half-step toward Mohd—watching the man's knuckles whiten around the pistol grip of the M-16, a volatile mix of anger and fear playing across his face.

Mohd shook his head, responding quickly to Soleiman in the same language—struggling to get a word in.

"He says that you are working for the military," the Moro responded finally, turning to look at Kruta, "that you are plotting to betray him to his enemies. They saw the soldiers leaving the hotel, the Americans with them."

What did you do, *Jack?* He suppressed an angry curse, glimpsing a couple of the younger militants out of the corner of his eye, moving in, weapons raised.

"Atras kamo!" he heard Mohd shout, the M-16's long barrel coming up in an action which translated the words more clearly than any 'terp. *Stay back.*

"Get back in the vehicle, Mr. Kruta," he said, glancing across at the former intelligence officer. "We're leav—"

It all happened so fast—the ragged burst of rifle fire striking his ears even as droplets of hot wet blood spattered across his face, the bodyguard's body jerking from the impact of even more rounds as Mohd crumpled backward into the bullet-riddled hood of the Datsun, half his face shot away. The rifle falling from nerveless fingers into the mud and gravel of the lakeshore.

There was no time to react, precious little to have been done if there were. Kruta saw the militants close in, rifles leveled—saw one of them kick savagely at Mohd's prostrate corpse. Saw it all, and raised his hands—another bitter curse escaping his lips as he fell to his knees in the mud.

Jack.

5:51 P.M.
Bud Dajo—the crater
Jolo Island, Sulu Province
The Autonomous Region in Muslim Mindanao (ARMM)

"He wants Manila to listen. To him," Annalyn Parada added softly, drawing the dark *terong* closer around her face as she squatted down by Charity's side in the shadow of an outcropping of volcanic rock, looking across at Shawn. "He told me as much, last night when—when we were. . .together."

She looked away as she said it, the words coming out choked—filled with emotion. Shawn's heart going out to her in that moment, despite their danger. She had already suffered so much.

"And if they don't?" It was Emmanuel who asked the question, sitting cross-legged on the ground a few feet away.

"Then. . ." Annalyn stopped, biting her lip—refusing to meet any of their eyes, seeming to try to summon up the strength to continue. "Then he's going to kill everyone—the adults, at least," she finished, looking over to where Dolores was playing with Faith, perhaps twenty-five or thirty feet away. They had insisted that the older girl take Faith away before they began talking, and she had complied—the fear visible in her big dark eyes. Fear still lingering from the chaos of the night before—from seeing her mother here, like this.

Death. Shawn ran a hand across his face, still struggling to accept their reality—the enormity of it all, far too overwhelming to grasp. Last night, when the first shots rang out, he had been so *sure* that God was delivering them. That, somehow, they were to be rescued.

But it hadn't been deliverance which came for them, out of the night.

The floor of the crater was thick with jungle and underbrush which had overwhelmed the burnt-out cinder cone over the centuries—only a few clearings remaining like this one, open to the sky. Reachable only by a handful of treacherously steep trails twisting and turning their way up narrow hogback ridges toward the crater rim. A few small huts scattered across the clearing, broken down and crumbling from decay. He suspected they would be sleeping outside once again.

The last five hundred feet of the climb had been a desperate scramble in the early-morning twilight, forcing most of them—hostages and captors alike—to crawl forward on their hands and knees to the top, his hand seizing Faith's in the desperate fear that she might fall. The view from there, staring down nearly three hundred feet into the jungle-covered bowl of the crater below them, might have been breathtaking under different circumstances.

As it was. . .well, the climb down had been nearly as difficult as the climb up—Khadafi and the others pushing them on throughout the descent, only allowing the shortest of rests, the ghostly ruins of burnt-out cottas, old fortifications from a century past, visible in the jungle just off the trail. Human bones emerging here and there through the undergrowth.

"They massacred our people," Khadafi had said when asked, more sadness than anger in the older Moro's eyes as

he pushed forward, cutting away brush with a long bolo knife where it threatened to obscure the path. He'd refused to say anything more.

Manong Soleiman had no longer been with them by that point, the militants separating into two parties somewhere back along the short drive from Maimbung to the foot of the mountain. *Why*, Shawn had no idea—and no one was talking, not even the shaken Aldam, who still seemed to be in shock over the bloodbath of the previous night. All of his rock stars, butchered in their sleep by his fellow Moros— even Abu Nazih, a man who had fought for his beloved caliphate.

That he had been spared, despite his seeming defection from Soleiman when the two groups had separated, was something of a miracle—and to the teenager's credit, he seemed to know it. Or perhaps his confidence had just gone out of him with the confiscation of his rifle.

The low, persistent murmur of Annalyn's voice seemed to die away just then, and Shawn looked up to see Khadafi standing there behind them—the older man's figure an imposing presence in the fading half-light, the setting sun already sunk low below the volcano's rim.

"You should keep your daughters close," the Moro observed simply, his dark eyes unreadable as he regarded them. "You don't want them wandering off into the jungle. There are many ghosts in this place."

He seemed on the verge of saying something further, but it was in that moment that the jarringly discordant buzz of a satellite phone sounded, and Khadafi turned half-away, plucking a scuffed, battered Thuraya from the knapsack slung over his shoulder. The phone Abu Nazih had been using just a few days before, Shawn realized. *Spoils of war.*

"The American? You have him?" the missionary heard Khadafi ask, casting a glance upward toward the heights above, the rim of the cinder cone where the trail, barely visible from this distance below, began to snake down into the bowl. "Good."

6:03 P.M.
Station Manila
The Embassy of the United States
Ermita, Manila
Philippines

". . .yes, it's coming through now," Darren Lukasik replied in a distracted aside into the secure line, his attention focused on the screens mounted on the far wall of Station Manila's small operations center as the satellite feed from NROC in Chantilly, Virginia came up, the KH-11 "Kennen" reconnaissance satellite moving into position over the Pacific, two hundred miles above the earth's surface, the lenses of its massive cameras focused in on the small island of Jolo, in the Sulu Sea.

It was like looking through the Hubble Telescope. . .at the earth. Four decades on since the first KH-11 launch, the satellites' true capabilities were still a closely-guarded state secret, with only a handful of photos ever released to the public—twice by people who later ended up convicted of espionage.

And small wonder, because the detail they revealed was. . .breathtaking. Night was already falling—as would have been obvious even in Manila had the operations center possessed any windows—but even in the gathering twilight, you could make out the figures of nearly twenty people out in the open, scattered around a small clearing near the northwest side of the Bud Dajo crater bowl. And at least three of them—a man, a woman, and a girl who couldn't have been more than five or six—were clearly Western.

The Braleys.

"Good going, Jack," Lukasik observed quietly, a smile creeping across his face as he muffled the phone's receiver against his chest. He glanced over and saw Matt Campisi's nod. They had located their people, thanks to Richards— and, as far as any one knew, their Filipino counterparts remained in the dark. That was going to make Washington very happy.

"NROC," he began, lifting the receiver once again as he scanned the incoming images. "What can you give us on IR?"

They didn't have a lot of time. Satellites didn't "hover" after all—in orbit, the KH-11 was moving at nearly eighteen *thousand* miles per hour. But its cameras could give them what they needed, even in a small window.

"One moment, sir," the tech in Virginia responded, a minute passing before the incoming feed on the screens changed to the haze grays of infrared thermal imaging, the mountain standing out in ghostly relief, beneath the wisps of cloud cover.

"What's this?" his deputy chief of station asked suddenly, Campisi's long finger stretched out toward the left of one of the screens. And there they were, beneath the canopy of the jungle—picking their way up the eastern face of Bud Dajo along a narrow ridgeline trail—a tight cluster of heat signatures. *Men.*

"Well, well," Lukasik murmured, his eyes narrowing. "Who do we have here. . ."

1:34 P.M. Central European Standard Time
The Marivaux Hotel
Brussels, Belgium

"You're sure?"

Arne Kornbech nodded, the phone clutched tight against his shoulder as he picked up another dress shirt off the hotel room's king-sized bed, throwing it into his luggage. "I am."

The former Jaeger was a stocky fireplug of a man in his late forties, standing no more than 5'6" in his stocking feet. His hair had once been a dark blonde, but it had begun to gray and thin not long past his fortieth birthday, and he had retaliated against the ravages of age by shaving it all off. Without bothering to check with his wife.

"Kruta has now missed his comms window by. . ." he checked his watch, a hard glance in his ice-blue eyes, ". . .four hours. And all my attempts to contact him have gone unanswered, ma'am. I'm getting nothing from his phone—it's dropped off our radar completely, may have been destroyed."

He zipped up the wheeled duffel bag, leaning it against the bed. He was due to have left already, headed home to spend Christmas with Clara and the kids at their home in Skaelskør, on the island of Sjælland, but that had all changed when Brent Kruta failed to make contact following his scheduled meeting with Manong Soleiman's militants.

"Then he's been taken," the Svalinn Security Group's CEO responded from nearly three thousand kilometers away in Istanbul, a grim edge in her voice, all emotion buried deep beneath the surface.

A former case officer for the Americans' Central Intelligence Agency, she was good at doing that. But she also had enough time in the field to know how this ended.

The *only* way this ended.

It wasn't as though any of them hadn't grasped the potential consequences of doing business with Hadjiman Palalisan. But in the end, it had been the call of the man in the field. The *wrong* call, as it happened. *Bad business.*

"I think we have to proceed under that assumption, yes."

"Where are our closest personnel, Arne?"

He had looked himself, the moment he realized there was trouble. "Peters is in Jakarta, there to interview a potential hire with the *Kopaska.* That's as close as it gets."

Their next nearest team was in the Helmand, on a training mission with the ANA, but he'd pulled the personnel files of the men there, and. . .*no*. Good men all, for the job they'd been assigned. Not this one.

There was a heavy sigh on the other end of the line. Then, "Get in touch with State—read them in. They'll be overjoyed to hear from us."

Chapter 19

10:09 A.M. Eastern Standard Time, December 23rd
CIA Headquarters
Langley, Virginia

Svalinn. Bernard Kranemeyer shook his head, turning away from the window with a heavy sigh. "This is confirmed?"

"Not independently, no," Ron Carter replied, standing in the doorway leading to the DCS' outer office. "All we have at the moment is Svalinn's report, delivered to the State Department by their operations officer, Arne Kornbech. Kornbech is a Dane, a former Jaeger who—"

"I know him," Kranemeyer replied simply, cutting off his lead analyst. As he knew so many of the senior staff at SSG, including their chief executive officer. *You've done well for yourself, haven't you?*

No question there was money to be made in the private sector—all the more so now, as the United States struggled to disengage after more than a decade and a half at war. Brent Kruta himself had sat in this very office not eight months before, laying out his reasons for leaving. *Finances, most of it.*

Kranemeyer had tried to dissuade him from going through with it, but the words had fallen on deaf ears. He'd had a daughter to put through college, and a wife with Crohn's whose medical bills were getting out ahead of what his Agency health insurance could reasonably cover.

He had needed more money, better benefits. Not hard to understand that, not hard at all. The Agency wasn't a place a man came to get rich.

But now he was in trouble, the DCS mused. And it wasn't going to be his company who got him out.

"Where are we with Imamović & Co.? Do we have a sitrep from Walker?"

"The prisoners were returned to Al-Jafr thirty minutes ago. They won't be going anywhere, anytime soon."

"Has regular contact been established with Richards and Granby on Jolo?"

"Not as of yet, no."

11:34 P.M. Philippine Standard Time
Bud Dajo—the crater
Jolo Island, Sulu Province
The Autonomous Region in Muslim Mindanao (ARMM)

"I'm sorry." Shawn Braley looked over to where the American sat, his back to a tree on the edge of the clearing— his shirt torn and bloody, hands secured behind him and around the trunk. His upturned face wet with the light rain now descending from the heavens, soaking them all to the skin. The thick fronds of the palms above, affording precious little cover.

They were the first words the man had spoken directly to

them in the four hours since he had been dragged into the camp by Manong Soleiman's fighters—thrown to the ground and beaten with the butts of the militants' rifles until Shawn had tried to intervene.

Khadafi had stopped him, his hand on the missionary's shoulder, a warning in the older Moro's eyes. *Don't interfere.*

Soleiman had been in a fury when the group had returned—screaming threats, his sword drawn. He had struck the newcomer once with the flat of its blade, the impact taking him once more to his knees.

Something had gone wrong out there, Shawn didn't know *what*, but it seemed to have pushed their captor over the edge.

"You don't need to be sorry for anything," he heard his wife reply, the strength in her voice surprising him. She had been using some of their precious drinking water—drawn from several 50-gallon drums which seemed to have been brought to the mountain weeks if not months before—to daub at the stranger's wounds with a torn strip of her *terong*.

"I came here to pay your ransom," the man went on after a long moment's pause, his body wracked by a sudden cough. The night air was all the colder, up here on the mountain, and the rain was making things worse. "To get you all out."

"Ransom?" Shawn shook his head, unable to grasp what he was saying.

"You didn't know?" A bitter, ironic half-smile played at the stranger's lips. "Perhaps it was all a lie, all along. . .Soleiman demanded a ransom, and your family, your church—everyone back in the States—people raised over three million to get you out. I was sent to handle negotiations."

And then he remembered—Abu Nazih's words on the afternoon before his death. The smirk on his face when he'd said it, raising Shawn's hopes and dashing them in the space of a breath. *"You Americans must learn a lesson. Not everything can be had for a price. . ."*

"And who are you?" Emmanuel Asuncion asked, a skeptical look in the Filipino's eyes as he crouched a few feet away, a sodden, threadbare blanket draped over his shoulders.

"A Marine," the American responded, choking on another cough. "Private security now. Name's Brent—Brent Kruta."

"What's been going on?" Shawn heard himself ask, still barely comprehending the situation. He shivered with the cold, hugging Faith closer—her small body warm against his chest. "What went wrong out there?"

"I'm not sure, exactly," Kruta replied, his voice low—casting a glance back through the darkness of the jungle night toward the sentries patrolling the perimeter—several visible by the glowing coals of their cigarettes. "A unit from the Special Action Force—Filipino spec-ops outfit—flew into Jolo last night. Near as I can tell, their arrival threw Soleiman into a panic. I thought our deal was still on, but when I showed up, he grabbed me instead."

"Your deal? Then you. . ."

Kruta met the missionary's eyes, nodding slowly. "After a manner of speaking."

Then all those people. . .

Shawn felt suddenly sick, remembering the dead man whose belly he'd stepped on in the chaos of the previous night—the fire and the madness. *Butchery.*

And it had all gotten them *nothing*.

"Mrs. Braley," the man was saying, shifting his focus over to Charity, "I saw your sister Debra in Manila, only a few days ago. She wanted me to assure you of her love and her prayers. . ."

12:04 A.M., December 24th
Camp Bautista, Jolo
Jolo Island, Sulu Province
The Autonomous Region in Muslim Mindanao (ARMM)

They should have all been asleep, Richards supposed—but it was hard to sleep on nights like this, tensions never far from the surface, the edge from the previous night, still not worn off.

It was Granby who was the center of attention in the middle of the rectangular concrete-block building which served as sleeping quarters for Segovia's men and which had been commandeered by the SAF—sitting there surrounded by a half-dozen of Mijares' commandos, a handful of playing cards poised carelessly between his dark fingers. A glass of brandy cut with wild ginger not far from his free, gesturing hand.

They were playing poker—had been for the last two hours—but Granby's focus wasn't on the game, his hearty, booming laugh filling the narrow confines of the room as he launched into yet another war story from his time in Afghanistan. *There I was. . .*

Bringing him along had been a good choice, Richards thought, glancing briefly to where Carson sat on the other side of the circle, going quietly over his cards.

They'd needed someone who could work a room, and it certainly wasn't going to be either him or Carson. *Hold everyone's attention.*

It was the secret of every good magic trick, focusing the audience's attention on one hand—while the other pulled off the "trick."

He waited until Granby had taken another drink—one of Mijares' sergeants taking advantage of the pause to begin a story of his own, something about an operation a decade before against Communist guerillas on Samar—before slipping out of the building unnoticed and into the night.

The rain was coming down steadily now—the same rain which had driven Granby and his newly-made friends off the camp's makeshift basketball court some hours previous. Wherever the Braleys were. . .it had to be a miserable night.

He made his way back there now, to the deserted court— glancing around briefly before pulling up the cuff of his Levi's to retrieve the stolen cellphone from his boot, taking the SIM card from his trousers pocket and slipping it into the back, powering the phone on.

There were two messages, both of them short and to the point—come in nearly five hours apart. The last, only thirty minutes before.

Theory proven right, read the first message. *Back-up on-station next 24, stand by for further orders.*

DEVGRU, presumably. And now they had a location— his hunch, paying off. He reached up, wiping droplets of rain from the screen with his thumb before scrolling down to the second message.

Our uncle now likely has a fourth guest. Our friend from the private sector has dropped off the map.

Brent. Richards closed his eyes, as if to shut it all out—
the night, the rain falling relentlessly down from the sky—
unable to escape the reality. *This was personal now.*

3:17 A.M.
The USS Michigan
The Mindoro Strait

"It's back, sir." The *Michigan's* CO took a sip of his coffee,
standing there in the sonar room in his shirtsleeves, his face
lit by the glow of the electronics.

"How long?" Piasecki asked, glancing at the screen in
front of the sonar technician. There were a *lot* of active
contacts—they were in the middle of a sea lane, after all—
more than a dozen cargo ships transiting the strait north and
south between Mindoro and Basuanga. A VLCC—the
literally named Very Large Crude Carrier—tanker no more
than fifteen miles off their starboard bow.

But there was only one which really interested them,
seven miles back—the contact tentatively designated Sierra-
59—nearly obscured on the display by another contact, all
but right on top of it, a slow-moving bulk carrier identified
as Sierra-67.

"I'm not certain, sir," the young sailor replied honestly,
a frown crossing his face as he removed his headphones. "We
first picked it up nearly an hour ago, but it was hard to be
certain. Even now. . .he's just hanging out there in the
baffles of the bulk."

Getting lost in the noise, Piasecki thought—the
commotion in the water generated by the bulk carrier's
massive fixed-pitch propeller effectively masking any sounds

their primary contact might be making.

"But you think it's him?" They had picked up traces of another submarine's presence the previous day—just traces, a stray contact slipping into the thermocline. That he had picked up them seemed almost a given, as hot as they were running. *If he was now shadowing them. . .*

A brief, hesitant nod from the sonar tech. "The way he's acting. . .I do, sir."

He knew without asking that they hadn't been able to ID the contact, not with all the white noise from the bulk carrier surrounding it, but in these waters—not much more than two hundred miles northeast of the Spratlys—it was likely Chinese, maybe one of their newer *Yuan*-class Type 039As, which would do a lot to explain the trouble they were having keeping track of it, even absent the bulk carrier.

"Get the SEALs' CO up here," Piasecki announced after a moment's reflection, turning to give the order to a sailor behind him. "Right away. I want him to see this."

Guilbeau was in the sonar room ten minutes later, his hair still tousled from sleep. "A Chinese submarine?"

"That's the working assumption," Commander Piasecki replied. "Right. . .here, shadowing us through the strait on the heels of this bulk carrier."

The SEAL glanced over the screens only briefly before directing his attention back to the captain. Here, he was just a passenger—didn't have the training or the inclination to argue the point with Piasecki. What mattered was what was to be done about it.

"I want to turn the tables on him," the *Michigan*'s CO replied when he put the question to him. He reached out, tapping the screen to indicate a sonar contact about five miles ahead, designated Sierra-77. "That's a container ship—I want to creep up and slow down, hide in its wake, use his own strategy against him to mask our exit from the strait. Find another ship if we can or, failing that, go down into the thermocline and sit there until he passes—let him chase the container ship for a few hundred miles until he realizes we're not there anymore."

"How long will that add to our ETA?"

"Hard to say, exactly. Five or six hours, most likely."

Guilbeau did the math in his head. "That would put us off Jolo after daybreak tomorrow, commander. My men would have to wait until after dark to go in—your five or six-hour delay means a twenty-four-hour delay on my end. That's unacceptable."

Piasecki took a step toward him, a warning light in the CO's eyes. "The security of my boat rests in its ability to remain hidden, senior chief. An ability now fatally compromised by this speed run. We need to shake this Chicom, and do it before exiting the strait. We likely can't outrun him, and odds are he's quieter than we are, too. That leaves us with misdirection."

"My orders are clear, commander," Guilbeau replied quietly, his eyes never leaving Piasecki's face. "And they don't admit of another twenty-four-hour delay. If you want to dispute them, take us to comms depth and take it up with the command authority."

Chapter 20

Bud Dajo—the crater
Jolo Island, Sulu Province
The Autonomous Region in Muslim Mindanao (ARMM)

The sky was just beginning to redden in the east, the sun still hidden well below the rim of the crater—its first few rays filtering through the trees to strike Brent Kruta's face where he sat, his back against the tree, his body weight straining limply against the ropes that bound him to its trunk.

The rain had stopped, hours before, but he was still drenched to the skin, his torn clothing plastered to his body—a chill running through him.

He ached from the beating he'd received at the hands of Manong Soleiman's militants—a beating which had started on the shores of the lake, and continued most of the way up the mountainside. His left eye had swollen shut overnight and it felt as though one or more of his ribs were broken, pain flickering through his body whenever he took a deep breath.

Soleiman had snapped. That was Kruta's professional

assessment as a former intelligence officer, watching his behavior the previous evening, all the way up the trail and in the camp itself—screaming out threats and brandishing that *kampilan* recklessly. His training forcing him to take stock of their situation, the logic struggling to filter its way through the pain.

This hadn't been the plan. And Jim Palalisan. . .as dangerous as working with him had been, he wasn't a part of this. The image of Mohd's bullet-riddled body collapsing back into the hood of the Datsun, still far too fresh.

Palalisan had lasted as long as he had in Mindanao politics by cultivating an intense personal loyalty among his fellow Moros. He wouldn't have put his own bodyguard at such risk.

Which left them with Soleiman going completely rogue, that worst of all options. *Off the reservation.*

Perhaps it had been the chaos of the night before—the fear of reprisals following his murder of Abu Nazih— perhaps it had been the arrival of the Filipino commandos, pushing him over the brink. How he had gotten here, really didn't matter—he was *here*.

And all bets were off.

2:45 P.M. Pacific Standard Time, December 23rd
The Westin
Henderson, Nevada

"Should I be hurt, Rick?" Steve Winfield asked, a quiet smile of amusement flickering across the casino mogul's weathered face as he glanced down the sofa at the President of the United States. "That you chose to stay all the way out here, rather than accepting my invitation to be my guest at the Bellagio?"

Norton grimaced. "Nothing of the sort, Steve. . .you know I would have loved nothing more. It's the optics of the thing, you know how it is—staying on the Strip itself when I'm in town to mark the anniversary of such a devastating attack. My advisors, they—"

"Are wrong, as they often are. This is Vegas—the show goes on. And what better way to send a message to the terrorists that they *failed* than for the President himself to spend Christmas at the resort they targeted, the very next year. You gotta stop listening to these people, Rick. They're leading you astray. You have good instincts, use them."

The President forced a smile. A long-time party donor, Winfield had thrown his support behind his campaign early in the primary—a decision for which he would be forever grateful—but there was far too much of the showman in him for the two of them to have ever become close.

Politics was just another show for Winfield, playing out on a bigger stage—not a principled *fight*. Not even now. One might have thought that last Christmas Eve would have changed him, but there was little sign of it in the man's eyes.

A moment later, he found himself revising that assessment.

"You're going to get them out, aren't you?" the casino mogul asked, stretching out an arm along the back of the sofa as he leaned toward the President. "The Braleys."

"Of course we are. The SEALs should be—" Norton stopped himself there, realizing the danger of saying too much, even here. With a friend. "We're going to bring them home, Steve. We always bring Americans home."

"Good." Winfield looked away for a long moment. "I gave half a million toward their ransom myself, you know."

He hadn't, and in truth, it surprised him, but Norton chose to acknowledge the words with a simple nod.

"They've been hostages for what now. . .three weeks? God, it's a disgrace."

The President bristled at the words, incapable of remaining silent. "We're doing all we can," he replied defensively. "*Everything* we can."

"I was a hostage," the casino mogul went on, as if he wasn't even aware Norton had spoken. "For a few hours. And I was even unconscious for part of it."

A laugh escaped his lips at the last sentence, as if overcome by the irony of it—a harsh barking laugh that died away in a reflexive shudder. "I still see those masked faces at night when I try to sleep, Rick. *Still.* A year later, and I didn't suffer as they have. Get them out."

7:13 A.M. Philippine Standard Time, December 24th
Bud Dajo—the crater
Jolo Island, Sulu Province
The Autonomous Region in Muslim Mindanao (ARMM)

So this was what it felt like. To meet Death. Their paths had crossed so many times over the years—Afghanistan, Iraq, Afghanistan again. . .a score or more countries with the Agency. A dance, a flirtation—ships passing each other in the night. But Death had always stopped at someone else's door, in the end.

Not this time. The humid morning breeze rippled through the trees, sending an involuntary shudder through his body as Brent Kruta looked up into the barrel of the old Colt M1911A1 clutched in Manong Soleiman's left hand, its worn, gaping muzzle only inches from his forehead—hammer back.

"This was the plan all along, wasn't it?" the guerrilla leader demanded, his eyes bloodshot and wild, gesturing angrily with the *kampilan* in his other hand. His English imperfect, but understandable enough. "To sell me out, to *betray* me. You bought Palalisan with the ransom, and he arranged to deliver me up into your hands."

Madness. He found himself only listening to Soleiman's harangue with one ear, his mind drifting absently back to his wife and daughter. Heidi had thought this work would be safer, a welcome change from his years at war.

More time for the two of them, together, even as Lauren went off to college.

He'd known it wouldn't be that simple, of course. That many of the hazards would remain the same, if better compensated. But it had seemed simpler just to let her believe.

And Death had found him, all the same.

The cool steel of the Colt's muzzle jammed into the thin skin of his forehead, bringing his attention back to his captor. ". . .you thought to bring me down," Soleiman was saying, pressing the gun in harder to emphasize each word, his finger curled around the 1911's single-action trigger, "and look where you have found yourself. At my mercy."

A breath of pressure, that was all it would take. Just a breath, and his brains would be spattered all over the ground. *Make him do it*, something within him urged. The void, calling out to him. *Oblivion.*

Instead he remained silent, refusing to meet Soleiman's gaze. That was what they taught you at the Farm. Don't antagonize, don't stand out. *Don't play the hero.*

Unlearning everything he had once been taught as a Marine. But it kept a man alive.

And that was when he heard Shawn Braley's voice, calling out across the clearing, raw desperation in its tones. "Please. . .please, just *stop.*"

7:19 A.M.
Talipao
Jolo Island, Sulu Province
The Autonomous Region in Muslim Mindanao (ARMM)

The smoke of a cooking fire drifted lazily in the humid morning air, the sun already beginning to burn down on the jungle as Jack Richards stood in the open door of the squat, Korean-built AFP utility truck, his eyes following the SAF commandos as they moved around the small *barangay*, talking with the locals.

The houses lining the rutted, muddy dirt road were a mix of modern concrete-block and more traditional Filipino nipa huts, most of the latter elevated off the ground—kids running around, more than a few of the boys in football jerseys, even as their parents did their best to keep them away from the soldiers. Richards saw one boy chasing after a half-starved mongrel of a dog, who was currently lifting his leg against the corner of a nearby house.

They weren't more than a kilometer now from the spot where the NICA drone had finally lost Manong Soleiman's vehicles in the jungle—the cinder cone of Bud Dajo visible through the trees to the northwest as Richards glanced cautiously toward its slopes.

There was little doubt that Soleiman's force probably now included Tausugs from this very village, he thought, keeping a wary eye on their surroundings—spotting Mijares about forty meters off, talking with a middle-aged, gray-headed man in a t-shirt and black jeans. Several older men— perhaps the local elders, it was hard to say—gathered around in a semi-circle of the ubiquitous plastic chairs he never seemed to get away from, no matter where he'd gone in waging the "War on Terror."

They were armed, now—pistols riding in the black leather holsters on their hips. A pair of Rock Island Armory 1911s for him and Granby, loaned to them by Colonel Segovia just before they left the base. Nichols would have approved—the venerable sidearm, for all its shortcomings, always a favorite of his. Carson had received a Glock.

It was a precaution which served as stark testament to just how quickly they all knew things could go pear-shaped out here.

Moro culture, Mindanao and points south, was a weapons culture that put even the strongest American defenders of the 2nd Amendment to shame. Once it had been blades, now it was guns, and *everyone* had one. Or more.

It was why they were here in force—very nearly the entire SAF detachment, plus the better part of a platoon of Segovia's soldiers. A footprint so massive that it ran hard against the grain of Richards' own counter-insurgency experience, but it was also too large of a force to easily challenge.

"Pantakasi" was the word the lieutenant colonel had

used, in their briefing for the operation the previous night. *Cockfight derby.* The call going out through the Jolo countryside for any man with a weapon—which was a quick way of saying anyone north of or nearing puberty—to turn out and swarm an isolated enemy.

The Minutemen of Lexington and Concord, Richards mused ironically. Except this time, they were the redcoats.

He shut the door of the truck, walking back along the length of the small convoy to where William Russell Cole stood by the rearmost vehicle, another Korean-built KM-450 Series, this time with an M2 Browning mounted in the truck's bed, a Filipino PFC posted up behind the machine gun. Sweat already beading on the young soldier's face in the humidity of the early morning, his right hand on the Browning's spade handle, a rosary wrapped around the fingers of his left—his lips moving softly in the familiar refrain.

Santa María Madre de Dios. . .

Richards knew it well, could *hear* it, even if he couldn't hear the soldier. You didn't grow up in the Southwest without knowing it.

Holy Mary, Mother of God, pray for us sinners, now. . .and at the hour of our death.

If anything kicked off, the man on that gun would be anyone's first target. And the kid probably knew it.

He turned to the FBI Special Agent, noting the skepticism in the older man's eyes, knowing he was still trying to place him from Vegas—probably knew he had lied. *No matter.*

"Tonight," Richards began, keeping his voice low as he glanced back up at the nervous private, "I'm going to need you to run interference for us. With the Filipinos."

7:22 A.M.
Bud Dajo—the crater
Jolo Island, Sulu Province
The Autonomous Region in Muslim Mindanao (ARMM)

He wasn't sure where he had found his voice—something breaking inside him at the sight of the man who had come to rescue them, there on his knees. The muzzle of Soleiman's pistol pressed into his forehead.

And Khadafi wasn't here to stop him, not this time. The older man, out on the perimeter—checking on the guards posted to cover the trail. He had seen him leave.

"He's done nothing wrong," Shawn Braley protested, taking a few steps away from his family and toward Manong Soleiman and the cluster of militants surrounding him. Aldam there, the teenager hanging on the periphery of the group, a dark look of hatred in his young eyes. "He only came to pay our ransom, to—"

"Go sit back down, Shawn," he heard Kruta warn weakly, saw Soleiman's hand move like a striking viper, slamming the butt of the pistol into the Marine's temple, sending him reeling back against his bindings.

And then he found the pistol aimed at his own head, Manong Soleiman advancing on him—rage in the man's eyes, the weapon's muzzle seeming to grow larger with each step. "What do you know, missionary? What do you know, of *any* of this?"

"He doesn't—"

"Shut up!" He cringed away from the man, hearing his daughter's scream of terror, feeling the cold muzzle of the pistol bite into his temple. *Oh, God. . .*

"You came to our land," Soleiman spat, his breath hot and foul against Shawn's face as he leaned over, as if trying to force the missionary to look him in the eye—the pressure of the pistol unabated against his skull, "as you Americans have done for the last hundred years, your false religion advancing behind your guns and bayonets. *Hiding in fear.*"

Soleiman took a step backward, the *kampilan* arcing through the air—the flat of its blade catching Shawn in the ribs, pain lancing through his body. The impact taking him to his knees on the hard ground.

"You don't have the guns now," he heard the man boast, and he felt the presence of the pistol there once again, aimed at his head—just out of sight, but he found himself incapable of looking up. *The shadow of Death.*

His breath was coming shallow and fast, the fear washing over him. The acid taste of bile in his throat—struggling to pray, the words refusing to come—Soleiman's mocking, taunting voice ringing in his ears, driving out all else.

"You don't have the guns," the terrorist repeated, "and the God you've turned your back on won't come down to save you from me. *Admit it.*"

He had. The realization hitting him in an agonizing wave of despair. Without ever meaning to, without ever realizing it, he had turned his back on God—trusting in himself, in *America*. He'd preached against the prosperity gospel, but he'd bought it himself, all the same—that feeling of *invincibility*, so uniquely the American birthright. *The hubris.*

But that wasn't what Soleiman meant. "Admit *what?*" he heard himself ask in a strange, cracking voice he hardly recognized as his own.

"That it's a lie, all of it," came the hissed reply, the death-cold muzzle of the pistol grinding once more into his temple, a relentless pressure as he ducked his head. "Admit it—Allah has no son. *Say it.*"

Denial. A thousand voices, screaming in his mind. Everything in him crying out against the blasphemy, but *survival* the loudest voice of all. It was so easy to think of martyrdom in the abstract, to praise those who had remained true to their faith in the face of death. *True to the end.*

Here in the moment, it was hard to think beyond the next second—the will to survive, overwhelming all else. The pistol's muzzle, cold against his skull. "God," he began, a quaver in his voice, his whole body trembling as if still clutched in the grip of the fever, "God had—"

"Shawn, no!" he heard a voice call out, close at his side. A hand on his shoulder, offering strength and comfort. *Manny.* "Don't deny your faith, my brother."

Brother. He felt the tears begin to flow unchecked down his face, shame filling him at the Filipino's words. He had come to help these people, to teach them the Gospel, but he was one who had needed to *learn*, after all—their faith, far stronger than his own.

There was a desperate earnestness in Emmanuel's words, his fingers squeezing Shawn's shoulder fiercely as he continued, "Remain true—hold fast to your faith, even to the death, and you will receive a crown of life. Our God is stronger than this man, than all of his threats. Than anything he—"

And the pistol was no longer at his temple, the pressure easing suddenly, replaced by an overwhelming sense of fear. *No.* He started to react, a hard edge of stone cutting into his knees as he struggled to rise, but it was too late. Far too late.

The next moment, the deafening blast of the .45 hammered his eardrums. . .

4:29 P.M. Pacific Standard Time, December 23rd
The Westin
Henderson, Nevada

". . .at least two hours to reach the summit, according to our estimates, which should put our men in position about 0400 hours local, about an hour before daybreak." On-screen, General Shulgach paused, glancing up into the lens of the camera. "That's not optimal, Mr. President."

"What alternative do you recommend, general?" Norton asked, running a hand across his chin as he glanced around at his team, wishing that Gisriel was here. They would teleconference later, but it wasn't the same as having his National Security Adviser at hand to consult in the moment.

Still, it wasn't possible to transport their entire national security architecture to Vegas for the holiday.

"I would suggest pushing our timetable back another twenty-four hours, sir," Shulgach replied cautiously. "In which case the *Michigan* would remain submerged off Jolo for the entirety of the day tomorrow, locking out her SEALs after dark. With the seven-kilometer hike to the foot of the mountain, and the climb. . .they should be able to reach the camp around 0200 hours on the morning of the 26th, which allows for a significantly greater margin of error while still assuring our forces the cover of darkness to carry out the operation."

"That would leave the Braleys in the terrorists' hands for

another twenty-four hours," Norton said slowly, finding himself torn by indecision. The thought was intolerable, and even so. . .

"That's correct, sir. I would not recommend it if I did not have serious concerns about our ability to pull this off successfully on the current timetable. A failed attempt will, after all, result in even more serious consequences for the Braleys."

"Of course," the President said distractedly. Making these decisions never came easy. The media would torch him either way, if something went wrong—they always did. And *losing* the Braleys, at this point, after all the media attention their case had garnered. . .the fallout would be devastating.

"I will consult with my advisers, general—and let you know my decision in the next few hours."

7:31 A.M. Philippine Standard Time, December 24th
Bud Dajo—the crater
Jolo Island, Sulu Province
The Autonomous Region in Muslim Mindanao (ARMM)

The echoes of the shot died away, crashing out into the jungle—the acrid smell of gunpowder filling Shawn Braley's nostrils as he glanced back over his shoulder to see Emmanuel fall back, his face distorted in pain, hands clutching at his right side, his shirt already stained dark with blood.

He could hear the lay pastor's moans of pain, Charity and Dolores screaming, Faith's smaller, high-pitched voice joining theirs in a wail of fear—could smell his own fear, raw and visceral, a sour, rancid odor, mixing with that of the gunpowder. And he found himself rooted to the spot, his mouth open in shock—simply staring at his wounded friend as though paralyzed, unable to help, thinking of his wife and children back in Mindanao. *No.*

The spell only lasted a moment, maybe two, and then he pushed himself to his feet, heedless of Soleiman's gun, scrabbling across the hard, rocky ground to Emmanuel's side. The Filipino's breath was coming sharp and fast as Shawn knelt beside him, his eyes already glazed with pain, dark red blood seeping from between his fingers as he pressed them hard to his side.

"Stay with me, Manny," he whispered, clasping his friend's free hand in a desperate grip—his eyes darting wildly around in search of someone, anyone, who could help. A thousand despairing prayers flickering through his mind. *Please, God, he's your servant—spare* him*, at least.*

His gaze met Kruta's, but the Marine's face was tight-lipped and grim, his arms still bound behind him, to the tree. No help to be found there.

It took everything in him to face Manong Soleiman, to look into that harsh, implacable face, framed by its wild mane of black hair. "Please," he heard himself beg, "whatever you ask, I'll do it. Just *help him.*"

"*No,*" he heard Emmanuel whisper, his grip tightening on Shawn's hand, shaking his head as he lay there. *Faithful to the end.*

But there was no mercy to be found there, in the terrorist's face—Soleiman's eyes holding Shawn's for a long moment before he looked away, seeking out Aldam on the edge of the crowd. "*Dali dinhi.*" Come here.

The teenager seemed frozen for a moment, as if

disbelieving that Soleiman had chosen to address him—then he shuffled forward, his long hair tied back from his forehead with a band, still not quite meeting his leader's eyes.

"You wanted to fight for Abu Nazih, *o-oh?*" *Yes?*

Even to Shawn, Aldam's response was unintelligible, and he saw the anger flicker in Manong Soleiman's face, the wicked blade of the *kampilan* glistening in the morning sun as its tip came up to rest against the teenager's Adam's apple, drawing a bright red line of blood as it scraped higher, forcing his chin up.

"Look at me when I speak to you. *Tu - Bag ga ko!*" Soleiman spat, glaring at his young follower. *Answer me.* "You wanted to fight for Abu Nazih? To kill the infidels who have defiled our lands?"

"O-oh." *Yes.* Louder this time, Aldam's eyes wide as he stared down the blade at the guerrilla leader, visibly shivering with fear.

And then the blade was gone from his throat, flashing in Soleiman's hand as he reversed the *kampilan* in his grip, extending the long, ornately carved wooden hilt toward the teenager.

"Then take this," Manong Soleiman barked, gesturing toward the prostrate Emmanuel, "and take that dog's head."

No. The words died in Shawn's throat, fear choking him as he watched Aldam reach out, taking the sword.

"This isn't necessary," he heard Brent Kruta protest from his position by the tree. "Your best chance of surviving this, Soleiman, is to hold onto your hostages. If you give the government reason to believe that you're just going to kill them all, they'll come for you—hard."

"I have all the hostages I need," was the contemptuous

reply, a flash of fury as Soleiman glared at the teenager. "*Buhuat ta!*"

Do it.

Shawn heard Dolores scream again, saw Aldam begin to walk toward them—the sword swinging carelessly from his hand. Threw himself over Emmanuel's prostrate body, as if he could shield him from harm, their eyes meeting in that last moment—and he could see the resignation in his friend's face, his eyes closed, his lips moving in silent prayer.

Then hands descended on his shoulders, strong, rough hands tearing him away—his fever-weakened body unable to fight them off. He saw Khadafi's face over his shoulder, heard himself plead almost incoherently with the older Moro to intervene, to do *something*.

But there was no help to be found there, Khadafi's face hard and impassive. An almost imperceptible shake of the head, his only response.

And the sword flashed in the sun.

Chapter 21

"Mr. Ambassador," President Luis Maskariño greeted, coming around the corner of his desk as one of his aides showed the pair of diplomats into the Rizal Room.

"Mr. President," Ruan Liangzhi, the Ambassador of the People's Republic of China to the Republic of the Philippines, replied, a warm smile spreading across his face as he reached out, clasping Maskariño's hand. "Allow me to introduce my colleague, Senior Colonel Liu Xinshe, our defense attaché."

"We've met." Maskariño smiled as he shook hands with the officer. "The New Year celebrations at your embassy, wasn't it?"

"Your memory is excellent, Mr. President," Colonel Liu responded with a smile that seemed somehow less genuine than Ambassador Ruan's. Then again, the latter had become a good friend over the last few years—a career diplomat who had spent nearly three decades in the PRC's Ministry of Foreign Affairs, Ruan had extended family in Manila and an unfeigned love for the islands which had endeared him to Maskariño.

"Even as a child," he had said at their first meeting, not long after Maskariño had taken office, *"my mother would tell me stories of our cousins across the sea—of the cultural bond we in China shared with the Philippines. Coming here, in the twilight of my career. . .has been like coming home."*

"Please, gentlemen, have a seat," the Filipino president said, gesturing to the sofa as he sank into the armchair across from it. He was dressed far more casually than his Chinese counterparts—a dark blue polo shirt and khaki slacks opposed to their finely tailored business suits. He had never been one to stand on ceremony. "What can I do for you this morning, Liangzhi? Your office was. . .unclear on the reason for this meeting, but it seemed urgent."

"Indeed it was, Mr. President," Ambassador Ruan replied, the smile now gone, his tone utterly serious. "Colonel Liu has the details."

Maskariño turned toward the defense attaché, who was busy retrieving a file folder from the briefcase at his feet. After a moment, Liu rose, extending it toward him.

"Late last night, Mr. President, PLA(N) naval assets picked up a submarine transiting the Mindoro Strait. We believe it to have been an American *Ohio*-class. Possibly one of the *Ohio*-class boats converted into a guided missile submarine in recent years, and used for deploying their Navy SEALs. . ."

10:04 A.M.
The USS Michigan
The Sulu Sea

". . .we'll lock out here," Jason Guilbeau was saying, circling the location on the map with his pencil, "off the north coast of Jolo. Take the SDVs in to the beach. Which is where the Agency is supposed to meet us."

One of his men let out a groan, and Guilbeau laughed. "Yeah, I know. Our old friends. . .Christians in Action. But those are our orders, such as they are. If the stars align, they're supposed to procure vehicles for us. If they don't, well, we're going to have to hump it in from the beach, seven klicks. And that's even before we start climbing the mountain itself. Take a lot longer."

"What's our ETA there if we *do* have to walk?" Dom Zamora asked, sitting on the bunk a few feet away. Dom always wanted to worst-case every situation, one of the attributes that made him an effective second-in-command.

"Around 0400, if we get off smoothly," Guilbeau replied, knowing the odds of that were vanishingly small. Out in the field, Murphy was ever-present. "If the *Michigan* gets us there on schedule."

That was somewhat more likely. They seemed to have lost the Chinese submarine on leaving the Mindoro Strait— at least the *Michigan*'s sonar techs had reported no further contacts—and Piasecki had finally relaxed an hour or so before. *No harm, no foul.*

Dom made a face. "That's cutting it close. If the intelligence estimates of Soleiman's strength are accurate, we're outnumbered nearly three to one."

"Are those even sporting odds?" one of the younger SEALs asked, grinning across the narrow space at Zamora. "Hardly seems fair."

Dom didn't laugh. "It's a lot of people to keep track of when you're trying to rescue hostages. We need every edge we can get, and our NODs are a big one. Op continues past sun-up, we're pissing that away."

He was right. Guilbeau knew that and yet. . .their orders were crystal-clear. All they had to do was find a way to execute them.

"Point taken. Styer," he continued, moving on— addressing the SEAL who had spoken up, "once we reach the summit, I'm going to post you and Farris up here on the rim of the volcano to provide overwatch with the long gun and IR illuminator. Should have a clear shot at anything that breaks cover in the bowl below."

The problem being that there was a *lot* of cover—near the entire bowl covered with jungle, from what they had seen on the sat photos. They'd make do with what they had.

"How far are we talking?" Styer asked, leaning over to glance at the map.

"Little over three hundred meters across, rim to rim."

A smile. "Easy shot."

10:24 A.M.
Talipao
Jolo Island, Sulu Province
The Autonomous Region in Muslim Mindanao (ARMM)

In field operations, it wasn't just that plans never survived contact with the enemy—they rarely made it past your allies.

Or Murphy, ever skulking around the next corner.

"I'm fine, boss," Nate Carson retorted, the tight grimace on his face as he leaned back into the seat of the AFP Humvee belying the words. "Just need some Motrin—I'll be good."

Richards shook his head, glancing up the dirt road toward the village, Segovia's troops continuing their operation. His problems had just gotten that much more challenging, the night's operation hanging in the balance.

"No you won't, Airman," he said quietly, turning back to his friend. "That's a bad sprain. You're not going to be putting any more weight on it than you have to, next few days."

Carson had been poking around an abandoned nipa hut on the outskirts of the *barangay* with Mijares' commandos when it happened, his foot plunging through rotten flooring. His weight carrying him to the ground, twisting his ankle.

It would have to be our medic. He and Granby both had the basics, but Carson's expertise as a pararescue jumper far surpassed any skill of their own. Having him there when they recovered the Braleys, well. . .he would have said it was essential not five hours before. Now it would have not to be. *Off the table.*

"Jack," Carson spat, gritting his teeth against the pain, "I know my limits. I can *do* this, can be right there with you when we—"

"No, you won't," Richards cut him off, seeing Mijares approaching from the other side of the convoy. "The only place you're going is back to base."

10:37 P.M. Pacific Standard Time, December 23rd
The Westin
Henderson, Nevada

The inner door of the hotel suite closed behind the President and his wife and he stooped down, unlacing his leather wingtips and kicking them off before padding into the luxuriously-appointed bathroom, fiddling with the clasp of his pre-tied bowtie as he went. He had never learned to tie those things. . .had tried once in college and once more when first running for the senate and given up in frustration both times.

It had been a long evening—a benefit dinner in Vegas itself for children of the 12/24 victims. Politicians, business leaders, and Hollywood celebrities, come together to pay homage to the fallen and raise money to help those who had survived them.

The result had been several hours of listening to tedious speeches, offering his own brief, carefully-prepared remarks, eating very little, and through it all, attempting to maintain an appropriately grave expression, no matter what was being said to him in the moment.

All the mainstream media needed was a single photo of him laughing or even *smiling* too carelessly at such a function—stripped of context, it could be his ruin.

He had excused himself from it all at the earliest possible opportunity, using his need to prepare for tomorrow's commemorations as an excuse, though it was true enough. As much as he wanted to go to bed, he would be up for another hour or more going over his speech. And he had deferred his decision regarding JSOC till the morning, despite his initial promises to Shulgach.

There had been simply too much demanding his attention earlier, and the *Michigan* wouldn't even arrive off Jolo for another eight or nine hours. It was a decision worth sleeping on.

He walked over to the toilet, letting out a weary sigh as he unzipped the fly of his trousers. He would be glad when tomorrow was over, when—

"Mr. President," he heard Dennis Froelich call from outside the bathroom door, a curse exploding from Norton's lips as he hastily re-zipped his pants.

"What in God's name is it, Dennis?" he demanded, walking over and throwing the door open to confront his chief of staff. "Can't it wait?"

"I'm afraid not, sir. You have a call—from the Filipino president."

2:43 P.M. Philippine Standard Time, December 24th
Jolo Airport
Jolo Island, Sulu Province
The Autonomous Region in Muslim Mindanao (ARMM)

". . .of course, sir," Lieutenant Gringo Mijares replied, the phone pressed tight to his ear as he stood on the cargo ramp of the parked Philippine Air Force Airbus C-295, its fuselage shielding him from the mid-afternoon sun. "I'll be conducting my briefing in twenty minutes, by which time the NICA should be able to provide aerial reconnaissance of the target."

"Good," was the response from his commanding officer, Police Brigadier General Reynaldo Gonzaga, back in

Zamboanga City, at WESTMINCOM. "How soon can you move in?"

That was the hard question. . .the question he'd been mulling over ever since the morning, and he still didn't have an answer he was comfortable with. "Tomorrow night, likely," he said after a pause. "No sooner—we need to ascertain their strength and determine our best route up the mountain. Segovia wants to move in, cordon off the area, but we don't want to spook Soleiman, provoke him into executing his hostages."

Another pause, as Mijares looked out over the runway toward Camp Bautista, a grimace passing across his smooth face. "This with the Americans, sir. . .is it necessary?"

"It is, lieutenant," came Gonzaga's reply, without a moment's hesitation. "Only till tomorrow evening, though. The *Apolinario Mabini* and *Miguel Malvar* are en route to Jolo as we speak, on the orders of Admiral Amparo, backed by the *General Mariano Alvarez*. Once those vessels are on-station, our concerns with the Americans will be at an end."

"Yes, sir."

10:59 P.M. Pacific Standard Time, December 23rd
The Westin
Henderson, Nevada

"He thinks he can talk like that to me," President Richard Norton seethed, shoving the secure telephone into Froelich's hands as he emerged from the bedroom of the suite, the door slamming back against its stop. "To *me!*"

He paced half-way out into the middle of the suite before pacing back, his motions agitated, his face distorted with anger as he darted glances at what remained of his staff, most already long departed to their own hotel rooms.

"Get Nathan back on the phone," he bellowed finally, glaring at his chief of staff.

"Mr. President," Froelich began, nonplussed, glancing at his watch, "it's two in the morning on the East Coast. The general is likely asleep."

"Then you'll just have to *wake* him!" Norton exploded, punctuating his words with a curse as he started pacing again. "I need him, Dennis, I need him *now*."

Froelich looked chastened, his attention turning to the phone in his hand. "But of course, Mr. President. What's going on?"

"Maskariño. He knows—Soleiman's location, the *sub*. He knows *everything*."

3:04 P.M. Philippine Standard Time, December 24th
Camp Bautista, Jolo City
Jolo Island, Sulu Province
The Autonomous Region in Muslim Mindanao (ARMM)

". . .based on intelligence I was given at *Barangay* Kahawa, we now believe Manong Soleiman to be holed up in Mount Dajo National Forest, likely in the bowl of Bud Dajo itself," Lieutenant Mijares continued, glancing around the table in the conference room of the base operations building. "Along with the hostages."

"Kahawa?" Jack Richards asked, working to control his face as he glanced up from the map spread out before them. *They knew.* He didn't look at Granby or Russ Cole. Carson was back in the barracks, clutching an ice pack to his injured ankle. "That was the first of the five *barangays* we visited. . .six hours ago, and you never breathed a word of this, Gringo."

Mijares just looked at him. "You've done this before, Jack—you know how this works. Intel has to be corroborated, bolstered by supporting intelligence. And if we'd stopped our circuit at Kahawa, having found our answers—Abu Sayyaf would have had little difficulty in figuring out where we'd found them. Even now, I only say this here—among my own men. I think even Colonel Segovia would acknowledge the high likelihood that Abu Sayyaf has paid off men in his own ranks for information."

Richards cast a glance toward the AFP lieutenant colonel, but Segovia said nothing—just stood there, arms folded across his chest, any trace of geniality long gone from his countenance. Clearly as unwilling to confirm Mijares' accusation as he was unable to refute it.

"The NICA have their UAVs in the air once again, and should be able to confirm the presence of our targets on the mountain." The commando officer leaned forward and pressed a button on the conference phone in front of him. "De Rosales, what is your status?"

"Should be coming up on your screens any moment," the voice of the NICA intelligence officer back in Zamboanga City replied over the phone. "We're over the mountain."

Another minute, and the small computer monitor behind Mijares came to life, the streaming video feed from the orbiting ScanEagle buffering for a long moment before it began to stream, its cameras focused down into the jungle-covered bowl of Bud Dajo's cinder cone.

"And there they are," Richards heard Mijares breathe, his

own attention focusing in on the clearing—the men with weapons, scattered around its periphery. *Soleiman had a perimeter out.*

On the trails, too—like as not, at least a handful of men, posted up where it would be almost impossible to see them until you had tripped over them. This was going to be a treacherous assault, no matter who undertook it.

But they were up there, and there was nothing for it but to go get them.

"My troops can have that mountain encircled by nightfall," Segovia spoke up from the back of the room, arms folded across his chest, the sleeves of his uniform shirt rolled above his elbows. "No one in, no one out."

Mijares turned, meeting the commander's eyes. "I've seen the terrain—that's a promise you won't be able to keep. Not without spreading your men far too thin, rendering them all too vulnerable. Manong Soleiman isn't alone, and there are other factions of Abu Sayyaf already jockeying to fill the void left by his assassination of Abu Nazih. Wiping out an isolated unit of your men. . .it would offer just the notoriety needed to accomplish that."

"My men are capable—"

"And if you panic Soleiman," Mijares continued, cutting off Segovia before he could finish, "he's just going to kill everyone anyway. We want to keep those people *alive*. To do that, we must keep the circle on this small, and our footprint light. Hit him before he knows we know."

"I agree," Richards spoke up, making eye contact now with Granby and seeing a nod from his fellow Marine. It was the only approach that made sense, that gave them *some* chance of success. You could never have certainty, not in this life.

If the commando officer heard him, he gave no sign.

"As for our American friends, Colonel," he went on calmly, without so much as glancing in their direction, his attention still focused on Segovia, "I must ask that you take them into protective custody until the successful conclusion of our operations."

Chapter 22

3:09 P.M., December 24th
Camp Bautista, Jolo City
Jolo Island, Sulu Province
The Autonomous Region in Muslim Mindanao (ARMM)

Richards just stood there—his tall frame rigid, his obsidian-black eyes narrowing into dagger points as he stared across the table at Mijares. He heard Granby swear in disbelief and frustration, but it was William Russell Cole who beat them both to the punch.

"I must protest this," the hostage negotiator began, shaking his head, "on behalf of myself and my agents."

It was possible that his omission of the Agency was an oversight, but it seemed unlikely. *Friends like these. . .*

But Cole wasn't done. "We are representatives of the United States government, here to coordinate and liaise on the return of the Braley family. We—"

"And so you will," Gringo Mijares replied, a courteous, professional smile affixed to his placid countenance. "When they are rescued."

Something had changed here, Richards knew, watching

the man's face closely—his eyes. Something *had* to have precipitated this. "What is this really about, Gringo?" he asked after a long moment.

"It's about my orders," the commando officer replied, turning finally to look at him. "And about the sovereignty of my nation."

"Which the United States respects," Cole began again, his voice rising from the other end of the table in an indignation Richards found ironic, given the conversation they had had only a few hours before at the side of the road in Kahawa. "As we have made clear many—"

"Which is why," Mijares interrupted once more, looking Richards in the eye, "last night, an American submarine was detected passing through the Mindoro Strait, en route to Jolo. Because the United States *respects* Filipino sovereignty."

And there it was. It was hard to know what to say to that, but this wasn't a moment for hesitation. He shook his head, forcing a tight-lipped smile. "That all sounds above my pay grade, Gringo."

"As this is above mine," was the reply. "Colonel Segovia's men will look after you all—make sure you're comfortable. If you want anything, just ask. This should only take a few days. I—"

Whatever he had been on the brink of saying was lost as an orderly came into the room in that moment, his face drawn and pale—his words hushed as he spoke to Colonel Segovia.

Mijares fell silent, the entire room waiting expectantly—straining as if to catch a stray word.

Then Segovia turned to face them all, a grim look on the lieutenant colonel's face. "We just received a video, from

Manong Soleiman. The footage—delivered on a USB thumb drive by a *habal-habal* driver who has been detained for questioning—shows a fourth American hostage. And a severed head identified as belonging to Emmanuel Rogelio Asuncion, one of the Filipinos originally taken hostage along with the Braleys. . ."

4:13 P.M.
Malacañang Palace
San Miguel, Manila
Philippines

President Luis Maskariño leaned back in his office chair, his eyes closed as he kneaded his brow with his fingers, letting out a weary sigh. It was days like this that a man felt his age, he thought, savoring the first few moments of silence he had known since Ambassador Ruan had left his office, hours before.

And the call with the American president. . .

A weary smile crossed his face as he reached forward, opening the top drawer of his desk and removing a small wooden box. He set it on the desktop before him, pausing for a moment before opening the lid. Despite his friendship with Liangzhi, he wasn't fool enough to believe that the Chinese had his best interests at heart—even if President Norton's fumbling, stammering response had confirmed they *had* told him the truth.

No, they were playing their own game here, as ever—not unlike the Americans, as far as it went. The great powers, and their Great Game.

They both viewed him as a pawn.

He lifted the lid of the box and removed a thin sheet of hemp paper, laying it on the desk before retrieving a small pouch of cannabis from within an inner recess of the box, shaking a gram or so of the finely-ground weed onto the paper.

They were both wrong.

The Philippines had spent centuries in the thrall of one power or another. *Spain. . .America*—one colonialist scourge, exchanged for another, the nascent First Republic crushed by Americans who believed their little brown brothers incapable of self-governance. All those dreams of independence, of *liberty*, dying with the betrayal of Emilio Aguinaldo into American hands.

Maskariño pinched the joint tightly between his fingertips, rolling it back and forth as his eyes drifted over to the framed photograph of Aguinaldo sitting on his desk—an austere, unsmiling figure in a white linen suit, a bowtie encircling his throat. *A visionary.* Sold, ultimately, like Christ for thirty pieces of silver.

A lesson to be drawn there, doubtless. *Watch your step.*

He raised the joint to his lips and ran his tongue along the top edge, sealing it, like an envelope. Marijuana was officially illegal in the Philippines—he had, indeed, been one of foremost crusaders against all such drug use, since his days in Mindanao—but there was no one to challenge him, here in the Malacañang. And a man had to allow himself *some* vices.

Retrieving a pen from the desk in front of him, he packed the joint, tamping it down firmly before reaching for his engraved silver lighter—his eyes reflective as he lit up and took his first hit, staring out into space.

There was only one way for a country like the Philippines to survive in an age of great power competition—and it was by playing those powers off against each other, using each for your advantage and maintaining a scrupulous distance from each, no matter how hard they tried to drag you into their bed.

The only way. He leaned back in his chair, watching smoke drift out into the room as he exhaled softly—feeling the marijuana slowly begin to relax him, to melt away the tension the day had brought.

It had been necessary to put the American president in his place, to remind him of Manila's sovereignty. Of the limitations of his authority.

One of these days, it was going to be Beijing's turn. . .

4:49 P.M.
Station Manila
The Embassy of the United States
Ermita, Manila
Philippines

"What's your situation, exactly, Jack?" Darren Lukasik asked, leaning over the conference table—his knuckles pressed into the hard wood. His wife had planned for the two of them to take the kids to Christmas Eve Mass at the Immaculate Conception in the walled city, but he'd sent her a message when the call came in from Langley. *Wasn't happening.* Not with this. "Are you and your team all right?"

"We are," came the Texan's typically laconic reply from the speakers of the conference phone. "Just. . .the guests of the AFP at the moment. Here at Camp Bautista. I reckon you know more about that than I do."

They did. The last couple hours had plunged Manila Station into a whirlwind, forcing Lukasik to call back in personnel who had, similarly, been looking forward to a peaceful Christmas. Well, no one was getting one of those at this rate.

Ambassador Garner and Karen Lipscomb were off to Secretary Guidote's office at the Department of Foreign Affairs for what promised to be a stormy meeting, and President Norton was, apparently, still awake in Nevada and demanding updates.

And in the middle of it all, WESTMINCOM had forwarded the latest video from Soleiman, confirming their fears of Brent Kruta's abduction and putting on the table a new set of demands, along with a new deadline.

Forty-eight hours. For the Filipino military to begin withdrawing all forces from Jolo and for the payment of a five-million-dollar ransom for the return of all the American hostages.

He'd had a passing acquaintance with Kruta, dating back to their time in Iraq—but Baghdad had been a big station, hadn't known the man all that well. Still. . .that was one of their own out there, with a jihadist's sword to his throat. *Changed the game.*

Word from the Malacañang was that the troop withdrawal was a non-starter for Maskariño, no willingness to even negotiate the appearance of it, as a fig leaf for their own operations.

Which were now totally in the hands of the Filipinos, with their own team on Jolo grounded.

"What is your assessment, Jack, of the situation there on

the ground?" he asked, glancing over at his deputy chief of station—catching Campisi's grimace. They knew this line wasn't secure—that the AFP was controlling all their communications with Richards and his people at this juncture. *Unless he still had the phone. . .*

"The SAF is prepping for its own assault on Bud Dajo, supported by NICA aerial ISR assets."

Intelligence, surveillance, reconnaissance. Likely the ScanEagle UAVs they'd been using earlier.

"On what timetable?"

There was a lengthy pause—*too long*, Lukasik thought—before Richards replied, "Before the deadline. I'm afraid I don't have specifics."

That was almost certainly something less than the truth, a suspicion all-but-confirmed in the next moment as Richards added, "The AFP is on this call, sir, as I'm sure you're aware, but that doesn't change my assessment of our current situation, or my recommendation."

"Which is?"

"I would let the SAF commandos handle the assault," came the unexpected response, Lukasik and Campisi trading looks. But Richards wasn't done. "They know the terrain we're working with here, have the home court advantage—and we trained them, sir. They're good men. In my professional opinion, right now they're the best chance the Braleys have."

"Duly noted, Jack," Lukasik said finally, taken off-guard. The White House wasn't going to like this one bit. "I will pass that assessment up the chain. All I can do."

"Sometimes you just have to know when to fold 'em," Richards went on after another moment, sounding unusually morose, even for him. "Like that op in Tunis, few years back—you remember the one, sir."

He did, very well, a highly-sensitive mission deep into the Maghreb in the wake of the Arab Spring. He'd been at Tunis Station under Hoadley at the time. *But what did that have to do. . .*

"Comes a time there's nothing for it but to walk away," Richards continued, with only the briefest of pauses. "I'd like you to send a plane down here, sir, if you can. Tonight, before Christmas—fly us out to Manila, pick up the rest of the team in Zamboanga City on the way back."

"I believe—I believe I should be able to do that," Lukasik responded cautiously, glancing over at Campisi—his mind racing as he stalled for time. "The Bureau still have their Gulfstream parked at Ninoy Aquino, and I should. . ."

It hit him then, the realization washing across him like a riptide. "Yes," he added, more decisively, "I'll find a way to make it happen, Jack. Hang in there and I'll get these wheels in motion."

"What was all that about?" his deputy chief of station asked a moment later as he ended the call.

"I'm going to contact Langley," Lukasik said urgently, ignoring the question, "see if they'll make contact with Chamian for the release of the jet. I want you to find parachutes. Several of them—three, at least."

"Parachutes?" Campisi demanded incredulously, staring at him as though he had grown a second head. "Where am I supposed to find parachutes?"

"I don't know—task someone with it, there has to be some skydiving available around here or out toward Clark. Just find me some parachutes. When that plane leaves, they need to be on it."

He could see the light dawning in his deputy's eyes, breaking through the weary skepticism. "Then, all that crap about the op in Tunis. . ."

"We didn't walk away."

4:55 P.M.
Camp Bautista, Jolo City
Jolo Island, Sulu Province
The Autonomous Region in Muslim Mindanao (ARMM)

"There you go, Gringo," Richards said heavily, pushing back his chair and rising from the small table, the secure conference phone now silent. "I've done what I could."

He doubted somehow that it would accomplish anything—the command authority's position on this remarkably consistent, from the beginning. *American hostages—an American rescue op.*

"Did you mean it?" he heard Mijares ask from behind him, as he turned toward the door and the pair of soldiers waiting to take him back across the camp to the barracks where they were currently locked down. "What you said?"

The Texan paused, nodding slowly as he looked back at the commando officer, still seated there at the table. "I did. The raid with Mostapa. . .your men earned my respect that night. They've got this."

A tight-lipped, grim smile. "Thank you. I regret that it's come to this, Jack, truly. But I have my orders."

"I understand," Richards replied simply. *As did he.*

He hoped Lukasik had understood the Tunis reference—that he would come through for them. That he *could.*

5:01 P.M.
Bud Dajo—the crater
Jolo Island, Sulu Province
The Autonomous Region in Muslim Mindanao (ARMM)

The sun had already sunk well below the crater's rim off to the west, the bowl descending into a gloomy half-light just short of true darkness, the night's chill already raising the gooseflesh on Shawn Braley's forearms as he huddled in the shadow of a coconut tree.

He heard the buzzing of a mosquito around his ears, the insects homing in on their warm bodies in the gathering cold, but lacked the energy to reach up and slap it away.

It felt as though he had died, sitting there—watching his wife and daughter a few feet away, little Faith still sobbing brokenly into her mother's chest. She had seen. . .*everything.* Things no child should have ever had to see—the death of a beloved friend.

She had loved Emmanuel, loved joining in the hymn singing he had led, even here, in their captivity—her high, childish voice lifted up in praise. And now he was gone.

He *should* have died, Shawn thought, feeling a cold shudder run through his body. Would have, if Emmanuel hadn't intervened, but. . .*no.* That was a lie.

He would have given in, denied his Lord to save his life, the pistol muzzle against his brow driving out whatever remaining reserves of courage he might have thought he possessed.

That was what Emmanuel had saved him from—his own cowardice—a tormenting, despairing thought. He had wept then, unable to save him—unable to muster the courage to tear himself away from Khadafi's restraining hands. Forced to look on, helplessly, as it happened.

And then they had made the video, dragging Kruta into one of the broken-down nipa huts to film it—Aldam laughing hideously as he tried to carry the severed head after them, his fingers struggling and failing to find a purchase in Emmanuel's close-cropped hair.

A grotesque horror show, all of it—burning itself into his brain as if with a brand. He saw it now, every time he closed his eyes.

God forgive me, he felt himself pray, hugging his knees tighter to his chest. *I have failed You so miserably, all through the years—even as I believed I was doing Your work. I went my own way, trusting in success and prosperity, rather than You. Forgive me, Lord, and watch over my family—protect them and keep them—*

He felt something cold and hard prod his knee and looked up to find Aldam standing over him in the semi-darkness—the teenager's teeth showing in a grin as he poked Shawn once more with the barrel of his rifle.

"Don't go to sleep now," he said, laughing as Shawn shrunk instinctively away from him, back toward his family as though he thought he could shelter them from the threat. "You don't have that much time left to waste. . ."

3:08 A.M. Pacific Standard Time
The Westin
Henderson, Nevada

It just wasn't right, President Norton thought morosely, draining the last of his cup of coffee before replacing it on the table in front of him, listening as his advisers went back and forth—General Gisriel's image, appearing unusually informal in a dark polo and jeans, occupying the right half of the suite's main television screen. A weary-looking Secretary of State, to his left.

He was as tired as Sorenson looked, and unlike the SecState, desperately needed to be fresh for the morning, for the day of memorial services and speeches as the nation gathered to memorialize the worst terrorist attack on American soil since 9/11.

It was a day which would no doubt define the close of the first year of his presidency—perhaps even his whole political career.

And yet here he was, hours after that ghastly dinner—still awake, still running on the fumes of coffee, torn by the indecision of a fresh crisis. And Gisriel had gone over to the enemy.

"I'm inclined to concur with the Agency's assessment, Mr. President," the general was saying, an old Marine Corps enlistment poster from the First World War visible on the wall of his office just over his left shoulder as he stared into the webcam. *First to Fight.* "President Maskariño has drawn a clear red line here, and appears prepared to do his best to enforce it, judging by the actions he has taken with CIA and FBI personnel on Jolo. Given the critical role to be played by the Philippines in our overall effort to restrain Chinese influence in the region, that's a line we should be careful about crossing. And as Director Voss noted in her comments, Maskariño does have a more than competent SF outfit on hand in the Special Action Force, a police unit we trained and worked with for years through JSOTF-P. I believe General Shulgach was there himself, at least for a time."

"I was," came the reply, the JSOC commander's voice coming over the secure conference phone in the center of the round table. "And I concur—they're a solid group."

"The importance of our alliance with the Philippines is a point I have stressed many, many times over the duration of this crisis, Mr. President," Sorenson droned, seeming half-asleep. *As if I needed the reminder.* "If it is the assessment of JSOC and the intelligence community that this. . .'Special Action Force' can effect the Braleys' safe recovery, then I would strongly advise—"

"And what if they *can't?*" Norton demanded, coming to the end of his patience with these deliberations. He needed sleep. "What if something goes wrong, and they come to harm, and it becomes known that I sat by and allowed some tinpot third-world thug to overrule me when I had the SEALs within striking distance? What then?"

There was a long silence as Norton glanced around at his advisors in the room—toward those visible on the television screen. *Nothing.*

Then he heard Voss—the woman from the CIA—speak up from the conference phone, "In that case, Mr. President, I think you—"

"No," the President interrupted, cutting her off. "I won't have that on my conscience. General Shulgach, where is the *Michigan* at this moment?"

"Six hours out, Mr. President."

"Send them in."

Chapter 23

"Then for God's sake have someone *wake* Chamian," Darren Lukasik snarled in exasperation into the phone, his weariness bleeding through. "Or at least raise someone with the authority to release their plane. No one's getting a holiday this year—why should the Bureau feel special?"

"Because they're the feds," he heard, glancing up to see Campisi standing in the open door of his office, a wry grimace on his face. The station was already clearing out, down to its skeleton crew, people heading home to spend Christmas Eve with their families. Those who could.

His own wife and kids would be arriving at the basilica shortly, to take part in the Mass of the Solemnity of the Birth of Jesus, along with thousands of other worshipers. A part of him wasn't overly distressed to be missing it—he had never been the most religious of men, and the tradition was more his wife's than his own.

On the other hand, Christmas Eve Mass *was* a tradition they had tried to observe with sporadic success ever since the children were small—and even at his most cynical, he had to admit there was something awe-inspiring about the sight of so many people, brought together in worship, the ritual seeming to awaken something ancient and primal, even in the heart of an agnostic.

He reached forward to press the *mute* on the base of his phone, half-listening as the mid-level bureaucrat back at Langley tried to explain the differences of time zones and how most of the Bureau's senior people would still be asleep.

As if he didn't have a clock on his own wall—set to Eastern Standard—to tell him that.

"Any luck with the parachutes?"

A nod from Campisi. "Downstairs. It took some. . .doing, but we have them. You don't need to know the details."

Fair enough. Hard to know who they'd had to bribe, but they only needed to carry this charade off for the next few hours—likely wouldn't matter in the long run. "And the weapons?"

"Lort's down sweet-talkin' the Gunny. May have to place a call to Bangkok before it's all over."

Likely enough, Lukasik thought, shaking his head. The embassy's Marine detachment reported to Lieutenant Colonel Brian Eigenrauch, a hard-bitten Fallujah veteran and the commander of the Marine Security Guard's Region 3, headquartered in Thailand. Odds on, they weren't going to "borrow" so much as a pistol from his people without his say-so.

Which meant breaking up someone else's Christmas Eve. "Get it done."

8:47 A.M. Eastern Standard Time
CIA Headquarters
Langley, Virginia

"And we don't know where they are, or when they left?" Bernard Kranemeyer asked, glancing up from his papers. First the uproar from Manila Station, ruffling the Bureau's feathers over the use of their Gulfstream, and now this. . .it might have seemed as though the day could only get better, but the DCS was far too seasoned a cynic to buy it.

A rueful shake of the head from a weary Danny Lasker, who had been due to go home two hours before. "The Philippines aren't a primary collection target in the region. . .most of our assets are focused elsewhere."

"Elsewhere" being primarily Beijing. Such were their realities, Kranemeyer thought, acknowledging Lasker's words with a grunted curse, but it didn't make the challenge of this job any easier.

It was a shortsighted man who thought you only needed to spy on your enemies. You also needed to keep tabs on your friends—prepared for those odd moments when they might not be your friends anymore.

"So we just know that they're at sea?" A nod. Kranemeyer flipped open the folder again, staring down the stats laid out before him. The *BRP Miguel Malvar* had begun life as the *USS Brattleboro*, an escort ship built by the Pullman Standard Car Manufacturing Company out in Chicago, and originally laid down in October. . .of 1943.

She had first made it to the Philippines the following year, supporting American operations in the Battle of Leyte Gulf, and had spent nearly twenty years in the Cold War navy before being decommissioned and sold to the ill-fated Republic of Vietnam in 1966. When the end came, following the fall of Saigon in '75, the *Ngọc Hồi*—as the *Miguel Malvar* was then known—had fled to Luzon and been absorbed into the Philippine Navy, along with most of the other remaining VNN ships.

And so here she was, eighty years on, still serving in the capacity of an "offshore patrol vessel" like the other two ships on Lasker's list. A relic from a bygone age. It was like finding the *HMS Victory* at Jutland.

Which didn't mean that she wasn't more than capable of causing them headaches. If any of these three patrol vessels was cruising off Jolo when the *Michigan* put Red Squadron's SEALs ashore. . .well, the Mk.22 3"/50 main gun on the *Miguel Malvar*'s forward deck might have been ancient, but it was more than enough to give anyone downrange a bad night.

He let out a weary sigh. None of them were getting enough sleep these days. "Flash JSOC and CINCPACFLT—make sure the *Michigan*'s CO what he could be in for. Let them know what we don't know."

10:04 P.M. Philippine Standard Time
Camp Bautista, Jolo City
Jolo Island, Sulu Province
The Autonomous Region in Muslim Mindanao (ARMM)

"I'm not pulling my people out," William Russell Cole replied firmly, punctuating the words with an emphatic shake of the head. Behind him, there was another poker game going on, but it was just Granby, Carson, and the FBI agents now—the few SAF personnel left after they'd been moved into the smaller of the barracks buildings, now simply looking on, unsmiling as the Americans talked and played.

Mijares might have expressed his own regrets, but for his men. . .things had changed. Richards found it hard to blame them, truly. You could understand betrayal, rationalize it—perhaps even sympathize with a person's reasons—but it remained betrayal, for all that.

The CIA liaison operation with the Special Action Force had been the work of months, and all that hard-earned trust had been scuttled by the revelation that for the last few weeks, their American guests had been working to undermine them—to subvert their operations in favor of their own. You didn't get that sort of trust back.

It was the sort of consequences Washington rarely seemed to consider when imposing its will—at least not until the next time they went to do something and found themselves strangely lacking the allies to accomplish it. *Too late.*

"As long as the Braleys are in captivity," the hostage negotiator continued, "I'll stay and we'll continue to do whatever they'll allow us to do to bring about their safe return."

Whatever we can still do after you people upset the applecart, his look said, though his words were studiously restrained. It was clear he held the Agency responsible for how things had unfolded.

"They're not going to let you negotiate," Richards replied evenly. They'd had their orders, as Cole had his. What might have been *wisest* didn't enter into it. "You heard Mijares—it's going to be an assault, sometime between now and the deadline. You might as well get on the plane with us and save your outfit the fuel."

It still wasn't clear just when the plane was coming, or if it would be in time, but Lukasik had made contact forty-five minutes earlier, and the wheels *were* turning.

Cole snorted. "The HRFC won't be picking up the tab for your flight, rest assured. Langley's getting that bill."

That good old spirit of inter-agency cooperation.

"You think I don't want to?" he went on after a moment, favoring Richards with a hard look. "I have a daughter in an abusive marriage who needs to get out—I'd hoped to have her and the kids spend Christmas with me this year, but here I am, on the far side of the world, and she's still with *him*."

There was anger there, lingering just beneath the surface—a raw edge to the man's voice. *He was going to be a lot angrier after this night.*

"But I have a job to do here, and I'm going to do it."

10:38 P.M.
The USS Michigan
The Sulu Sea

"But they don't know where any of them are." Jason Guilbeau just stared across at the *Michigan's* CO, Derrick Piasecki, shaking his head in rueful disbelief. He caught Zamora's eye and swore softly. "What *was* the CIA able to give us?"

"Simply that all three of these 'offshore patrol vessels' have left port in the last twelve hours and are currently unaccounted for. The nearest is the *BRP Miguel Malvar*, which departed Naval Station Juan Magluyan in Tawi-Tawi, sometime between 0700 and 1400 hours today."

"That's quite a gap," Zamora observed, the irony rich in his voice. It was better than knowing nothing, but not by much.

Piasecki nodded. "It is. The *Miguel Malvar* is an old ship, but even so. . .she could well be ahead of us. Or at least will be, by the time your men are ready to lock out."

"How old of a ship?" Guilbeau asked, rubbing a hand across the rough stubble of his beard.

"Second World War." Piasecki caught their looks of surprise and shrugged. "One of ours, originally—decommissioned in the '60s and sold off. Ended up in the Philippines."

"Armament?"

"About what you'd expect from World War II. A three-inch main gun on the foredeck—handful of Bofors and Oerlikon guns."

More than enough. They would be locking out at depth,

so the presence of an old corvette didn't pose much of a threat to the *Michigan*, but the process was going to take the better part of an hour. And if it stumbled across his men in the water—or perhaps worse, regrouping on the beach. . .

"Just get us in place," he said finally, turning away from Piasecki. "We'll take it from there. They can't shoot what they can't see."

10:53 P.M.
Ninoy Aquino International Airport
Pasay, Metro Manila, Philippines

It *had* taken a call to Bangkok, but in the end, they'd gotten the cooperation they needed. Darren Lukasik hefted the long case on his back as he trudged up the stairs of the FBI Gulfstream G550, ducking his head as he entered the aircraft. The pilot and co-pilot were visible through the open door of the cockpit, going over their pre-flight checklist.

The Marines had loaned them a pair of M9 Berettas, packed along with a pair of mags for each in the hard case in Lukasik's right hand—as well as a couple M4 carbines and an 870 Modular Combat Shotgun, all with Aimpoints mounted on their tactical rails. The Manila detachment commander—a short, powerfully built Marine gunnery sergeant named Pociask—and a couple of the watchstanders had helped them jury-rig makeshift weapons cases for the jump, the more graciously once they'd realized two of the CIA officers they were ultimately helping were Corps alumni.

Semper fi.

"Thanks for taking this on, Matt," he said, straightening

to face his deputy as he shrugged the long guns off his shoulder, dropping them onto the sofa which ran along the interior of the Gulfstream's fuselage. There were a pair of encrypted tactical radios in the case as well, Agency-issue and set up with the freqs for DEVGRU's Red Squadron. Once the SEALs locked out and started in for the beach, they'd have comms.

Campisi just smiled in reply, accepting the pistol case from him, that weary, enigmatic smile of his which rarely betrayed anything more than cynicism. It was no different now. "Why not? Not every Christmas you actually get to be Santa."

11:37 P.M.
Bud Dajo—the crater
Jolo Island, Sulu Province
Autonomous Region in Muslim Mindanao (ARMM)

He should have been asleep. He knew that—if there was one thing his years with the Corps had taught him, it was the importance of sleep. Whenever and wherever you could get it. He'd slept on rocky Afghan hillsides, in the back of Blackhawk helicopters on exfil from a target—through mortar fire raining down on a FOB in Kandahar. Even standing up, once or twice.

But as Brent Kruta shifted restlessly against the bindings lashing him to the coconut palm, he knew sleep wasn't going to come.

A man saw a lot of things in more than a decade and a half at war—he'd stood in the aftermath of more than one suicide bombing, a street awash in blood and gore. Been there when a Marine in his squad was caught in the blast of an IED, a nineteen-year-old kid clutching the shredded remains of his thigh, screaming for his mother and mercy and Jesus Christ as they struggled to stabilize him.

They'd gotten him out, gotten him home—back to his family and his fiancee. *To recovery.* Three years later, not six months after the birth of his second daughter, he'd taken a pistol, gone out into the woods back of his parents' Ohio home, and shot himself. That was war.

But seeing a man beheaded in front of him, that blade slicing down through the air. . .there was something about it that defied reason, a raw, visceral fear that went beyond anything he had ever known before.

Even now, reflecting on the events of the afternoon—it sent a shudder through his bruised, battered body that had little to do with the cold. The Filipino woman—Annalyn, he had heard Charity Braley call her—had brought a blanket over to him as it had gotten dark, but the teenaged fighter they called Aldam had kicked it away not long after, laughing as he did so before swaggering away with his rifle held over his shoulder. *Power.*

He had seen it the world over, in conflict zones from Latin America to Africa, the Middle East and Afghanistan. Stick a gun in a kid's hand and he thought he was king of the world. No—*god.*

Give him power over people who couldn't fight back. . .and you created that most dangerous and unpredictable of monsters—one with no sense of his own limitations.

I'm sorry, he thought, his mind wandering, conjuring up an image of his wife, Heidi. The last five years had been hard for her, since the Crohn's diagnosis—the career change to Svalinn had been meant to bring them both financial stability and comparative peace of mind.

Instead it had brought him to his death. *The irony*. Life was funny like that—nothing ever so certain as its end.

An end, Kruta realized as he shifted position once again, his bruised and battered body protesting against the exertion. . .which had finally arrived.

8:16 A.M. Pacific Standard Time
Las Vegas Metropolitan Police Department Headquarters
Las Vegas, Nevada

"But of course, Mrs. Zimmerman," President Norton murmured sympathetically, taking the widow's hand in both of his own, the hubbub in the lobby of the LVMPD Headquarters' Building B swelling around them. "I remember meeting you and your son last January, on my first visit after the attacks. Your husband was a brave man, and a credit to both this department and his country."

It seemed as though he had said those words a dozen times already in the few minutes since he had entered the building—his Secret Service detail cutting through the sea of police khaki around them, serving LVMPD officers and the families of their fallen, all gathered here this morning to meet with their President.

And there had been *many* of the fallen, last Christmas Eve. Responding to the downing of Delta Flight 94 by a shoulder-launched missile, Metro's Zebra units—the LVMPD SWAT—had rolled right into an ambush just off State Route 589 down in Winchester and been utterly disemboweled by the ferocity of the attack. RPGs, automatic weapons—a *car bomb*—the SWAT officers had found themselves in the middle of a war without warning, and the 40-man Zebra unit had suffered nearly 80% casualties, burying eighteen of their own in the days and weeks that followed.

He couldn't remember if Wayne Zimmerman had been caught in that ambush or not—he didn't, actually, remember meeting his widow or her son the previous January at all, despite his words of comfort—but laying a wreath and giving a speech at the ambush site was on his schedule for late morning. Another ceremony among the many this day.

Hopefully then, as here, his staff would do their best to ensure that he got everyone's name. Maybe by then he'd have news from the Philippines. So long as no one screwed up.

God, help no one to screw up, he found himself thinking anxiously as he moved down the line, shaking a grim-faced officer's hand—stooping to look a little girl in the eye. *I need a win.*

12:23 A.M. Philippine Standard Time, December 25th
Jolo Airport
Jolo Island, Sulu Province
The Autonomous Region in Muslim Mindanao (ARMM)

The runway lights were lit tonight for the first time since the Filipino military had locked down the airport following the SAF's arrival—a long double line of lights stretching out into the night.

The Gulfstream, already on final approach—somewhere out there in the darkness.

"What are our odds, you think?" Titus Granby asked quietly, glancing over at Richards from where he leaned against the hood of a US military surplus deuce-and-a-half, the shadows of the big truck looming large in the airport lights.

"I think it's going to be the toughest jump of our lives." Richards caught Granby's look of surprise and found himself suddenly wondering just how many jumps his partner even had under his belt.

It had been a part of his training with MARSOC, for sure, but if his time in the Corps had been anything like Richards' own. . .the actual combat jumps had been few and far between. Most of his jumps were with the Agency, and Granby wasn't that long out of training.

"Wish I was going with you two," Carson said regretfully, his face pained in the glare of the runway lights. His ankle was still swollen, despite the hours of ice, and he stood awkwardly, trying to keep his weight off it.

So do I, Richards thought. As a PJ, Carson probably had more career jumps than the rest of them put together. Parker or even Ardolino would have been a better choice than Granby for this end of things, and he would have felt better about this if they had been along in any case—but he'd felt the risk of the Filipinos getting wise to their plans was far too great if the Gulfstream had stopped in Zamboanga to pick up the rest of the team. Hopefully Lukasik had arrived at the same conclusion. If—

"Jack," he heard a voice call out, turning to see Gringo Mijares walking across the tarmac toward their position, his hand extended as he approached Richards.

"Have a good flight back to Manila," Mijares said, a tight smile on his face as he shook first Richards' hand, then Granby's and Carson's—the approaching whine of turbofans growing in intensity as the FBI's Gulfstream G550 descended out of the night, the white smoke billowing out from its tires visible in the runway lights as it touched down, racing toward them with seemingly undiminished speed.

Richards nodded by way of reply. "Best of luck out there," he added after a moment, staring earnestly at his counterpart, "with the Braleys. Bring them out safe."

"Of course, Jack. My men won't let you down."

"I know they won't." *The final betrayal*, Richards thought, with a distinct sense of regret. That statement, at least, honest enough.

But the Gulfstream had already taxiied to a stop, not fifty meters away—its stairs folding out from the fuselage. A final handshake and he turned away, slapping Carson on the shoulder. "Come on, let's go."

Chapter 24

12:38 A.M. Philippine Standard Time, December 25th
Jolo Airport
Jolo Island, Sulu Province
The Autonomous Region in Muslim Mindanao (ARMM)

"So you understand what I need you to do?" Jack Richards asked, adjusting the straps of his parachute as he stood in the open cockpit door of the Gulfstream, his gaze shifting between the pilot and co-pilot.

"I do," the FBI pilot replied, his face twisting in a look of discomfort. He was maybe ten years Richards' senior, his dark hair already streaked with gray. *We'll add a few more of those tonight.* "But I've never done anything like this before, ever."

"And that's why I need you to listen carefully—because I have." He reached down, making sure the Beretta M9 rode securely in its holster on his right hip. The long guns were going to be the issue in this jump, first getting them out the Gulfstream's baggage door without getting hung up, second getting down with them. Station Manila's jury-rigged weapons cases were. . .just that. Better than nothing, he supposed. "We don't have much time before the tower's going to start asking what's up. You're going to take us up to ten thousand feet before heading west along the coast—the drop point is only six miles out."

A heartbeat, in this plane. "As we near the drop, you're going to need to cut your speed down to just above stall, maintaining altitude just north of ten thousand. That's when we—"

"I don't think we should be doing this at all," the co-pilot interjected, the words directed not at Richards, but his colleague. "Nothing was said about any of this back in Manila, before we took off, and it has to be a violation of Filipino sovereignty to—"

"It is." Matt Campisi cut him off, shouldering his way past Richards and into the cockpit. "One that has been sanctioned by the command authority. So get us in the air."

12:44 A.M.
The BRP Miguel Malvar
The Sulu Sea, three miles northwest of Jolo

In the skies above, the moon played hide-and-seek among the clouds, the foam of the *Miguel Malvar*'s wake glistening white in its faint rays. Off to starboard, the lights of Jolo City—what there were of them—glittered in the darkness. The island was under a strict curfew, part of the martial law imposed on Mindanao and points south not long after Luis Maskariño had come to office.

Teniente de Navio Adrian Bolaños, the *Malvar's* executive officer, stood on the ship's darkened bridge, hearing the soft murmur of voices around him as the ratings went about their work, grey ghosts in their newly-issued CAMOPAT uniforms, the faint glow of the electronics providing their only illumination.

On a normal night watch, the mood in the bridge could be quite light—men exchanging banter and barbed insults as they carried out their duties, in the way of sailors since time immemorial. Tonight was different, and you could *feel* it as well as hear it. They were at battle stations, for the first time in some of these young sailors' lives, and this was no drill—as the live ammunition being carried forward to the 3-incher on the foredeck bore witness, the shadowy figures of sailors manning the 20mm Oerlikons on the bridge wings.

The orders to sail out from Tawi-Tawi on Christmas Eve had come as a surprise to Bolaños—and everyone else onboard—their mission objective, all the more so. He had a cousin in the United States, living with his family in the suburbs of Orlando—had visited them himself only the previous summer.

It seemed inconceivable that his ship could possibly be heading into a confrontation with an American vessel, and yet. . .he had read the orders himself, their wording crystal-clear.

What was far less clear was what they were expected to do in the event of such a confrontation, should it take place before they effected a rendezvous with the newer ships due on station in the morning and late afternoon. What little anti-submarine capacity the *Miguel Malvar* had once possessed had been stripped out in a refit in the early '90s, when Bolaños himself had still been a small child, leaving them with only the guns. Perhaps if they caught the Americans on the surface. . .

The odds of that seemed vanishingly small, their Raytheon surface-search radar still displaying no unaccounted-for contacts. Still, there was no way of knowing when that might change.

Bolaños felt the ship shudder beneath him, its diesel engines pushing power to the twin propellers as it turned, the petty officer first class behind him announcing their new heading. *Seven-two*, bringing them east-northeast along the northern coastline of Jolo. . .

12:47 A.M.
The USS Michigan
The Sulu Sea, four kilometers north of Jolo

The water was surprisingly warm, enveloping Guilbeau's face as he leaned back up against the metal side of the Dry Deck Shelter bolted onto the upper hull of the *Michigan*, his hand on the pistol grip of his short-barreled HK416 rifle—breathing steadily through his Draeger rebreather as he and his men waited for the water pressure inside the chamber to equalize with the ocean without.

It was pitch-black in the DDS, and he could sense, rather than see, the presence of the men surrounding him—the seven men of his assault team, plus a pair of drivers from the SDVT-1 task unit, the minisub itself resting on the "floor" before them, so close he could have reached out and kicked it with a flippered foot.

Zamora was with the remaining SEALs and the other SDV in the opposite shelter, the second of the two disturbingly-coffin-like chambers which clung like barnacles to the *Michigan*'s hull.

It felt as though they had been enveloped in darkness for an eternity now, though he knew it couldn't have been much more than twenty minutes since they'd entered the chamber as the *Michigan* crept ever closer to the Jolo coast. Ahead of schedule, if ever so slightly. Guilbeau reached up self-consciously, touching the slight bulge of the crucifix around his neck, beneath the wetsuit. Perhaps God was smiling on them this night.

They were, after all, going out to bring His people home.

The doors of the chamber opened then, and Guilbeau felt the man next to him kick away from the wall, disappearing out into the watery void beyond.

Guilbeau followed him out, just making out Zamora's team exiting their own chamber across from them, vaguely human shapes recognizable only by their movement.

Above and behind them, the *Michigan*'s sail loomed large in the murk-dark waters, an imposing presence—its dive planes looking like the fins of some great fish.

He took his hand off his carbine, letting it hang free from its sling as he turned back toward the deck shelter, helping his men tow the SDV out onto the deck of the now-motionless *Michigan*. Each minisub held six men—the pair of SDVT-1 drivers and four passengers. It was going to take two trips to get everyone on the beach.

It took several men on the tow ropes to draw the minisub from within the chamber, the weight of the submersible itself and the water resisting their efforts as they brought it out.

Whaley and Schrom, the SVDT-1 operators, took their positions almost immediately, going over the pre-mission checklists and checking their instruments.

And that was when he felt a hand descend on his arm—looked up into another goggled face, only inches from his own. *Dom.*

Only the man's eyes were visible, and those just barely, but he knew, without a word being spoken. *Something was wrong.*

12:48 A.M.
The Gulfstream

The slipstream howled through the open baggage door of the business jet, a cold wind that stung Richards' face as he stooped down in the opening, the Remington modular shotgun in its weapons case strapped to his side, his tall, lanky frame bent nearly double in the Gulfstream's cramped baggage compartment.

The whine of the jet's Rolls-Royce turbofan was deafening now, drowning out all else, the left engine nacelle literally right *there*, scant feet away from his face. So close it seemed as though he could reach out and touch it.

Going out the baggage compartment and under the nacelle was the only safe way to make the jump—even assuming they'd been able to open the forward door in flight, anyone attempting to jump from it would run the risk of getting sucked back into the engine. Not the best way for a man to die.

He felt the Gulfstream nose up, cutting even more airspeed as they approached the drop point—moving until he was crouched in the door itself, gazing down into the night. The dark water and darker land, stretched out below him. *Any moment now.*

And then he felt Granby's hand descend on his shoulder, squeezing firmly once, then twice, and he pushed himself away from the aircraft, hurtling out into nothing, the abyss reaching out to enfold him.

The wind tore past his helmet as he fell through the sky, the curiously weightless sensation of freefall enveloping him. It felt as though a man could fall forever in moments like this—no longer a creature of earth, but the heavens. A strangely seductive feeling.

In reality, a clock had started ticking the moment he kicked free from the plane—a clock that could only run so long without ending in his death. His mind, counting down the seconds with remorseless precision. *Twenty-three. . .twenty-four. . .*

Granby should be following him down—somewhere in the darkness above, running a similar count, a few seconds behind. Protocol would have said he should have jumped first, with Richards—as senior officer—bringing up the rear, but after assessing the dimensions of the Gulfstream's baggage compartment, they'd reversed the order. *Tall guy first.*

*Twenty-eight. . .twenty-nine. . .*when the mental count hit *thirty*, Richards reached back, seizing the handle of the pilot chute in its pouch on the back of his right leg strap, throwing it forcefully out and away from him—the pilot chute billowing up into the night behind him, pulling his primary from the pack on his back.

A heartbeat, and he felt the primary chute deploy, pulling back against his shoulders as it brought him upright. He looked up to see a neon-orange sport canopy unfolded in the sky above, and shook his head at the irony of it all.

We're not in Kansas anymore.

Below him, the line of breakers were visible now, white foam against the billows—the dark jungle beyond the beach, houses scattered amid the tree cover. They were going to come down in someone's backyard, like as not.

Nothing for it but to settle in for the ride. And hope they didn't have dogs.

12:53 A.M.
The USS Michigan
The Sulu Sea

The second SDV wouldn't start. It was impossible to know why, whether something had gone wrong in how it was stored in the dry deck shelter on the long voyage down from Fleet Activities Yokosuka, or if there could possibly have been a defect in the submersible's lithium-ion batteries developing earlier—even back to the flight out from Pearl, though Guilbeau respected the professionalism of the SDVT operators enough to think they would have run equipment checks at Kadena and since.

The only thing he knew for certain as he stood there on the deck of the guided missile submarine, sixty feet beneath the waves, was that Murphy had pounced—ever that bane of field ops. Whatever advantage their early arrival on-station had conferred, already slipping away, faster with every passing moment.

Comms with the *Michigan* were nearly impossible—at least without sending a man back in, which would waste even more precious time. And falling back on the lone remaining SDV would require four trips in and back, isolating a small group of SEALs on a hostile beach for far too long. Leaving them exposed, and delaying their ETA at the mountain, possibly well past sun-up. *Unacceptable.*

Their only other option was. . .risky, in light of the intel reports about the Philippine Navy units converging on the island. Then again, how many times over the years had the CIA been wrong?

Lots.

Guilbeau allowed himself a tight smile behind the facemask, and reached out, putting a hand on Zamora's shoulder and gesturing back into the dark caverns of the dry deck shelters, making his intent as clear as he could without words.

Launch the Zodiacs.

12:56 A.M.
Patikul
Jolo Island, Sulu Province
The Autonomous Region in Muslim Mindanao (ARMM)

The deserted road came rushing up to meet Richards' feet as he guided himself in through the gap in the trees, the light northeasterly breeze on his face as he pulled down on both of the parachute's steering toggles in unison, slowing his descent.

His boots hit the dirt with a *thud* and he took a few running steps forward, burning off the last of his momentum as the square chute began to collapse behind him, its garish orange canopy still tugging weakly at his shoulders.

He turned back, pulling it down after him before shrugging off the harness and removing his helmet—just in time for

Granby to come into view maybe twenty meters further down the road, flaring out as he descended below the treetops.

The jungle was dark around them, the fronds of the palms scattered along both sides of the road looming ominously in the night, the road rutted and muddy from the previous day's rain.

They couldn't be more than half a klick in from the beach, but it was a half-kilometer of jungle sprinkled with countless small huts and outbuildings, as Richards had observed, gliding in over the trees.

And they were deep in Abu Sayyaf territory here, just a few kilometers from Jolo proper. All Segovia's warnings of a *"pantakasi"*—cockfight derby—coming back to mind as Richards pulled his parachute off the road, burying it in the vegetation until the orange fabric was nearly invisible. They needed to link up with DEVGRU's people, and fast.

By the time Granby rejoined him, he'd retrieved the Remington 870 from its weapons case and racked a shell into the chamber, fully extending the stock back against his shoulder.

"You good?" the younger man asked as he came up, his M4 carbine held at the low ready.

"I'm good. Let's go steal a car."

1:07 A.M.
The USS Michigan
The Sulu Sea

"How long have you had the contact?" Commander Derrick Piasecki asked, leaning over his sonarman's shoulder to look at the screen.

"No more than two, three minutes, sir," the young man replied. "I sent for you the moment we identified it."

"You think it's the *Malvar*?" Piasecki asked skeptically, eyeing the contact, now designated Sierra-73 on the screen before them. *Bad time for it to show up.*

"It fits the profile, yes, sir. Twin screws, and about the right size for a corvette. And we're well out of the sea lanes here."

That much was true enough, the *Michigan*'s CO reflected. The last few hours, on the final inbound track toward Jolo, they'd encountered no major traffic and few contacts at all.

And now they had swimmers out, with no way to communicate with them.

"How long before she's on us?"

"Fifteen minutes."

1:13 A.M.
The Sulu Sea

Water sluiced off Jason Guilbeau's wetsuit as he heaved himself up and over the gunwale of the Zodiac CRRC— Combat Rubber Raiding Craft—rocking gently in the ocean swells.

Getting the SDVs back in their shelters and the Zodiacs inflated and on the surface in under twenty minutes had been a herculean undertaking, but they had pulled it off. *Now the real fun begins.*

Their mission, only beginning. He spat out the rebreather and pushed up his face mask, glancing across to Zamora, who was acting as coxswain of the other Zodiac.

"All right," he began, "we're going to take the boats in to a klick out from the beach, cut the engines and paddle the rest of the way in. Hundred and fifty meters out, we'll hold up and try to raise the Agency—see if they're in position. If not. . ."

He gestured to Styer, lying on the gunwale to his right and Melhorn, one of the SEALs in Dom's boat.

"You two will swim in and secure the beach. Everyone copy?"

"Solid copy, Senior."

He took his position near the bow, his carbine trained outward as the Zodiacs' outboards sprung to life, the rhythmic sound of their four-stroke motors filling up the night. *Time to do this.*

Time to go bring the Braleys home.

Chapter 25

1:19 A.M.
The BRP Miguel Malvar
Three kilometers north of Jolo

"Sir, you need to take a look at this." There was a curious edge of worry in the radarman's voice, and Bolaños pushed himself out of his chair on the *Malvar*'s bridge, moving to where the man stood, monitoring the screens of the AN/SPS-64(V)11 surface-search radar.

"What is it?" It had been a quiet night thus far, but something deep within his gut told the executive officer that was about to change.

"It's this," the radarman replied, gesturing to the screen. "We have a contact, right. . .there, sir. About fifteen hundred meters off the starboard bow. It's not a ship, or even a fishing boat—the signature isn't even close to right, and if there was, we would see it, but there's something out there, all the same. It—"

He could feel the prickle of danger dance up and down his spine, a premonition that bordered on certainty. But there could be no hesitation, not in this moment.

"Wake the captain," Bolaños spat, turning on a surprised ensign standing there a few feet behind him. "Do it—*now*."

1:21 A.M.
Patikul
Jolo Island, Sulu Province
The Autonomous Region in Muslim Mindanao (ARMM)

Almost. . .there. Richards clenched the penlight between his teeth, aiming it at the mess of wires emanating from the ripped out side of the old Toyota HiAce's steering column.

They'd already jacked an old four-door Accord, back closer to the main road, but they needed capacity—and a family car just wasn't enough to transport sixteen SEALs to their target.

Which is how they had ended up here, less than ten meters from an almost-certainly-occupied house, hotwiring an old passenger van. At least there hadn't been any dogs. *Yet*.

Richards raised his head, glancing through the spider-veined glass of the windshield to make out Granby's figure on the other side of the truck by the hood, his carbine held across his chest, at the ready. They'd put the van in neutral and pushed it as far away from the squat concrete-block residence as they could, but the lane was as rutted as the road had been, and the logistics were difficult to manage. . .a nipa hut along the alley back to the road cramping their maneuver room. In the end, you only had so much time—and some risks you had to take.

He brought the edge of his knife back against the bunch of wires in his gloved hand, cutting them loose from the

350

ignition cylinder before beginning to strip away their protective rubber coating.

Madness. All of this was madness, the rational part of his brain protested—knowing that if there *was* a disturbance, they were likely dead men. Lukasik had gotten them weapons, yes, but no suppressors. The minute a shot was fired. . .

He had been part of some dicey operations over the years, but this was in the hard running for first place. *And all of it so easily avoided.*

But that wasn't getting this van hotwired any faster. He separated the ignition and battery wires, the naked wiring glinting in the gleam of the penlight, preparing to wrap them together. . .and that's when he heard a man's voice call out anxiously into the darkness from the door of the nipa hut, *"Kinsa ang naa diha?"*

Richards' head came up, his fingers releasing the wires as if he'd been shocked—dimly making out a slight figure standing just outside the hut, behind the low fence, in the split-second before he hunched down behind the Toyota's wheel, trying and failing to make himself small. He spat out the light and switched it off, praying the man hadn't seen the flash.

Go back in, you fool. The knuckles of his right hand turned white around the knife—the Remington in his left. *Just turn away.*

Granby had vanished, probably taking cover on the far side of the van, but he was exposed—the door of the van conspicuously open, and in the man's line of sight.

"Kinsa ang naa diha?" the man repeated, taking a few steps out and away from his house. The translation was lost

on Richards, but he could guess. *Who's there?*

Turn around—go back inside and lay back down beside your wife. There's nothing for you here.

He didn't want to have to kill a man for just protecting his own. Didn't want to—but knew he would, the knife cold in his hand. *To protect* his.

Every fiber of his body tensed, his muscles coiled for action as the man advanced closer, coming even with the front of the Toyota.

It was clear the Moro knew something was wrong, that he was expecting trouble—his approach tentative, as though he sensed a trap.

"Paghunong diha!" Granby's voice, no louder than a low hiss, even as he appeared around the front of the van—his weapon raised in the darkness.

The man froze in place, his mouth opening as if to utter a cry of surprise—and Richards was out and around the door, slamming the buttstock of the Remington into the side of the Moro's skull.

He went down hard, a soft, strangled moan escaping his lips as he crumpled unconscious into the dirt and mud.

Richards stooped over him as Granby circled the front of the HiAce, checking to make sure he was out.

"That was close," Granby announced softly, lowering the M4. "I thought for su—"

He never finished his sentence, a distant sound from out to sea striking both their ears, like a clap of thunder or the report of a gun.

A very big gun.

1:24 A.M.
The Zodiac
The Sulu Sea

The shell went high and wide, exploding nearly sixty meters off to port in an angry black-orange burst of fire, Guilbeau's face blanching beneath the greasepaint. They had cut the engines when the corvette first appeared, still nearly two klicks back out to sea, hoping to reduce their sound profile and visibility, eliminating the telltale white wake of the outboards.

It hadn't worked—the Filipino warship closing the distance steadily until they heard the call over the loud hailer, ringing out across the waves. *Stop.*

He had elected to ignore the order—every stroke of their paddles bringing them closer to the shoreline, still well over a kilometer away. Every moment they could buy, precious.

And that was when the shell had come roaring in, quite literally across their bow.

"Start 'em back up," he bellowed, rising up from his position on the forward gunwales, his carbine clutched in his right hand. There was no time for indecision, not now. Flight or surrender, their only alternatives, staring down the muzzle of the corvette's deck gun—the latter, unacceptable.

"Dom!" he called across to the other boat, raising his voice as Shing restarted the motor and their outboard roared back to life, "take your people out of here!"

The small craft seemed to leap forward, churning through the water—the jolt taking Guilbeau back to his knees—hugging the hard rubber of the gunwale as they veered away from the other Zodiac, making for the beach at top speed.

They had a chance, the senior chief thought, the spray lashing his face as he pressed himself into the gunwale—they were small targets, and fast. If it was the *Malvar*, if the CIA's intel had been accurate—they were on the receiving end of an eighty-year-old artillery piece.

No less deadly for its age, but manually aimed—and loaded. *Slow.*

It was a small edge, but it was all they had. It would just have to be enough.

And then he heard it, that unearthly, whistling sound coming in again—like an oncoming freight train.

1:26 A.M.
The BRP Miguel Malvar

"Another miss," the gunner's mate serving as spotter announced, marking the white shell splash against the darkness of the sea. "Down five degrees, over two."

Seaman First Class John Carl Reyes tossed aside the smoking hot shell casing, stepping back to let his fellow loader slam another 24-pound shell into the breech. Metal scraping against metal as the petty officer on the gun cranked it vigorously into position.

The Americans' boats had split up now, seeming to dance over the waves at top speed as they raced for the beach, once again ignoring *Teniente* Bolaños' order to stop over the loud hailer.

Reyes' pulse beat faster with excitement at the sight and he raised a hand to cup his ear as the chief took the lanyard in his hand, pulling it back—hard and quick.

The report reverberated across the deck, the young

seaman's ears still ringing as he scooped up a shell—hurrying it forward to the breech. He'd joined the navy right out of high school three years before—had been on the *Malvar* for the last two—but he'd never seen its guns fired outside of training.

Until tonight.

9:31 A.M. Pacific Standard Time, December 24th
Desert Springs Hospital Medical Center
Las Vegas, Nevada

". . .the debt this country owes to you and your staff, Dr. Bala, is one it can never fully repay."

It seemed as if he had said those words so many times already this morning—and would say them again so many more. It all seemed so. . .insincere, somehow, the repetition of the same thing, over and over again. As a politician, he should have been used to that, and yet he had worked so *hard* to convince himself that he was different.

Many of the wounded and dying from the Bellagio had been brought here, last Christmas Eve, to Desert Springs—all but overwhelming its emergency room's staff. It was due to their skillful treatment that Representative Gilpin had survived her own injuries.

"It is my honor to—"

"Mr. President." It was Froelich—the President struggling to conceal his annoyance at the interruption as he turned toward his chief of staff.

"What *is* it, Dennis?"

"It's urgent, Mr. President—I need to speak with you at once. Privately."

"Dr. Bala," Norton said, forcing a tight smile to his face, "would you give us a moment? May we have the use of your conference room?"

His Secret Service detail led the way, the door barely closing behind the group before the President turned on Froelich. "What is it that couldn't wait, Dennis? You know how important this is—the media is here, and—"

"We've received a CRITIC from CINCPACFLT, sir—forwarded from the CO of the *USS Michigan*, not more than ten minutes ago. A Filipino naval vessel was, at that time, closing on their location and potentially endangering the DEVGRU team." Froelich paused, weighing his words as if not quite believing them himself. "Mr. President, the *Michigan*'s CO has requested authorization to engage, and if necessary, sink the Filipino warship if the SEALs' lives are placed in jeopardy."

He thought for a moment that he had misheard, and then his chief of staff's words sunk home, in all their horrifying reality. "You're asking me to—I mean, that. . .what he's suggesting would be an act of war."

"That is CINCPACFLT's assessment, yes, Mr. President. But if Red Squadron's men *were* in harm's way. . ."

It was unfathomable. Norton just shook his head, staring at Froelich as though he expected to find some reassurance in the man's eyes. "No," he said finally, "no. . .absolutely not. Authorization denied. The Filipinos—they wouldn't *dare*."

1:32 A.M. Philippine Standard Time, December 25th
The Zodiacs
The Sulu Sea

Just ahead, not thirty meters off, the white foam of the breakers glistened in the pale light of an unfriendly moon—pain shooting like fire through Guilbeau's shoulder as he swam forward, stroke after agonizing stroke—a crimson stain blossoming out through the waters.

They'd come *so* close, he'd almost thought they were home free. And then that last shell had come screaming in, exploding not far off their bow. Shrapnel spraying the Zodiac, shredding a handful of the raft's airtight inflatable chambers—a hunk of hot, sharp metal burying itself in Guilbeau's shoulder.

The raft had begun to lose integrity almost immediately, and everyone had ended up in the water in a confused, struggling mass.

A breaker caught him in the face and he shook his head to clear his eyes, gritting his teeth against the pain as he threw himself into it. *Almost there.*

He hoped Zamora had known better luck—hoped his own men were all still alive. It had been impossible to tell in the water, chaos reigning supreme as the Zodiac went down and the Filipino corvette closed, edging in even closer to the coastline.

There was barely fifteen feet of water out there—they had all studied the depth charts extensively preparing for their run in with the SDVs—but it didn't matter. The *Malvar* drew less than ten.

No salvation to be found there.

Even now, as he collapsed on the dirty sand of the narrow beach, his ears still ringing from the explosion, he could hear it—the officer's voice calling out over the *Malvar*'s loud hailer. Calling on them to stand down. *Surrender.*

Guilbeau rolled over on his back in the sand, clutching the H&K to his chest. The piercing beam of the corvette's searchlight sweeping through the night about ten feet over his head. They needed to regroup, orient themselves—get back on mission.

If they could.

Footsteps there, off to his right—he felt the presence more than he heard it, his shoulder burning as he threw himself into position, bringing the carbine up as a tall figure emerged out of the darkness, a weapon visible in the man's left hand.

"Easy," the man said, raising his empty right hand toward Guilbeau, his voice ever so faintly tinged with the accents of south Texas. "We're friends."

Chapter 26

Spend long enough running field operations, and you were bound to have one go wrong from time to time. If you got lucky, you managed to cut your losses and pull your people out before you started paying the blood price for your hubris.

Tonight wasn't going to be one of the lucky ones, Darren Lukasik realized, pushing up his glasses to rub his eyes wearily. Not if the intel they were receiving from CINCPACFLT courtesy of the *Michigan*'s CO was accurate.

"Do you have anyone you could reach out to at the NICA, Carla?" he asked, opening his eyes again to look up at the screen at the end of the room. He was alone in the conference room right now—Station Manila all but deserted at this hour—but Ambassador Garner was on his way in. The White House had seen to that. "Anyone with the connections to help clear up this mess. . .before we lose any more men?"

One of Red Squadron's boats had been hit, at least, according to Piasecki. Hard to know how many survivors there could have been. What wasn't clear to Lukasik—like all VLF traffic, the CO's message had been the soul of brevity—was why the SEALs had even been *using* their boats to begin with. He'd been read in on all the interagency briefings with JSOC—knew that hadn't been part of the plan. No word from Richards, not yet, though Campisi had taken a satphone to give to him. Like as not, he was in the middle of the chaos.

On-screen, Carla Souders paused for a moment before leaning toward the camera, into the glow of her laptop's screen. She looked worn in the pale light, the room dark around her—a housecoat wrapped tightly about her body, sleep still not entirely driven from her eyes.

Neither one of them had gotten much rest—he'd been due home hours ago, but all of this just *kept* escalating. And Campisi wasn't back yet—wouldn't be for the better part of an hour.

"No, I'm afraid not," she replied slowly, seeming to consider her response carefully. "If the PN had authorization to open fire on our boats. . .that decision was made at a far higher level than any of my contacts. This could well be out of our hands, Darren."

A grimace passed across Lukasik's face, knowing what she meant without her saying it.

Maskariño.

1:56 A.M.
Patikul
Jolo Island, Sulu Province
The Autonomous Region in Muslim Mindanao (ARMM)

Guilbeau bit down hard into the brass of the 5.56mm NATO cartridge between his teeth, his eyes watering as Reiner dug the chunks of shrapnel out of the meat of his left shoulder. He could have used a shot of whiskey, anything to take his mind off the pain, but Motrin was all they had with them, and it had yet to kick in.

He was lying flat on his stomach in the stripped-out back of the Toyota HiAce, on eye-level with a crumpled pack of Fortune cigarettes displaying a jarring image of a gangrenous foot as Reiner—their combat medic—went about his work, the black Agency officer holding the light for him.

Reiner had made it out, at least. Shing, the coxswain of his Zodiac, was still MIA, along with Howett and Wilkens. They'd both been on the port gunwale with him when the shell exploded off their bow, but in all of the confusion. . .

No. The senior chief closed his eyes, shutting it out. They had to be alive, had to still be out there somewhere. Shing and Wilkens were relatively new, but Howett. . .Chris Howett had been with him and Dom since their time in Team Three. Their wives were best friends, and his son Dave had grown up with Howett's little girl—the two of them had even dated for a while, in high school.

Dom had made radio contact—they'd beached their raft about a klick and a half up the coast and were on their way in. That would bring their effective strength up to eleven, not counting the CIA officers.

The CIA.

He heard the low soft drawl of the lead Agency officer—Wilson, or whatever his name really was—coming from the rear of the van, where he stood guard with Styer, one of the walking wounded. Knew what he was saying, likely enough.

What he'd been saying—ever since he and his partner had pulled Guilbeau off the beach. But he wasn't in command here—this *wasn't* his op.

"There you go, Senior," Reiner said, binding the field dressing in place over the torn flesh. "Last one out."

He gave Guilbeau his hand and helped him to one knee in the back of the van, giving him a hard look as the CIA officer killed the light. "You good?"

"Will be, Doc. Will be." He figured they both knew it was a lie. At least it wasn't his right—he could still shoot, and just now, that's what counted.

Reiner handed him another Motrin, brusquely ordering him to take it as he dismounted awkwardly from the Toyota, nearly losing his balance.

They were pulled just off the rutted, desolate jungle road, not much more than a klick in from the beach—the Honda parked maybe fifteen meters in front, a darkened, angular shape against the undergrowth. Radakovich was up there, pulling security—his torn-up left thigh bandaged and wrapped to stop the bleeding. *"A couple inches higher and we might have had problems,"* he'd joked as Reiner patched him up, but he couldn't put his full weight on it. Wasn't going to be able to make the climb. *No matter what he said.*

McCalley was in the same boat, complicating their situation even further—his left knee badly mangled by shrapnel, and a jagged piece lodged in his side, just below the ribs. Wasn't much they could do for him here, other than staunch the bleeding and keep him stable.

"As soon as your other team gets here, Senior," the lead CIA officer began as soon as he stepped out of the van, "we're going to need to push on out."

Guilbeau winced, gritting his teeth against the pain as he looked up at the tall man. "This isn't your op, Wilson. I still have three people unaccounted for—not going to leave them behind, not here in Indian country."

A strange shadow passed across the Agency man's face at the words, but it was gone in a moment. "If you don't, you may not leave at all. We're living on borrowed time just now—we are, as you say, neck-deep in 'Indian country'—and the cavalry isn't any friendlier. You think you're going to recover your guys—or their bodies—with that warship on the prowl?"

Even as he spoke, Guilbeau could see the ghostly finger of the *Malvar*'s searchlight, off in the distance—stabbing through the trees. But he wasn't done.

"We stay here, it's a coin toss who sweeps us up first, the AFP. . .or Abu Sayyaf."

It was hard to argue with the logic of that. Yet logic could be such a liar. Guilbeau shook his head, knowing it was ultimately his decision—a burden that rested on his shoulders and his alone. The burden of command. *And yet*. If there was any chance of bettering the odds, for all of them. . .

"You have a satphone?" he asked after a long moment. Their long-range comms equipment had gone down with the Zodiac, leaving them unable to reach out beyond the limited range of their personal radios. At least till Dom arrived.

The CIA officer nodded, his face hardly visible in the darkness as he brought it out of his pack, handing it over. "Be my guest."

1:03 P.M. Eastern Standard Time, December 24th
JSOC Headquarters – Pope Field
Fort Bragg, North Carolina

He had known when the word first came in from CINCPACFLT that this wasn't going to be a good day. Listening to Senior Chief Petty Officer Guilbeau was only confirming that assessment.

A heavy sigh escaped General James Shulgach's lips as he leaned back in his chair at the head of the conference room's long table, listening to the SEAL's voice over the satphone. An SF veteran who had served with the B Squadron of the 1st Special Forces Operational Detachment-Delta in Iraq, he had spent the better part of the last twenty years either leading men in combat or sending them there—and they hadn't all come back.

He remembered every one.

The memory of what it had felt like to stand in the senior chief's shoes was painfully fresh, yet it didn't change the reality of their situation. The mission they had been tasked with carrying out.

"Senior Chief," he began, clearing his throat as he glanced around the room into the faces of his staff, "if it is your decision to pull the plug on this op, please know that you will have my full support. But our directive from the command authority remains in place—rescue the Braleys."

There was a long silence from the other side of the world,

so long that for a moment he almost thought the sat call had dropped. Then, "I understand, sir."

Simple as that. "To that end," Shulgach went on after a pause, "State is liaising at the highest levels with their counterparts in Manila—working to get the Filipinos to back down and stand aside. We will do everything in our power to support your mission. *Everything.*"

2:15 A.M.
Patikul
Jolo Island, Sulu Province
The Autonomous Region in Muslim Mindanao (ARMM)

One of the headlights of the HiAce was out, the remaining beam illuminating only the middle of the road as Richards drove—trying to use what little moonlight filtered through the clouds and the tree cover to keep from going off the road completely. They had the road to themselves for the moment, thanks to the curfew—the Honda with Zamora and several of the remaining SEALs following behind—but that only made them more conspicuous, if anyone showed up to care.

He felt Guilbeau's eyes on him—could still hear the pain and anger in the SEAL's voice, back there along the roadside. The two of them, moving away from the group. *"I don't leave men behind—that promise is all you have out in the field, the knowledge that someone is always going to come for you, no matter what. And those men are my brothers."*

The senior chief had paused for a moment, his eyes growing hard. *"But you don't understand that, don't know what it's like. There's no code for you spooks, is there? Only whatever it takes to get the job done—whatever and* whoever *you have to sacrifice along the way."*

"*I was in the Corps,*" he'd replied, never quite realizing till he spoke the words just how long ago all that seemed. *A lifetime. "And one of my brothers is up on that mountain. I get it. But there are a thousand men with guns within the sound of a rifle shot, and more of them are loyal to Abu Sayyaf than not. You stay here, try to recover your men, you'll just lose them all. You get lucky, maybe the AFP gets to you first. The Braleys are dead either way."*

"*Intel said the Filipinos had their own plan."*

"*They did."* It had been his intel, after all. *"Might have even been smarter to let them run with it. But our betters decided otherwise, so here we are. And the Filipinos' plan isn't going to last past sun-up, when Manong Soleiman learns of what went down tonight and decides his only way out is to kill everyone and melt into the woodwork. We either get them, or no one does."*

It was that simple, in the end—a harsh reality even the SEALs couldn't deny, no matter how much they wanted to.

"Turn-off is just ahead," Granby announced, consulting their maps with the penlight. He had shotgun. "Five-six hundred meters, past the point where the road curves back west."

That was as far as they could take the vehicles—after that it was three klicks through the jungle, following narrow trails to the base of Bud Dajo. *And then the climb.*

Guilbeau had made the decision to leave the wounded with the vehicles—have Styer take the Honda and drive Radakovich and McCalley into Jolo itself once they'd gotten clear. A hard decision, but the right one.

Segovia would likely throw them all in the brig, but they'd get medical attention. And protection. Best they could hope for.

Richards cleared his throat, glancing in his mirror to catch the senior chief's eye. "All right, we're coming up on the drop-off. Get ready to—"

A loud curse from Granby cut him off, even as light washed across Richards' vision—the contrast nearly blinding him as they came around the curve of the road.

There, spread out before them not two hundred meters in front, was a line of military trucks blocking the road ahead, a powerful floodlight in the bed of the leftmost truck lighting up the terrain all around, illuminating at least a score of soldiers milling about and the mounted machine gun in the bed of the truck beside it.

The AFP. Richards slammed on the brakes hard, hearing a groan of pain from one of the wounded SEALs in the back as he did so—grabbing up his Remington from the seat beside him.

"Everybody out, everybody out!"

2:18 A.M.
Bud Dajo—the crater
Jolo Island, Sulu Province
The Autonomous Region in Muslim Mindanao (ARMM)

Something was going on. It was impossible to know what, but there was no mistaking the increase in activity around the small camp—the guards flickering back and forth like mute ghosts in the darkness, Manong Soleiman appearing from within the main hut at one point to place a call on the satphone.

Brent Kruta shifted his position against the coconut palm as much as the ties would allow, struggling to find a comfortable position with his hands behind him. He hadn't slept—*wouldn't*, at this rate.

It had all started maybe an hour before—it was hard to keep track of the time exactly, the weariness and fatigue playing tricks with his mind. A series of muffled *krump*s from off away to the northeast seeming to herald the beginning of everything else.

He saw the older Moro—the one they called "Khadafi"—cross the clearing to Soleiman's side, the low murmur of their voices drifting through the cold night air. Kruta couldn't make out the words, wasn't sure it would have helped if he could have. His several years' worth of Arabic—never mind his *immersion* in the language during his time in the sandbox—hadn't proven any help since coming to this island.

There was an irony in that, along with so many others. Language, like all the rest of his skills, utterly useless to him here, in the place he would end his life.

A glance over toward the missionaries told him they hadn't been roused—Shawn Braley lying there asleep with his back up against the tree, looking as uncomfortable as Kruta felt, his little daughter snuggled up in his arms, her face pressed against her father's chest—her hair dirty and matted from the weeks of confinement.

Kruta smiled, despite himself—despite the pain still racking his bruised and battered body. He could remember, vaguely enough, when Lauren had been that age.

He'd spent most of that time in Afghanistan.

It was strange how bittersweet all those memories

seemed, looking back—watching another father now with his little girl. *The mistakes we make.*

God, he whispered, looking up into the dark, cloud-strewn sky, *if You're up there. . .watch over that man.*

2:19 A.M.
The road in Patikul
Jolo Island, Sulu Province
The Autonomous Region in Muslim Mindanao (ARMM)

Surrendering didn't come naturally, Nathan Styer thought, holding his empty hands out and away from his body as the Filipino soldiers closed in, their rifles leveled, a kid who couldn't have been more than twenty-two waving an M-16 in his face and shouting at him to get down on the ground. *Never would have imagined it.*

He'd handed off his Knight's Armament DMR—designated marksman rifle—to the lead CIA officer, and left his Sig P226 on the driver's seat of the Honda, but he obeyed the order grudgingly, pain from a still-embedded piece of shrapnel shooting through his thigh as he knelt in the gravelly mud of the road.

Parting with the rifle hadn't been without a pang, but it was better than losing it to the AFP. He heard someone else screaming at Radakovich, heard Radak's gruff reply. McCalley was drifting in and out of consciousness, nearly delirious with the pain.

*As for the others. . .*he understood Senior's decision, but it still felt like a betrayal. They could still be out there, somewhere, long though those odds seemed.

"Petty Officer Nathan Styer, United States Navy," he

heard himself say, responding to someone's demand for his name. "I request medi—"

Warm blood spattered over his face before he could finish the sentence, the sound of a ragged burst of rifle fire striking his ears even as he looked up to see the young Filipino soldier standing there before him, swaying ever so gently in the night breeze, half his skull shot away.

The M-16 dropped from suddenly nerveless fingers, and its owner followed it down into the mud a split-second later, the impact of the body coinciding with another scattering of shots, the AFP soldiers beginning to react—far too slowly—as fire broke out all along the treeline.

The soldiers around him scattered, seeking cover, and Styer hurled himself forward into the mud, ignoring the pain as he dove for the soldier's rifle.

They were under attack.

2:25 A.M.
The jungle in Patikul
Jolo Island, Sulu Province
The Autonomous Region in Muslim Mindanao (ARMM)

Spend long enough at war, and the sound of automatic weapons fire became unmistakable. A grimace passed across Richards' leathery face as he heard that familiar, crackling sound off to their rear. *Back toward the AFP roadblock.*

The SEALs had heard it too. Dom Zamora had point and he held up, his fist raised as he dropped to one knee in the dirt of the trail, the strung-out formation of men freezing in place, listening, every muscle tensed—weapons trained outward, eyes searching the darkness. The jungle itself had gone quiet, the song of the night birds fading away—only the thin, homing whine of the ubiquitous mosquitoes remaining, droning about their ears. And the sound of the guns.

There were lights off to their northwest, through the jungle, maybe two hundred meters out. Perhaps a house or something, Richards thought, until he saw them move. Coleman lanterns, flickering through the trees as the men carrying them advanced, on a trajectory that would bring them across the SEALs' line of retreat, closing on the road and the AFP positions.

Pantakasi. The cockfight derby had begun.

He saw the look on Guilbeau's face, knew what the SEAL was thinking. His men were back there, too. His *wounded.*

"You can't do anything for them just now," he said quietly—earning a sharp, angry look from the senior chief. Turmoil and anguish there, beneath the greasepaint. The night's hard decisions were far from over.

Guilbeau didn't say a word, just lifted his hand and gestured up the line to Zamora, motioning him forward.

Richards reached up as he rose once more to his feet, shifting the Remington 870 to his left hand to adjust the strap of the Knight's Armament M110K3 DMR slung over his shoulder, the long can of its suppressor poking up above his head. A good rifle, but right now it was just another weight on his back—and they still had a lot of ground to cover. *Move on out.*

10:33 A.M. Pacific Standard Time, December 24th
The presidential motorcade
Las Vegas, Nevada

"He did it," President Norton repeated, more to himself than anyone else, looking out through the thick, bullet-resistant glass of the Cadillac as the presidential limousine rolled through Vegas on its way to the next event, the lights of their police escort flashing red, white, and blue, each side street they passed, blocked off by the LVMPD. "He actually did it."

It seemed impossible to believe, even now—the better part of an hour since he had received the news, the utter paucity of detail contributing to how surreal it all felt. *SEALs were likely dead*, that much everyone seemed to agree on, but who and just how many. . .his only even relatively clear information had come through JSOC, the CIA proving as useless as ever.

But he had sent men into harm's way, and an *ally* had dared open fire upon them. Even after experiencing Maskariño's arrogance first-hand, it seemed unfathomable.

"I want him on the phone," he snapped, shooting a dagger-sharp look across the limousine at Froelich. How was he expected to focus, to concentrate on the events of this day—the speeches he was supposed to give—with all this going on, consuming his thoughts?

His chief of staff looked a question at him. "Maskariño, of course," Norton shot back impatiently. "I want to speak with him, before my speech at the LVMPD SWAT memorial."

"Mr. President, it's two in the morning on Christmas

Day in Manila," Froelich protested, shaking his head. "State's people are having a hard enough time just getting in touch with their opposite numbers. We won't be able to set up anything with President Maskariño for. . .hours, even if he would agree to a call."

"Then try harder."

2:37 A.M. Philippine Standard Time, December 25th
Camp Bautista, Jolo
Jolo Island, Sulu Province
The Autonomous Region in Muslim Mindanao (ARMM)

Without the audio, the flicker of the muzzle flashes coming over the dark, grainy video feed from the overhead UAV was almost beautiful—a twinkling iridescence which reminded Gringo Mijares of the time he had taken his ex-wife to the Donsol River in the Sorsogon back during their engagement. Ten thousand fireflies lighting up the mangrove forest all around as their boat slipped silently through the night.

A magical moment—but then, as now, the reality had been far less so. Out there, men were dying. He pulled the plate carrier over his head, fastening the straps and drawing them tight to his body.

He should have seen this coming—should have *known* the Americans wouldn't give up so easily. Close a door, and you'd find them breaching through an adjacent wall—it was the American way.

And tonight, it was getting people killed.

"My men are ready to roll out with your convoy, Colonel," he announced, picking up his IMI Galil as he walked over to where Lieutenant Colonel Segovia stood by the map table. They'd thrown out a series of roadblocks to stop and apprehend the American SEALs after they made it ashore, and one of them. . .one of them had become the focus of a coordinated attack from the Abu Sayyaf, isolated and vulnerable out there in the jungle west of Bud Dajo.

He could tell from the look in Segovia's eyes that he wanted to fight him over it, but in the end, it didn't come to that—his forces were spread thin this night and whether the army officer would ever admit it out loud or not, none of his men were the equals of Mijares' commandos. He *needed* them.

"All right," he said finally, grudgingly, "have your men ready to mount up. We push out in five."

2:40 A.M.
The road in Patikul
Jolo Island, Sulu Province
The Autonomous Region in Muslim Mindanao (ARMM)

They had managed to fall back the two hundred meters to the AFP roadblock without getting killed—somehow, Styer still wasn't sure how, kneeling behind the engine block of the military truck as he pushed a new magazine into the mag well of the scavenged M-16.

The big Browning machine gun in the truck's bed was silent—the lifeless body of a young Filipino soldier lying in an awkward, mangled heap just beneath the mount, his eyes wide open and staring up into the night, the beads of a rosary twisted around the fingers of his left hand. He'd likely been killed in the first bursts of fire.

Bullets whined through the air above his head as Styer pushed himself to his feet, flipping down his NODs and watching the landscape turn green around him as he searched for targets.

He had carried McCalley back into cover with them—Radak hobbling along on his bad leg beside them, firing the rifle to cover their retreat and screaming curses in at least three languages back at the enemy. *You can take a man out of the Balkans. . .*

The AFP were putting up a tough fight, but the darkness wasn't their friend, and he could feel the fight shifting around them as the numbers of enemy fighters swelled, flanking them hard from the north, around the roadblock.

Styer shouldered the rifle and moved north himself, across the road toward the bullet-shredded wreck of an AFP jeep, ignoring the stabbing pain in his left bicep—picking out a small group of hostiles in his night-vision, maybe fifty meters out in the jungle. Four to five guys, no more. Moving cautiously, edging their way around the soldiers' defenses.

"Radak!" he called out, raising his voice over the chaos of the battle—catching his partner's attention. "Contact left!"

He fell into cover near the front of the destroyed jeep, raising the scavenged M-16 over the hood—missing the absence of the PEQ-15 IR laser he would have customarily used as he picked out the rearmost target among the trees. And fire blossomed from the rifle's barrel. . .

1:51 P.M. Eastern Standard Time, December 24th
CIA Headquarters
Langley, Virginia

"I understand, Darren. Let me know the moment you have something—*anything*—from State's people." Bernard Kranemeyer returned the secure phone unit to its cradle on his desk, letting out a heavy sigh. Ambassador Garner's team in Manila was slowly re-assembling, fighting sleep and traffic to get back in to the embassy and put together a plan—on Christmas morning.

If they could secure the cooperation of the Filipinos—at least convince them to *stand down*—it would improve the SEALs' chances of success immeasurably.

If they could have secured that cooperation prior to *launching* the operation, well. . .Garner's small cadre of foreign service officers would still be abed, and all of Red Squadron's SEALs would likely still be alive.

But that ship had sailed, and now they were left to pick up the pieces. Best they could. Kranemeyer closed his office door behind him, making his way down the corridors toward the Clandestine Service's operations center.

They were, in so many ways, victims of their own success. More than a decade and a half of remarkably successful "kinetic" counterterrorism operations—most of them carried out in more-or-less failed states where the United States was far and away the biggest player on the block—had left policy-makers with an undue impression of their own invincibility. The belief that they could impose their will on enemy and ally alike, even in corners of the globe that *did* very much value their own sovereignty and had the capacity to do something about it.

Perhaps men in his position had simply done a bad job of communicating the reality to them. No one ever liked telling a principal that what they wanted was impossible, lest someone else find a way to *make* it possible and make off with your budget in the process. Truth to power, after all, was a double-edged sword.

All of which brought them to where they were now—making a desperate last-ditch effort to salvage a situation they never should have found themselves in to begin with.

The op-center was bustling with activity when the DCS arrived—not just the Jolo op, of course—they were tracking ongoing operations in Afghanistan and Syria, and Rineer had just landed in the Sahel with his team.

But the Philippines did have marquee placement.

"Do we have comms up with the SEALs?" he asked, walking over to where Ron Carter stood beneath the main central screen on the far wall.

A nod served as his response for the moment, Carter tapping something into the tablet in his hand. "JSOC patched us into their comms network with Red Squadron. We're getting it as it comes in."

That was an improvement—one of the benefits of that decade and a half's worth of CT operations was greatly enhanced cooperation and coordination between the CIA and the spec-ops community, on a level that would have been well-nigh unthinkable during his own early days with Delta.

"And the satellite?"

"Will be coming on-station in forty."

2:53 A.M. Philippine Standard Time, December 25th
The main road
Jolo Island, Sulu Province
The Autonomous Region in Muslim Mindanao (ARMM)

Gringo Mijares leaned back into the rear seat of the up-armored HMMV, his rifle slung across his chest as they rolled out along the main road, the M113 armored personnel carrier at the head of the column setting the pace—the city lights still visible in the rear-view mirrors of the Humvee.

His monocular Aselsan A100 was flipped up on the front of his helmet, as were those of most of the rest of his men. The new Turkish-made NODs alone gave his men an edge over Segovia's regulars. Night-vision equipment still was far from standard-issue in the AFP, and it left them at a serious disadvantage on nights like tonight.

With any luck, the SAF's presence—and the firepower of Segovia's APCs—would be enough to turn the tide of the ongoing firefight at the roadblock. And then they were going to have to go looking for the Americans.

Mijares' face darkened. The last radio reports—pre-contact—from the AFP detachment manning the roadblock had indicated they were preparing to stop a pair of suspicious vehicles. *The American SEALs?*

That was a question they hadn't gotten answered—the detachment coming under fire before they could report back. But sooner or later, he and his men would be tasked with going after them.

It wasn't a prospect he looked forward to. His men were good, but the SEALs. . .even he had to admit they probably had the edge, and better kit to further skew the odds in their favor. That, and he had spent most of his career carrying out CT operations alongside American advisers—some of them SEALs—during JSOTF-P's tenure. It was help he would far rather his nation not found itself forced to accept, but he bore little ill will toward the advisers themselves.

He did, after all, have a healthy grasp on the

shortcomings of his own country's counter-insurgency efforts, plagued as they were by the kind of corruption which had always been rife throughout the Philippine security forces.

At least Jack was away. He had come to genuinely like the big man over their months of working together, even if the revelations of the last twenty-four hours had come as a disappointment. Having to draw down on him. . .well, he was back in Manila now. It wasn't going to come to that. It wouldn't—

The explosion came without warning, Mijares' hand immediately on his gun, looking forward through the windshield of the Humvee to see a ghastly pall of oily-black smoke and fire billowing up into the night, the lead M113 just two vehicles ahead blown half on its side, ripped open as though someone had taken it apart with a can opener.

IED. "Get out!" he heard himself shout, putting out a hand and shoving the heavy armored door open with all his might—bringing the Galil up in his other hand as he stepped out onto the road. *"Everyone out!"*

Chapter 27

3:02 A.M.
Patikul—the jungle
Jolo Island, Sulu Province
The Autonomous Region in Muslim Mindanao (ARMM)

Based on the GPS data displayed on the dimly-lit screen of Zamora's DAGR, they had reached the foot of Bud Dajo. "Foot" being defined as the low end of the southernmost of the three main hogbacks snaking their way up the increasingly steep volcanic mountainside, the thin trails running their length offering the only way to reach the summit, at least without climbing equipment.

It was good they had the "Dagger"—otherwise one would never have known, Richards thought skeptically, glancing at the jungle canopy above their heads, shutting out the sky and any sign of the mountain above.

Hardly a breath of wind was moving between the trees, the chill night air humid and close. A few minutes before, another massive explosion had struck their ears, somewhere off to their southwest. Not the roadblock, not this time—though they could still hear the fire from that engagement, filtering through the jungle. This was something else. . .yet another of the fruits of a night that was going from bad to worse.

They had dodged at least three more groups of armed fighters on their way to the mountain—all of them, fortunately, headed *away* from Bud Dajo. Whatever else might be happening, it didn't seem as though anyone was racing to Manong Soleiman's rescue.

"With the way the trail twists and turns along the ridge," Granby was saying, the faint glow of the tablet in his hand illuminating his face as Guilbeau and Zamora clustered around, "it's just over another klick to the top."

They wouldn't have actual real-time sat coverage for another thirty minutes—and only for a brief window when they did—but Lukasik had helpfully downloaded all of their existing satellite map overlays onto the encrypted tablet. Combined with the GPS information of the SEALs' DAGR, it was possible to pinpoint their own location, and map out the path to their objective.

". . .the trail is steep but passable most of the way up," the former Marine Raider continued, using two fingers to zoom in on the map, "until the last hundred and fifty meters or so, when it becomes a sixty-degree slope up the side of the cone. That's where life gets fun."

The American soldiers assaulting Bud Dajo back in 1906 had crawled to the top on their hands and knees, harassed by heavy fire, including makeshift "grenades" made from conch shells filled with gunpowder. But that hadn't been in the dark.

A mosquito whined about his ear and Richards reached up, smashing it savagely against his neck and smearing his grease-painted skin with its blood and his own. *Mosquitoes.* Wherever he'd gone in the world, wherever he'd fought— they'd been there waiting for him.

"All right," Guilbeau said quietly, rising from his knee in the dirt, "let's see what's waiting for us up there. Dom, get the first Hornet in the air."

A nod from Zamora and he motioned one of the other SEALs forward, the man removing a small ruggedized case from his backpack and setting it on the ground—opening it to reveal the screen of a small terminal, a handheld joystick, and, embedded in the foam interior of the case, a pair of tiny nano-UAVs.

Black Hornets, Richards thought, watching the man extract one from the foam with his thumb and forefinger, the drone measuring barely seven inches from tip to tail. Much smaller than any of the smallest UAVs he'd even imagined having access to, years before in the Corps, he had used these in Egypt with Nakamura, back at the beginnings of what had become the QUICKSAND op.

They were a truly revolutionary piece of kit—a genuine "force multiplier" in a business which abused that term far too freely.

A light whirring noise filled his ears as the SEAL held the small copter aloft, its rotors spooling up in the darkness as he fiddled with the joystick.

A few moments passed, and then the nano UAV rose up from his hand, twisting and turning in the darkness until it rose out of sight. . .

3:14 A.M.
Talipao—the roadblock
Jolo Island, Sulu Province
The Autonomous Region in Muslim Mindanao (ARMM)

McCalley was dead. It seemed hard to fathom, the impact still not fully sinking home as Styer knelt behind the wheel well of an AFP Humvee, reloading a magazine for the M-16—feeding cartridges one by one between its metal lips.

The acrid, oily smell of smoke filled his nostrils, nearly choking him, along with the sickening odor of seared, burning flesh—one of the big military trucks which had formed part of the original roadblock on fire, its flames lighting up the scene like a torch, rendering his NODs all but useless.

There was still a sporadic scattering of shots coming from the surrounding jungle—enough to keep them on edge, to force the small handful of men dragging the bodies of their fellow-soldiers from the burning wreck into cover, but most of their attackers seemed to have faded away. Moving on, seeking other targets perhaps—they could hear heavy firing off toward Jolo and from what little he had been able to determine of the radio reports the Filipino personnel were getting, it seemed as though their QRF had itself come under attack.

He and Radak had done their best to get McCalley under cover when they carried him back into the roadblock, but he'd been half-delirious even then, and with the fight flowing around them, there was no place of safety to be found.

Styer had returned to check on him only to find that

sometime in the previous thirty minutes, he had taken another pair of rounds to the chest, dying lost in the haze of delirium—bleeding out.

Mac. He'd come to the Teams from the High Plains of southeastern Wyoming, about as far from the sea as a man could get. Still had a battered Stetson stowed in his equipment locker back at Little Creek. Unmarried, and more of a loner than most, he'd lived for his motorcycle and the open road, going through a never-ending string of girlfriends—Frog Hogs, most of them, the kind of women who hung around Little Creek, looking to share a night with a SEAL. Not Styer's thing, but Mac hadn't cared. He'd been a good guy to have a beer with, better guy to have at your back in battle.

And now he was dead. Yet another brother lost this night.

Styer topped off the mag with one last cartridge, tucking it into the pouch on his chest rig as he rose, his eyes once more searching the darkness of the jungle bordering the road. The night wasn't over just yet.

2:27 P.M. Eastern Standard Time, December 24th
CIA Headquarters
Langley, Virginia

The ocean was dark and cold in the lens of the KH-11's IR cameras as the reconnaissance satellite swept in over the West Pacific, the NRO's technicians focusing in on the island of Jolo, itself barely a speck in the sea from two hundred miles up—and the mountain of Bud Dajo.

Kranemeyer took a last sip from his cup of coffee and set

it to one side on the desk of an abandoned workstation as the cameras zoomed in on the volcano's crater, picking out its features in stark relief—spectral, ghost-gray human figures moving jerkily here and there across the bowl.

If they'd hoped to catch Manong Soleiman's men sleeping, well. . .that wasn't going to happen. They might be distracted, disorganized, and there was no recognizable perimeter, but they *were* awake.

No perimeter. . .Kranemeyer's eyes strayed to the edge of the screen, and his breath caught in his throat as he rapidly reconsidered that assessment, making out the thermal signatures of men beneath the jungle canopy on the volcano's rim, standing guard over the narrow approach up the hogback. And below them, maybe three hundred meters down the mountainside, toiling their way up—Red Squadron's SEALs.

"Push this out to the ground team," he ordered, shooting a look over at Carter. "Make sure they're seeing this."

3:34 A.M. Philippine Standard Time, December 25th
Bud Dajo—the approach
Jolo Island, Sulu Province
The Autonomous Region in Muslim Mindanao (ARMM)

"We're looking at 'em," Richards replied softly, laying on his back in the tall grass—the satellite phone pressed to his ear. The SEAL with the UAVs—Melhorn was his name, a short man with a heavy Boston accent—lay beside him, the terminal's screen just visible to Richards as he manipulated the joystick, pulling the Black Hornet into a hover just below the treetops up on the volcano's rim.

There were three men visible in the nano UAV's infrared camera—long guns in their hands, huddled in the broken-down ruins of a large cotta perched at the very top of the trail. The structure, like as not one of the Moro fortifications from the original battle, was crumbling and all but reclaimed by the jungle—barely offering so much as a breastwork to the men now sheltering in its shadow. But it still had command of the trail.

He glanced over at Granby's tablet, displaying the satellite imagery from Langley. It was no different at any of the other approaches—Manong Soleiman had his men disposed well, if you took his relatively small numbers into account. And the main camp was abuzz with activity. *So much for the element of surprise.*

That had gone straight out the window with the throaty report of the *Malvar*'s main gun—along with so much of the rest of their plan.

"We're going to need to take the rest of them down before we strike at the camp," he observed quietly as the senior chief came over, half-crouched in the grass, making his way along the slope.

Just above them, itself now nearly obliterated by the encroaching jungle, lay the vestiges of the lateral trail "Black Jack" Pershing had cut back in 1911, during the *second* siege of the mountain, girdling the entire circumference of Bud Dajo and cutting the besieged locals off from access to the countless smaller trails they had used to bring in supplies.

After that, they'd barely have a hundred meters more of trail to go before the going started getting far tougher—the slope of the volcano's cone already rising precipitously into the night sky above their heads.

Guilbeau glanced at the dispositions laid out in the satellite imagery and nodded wordlessly. No way they could risk those sentries coming back down after them once they took down the camp.

"All right," he said quietly, motioning Zamora forward. "Here's what we'll do. Dom. . .you take two of your men and use the lateral trail to make your way across the mountainside to the east approach. Wilson, you two do the same, take the guys on the west." He withdrew the suppressed Sig-Sauer from his rig, handing it over to Richards and motioning for Melhorn to do the same for Granby. "Keep things quiet, stay on comms. I'll push on ahead with the main body, and we'll keep eyes up with the Hornets."

"Solid copy."

3:49 A.M.
DILG-NAPOLCOM Center
Quezon City, Metro Manila
Philippines

"I should be with my family right now." The young office assistant who had ushered them into Ismael Robredo's office had still been blinking back sleep, and the Secretary of the Department of the Interior & Local Government wasn't in much better shape—he was dressed far more casually than Katherine Lipscomb ever remembered seeing him, and several long hairs were sticking up from the back of his head where his attempt to comb them flat had failed.

"So should we all, Mr. Secretary," Ambassador Reuben Garner acknowledged gravely, extending his hand toward their Filipino counterpart. This hadn't been the original plan, but they'd proven utterly unsuccessful in obtaining so much as a call with Secretary Guidote or a meeting with any other sufficiently senior official at the Department of Foreign Affairs. *So here we are.*

Robredo seemed not to see the ambassador's hand, wearily gesturing for them both to take a seat. She saw Garner's face flush, but he took the indicated seat and she followed suit, mirroring her principal.

"My children will wake up in a few hours," Robredo continued, circling back around the rear of his desk. "Christmas morning, and where will I be? Here with you."

There are children who will never *see their fathers again,* Katherine Lipscomb thought, anger flaring behind the mask as she stared mutely across at the interior secretary. The news still didn't seem real. . .at least three US Navy SEALs missing in action. *Likely dead.* And more wounded.

And all of it. . .so *unnecessary.* She had confronted the reality of death many times over the course of her career as a foreign service officer, but it rarely came without a feeling of failure. That diplomacy had failed—that *she* had failed.

As they had here.

"There is," Garner began, "as you are likely aware, Mr. Secretary, a detachment of US military special-operations personnel currently on Jolo, tasked with recovering the Braleys. Earlier tonight, they came under fire by AFP units, and—"

A heavy sigh escaped Robredo's lips. "I am indeed aware, Mr. Ambassador. *Well* aware. Your military's actions have sparked a brushfire of engagements with Abu Sayyaf all across the western end of Jolo, and the AFP commander on the island is taking losses of his own as he tries to contain the situation."

The ambassador looked stricken and Lipscomb struggled to control her own face. Their intel briefing hadn't said anything about *that*. *From bad to worse.*

"What's done is done, Mr. Secretary," Garner said finally, recovering himself. "However we might wish it otherwise. Neither of us can bring back our dead. The American team is on Jolo, and they are closing in on Manong Soleiman. All the administration asks is that your security forces stand aside and allow the rescue to take place."

Robredo shook his head wearily, shifting his attention from the ambassador to her. "The man you have in your White House—those tweets of his, his threats to 'send in the SEALs,' they weren't empty bluster. It wasn't just about putting public pressure on my government, as you once sat here and told me. He meant them, and you would do well to recognize that. The game has *changed*."

So Russ had warned her. She hadn't listened, had chosen to believe that the old rules still applied. *Against all the evidence.*

"My president warned yours to allow us to handle this," Robredo went off after another long moment, glancing shrewdly between her and Garner. "Of the *consequences* if you did not. He meant those words as well. But it is possible that we may be able to reach a deal acceptable to the Malacañang."

4:05 A.M.
The roadblock
Jolo Island, Sulu Province
The Autonomous Region in Muslim Mindanao (ARMM)

"I understand. Bring them back to my position as soon as you can," Gringo Mijares ordered, toggling the mic on the radio attached to his chest rig—the glare of the still-burning truck casting strange shadows across his face as he stood there in the darkness of the early morning, hand on the Galil's pistol grip. The sun was going to begin coming up in another hour, giving them a better look at their situation, but he knew already it wasn't good.

Eight soldiers had died in the massive explosion which had destroyed the APC, with more wounded—and he'd had two of his own officers wounded in the firefight which had followed.

But Abu Sayyaf had been gambling on ambushing Segovia's troops, not the Special Action Force, and his officers' night-vision and superior training had slowly but surely turned the tide of battle, sending the militants running in the end, dragging their dead and wounded with them.

From there, they'd proceeded four kilometers on foot from the ambush to the roadblock, relieving the soldiers there and scattering what remained of their attackers. And finding even more casualties.

But the AFP had detained a couple of the Americans. That might net them some intel—if they would talk.

"Sergeant Dalisay!" he called out to a stocky, muscled man posted up about eight meters to his left. One of his commandos. "Get the men back together, make sure their ammo supplies are topped off. Once Segovia's personnel are on their way back to base and we've debriefed the Americans. . .we're going to need to go out after the rest of their team."

Go hunting, he thought, the NCO's acknowledgment in his ears as he half-turned to look up toward the towering summit of Bud Dajo, just visible off through the palms lining the road, its jungle-covered slopes somehow dark even against the night. This night was going to get a lot worse before it got better. *If* it did.

Just then, his radio squawked with static, Segovia's voice coming through. "New orders for you, lieutenant. Just in from WESTMINCOM. You're to stand down."

4:13 A.M.
Bud Dajo—the rim
Jolo Island, Sulu Province
The Autonomous Region in Muslim Mindanao (ARMM)

One misstep here and it was over the edge, Richards realized, picking his way carefully along the slope—barely raising himself from his knees as he half-crawled forward, Granby following just behind.

"You're almost on them," a voice in his ear informed him. *Melhorn*. Watching from above with the UAV. "Another ten meters and you'll be able to flank them from the west."

Ten meters. The Texan glanced out along the slope and winced. It sounded so simple, but in practice. . .the incline was only getting more precipitously steep the farther they got from the trail. He shuffled a boot forward, testing for a foothold, wrapping a free hand around the trunk of a tree towering above them in the darkness—trees grew here, somehow—the shotgun slung across his chest, the sniper rifle on his back.

One step, and then another—the precipice yawning down into a strange greenish-blackness below him as viewed through his NODs, the tops of the trees twenty meters down waving gently in the night breeze. Fall here and you would bounce down the tree-strewn slope for a thousand feet or more, smashed against one trunk after another until your mangled corpse managed to come to a rest. Best not to dwell on it.

He glanced up, gauging the distance from where he stood to the rim, no more than five meters at most. They were there, just up from the trail—another four militants, clustered in the dark. *Waiting*. They—

His foot slipped in that moment, loose dirt giving way beneath his boot, catching him off-balance. He pitched forward, dirt and stone skidding downhill as he clawed desperately for a purchase. The fingers of his right hand found an exposed root and closed around it, pain shooting through his body as he jerked to a sudden stop, the jolt almost certainly dislocating his shoulder, his feet scrabbling for support.

He bit down hard, struggling not to cry out—feeling the metallic taste of blood fill his mouth.

"Hold on, Jack." Granby's voice, barely above a whisper, as the former Raider scrambled across the mountaintop toward him, choosing his footholds carefully—letting his carbine hang from its sling as he advanced. He stripped his belt out of its loops, wrapping it around the slender trunk of a small tree just up the slope—twisting it around his hand and testing it with a hard jerk.

"Give me your hand. . ."

3:15 P.M. Eastern Standard Time, December 24th
The Harry S. Truman Building (State Department Headquarters)
Washington, D.C.

"And they honestly expect to be hailed as the heroes of this rescue after this?" President Richard Norton demanded, his voice coming clearly through the conference phone on the SecState's desk. "After all they've *done* today?"

"It's a rescue which hasn't happened just yet, Mr. President," Aaron Sorenson replied, turning back toward his desk from the window. Outside it was clear and cold, a bitter wind whipping across the Potomac from the west. "And may not, if the Filipino military chooses to take a hand. What we are being offered is a chance to save face—for everyone involved in this."

In this debacle, he nearly said, but it was clear from the President's tone that he wasn't ready to hear that. Might never be.

"Red Squadron's people are down there alone," he added after a moment that seemed to stretch out forever. "Cut off."

"They're SEALs," Norton retorted, his voice sharp and impatient.

"They are, Mr. President," the Secretary of State acknowledged, running a hand across his face, "but as I believe Nathan will attest. . .they are only men."

And they die just like any others. As they had already learned today. He heard Gisriel chime in with agreement, gently prodding the President. If there was anyone in Norton's cabinet who could move him, it would be his National Security Advisor. The former Marine general was one of the few people in Washington who truly seemed to command the President's respect.

". . .even if that were the case, Mr. President," Gisriel was saying, "we will need to exfiltrate the Braleys from the mountain after the rescue. We can't do that without the cooperation of the Filipino government, not after what's happened. This deal Ambassador Garner has brokered is our best chance of seeing this through and bringing them home."

"And how do I explain those. . .those who have died?" the President asked after another long moment. They still didn't have a clear picture of the casualties from JSOC, but it seemed clear they had lost people. *Already.*

Sorenson cleared his throat, but it was Gisriel who took the question. "Quite simply, Mr. President, the operation to recover the Braleys was a joint US-Filipino mission. Our people took casualties. That's close enough to the truth—all the families need to be told."

"All right," Norton said finally, the reluctance audible in his voice. "See that it's done."

4:19 A.M. Philippine Standard Time, December 25th
Bud Dajo—the rim
Jolo Island, Sulu Province
The Autonomous Region in Muslim Mindanao (ARMM)

Fire spasmed through Richards' right shoulder, seeming to shoot tendrils of pain down his arm as he moved cautiously through the trees and undergrowth, wishing for the thousandth time for a machete, or even a tomahawk like the one Zamora had been using to clear his way up the trail, further down the mountain. Not that he would have been able to swing either effectively. . .

Still, he was alive. Thanks to Granby. *Ooh-rah.*

"Dom, you have eyes on?" he heard Guilbeau ask over his earpiece, the question followed almost immediately by a *click-click* of acknowledgment. "Jack?"

But he didn't, not yet—the borrowed Sig-Sauer P226 clutched in his left hand as he pressed forward, the pistol's long suppressor leading the way. He could feel rather than see Granby off to his right, moving with him, the NODs restricting his peripheral vision.

The jungle had gone quiet around them, and he had to wonder if the men waiting for them had sensed it too— Death stalking the jungle this night. He pushed through a thick mass of ferns and dropped slowly to one knee, raising his right hand awkwardly in a clenched fist, bringing Granby to a halt.

There they are. He blinked his eyes against the blinding flash of pain, the low murmur of men's voices reaching him as he made out the figures of four men clustered very near where the UAV footage had placed them more than a half-hour before, in the desolate ruins of yet another fortified cotta—the remnants of vine-covered and half-rotted-away abatis strewn out in front, toward the trail approach, the logs' sharpened ends dulled by time and weather.

One of the men was smoking, no doubt relying on the nicotine rush to calm his own nerves—the cherry of his cigarette a bright flash in Richards' NODs. He glanced over to see Granby gesture toward him, picking out his targets. They'd take the ones in the back first. *Then the front.*

A nod, and Richards reached up, toggling his mic twice in rapid succession. *Click-click.*

"Take 'em down."

Guilbeau's transmission had barely ended when Richards brought the Sig up in his left hand, acquiring only the briefest of sight pictures before he squeezed the trigger once, twice—sending a pair of 9mm rounds through the right temple of the smoker. *Lights out.*

And then he was transitioning, bringing his weapon to bear on his second target—seeing Granby's fall. He'd never been as good with his left hand as his right, but you trained to compensate all the same. For nights like this.

But his target was already turning as he squeezed the trigger—*slow, too slow*—no doubt alerted by the sound of the bodies of the other men collapsing around him. The bullet going wild, cutting a path through the empty air past the man's head.

And he saw the face of his target, greenish-tinted in the lens of the night-vision, distorted in horror and fear. A young man—no more than nineteen or twenty—his mouth opening in shocked surprise, his eyes searching the darkness wildly. *In vain.*

A second bullet from Richards' Sig caught him in the throat, his cry of alarm muted to a gurgling choke as he reeled backward, struggling to raise his weapon.

They both shot him then, the rounds striking him high in the chest—depositing him in a crumpled heap in the shadow of the crumbling cotta wall.

Richards paced forward, the Sig-Sauer still outstretched in his hand, checking each of the bodies in turn—his ears alert for any sign that they had been compromised. *All clear.*

He hit the mag release, wincing with pain as he fished a fresh mag from his pocket and slid it into the butt of the pistol—walking over to the rear wall of the cotta and staring down through the trees, the bowl of the volcano's crater spread out before them.

It was, ironically, just as good an overwatch position as it had looked on the sat imagery. *That* never *happened.*

"All clear," he announced, toggling his mic and hearing Guilbeau's acknowledgment. "We're in position."

He turned back toward Granby, a grimace passing across his face. "All right, let's get set up. And. . .I'm going to need you to put this shoulder back where it belongs."

4:23 A.M.
Bud Dajo—the crater
Jolo Island, Sulu Province
The Autonomous Region in Muslim Mindanao (ARMM)

"Shawn." Shawn Braley felt his young daughter stir restlessly against his chest at the sound of his wife's sleep-choked voice. "Shawn. . .what's going on?"

He found himself unable or unwilling to answer her, a

curiously numb sensation seeming to possess him as he watched men hurry back and forth across the clearing—flashlight beams flickering in the night. Something had happened, that much was clear, the noise and commotion waking him from what had been a fitful sleep. Aldam was visible just on the other side of the huts, shouting at someone else—the teenager's rifle slung across his chest.

When he closed his eyes, he could still feel the muzzle of that rifle jabbing into his chest, cold through the ripped, thin shirt he had worn ever since that fateful morning in church—a shudder rippling through him at the memories. *Looking into the face of Death.*

He saw Khadafi then, stopping to speak to one of the other militants before coming toward them, the beam of his flashlight swinging as he walked. The older Moro stopped before them, his face shrouded in the darkness behind the light.

"Give her to me," he said quietly, a strange note of regret in his voice, the flashlight playing across Faith's matted golden curls as she lay in her father's arms.

It took a moment for Shawn to process the words, but Charity reacted immediately, her raw, wounded cry of *"No!"* rousing Dolores from where the fifteen-year-old rested on the other side of his wife.

"I will keep your daughter safe," Khadafi went on, ignoring her outcry as he stooped down to look Shawn in the eye, "and make sure she comes to no harm. She doesn't need to see this."

He shook his head, opening his mouth to ask the older man what he meant—but then he looked out past Khadafi's shoulder to see Manong Soleiman emerging from the main hut off toward the west end of the clearing, flanked by a pair of his guards. The long blade of the *kampilan*, visible in his hand. . .

Chapter 28

4:26 A.M.
Bud Dajo—the trails
Jolo Island, Sulu Province
The Autonomous Region in Muslim Mindanao (ARMM)

They were running out of time, Jason Guilbeau realized, casting a critical glance up at the brief snatches of sky which could be made out through the cover of the jungle above as he and his men pressed forward, weapons raised—greenish-gray ghosts flickering through the jungle, down the steep mountain trail descending into the bowl.

Dawn was coming, less than an hour away now—and with it, their biggest tactical advantage was on its way out.

"I have eyes on the hostages." It was the lead CIA officer, his voice coming clear through Guilbeau's earpiece. "They're near the center of the clearing, under a copse of coconut palms."

There was a moment's pause, and then the man went on, a peculiar strain entering his voice. "We have a lot of activity around them, Senior—at least seven-eight MAMs, all of them armed." *Military-age males.* "Lead guy, may be Soleiman, has a sword."

Guilbeau grimaced, taking his hand off the forend of his weapon to toggle his lip mic. "What's your status, Dom?"

"Hundred and fifty meters out," Zamora replied a moment later, a burst of static accompanying the words. He and his element were pushing down the trail from the east approach, moving in rough parallel to Guilbeau's own.

The Black Hornets had been pulled back down, recharging as they advanced for one final use as they closed on the objective. Hard to say whether they were going to have that kind of time.

"Copy that," the senior chief acknowledged, his eyes scanning the darkness ahead. They were close. *But was it close* enough?

4:28 A.M.
Bud Dajo—the rim
Jolo Island, Sulu Province
The Autonomous Region in Muslim Mindanao (ARMM)

"You seeing what I am?" Richards asked quietly, lying prone on top of the rear wall of the cotta, the M110K3's bipod unfolded and anchored in the soft earth in front of him, its stock snug against his injured shoulder.

The recoil was going to hurt, but there was no help for it. He had far more time on the long gun than Granby. *Thomas, where are you when I need you?*

But he knew—Parker was still back in Mindanao, carrying out his orders, best he could. No one's fault, just the way their dice had landed.

"Yeah," Granby replied, the SEALs' IR illuminator set up beside him and turned on, night-vision binoculars pressed to his face as he scanned the crater below, serving as his spotter. They were Marines, after all, and that was the way the Corps did it—unlike the Army, which would have put the most experienced man on the glass, and the junior member of the team on the gun. "They're panicking, looks like."

It hadn't been meant to end this way—the plan had been to hit the camp while everyone was asleep, even the outpost sentries nodding off in the stillness of the early morning. The Braleys rescued, their captors dead before they knew what hit them.

But few ops ever went according to plan. Richards shifted restlessly atop the crumbling wall, reaching over to massage his shoulder. Moving the rifle into position, he'd tripped over something in the darkness, looking down to find an exposed human femur poking out of the cotta's charred ruins, vestiges of the battle which had once been fought here. *The massacre.*

There were all kinds of ghosts in this place.

Richards centered the DMR's reticle on the face of the man with the sword, studying him through the night-vision scope, picking out the mane of wild black hair streaming back over his shoulders, secured around his forehead by a headband. *Soleiman?*

It seemed likely, though neither the CIA nor their Filipino counterparts had a photo on file. He traversed the rifle on its bipod, following the man as he stalked back and forth before the hostages, one hundred and eighty-three meters away, according to the laser range-finder Granby was using—the Moro gesturing angrily with the sword back toward one of his men.

It was impossible to hear what he was saying from their overwatch position on the crater's rim—but the anger was unmistakable.

"There's Kruta," Granby announced quietly, the infrared dot of the laser winking out through the darkness to indicate his mark. "They're bringing him over to the rest of the group."

The former CIA paramilitary's face was visibly bruised and battered as Richards glassed over him, and he seemed to stagger against the man escorting him as if he might fall.

We could have worked this out, Brent, Richards thought, grimacing at the sight of his former colleague. *Didn't have to go this way.*

He saw the guard shove Kruta to the ground near Soleiman, saw the militant leader turn on him—his face distorted with anger, the sword raised in his hand.

Richards' face tightened into a grimace, refocusing the rifle's reticle on Soleiman's back, just between the shoulderblades. *Easy there.*

As if in answer to the whispered injunction, he saw Soleiman halt, half-turning away from the kneeling Kruta— lowering the sword for a moment as he pulled a cellphone from the pocket of his fatigue pants, raising it to his ear.

The next moment, a ringtone began to blare from a dead man's pockets somewhere behind them. . .

4:31 A.M.
Bud Dajo—the trails
Jolo Island, Sulu Province
The Autonomous Region in Muslim Mindanao (ARMM)

"You need to get in there, *now*." The CIA officer's voice once more, harsh and urgent. "He's calling the outposts."

Guilbeau swore softly, his eyes scanning the darkness— the clearing now just visible ahead of them through the trees. They weren't going to have time to set up, to perform a final recon. And they were outnumbered more than three to one.

Soleiman might write off a single outpost not responding as a fluke—phone batteries died, after all, but once he tried *all* of them. . .

People were going to start dying.

"Contact front," he heard Kuznicki—their pointman— hiss over his earpiece, the words coming simultaneously with a sharp metallic snapping from twenty meters out, near the borderline of the jungle. *People already were.*

4:33 A.M.
Bud Dajo—the crater

"This isn't what you want to do," Shawn heard the Marine say, his voice thin and weary as he knelt there on the hard volcanic ground. "The only hope you have—"

"They're not answering?" Khadafi this time, the Visayan filtering through the missionary's brain. "None of them?"

"None." There was rage in Soleiman's voice, rage and. . .*fear*, a strangely dissonant sound. Shawn glanced over to meet his wife's eyes, seeing his own confusion reflected in her face—

Faith now awake and huddled in her mother's arms, turning away from the men now gathering round. At least a dozen Abu Sayyaf fighters filled the space between them and the nearest hut—with more scattered out across the clearing.

"They're here," Soleiman spat, cursing angrily as he threw the phone away, sending it bouncing over the hard ground. "They are *here!*"

"Give her to me," Khadafi warned, taking a step closer to Charity. "Now—this is your last chance to protect her. I will take care of her as though she were my own. I will—"

"Your only chance of saving yourselves," Kruta pressed, raising his voice—undeterred by the guard's rifle aimed at his head, "lies in negotiation. You can only negotiate so long as you keep us alive. *All* of us. We are your only—"

"Enough!" Soleiman's dark eyes flashed with a wild light as he wheeled on the Marine, the long, wicked blade of the *kampilan* extending from his hand. *No,* something within Shawn screamed, all the memories of Emmanuel's execution flooding back through his mind—everything within him screaming to stand up, to do *something*. To take his place.

And yet he seemed rooted in place—*frozen*—even as Soleiman took a step closer to Kruta, raising the sword in his right hand.

"This is your doing, all of this," the militant leader raged, a mad fury in his voice as he brandished the blade toward the Marine's head, "You have brought—"

His words died away suddenly, a harsh wet *thud* striking Shawn's ears, followed by another, far more distant sound— like a single handclap. Soleiman seemed to sway unsteadily, the *kampilan* dropping from his fingers as his arm fell to his side.

Then he pitched forward, falling face-down in the dirt—the impact of his body seeming to jar everyone from their trance.

Khadafi moved first, unslinging his rifle from his shoulders, the light of someone's flashlight beam glinting off the older Moro's silver hair as he advanced on Charity and Faith, stooping down—

And then he was on his back in the dirt, struck down as if by from some hand from on high, moaning in pain and clutching at the dark, damp circle blossoming outward through his shirt from the ragged hole over his chest.

Madness. Everyone reacted then, men scattering, scrambling for cover—a ragged burst of rifle fire echoing out through the night as someone fired wildly up at the rim.

Out of the corner of his eye, Shawn saw one of Kruta's guards go down, saw the Marine lurch to his feet, stumbling toward the man's dropped rifle.

He was there—his hand closing around the receiver—when Shawn sensed movement, off to his left. Looked up to see Aldam, not fifteen feet away—the teenager's rifle barrel swinging upward in an unstoppable arc.

A strangled cry of warning escaped Shawn's throat, a raw visceral sound. *No.*

He wasn't going to watch this happen, not again. Not after all they'd been through, after all the suffering. . .

Something seemed to snap within him, all the grief and fear of the weeks of captivity pouring forth, like water through a broken dam. Shawn was on his feet almost before he even realized it, staggering toward Kruta—arms outstretched, a wild, alien scream ringing in his ears. *A voice he barely even recognized as his own.*

He hit the stooping Marine at a faltering run, the impact taking Kruta off-balance and knocking him backward, out of the line of fire. A strange euphoria seeming to wash over him—as though he'd recovered something of himself in that moment, something thought forever lost. He'd *stood*. He'd failed in so many ways through the years, failed himself, failed God, failed the people he had come to save, but here—*now*—he had stood. He'd—

And he was falling—a series of sledgehammer blows pounding into his back, the earth rushing up to meet him, folding him into its dark embrace. He tried to move, but he seemed unable to lift so much as a hand, a strange creeping numbness seeming to wash over his body as sight and sound slowly faded away. And somewhere ahead, it was as though he saw a small boy running out of the jungle—into a field of flowers. . .

Chapter 29

4:35 A.M. Philippine Standard Time, December 25th
Bud Dajo—the crater
Jolo Island, Sulu Province

Chaos. Blood and fire, filling the night. Brent Kruta rolled over onto his belly, wresting the Chinese-made Type 56 from the nerveless fingers of the dead militant, even as he heard another burst of rifle fire ripple out through the darkness.

Flecks of blood spattered his face and he saw Shawn Braley sway for a brief, heart-wrenching moment before collapsing face-down in the dirt at his side, the back of his shirt torn by bullets and stained with blood.

He felt time itself seem to slow down as he stared, frozen, at the missionary's body—unable to process the reality of what he was seeing. That his own life had been saved. . .at the cost of the life of the man *he* had come to rescue.

His own words to Richards, back there in the hotel room in Cotabato, ringing over and again through his ears. "*The family doesn't want a raid, they don't want pipe-hitters kicking down doors. They just want their loved ones back.*"

But that was the one thing to be denied them, in the end. All of those prayers, his own feeble words among them, ending in a broken body in the dirt. *Why?*

It seemed like an eternity, but only a second or two could have passed before he looked up, staring past Shawn into the eyes of the killer—a boy, really, still not out of his teens—seeing the fear and hatred written there, the muzzle of his rifle coming back to bear. *Aldam.* The swagger was long gone, but the power. . .oh, he'd had the power. *Of life and death.*

He found the safety of the Type 56, a rage filling his body, consuming him. Flipping it off with wooden fingers, knowing even as he began to bring the weapon up that he was too slow—that his own death lurked in that rifle's chamber.

But neither of them ever got the chance to fire—a round from somewhere out in the night smashing into the teenager and dropping him where he stood, the rifle clattering from his fingers.

Kruta pushed himself up, preparing to put another burst into the kid's body—to be *sure*—when he felt a bullet whip by his own head, the buttstock of the rifle coming up against his shoulder as he turned on one knee, seeking targets. The bitter staccato of automatic weapons fire filled the night, men falling all around—the sound swelling to fill the amphitheater-like bowl of Bud Dajo's crater. Off to the northeast, a large gout of flame spurted from a rifle's barrel as its owner emptied it into the night.

He caught sight of an Abu Sayyaf militant taking cover behind a cluster of rocks and squeezed off a ragged burst—but it was too far, the night still too dark, to see whether his shots had taken effect.

And he needed to get in cover, fast. He didn't know who was out there—the Filipinos, the SEALs, or the CIA—but he knew what he had seen. They had a sniper up, and from that distance, at night, he was just another man with a rifle.

A loud, keening wail struck his ears in that moment—the sound of a child crying out for her father, piercing him to the heart. He turned to find little Faith Braley running toward her father's body, heedless of the danger or the chaos swirling around them.

Kruta staggered toward her, leaning down to sweep her up with his free hand before she could reach the bullet-riddled corpse—holding her tight as she beat against his chest with her small fists, howling out her sorrow and despair.

Loss. It was a heart-wrenching feeling, that nothing would or could be the same—ever again. He made it as far as the copse, the rifle in one hand and the child in the other, colliding with Charity Braley as she emerged from its shadow—the impact bringing him to a halt, tears streaming down her dirt-smeared cheeks. *"Shawn,"* he heard her moan desperately, trying to move past him toward her husband's exposed body, but he blocked her path.

"I need you to sit back down, ma'am," he ordered, raising his voice over the chaos, trying to get her to look him in the eye. "There's nothing you can do for your husband. I'll protect you both until—"

He felt something bite into the back of his thigh—a red-hot burst of pain lancing through his body—and his right leg seemed to stop working. . .

3:37 P.M. Eastern Standard Time, December 24th
The R.C. Worley Prayer Chapel
Liberty University
Lynchburg, Virginia

". . .as Lord, we pray that you would watch over our brother and sister, Shawn and Charity, this night," Adam Cardwell intoned, his eyes closed as he knelt on the platform, shoulder to shoulder with members of the university faculty, including Donald Susich, who had been Shawn's professor of Biblical studies at Liberty. "Their little daughter Faith, whose very name reminds us of what will carry them through this time of crisis, and those Filipino believers still with them. Father God, we know that You are a man of war, and we pray that You would be a rock to those who would save them, that You would teach their hands to war, and their fingers to fight, in this Your holy service. Give them the strength to overcome, and strike down the wicked in the power of Your blessed name."

The lapel mic carried his words to every corner of the chapel, and he heard a murmured swell of *"Yes"* and *"Amen"* rise in answer.

The chapel was already near-capacity this Christmas Eve, and more were still arriving—come to keep vigil as they prayed for the Braleys' safe return.

They would be returned safely, Cardwell thought, his voice rising as he continued to pray. He had the utmost faith in that. He had brought all the influence accrued over years of prominence in evangelical political circles to bear over these last few weeks, keeping their case front and center before both the media and the President. His last conversation with the President—the night before—had been vague, but there had been enough left unsaid there to be certain the wheels were in motion. That deliverance was finally on its way. *God bless America. . .*

4:38 A.M. Philippine Standard Time, December 25th
Bud Dajo—the rim
Jolo Island, Sulu Province
The Autonomous Region in Muslim Mindanao (ARMM)

The M110's two-stage match trigger broke at four and a half pounds, sending its stock recoiling into Richards' injured shoulder as a bullet crashed from its muzzle. He winced against the pain, his ears ringing with the shot, the action cycling—feeding another long 7.62x51mm NATO cartridge into the chamber of the DMR.

"You got him," he heard Granby announce. "Center hit, stand by."

"Center-hit, stand by," Richards acknowledged, grimacing in the darkness. The Abu Sayyaf fighters were struggling to rally, disorganized but still dangerous—taken off-guard by the suddenness of the attack. Their leader now lying dead. A handful had formed a rough skirmish line off to the north, the muzzle flashes of their rifles sparkling in the night as they tried to hold off Guilbeau's SEALs.

He had lost track of Shawn Braley in the chaos unfolding after the first shots were fired, but he had to still be down there somewhere, hopefully near his family—he'd last spotted Charity near the trees, her head covering askew, along with one of the Filipino women. DEVGRU needed to get in there and secure them, most ricky-tick, but that required cutting through the remaining Abu Sayyaf.

Firing early had been a mistake, he knew that—had thrown everything else off, injected a deadly chaos into their battle plan. But the alternative had been to sit there and let Brent die. *"Those men are my brothers. . ."* Guilbeau's words, earlier this night. *"But you don't understand that, do you?"*

Except that he had, all too well.

"Fighter behind the rocks, reloading an AK, one-nine-three meters," Granby announced, his voice clear and calm, the laser stabbing out once more through the darkness like an accusing finger. "Hold quarter-mil right."

Richards traversed the rifle on its bipod, picking out the laser dot—the target there, clear in the rifle's night-vision scope—huddled down behind the rocks, feeding rounds from a chest bandolier between the steel lips of his AK's mag. His movements desperate, frantic even, but determined, for all that. Determination which would seal his fate.

And the CIA officer sucked in a slow, deep breath, his finger curling around the DMR's trigger. . .

11:42 P.M. Pacific Standard Time, December 24th
The Route 589 Memorial in Winchester
Las Vegas, Nevada

A cold December wind whipping across the open intersection buffeted the clear wall of bullet-resistant glass rising up in front of the stage as Richard Norton leaned forward into the microphone, his hands resting on the sides of the "Blue Goose"—the large, similarly-armored lectern which accompanied the President everywhere he spoke.

The strip mall behind the stage, anchored by a 7-Eleven

at its western end, was closed, as was the Pollo Loco across the intersection to the southwest, the restaurant's parking lot now packed with people, gathered to commemorate the fallen. Directly across from State Route 589 itself from where he stood, the city's memorial to the fallen SWAT stood in the parking lot of yet another small strip mall, shuttered since the attacks.

Since a handful of Pakistanis had bailed out from an idling SUV waiting by its storefront, one of the passengers aiming an RPG at the door of the lead SWAT Bearcat as it rolled past, responding to the shootdown of Delta Flight 94. Three officers had been killed instantly. And they had only been the first. . .

". . .Sergeant Albert Nakhla. . .Officer Jim Basilotta. . . Officer Ciprian Popescu, and Officer Nathan Tufteland."

The President finished the last of the eighteen names rolling across the teleprompters on either side of the lectern, looking out across the sea of people filling the closed intersection. Friends and family members of the fallen, neighbors. *Fellow citizens.*

"These brave men, the fallen of the LVMPD's Zebra Team, embodied the finest traditions of this country on the night they gave their lives, one year ago today. With their city under attack, they did not flinch, or quail from the danger. They ran to the sound of the guns. . ."

4:44 A.M. Philippine Standard Time, December 25th
Bud Dajo – the crater
Jolo Island, Sulu Province
The Autonomous Region in Muslim Mindanao (ARMM)

A burst rippled from the suppressed muzzle of Jason Guilbeau's HK416, tearing through the side of a young Abu Sayyaf fighter and turning him half-round before he collapsed onto the hard volcanic ground. He somehow still tried to lift his weapon, and the senior chief put another three-round burst through his head, ending the threat.

He heard the soft hammer of Reiner's suppressed weapon off to his left as the small assault team swept out into the clearing, moving like ghosts in the growing half-light.

What remained of the Abu Sayyaf resistance was crumbling before their advance, taken from two sides by his element and Zamora's and hit from the rear and above by the ad hoc Agency sniper team. Several militants had already thrown down their weapons, surrendering—overwhelmed by the suddenness of the attack.

"Kuznicki! You, Melhorn, Farris, get in there and clear those huts," he ordered, dropping to one knee—gesturing to the small cluster of buildings on the west end of the clearing.

"Two-Two, this is Two-One Actual. Do you have eyes on the hostages?"

"Negative, Two-One." Zamora's voice—the petty officer and his men, one of them limping noticeably, moving into view at the eastern edge of the clearing. Reiner had himself taken a bullet in the side during the opening exchanges of fire, but the medic wasn't letting it slow him down. Those two, the only casualties of the assault.

"Two-Three?"

"Last visual put them near the copse," the CIA officer responded. "No eyes now."

"On me," Guilbeau announced, gesturing to his remaining men to follow as he moved toward the trees. Only the moans of the wounded and dying now audible across the clearing, in place of the loud crackle of gunfire.

He found them not far from the copse, huddled against a pile of small boulders shadowed by a coconut palm—the women clustered close together, a Type 56 assault rifle in the hands of Brent Kruta, the former CIA officer, as he leaned back against the rock, his face twisted in a grimace of pain.

"You can stand down, Mr. Kruta," Guilbeau announced, pushing up his NODs as he advanced on the group—his SEALs fanning out, weapons at the ready. "Go ahead and give me the gun."

A mute nod, and Kruta ejected the Type 56's magazine, letting it clatter to the ground as he reached up, pulling back the charging handle to clear the chamber before handing it over.

"Where's Shawn Braley?" Guilbeau asked then, the look he got in return chilling him to the bone. *No. . .*

Chapter 30

"Yes. . .I understand," Bernard Kranemeyer responded heavily, the receiver of the secure telephone unit pressed to his ear. "Of course. . .see that you bring our field team out at the earliest opportunity. Of course, yes—thank you, Darren."

He returned the phone to its cradle, feeling the silence of his office settle over his shoulders like an oppressive burden. It was a long moment before he raised his eyes to look over to where Olivia Voss sat opposite his desk. She'd arrived to take over the night watch just as the call came in, and had ended up waiting.

"That was Lukasik," he said needlessly, as if the words were needed to fill the space. "WINDBREAK is a wrap. Brent Kruta has been rescued, along with Charity and Faith Braley—as well as a couple Filipino nationals taken hostage along with them. Shawn Braley. . .died in the assault."

"My God." Voss looked stricken, his own turmoil

417

reflected in her eyes. "His poor wife and kids. . ."

It wasn't the finish any of them had hoped for—the feeling that they had taken far too many wrong turns along the way, impossible to escape. All of it, so *avoidable*.

Or perhaps it hadn't been. They had no guarantee that the Filipinos would have known any better success.

"Has anyone told the President?"

"Not yet." Kranemeyer glanced at his watch. "He's just closing out his speech in Winchester. JSOC will be communicating with his team."

5:13 A.M. Philippine Standard Time, December 25th
Bud Dajo – the crater
Jolo Island, Sulu Province
The Autonomous Region in Muslim Mindanao (ARMM)

The eastern sky was beginning to brighten with the first few rays of the dawn, filtering their way slowly through the trees up on the rim of the crater.

"The AFP will be with us in ten," Senior Chief Jason Guilbeau announced, walking over to where Richards and Granby stood near the huts. "They want us to secure a landing zone."

Richards just nodded, casting a critical eye over the clearing. There were still bodies everywhere, lying where they had fallen—scattered across the dark volcanic soil.

Five or six militants—the only survivors who hadn't fled into the bush—knelt not far away, their hands zip-tied behind their backs. The youngest of them couldn't have yet been out of his teens, a baleful glare in his dark eyes whenever Richards looked his way. He'd taken a round through his shoulder, but Reiner—the SEAL medic—had patched him up, cleaning both the entry and exit wounds and staunching the bleeding. He was young—he'd survive.

A couple of Guilbeau's SEALs stood guard over them, with another couple watching over the Braley family—the rest spread out to form a perimeter.

"They found Shing," the senior chief went on after a moment, his face hardening into a mask of barely-suppressed anger, "washed up on the beach near Patikul. And McCalley died at the roadblock—took another couple bullets and bled out."

Richards grimaced. Leaving the three wounded SEALs behind to surrender to the AFP had been a sound tactical decision—there was no way they could have made that climb up Bud Dajo. But in the end, others always paid the price for your calls. *Like Shawn Braley.*

The missionary's body lay not far away, off to itself—covered over with a tattered blanket they'd retrieved from one of the huts. If he'd held his fire, sacrificed his old colleague, would he still be alive? Would their mission have been a success?

You held human lives in your hand, watching the balances rise and fall. And when you tilted the scales, you could never be quite sure where they would end up.

"I'm sorry," he replied quietly, looking Guilbeau in the eye. The SEAL just stared back for a long moment before turning away without a word, moving off to check on his perimeter—get an LZ marked out.

Granby shook his head. "That went well."

"He's right," Richards said, forcing himself to acknowledge the bitter truth. That all of this couldn't have gone much more wrong. "Right to be angry—his duty is to his men, and they paid a heavy price tonight. Thanks to us."

He turned away from Granby to find Brent Kruta standing there not far away, favoring his right leg—a curiously enigmatic look on the former CIA officer's face in the half-light of the early dawn.

"I hardly know whether to thank you or curse you, Jack," Kruta said finally, taking a faltering step toward them—a grimace of pain distorting his face at the movement. "I came here to do a job, and. . .I'm going home with it half-done."

"But you *are* going home."

"Small thanks to you. It was your grandstanding—that military raid on the hotel in Jolo—that pushed everything over the edge. Soleiman got wind of it, thought I was working with the AFP. He snapped. I got close, Jack." He was looking up at Richards now, and the pain in his eyes was far more than physical. "I got so *very* close. Could have taken them *all* home."

Richards took a deep breath, absorbing the words like a physical blow. Somewhere off in the distance, it seemed as though he could hear the sound of helicopter rotors, coming closer. Their Filipino counterparts, on their way. Ahead of schedule.

Something inside him wanted to lash back, to defend himself—Kruta had *done* this job, he knew how it went, well as any man alive. But the words wouldn't come.

Over his shoulder, he heard the senior chief calling out to Zamora, ordering him to move the prisoners closer to the LZ. Clearly he had heard the helicopters too.

All that had happened tonight. . .well, he was just going to have to find a way to live with it, somehow. As you always did.

Kruta stood there for a long moment more, looking up at the big man. Unable, as he'd always been, to sort out just what was going on behind those expressionless eyes—dark as coal. Richards had always been a hard one to figure.

Didn't matter. Shawn Braley was dead, and that wasn't going to change—no matter what anyone managed to tell themselves.

He glimpsed the SEALs off to their left, near the huts, getting the prisoners on their feet none too gently—shoving and cursing those who balked. The mood had changed with the confirmation of their casualties, darkening as the reality settled in. They would be going home to funerals—taking brothers home with them in body bags.

He had done more than enough of that himself over the years—more than any man should have to do. Knew all too well how it felt.

A tomahawk was hanging from Zamora's belt, the Marine noted with a wry grimace. *SEALs*. To be one, you needed either good hair or a flair for the dramatic, and judging by the chief petty officer's buzz cut. . .it wasn't the former.

Kruta felt someone's eyes on him and glanced over to meet Aldam's gaze—the teenager's eyes radiating hatred as one of the SEALs shoved him forward, stumbling across the hard ground toward the LZ.

"Move it along," he heard Zamora call out, punctuating his words with a curse as he moved alongside the prisoners.

I should have put another bullet into you when I had the chance, Kruta thought, meeting the young fighter's stare. Recognizing the monster Manong Soleiman had created, still lurking there in the kid's eyes—undaunted. *Unconquered.*

It was hard to know whether a few years in a Filipino

prison would change any of that. . .or whether he would come out harder and more fanatical than ever. Someone they'd be coming back for, ten years on.

Yeah, definitely should have made sure to finish him off.

Shing. McCalley. Jason Guilbeau ran a hand over the rough stubble of his beard, staring out toward the eastern horizon, watching the dawn's faint glow begin to pierce its way through the jungle up on the rim. *Christmas morning.*

And here they were.

The AFP was on its way—he could hear the sound of their helicopters' rotors, off in the distance, but growing ever closer. He was going to have to begin placing the calls, in another few hours—once he was cleared by the command authority. Neither Mac nor Shing had had kids, but Howett and Wilkens were still out there, somewhere—and both of them *were* family men. And their families deserved to know. *Gail.* Howett's wife was a tough woman—you had to be, to be a Team wife—but she was going to take this hard.

He closed his eyes—as if he could shut out the reality for another few precious moments, but he knew better. Knew and struggled to repress the anger that came with the knowledge—anger at Abu Sayyaf, at the CIA, at the command authority, at whatever blind, unreasoning fate had landed them all here together.

The senior chief glanced over to see Zamora bringing the prisoners over, filing past the blanket-draped corpse of Shawn Braley. His own anger was reflected in Dom's dark eyes, a fury there, hovering just beneath the surface. Dom's wife Patti was close to Gail, well. . .all of their families had been, ever since Team Three days on the West Coast, and he was taking it all personally. Along with the failure of their mission.

That was when he saw one of the prisoners—a kid, couldn't have been out of his teens—lean over and spit on the body as he passed, kicking Braley's corpse in the ribs with a sandaled foot.

Rage surged across Guilbeau's face, watching it happen, but Kuznicki reacted first, before he could call out, slamming the butt of his carbine into the prisoner's stomach—sending him staggering back.

He never saw Dom's hand go to his belt, but the next moment, the tomahawk was in his hand, the curved gray-black steel of its head burying itself deep in the back of the young militant's skull, blood spraying over Zamora's face as the kid collapsed to his knees, the life going out of him.

An angry curse escaped Zamora's lips as he put his boot into the militant's back, using it as leverage to free the tomahawk.

The kid's lifeless body slid the rest of the way to the ground as the tomahawk came free, his hands still zip-tied behind his back, leaving Dom standing there over him, breathing heavily—reaching up to wipe the blood from his face but only succeeding in smearing it over the greasepaint.

The senior chief just stood there for a long moment, frozen in shock—recognizing the looks of surprise and astonishment in the faces of the CIA officers across the way, knowing it was too late, far too late to intervene, to do *anything*. Knowing a line had been crossed which was bright and red.

He heard the helicopters again, the sound breaking him from the trance—closer now. *Much closer*. And he knew then what he had to do.

"Come on, Dom," he began, hurrying over to where his second-in-command stood, the tomahawk clutched loosely in his right hand, gore still dripping from its blade. "Get it together. And get those zip-ties off his hands. Do it *now*!"

1:15 P.M. Pacific Standard Time, December 24th
Winchester
Las Vegas, Nevada

There had been no applause. He was used to applause at the close of his speeches, Richard Norton thought, struck curiously by its absence as he walked toward the Presidential limousine, Curt Hawkins holding open its heavy door for him.

But the audience here in Vegas had been quiet—eerily quiet, as if the ghosts of the murdered SWAT officers had still walked among the crowd. A city still haunted, a year later, by the sheer magnitude of its loss.

It had been unnerving, as a speaker, and even with the twin glass panels of the teleprompters flanking the lectern, Norton had found himself wandering more than once during the speech.

He had to prepare to face the same thing again more than once in the next few hours, both at the crash site and during his main speech at the Bellagio—the most critical speech of his first year, perhaps his entire Presidency. The one that would go in the history books.

Dennis Froelich was waiting for him, within the limousine—fidgeting with his wedding band, the chief of staff's face curiously pale.

"Mr. President," Froelich began, twisting the band back

and forth—refusing to look him in the face. "We've heard from JSOC. Operation WINDBREAK is. . .well, Mr. President—"

"What is it, Dennis?" Norton demanded, feeling an ice-cold hand run down his spine, the interior of the presidential limousine growing somehow darker. *No.* He refused to accept it—it wasn't *true.*

"Shawn Braley, uh, Mr. President. . .Shawn Braley was killed in the assault."

5:23 A.M. Philippine Standard Time, December 25th
Bud Dajo – the crater
Jolo Island, Sulu Province
The Autonomous Region in Muslim Mindanao (ARMM)

"You." That was the first word out of Gringo Mijares' mouth as he stepped from the door of the Special Action Force UH-1H, walking out from the makeshift LZ toward the cluster of nipa huts. Stopping short as he recognized Richards' tall figure.

"Good to see you too, Gringo." Except it wasn't, and both of them knew it. Their past working relationship was water under the bridge, but after this night. . .there was a lot of blood in that water. On both sides.

Mijares looked between Richards and Granby, then back toward the helicopters—his men spilling out to take up positions, reinforcing the SEALs' perimeter. Guilbeau and his men ushering the rescued hostages, American and Filipino alike, toward the waiting helicopters—little Faith Braley in the arms of Reiner, the medic.

"If there was any justice here, I'd put you both on that

helicopter and take you back to WESTMINCOM in cuffs," the commando officer said finally, shaking his head in disbelief. That was truer than he knew, and for more than just them, Richards thought—his face impassive as he held Mijares' stare, feeling Granby's attention drift off out toward the brained corpse of the young militant, now dumped near the edge of the clearing, among the rest. A Type 56 once more slung around his shoulders.

"But I have my orders," Mijares continued, the reluctance with which he would follow them evident in his voice. SAF commandos approaching them with a stretcher for Shawn Braley's body. "So go on, Jack. . .*leave*. You've done enough. More than enough."

12:48 A.M. Turkey Time
Ulus 29, Beşiktaş
Istanbul, Turkey

The strait was never more beautiful than at night—lights glittering over the surface of its waters. From the windswept hilltop terrace, looking out toward the Bosphorus Bridge, you could see the pleasure yachts in close to the shoreline, sleek palaces of the waves—gleaming with light from stem to stern, and no doubt pulsating with music on a night like tonight, if she had been close enough to hear them.

But she wasn't. The only thing that carried at this distance was a sonorous horn blast from the bulk carrier now approaching the bridge from the south, being ferried toward the Black Sea by a cluster of small tugs. *Through the gates of Asia.*

Byzantium. Constantinople. *Istanbul.* A nexus of human

trade and conflict for thousands of years.

The same things which had brought her here tonight—because there were few trades as eternal as conflict itself.

Another gust of wind swept across the restaurant's deserted terrace, rippling through the woman's dark hair and forcing her to duck her head to hear the caller's next words. It was cold out here, her free arm hugging her coat tight to her body—but the privacy was worth it.

"Of course, Arne. . .I understand. We got him back—that's the important thing just now. Cut our losses, move on." You didn't win every battle, as she had found to her sorrow over the years. Nor could you rescue everyone you set out to. "See that Kruta gets that leg looked at, and make sure the Braleys get their money back. . .all of it, Arne," she insisted, hearing the former Jaeger's protest from the other end of the line at his home in Skaelskør. "We *failed* them. We'll take the loss."

That was just good public relations, she reflected, listening to Kornbech for another few moments before signing off, returning the phone to an inner pocket and nodding toward her bodyguard as she prepared to go back inside.

"My apologies—a business call," she said, returning to her table to find Michael Hignett still sitting where she had left him, idly picking at his baklava.

In his early fifties and long ago gone bald, Hignett had once—ten years before, when they'd both been Agency—been the CIA's Chief of Base here in Istanbul. Twice married, twice divorced, he'd elected to stay in place at the end of his career, taking up permanent residence in a city he had come to love. He was out of the game now, or so he said, but he remained one of the foremost experts on the region.

"Of course," he replied with an easy smile, taking a sip of his coffee. He'd always been good with people—if not relationships—one of the things which had made him an effective chief.

She took off her coat to reveal the sharply tailored navy blue pantsuit beneath, draping the coat over the back of her seat before sitting back down. "Now where were we?"

"The general."

"Ah yes." A smile. She hadn't forgotten. "Can he be trusted?"

Can we do business, she meant—not "trust" in the absolute sense. She didn't even trust Hignett *that* far.

There was a pause before he replied, as the former chief of station took another bite of the delicate, honeyed pastry, seeming to contemplate her question carefully.

"I wouldn't."

Epilogue

"All right, listen up," Jason Guilbeau announced, raising his voice over the noise of the Globemaster's engines, vibrating through the thin hull of the airframe. They had the transport's cavernous hold to themselves, for the time being. Just them. . .and four body bags.

Mac. Shing. Wilkens. *And Howett.* The hardest single loss DEVGRU had taken since the downing of Extortion 17, and it had been on his watch. *His command.*

The last three days had been the worst of his life, and the after action review on this op. . .well, that was why they needed to get things settled, *now*. Because things had the potential to get even worse from here on out.

"We have two hours till we land," the senior chief continued once he was sure he had everyone's attention. Dom didn't meet his eyes. "And that's how long we have to get our story straight. Styer, Radak, you weren't there, you weren't involved—go on up and pester the flight crew. You don't have to be a part of this."

"No way, boss," the lanky Styer replied, and Radakovich shook his head. "We're a team—we're in this together."

A grim smile creased Guilbeau's face—it was moments like this which made it impossible to leave the Teams. A feeling of *brotherhood*, like you could find nowhere else in the world.

He looked over at Doc Reiner, saw the look on the medic's face, and the smile died. This wasn't going to be easy. . .but nothing ever was.

"The responsibility for the deaths of those men," he said heavily, gesturing back toward the body bags, "our brothers—rests on my shoulders and mine alone. I—"

"It wasn't your fault, Senior," he heard Melhorn protest—several of his teammates joining in. . .but it wasn't true. They were *all* his responsibility, the burden which had come with rank.

"I will take whatever consequences come my way," he continued, squaring his shoulders as he looked from one man to the next, "but I'm not willing to see one of my men get taken down for something done in the heat of the moment, in the aftermath of a battle. This team has lost enough. Give it another day, maybe two, if they're not in the ground already. . .someone in the AFP is going to start looking over those bodies and begin asking questions. Or one of the remaining prisoners talks. By the time that filters its way through to our command, we need to be prepared with what to tell them. That's a decision we're settling before we get off this plane."

"We need to come clean," Reiner announced, barely

waiting for him to finish, a dangerous light shining in the medic's eyes. "There's a line there, and it was crossed. We can't hide that, can't make it go away. Best thing any of us can do is face the music."

Kuznicki nodded. "I agree."

Guilbeau shook his head, feeling anger boil up from within him. "So we go back home, bury our dead, and then drag our families—*all* our families, because you know JAG's not going to stop with Dom once they get rolling—through an investigation?" He stared Reiner hard in the face. "That's what *you* would do? And for what? You saw what that scumbag did. . .he *spat* in the face of our dead. A fellow *American*, Doc. If that had been you lying there, he would have done it to you. What Dom did, every last one of us *wanted* to do."

"Doesn't make it any less wrong," the medic replied quietly, refusing to match Guilbeau's tone.

"'Wrong'?" Guilbeau exploded, punctuating his words with an angry curse. "You want to see what's *wrong*, Doc, go take a look inside that body bag. *Look* at Chris, and tell me if you still think what happened up on that mountain was 'wrong.'"

Reiner flinched at that, the color going out of his face. Wilkens had, like Shing, been found by the AFP, washed up dead on the beach outside Jolo, but Howett. . .well, they didn't know. Had no way of knowing. He hoped Chris had been dead long before anyone got to him, but his mutilated body had been found four klicks in-land, the previous night, in the aftermath of an AFP raid. There would be no viewing, not even for his wife and kids.

Logic told him there was nothing he could have done,

that once they were in the water all bets were off—that the CIA officer had been right, and staying to try to rescue Chris and the others could have cost him his entire command. But logic wasn't going to comfort anyone's family.

"I'm with you, boss," Melhorn announced, raising his hand. "What Dom did, well. . .I don't want to think I would have done it, but I don't know. Not my place to judge. He's a brother—that's all that matters, in the end."

A slow nod from Radakovich, and Farris cleared his throat. "I talked with that contractor before we left Zamboanga. . .that kid's the same one who beheaded the Filipino a few days back. Spent the rest of his time since swaggering around like he was king of the hill. I say Dom did the world a favor."

"We keep our mouths shut," Melhorn went on after a moment, looking around. "We killed a lot of jihadis that night, what's one more? It happened in combat, that's all we need to say. One or two of the other detainees may try to cause problems, but we deny it. Our word against theirs. Who's going to say otherwise?"

"The Agency?" Kuznicki, this time—he was wavering, Guilbeau could see it, noting the doubt in the younger SEAL's eyes. He was a relatively recent transfer to DEVGRU, in from Team Five. Still dealing with the shift in culture.

"Christians in Action?" Radakovich sneered, shaking his head. "They're a black hole. Everything goes in, and nothing comes back out. We're safe."

More nods, the rest of his men slowly joining in—some more reluctantly than others, but nodding all the same. "Doc?" Guilbeau asked finally, shifting his attention back to Reiner.

The medic shook his head slowly. "It's the wrong call, boss. . .but I'm not going to throw the whole team under the bus. If that's our story, I'll stand by it."

4:03 P.M. Eastern Standard Time
Rockville, Maryland

The small two-story brick house there at the end of the road had been home for the last ten years of his marriage, William Russell Cole reflected as the Uber slowed to a stop outside, its wipers beating futilely against the late December rain. It would be sleet if not outright *freezing* rain in another hour, as night fell and temperatures plummeted right along with it.

The *best* ten years of his marriage—as the Bureau had shifted him to Headquarters and stopped yanking his family around the country. Even if the pace they set for him had never really changed.

But the Philippines. . .the Philippines had been a mess, even by the standards of a career that had known its share of bad moments. He had found himself turning livid as the news began to trickle into Camp Bautista, and when the pair of CIA officers had come walking back in the next morning. . .he'd exploded in a display of fury few of his colleagues had ever seen, knowing by that time that he had failed. That Shawn Braley was dead.

All the work he and the fusion cell had done, trying to work with the Filipinos, to leverage what access and influence they had to get the Braleys out. . .all of it sabotaged in a night's time.

He thanked his driver and got out, the rain beating down

upon him as he trudged down the walk toward the house, past the little wind-tattered American flag still planted on its stick beneath the naked limbs of the maple in the front yard.

His entire team had been kicked out of the country a day later, mostly over the Agency's use of their jet—a flagrant breach of inter-agency protocol which had reportedly precipitated an angry call from Director Chamian to David Lay.

A light was on in the kitchen, he realized somewhat belatedly, walking up to the door, already fumbling for his keys. *Still locked.*

The sound of the TV from the living room arrested his attention as he entered and he poked his head in, finding his two grandsons curled up on the couch, watching anime.

A smile creased the hostage negotiator's weary face and he stood there for a long moment, just watching the boys— before turning away. He found their mother in the kitchen, making sandwiches, spreading out peanut butter from a jar he hardly even remembered he'd had. "Tiff."

"Dad." She came over and hugged him then, the ache of the last few days seeming to melt away in his daughter's arms. "Merry Christmas."

It felt as though he could have stood there forever, just holding her, but he had to *know.* To be sure. "You left?"

She pushed away from him then, pain and uncertainty still visible in her eyes. "No. . ." she said hesitantly, turning from him. She was still wearing the long sweaters. "I'll be going back, Luke and I. . .we just need need space right now. That's all."

It was hard to know what to say to that, and in the end he elected not to say anything, just watching her as she went back to the boys' sandwiches. Thankful for a victory, no matter how small—or how temporary.

Merry Christmas.

8:51 P.M. Pacific Standard Time
Sierra Inn Dining Facility(DFAC)
Travis Air Force Base
Solano County, California

It had been a long flight across the Pacific, the team flying a charter from WESTMINCOM out to Guam, and hitching a ride on a 515th AMOW C-5 Galaxy from there. The Braleys had gone home first class, a State Department jet out of Ninoy Aquino.

Those who rescued them. . .had taken a longer and much more uncomfortable route. But that was show business.

Richards raised the mug in his left hand, draining the last of his coffee as he looked past Granby and out over the rest of the base dining facility, marking out the small groups of airmen still gathered around tables scattered across the room. A long flight and a quiet one, at least where Granby was concerned, though the brooding silence had warned him what was coming.

All that had changed five minutes ago—Parker and Ardolino off in search of a hot shower, Carson, his ankle nearly fully recovered, heading out to meet with a friend from his own Air Force days.

Leaving Richards finishing his coffee, Granby his pizza.

Richards pushed the cup away, wincing as he reached up to adjust the strap of the arm sling where it dug into his shoulder, before finally looking over at his colleague. "Are you sure this is a bridge you really want to cross?"

A nod. Granby was getting as taciturn as himself.

Richards shook his head. "I wouldn't. No one, Titus, wants more daylight shed on the details of how this operation went down. Not Manila. Not Washington. They struck a deal."

A deal which hadn't prevented Darren Lukasik from being PNG'ed and put on the first flight out of Manila, per last word from Langley—but it looked like that was about as visible as the repercussions were going to get. *For now.*

But the spin was already in motion, the news reporting they had seen during their stop-over in Guam, skewed as far as possible away from the truth—including a public statement from Filipino president Luis Maskariño, lamenting Shawn Braley's death while lauding the joint US-Filipino effort in the hostage rescue.

"You take this to JAG, lots of questions are going to get asked that no one wants to find the answers to. You're not going to make any friends, in high places or low. And a community that just lost four of its own is going to take another punch to the gut. Think about that, long and hard."

"I have," Granby replied, looking him in the eye. "And I still remember what you said, Jack, back there in Cotabato, about the hard choices we make in this business. The times when doing the right thing doesn't work out, but you have to do it anyway—and find a way to live with the consequences. *Somehow.*"

The End

An author lives by word-of-mouth recommendations. If you enjoyed this story, please consider leaving a customer review(even if only a few lines) on Amazon. It would be greatly helpful and much appreciated.

For news and release information, visit
www.stephenwrites.com
and sign up for the mailing list.
Stay in touch and up-to-the-minute with book news
through social media.

On Facebook:
https://www.facebook.com/stephenenglandauthor

Join the Facebook group to discuss the series with other
fans:
Stephen England's Shadow Warriors

On Twitter:
https://twitter.com/stephenmengland

Author's Note

Some stories you set out to write, and when you look back at the end, you marvel at the extent to which they took on a life of their own and went in directions you had never quite expected, going in. *WINDBREAK* is one of those stories, a novel which grew well beyond its intended scope over the course of research and writing, and ended up finished in the middle of COVID-19's lockdowns, in a very different world than any of us might have imagined.

A nearly-unexplored front in the War on Terror, the Philippines provided a challenging new setting for the *Shadow Warriors*, offering a look at a counter-insurgency effort with far different tensions than those found your typical Middle East-centric thriller, tensions shaped by the century of history between the United States and her one-time unincorporated territory.

That history forms a great deal of the underpinnings of this novel, and proved endlessly interesting to research and explore. Special thanks for helping me get a grip on the conflict which first brought American soldiers to the southern islands of Mindanao, Basilan, and Jolo goes to

James R. Arnold and his fantastic 2011 history *The Moro War*. And to the late Leon Wolff, author of the classic history *Little Brown Brother*, for the in-depth look he provides into the broader conflict.

To Zachary Abuza, whose work on modern security issues in Southeast Asia provided many interesting insights across the months of research.

A great debt of thanks is also owed to American missionary Gracia Burnham, for recounting her and her husband's own harrowing year of captivity by Abu Sayyaf, a story told in her book *In the Presence of My Enemies*.

Perhaps the greatest thanks of all, however, goes to long-time *Shadow Warriors* fan Andre Lim Lo Suy and his father George—the latter, a Mindanao native—for fielding an incessant stream of questions about the islands and providing countless bits of local color from information on the vehicles used by Moro politicians, to the snatches of Visayan dialogue scattered throughout the novel. *WINDBREAK* would not be what it became without the knowledgeable input of these two gentlemen, and I am deeply grateful. Whatever mistakes remain are mine, and mine alone.

Thanks also goes out to Shawn Hinck, returning once more to help keep my marksmen on target, and to my colleague Steven Hildreth, Jr. for his input on the military side of the story—a great thriller writer, in his own right, and one whose books you should be reading.

Thanks to the artistic genius Louis Vaney for creating another fantastic cover for the series, working as ever, from the loosest of ideas and turning it into exciting art.

And to the members of the *WINDBREAK* ARC team—

Bodo Pfündl, Andre Lim Lo Suy, Steven Hildreth, Jr., Paula Tyler, Diane Goldhammer, Sean McCormick, and Joanne Elmore, for their diligence in sifting through the pre-publication manuscript, looking for errors.

A warm thanks to my many friends in the military and intelligence communities for their help, encouragement, and insight over the years. It has been greatly appreciated.

And last, but far from least, to my readers, whose enthusiasm for this series continues to be both gratifying and humbling.

May God bless you all, and may God continue to bless America.

Printed in Great Britain
by Amazon

40603818R00253